VIVID AVOWED

THE EVELYN MAYNARD TRILOGY - PART THREE

KAYDENCE SNOW

Cover design © Fantastical Ink

Editing by Kirstin Andrews

kaydencesnow.com

For anyone who has ever felt alone

PROLOGUE

Sneaking around Bradford Hills Institute at night with Davis always sent a thrill of rebellious exhilaration through Joyce. Doing *anything* with Davis had an edge of adrenaline to it.

He was the model student during the day—even friendly with some of the lecturers—but at night, he was a bad boy. And he spent most of his nights with Joyce. That made her feel special, as if she were the only one who knew who he really was, the only one who saw his dangerous side.

"Where are we going?" George was keeping pace with them, walking slightly behind as the trio navigated a dark curved path by nothing but moonlight.

Davis hushed him. "Keep your voice down. We're going to the construction site."

"Oh." George's steps faltered. "Aren't students banned from there?"

Joyce detangled herself from Davis to loop her arm through George's. "Yeah, but that's what makes it fun." She grinned and pulled him along. "It's not like we're gonna do anything bad—just have a few drinks and check it out. It's totally safe, I promise."

Construction on what would be the new admin building had begun several weeks ago. During daylight hours, the area was teeming with contractors, buzzing with the noise of power tools and manual labor. At night, it was pretty much abandoned. Joyce and Davis had snuck in there a few times already, having sex up against the rough concrete of the structural walls and smoking pot, feeling on top of the world.

When Davis had suggested they invite George, Joyce had been surprised. She had Variant Studies with the smart, shy seventeen-year-old and had chatted with him a handful of times—they'd even done a group project together once—but she couldn't recall Davis ever speaking to him. George didn't really speak to anyone. His mind-reading ability made it difficult for him to be around people, and most students steered clear, worried he might expose their deepest secrets.

It was really sweet of Davis to notice the kid needed some friends. Joyce had agreed readily and invited him herself.

Davis placed the six-pack of beer he was carrying on the ground and held the chain-link gate wide enough for them to squeeze through.

They climbed to the third floor on staircases without railings and sat with their legs hanging off the edge of the building. The faint lights of the town twinkled past the treetops as they drank their beers and chatted about classes, gossiped about their classmates.

George kept pretty quiet at first, but the beer and easy conversation soon loosened him up.

"Hey, Georgie." Davis had started using the silly nickname as soon as they'd picked George up at his res hall, and he hadn't dropped it since. "You know, Joyce here is a bit special—like you."

"Really?" George's eyes flicked between the couple as Davis slung an arm around his girlfriend's shoulders. "You have an ability? I thought you were a Vital."

"Yeah, I am." Joyce nodded but eyed Davis. He had that look in his eyes—the one he always got just before he pulled something really daring. Usually it was fun, but sometimes . . .

Davis was the only one she'd told about her Vital status, about the way she sometimes glowed, but he wasn't in her Bond; there had been no spark between them when they touched. His ability hadn't even manifested yet—a sore subject for him.

"Wait, how did you know I'm a Vital?" Joyce asked.

George tapped the side of his head. "Heard you think it once or twice."

"Right." Joyce laughed. "I almost forgot."

"She's not just any Vital." Davis leaned forward, tipping them almost dangerously over the ledge. "She's a *special* kind of Vital. She can do things other Vitals can't."

"Davis." Joyce leaned them back to a safe distance. What was he doing? He knew how stressed she was about the glowing, how much she worried there was something wrong with her. Wasn't he the one who'd convinced her not to say anything to the social worker or the nurse? They might treat her like a freak, even take her away from him if they thought she was dangerous.

She couldn't risk that. She loved her life and her friends too much. She loved Davis too much to even think about being away from him.

"It's OK, sweets." Davis kissed her on the cheek. "Georgie won't tell anyone. I just want to help him."

"Help me?" George asked at the same time as Joyce said, "How?"

"You see, Joyce can draw Light from any source, including other Variants. And when she does, she can temporarily transfer the Variant's ability to another Variant."

George's eyes narrowed, as if he couldn't quite figure out what Davis was saying . . . or thinking.

"Davis." Joyce shrugged his arm off her shoulders and fixed him with a firm look. "What are you getting at?"

They'd used her glowing Light a handful of times. She'd once drawn from a shape-shifter and transferred to Davis so he could make himself look older and buy them beer. Harmless fun, but it took a lot out of her. Any time she used the glowing Light she felt drained and weak, and it took days to feel like herself again. But

Davis loved having an ability for a little while, so she did it whenever he asked.

"He wants you to take it all," George answered for Davis.

Joyce wasn't entirely sure whether George's ability had clued him in to what Davis wanted or if he was just smarter than her and had figured it out quicker—most people were smarter than her—but it suddenly made perfect sense.

"You want to take his ability permanently?" Joyce stared at Davis with wide eyes. "We don't even know if that's possible. We don't know what it'll do to George. I may not even be able to do it. I'm not that strong."

"Yes, you are." Davis said it with such conviction, such certainty, the doubt almost completely evaporated. He fixed her with that look she loved, the one that made his eyes shine, that made her feel as if they were the only two people in the room—in the *world*.

He cupped the side of her face, his hand warm, and she instinctively leaned into the touch. "I know you can do this, Joycie. I love you."

"I love you too . . . but . . ."

"Please try." George's plea reminded her they weren't actually alone in the dimly lit construction zone.

"George, I don't know what it might do to you."

"I don't care. Even if it doesn't work. Even if it only works for a little while. Do you have any idea what it's like to have voices constantly in your head? To not be able to sleep until everyone else in the building is asleep? To not be able to make friends because . . . because you're a *freak*? Just try. *Please*."

His eyes pleaded with her as much as his words. He was desperate.

Joyce chewed on her lower lip. Davis wanted this. George wanted this. Who was she to say no?

"OK." She nodded.

Davis clapped his hands once, the sound bouncing off the concrete. "Excellent!"

Joyce took George's hand and concentrated hard. She'd never tried to pull *all* of it before—she had to focus.

It took time, but eventually the Light became the only thing she saw in her mind's eye, the only thing she felt. She pulled harder than ever before.

She was so focused on her task, so determined to give them what they wanted, she didn't notice when George tried to pull his hand out of her grip, when he whispered weakly for her to stop. She didn't see Davis place his hand over George's mouth, holding him in place.

When she'd pulled all the Light out of George, she gasped and her eyes flew open. Her body and mind couldn't handle the pressure, the overwhelming weight of that much pure power.

She passed out.

Davis caught her before her head hit the concrete and lowered her gently down. Then, when he was sure George had no pulse, he kicked the young boy's body off the edge, hoping it would look like an accident.

"Fuck." With a growl, he grabbed two fistfuls of Joyce's coat and shook her. "Wake up."

This *had* to work. He hadn't put in months of effort hanging out with this desperate, pathetic chick for it to all be a waste.

"You better not be dead." He huffed and unzipped her coat, reaching for her neck to check for a pulse.

As soon as his skin connected with hers, he felt it. There was so much Light coursing through her she didn't even need to be awake to transfer it to him. It was *gushing* out of her.

A manic smile spread over his face as the sheer power coursed into his veins.

He considered throwing her off the edge along with George— he couldn't risk her freaking out and telling someone about what had happened—but he dismissed the idea. He had to make sure it was permanent first. And if it was . . .

He resolved to keep his new ability a secret as long as possible; he'd reveal it only at the most opportune time. He was already in his early twenties—no one expected him to manifest an ability at all.

As Davis lifted Joyce into his arms and climbed down the stairs, he allowed himself to think about what this could mean for him. He would be the most powerful man in America, maybe even the *world.*

Oh, the mind reading would certainly help, but it wasn't as if the ability was unique. No, the real prize was lying unconscious in his arms.

If he was right and Joyce really could take an ability and give it to someone else, he'd have to make sure he kept her close for a long, long time. He was a bit young to be a father, but if that's what it took to lock her into his life permanently, he'd start poking holes in condoms as soon as he got her back to his place.

ONE

One of Josh's carefully curated playlists drifted softly from the high-tech system in the corner of my room. Although it had taken him all of five minutes to throw it together, he knew exactly which songs to choose, and they were all perfect "getting ready" songs.

It had been way too long since one of Ethan's epic parties, and apparently the masses were getting impatient. Plus, my big teddy bear loved to throw a big party.

Dot unclipped the last little chunk of hair at the top of my head and separated it into sections. I was seated between her legs on the floor, my back leaning on the mattress as she meticulously straightened my hair. I hadn't cut it more than a trim since my mother's death. When straightened, it nearly reached my ass.

"Should I put it in a ponytail or something? It's getting really long." My nervousness about this party was manifesting as self-consciousness.

"What're you nuts?" Dot bent around me to look into my face, her brow creased. "I just straightened it to perfection. Girls would kill for this kind of hair."

"OK, OK." I held my hands up but chuckled. It was nice to

see her spunk back. Her vibrant, loud, over-the-top personality had faded each day her brother and Vital had been missing.

Charlie had been rescued over a month ago, along with dozens of other Vitals. He sat on the bed behind us, leaning on the headboard, flicking through my latest edition of *New Scientist*. He must've found something to hold his attention, because we hadn't heard a comment or a page flip in a while.

Bradford Hills Institute had given him the rest of the year off; he was to resume his studies for his master's the following year, but for now, he was spending most of his spare time with us. He'd obviously missed Dot. I couldn't imagine what he'd been through, locked up in a little cell for so long, never knowing when he might be dragged off to the lab of horrors.

It made me sick to my stomach.

"Apparently neural stem cells from Variant donors are seventy-six percent more effective than those from human donors in treating patients with chronic spinal cord injuries. The transplanted stem cells develop into new neurons that replace severed or lost nerve connections and almost completely restore motor and sensory function," Charlie piped up from behind us, solving the mystery of what had him so engrossed.

"Oh, really? I guess it makes sense when you consider the accelerated healing and better resistance to injury and disease in people with Variant DNA," I answered, itching to read that article myself.

Dot nudged my head to face forward again. "No nerd talk! Stop moving. I've only got one section to go."

I kept still as she dragged the last section of my chocolate-brown hair painfully slowly through the straightener. I had a feeling she was doing it just to bug me.

"There. Done," she declared, finishing it off with some anti-frizz shit that smelled sickly sweet and made me sneeze. She went straight to my closet and flicked through the hangers. "You sure I can't convince you to wear a dress?"

Hanging next to my mother's poppy-print dress were rows of

clothes I'd purchased on a recent trip to the city with Dot. Charlie and Ethan had come too, as well as a full Melior Group security detail. We were able to pretend the agents weren't there for most of it, and I'd learned how enjoyable spending money could be when you didn't have to worry about packing all your purchases into one easy-to-carry bag.

For tonight, I'd opted for skinny jeans and a blood-red sweater with a V-neck. My suede ankle boots—one of *three* newly purchased pairs of shoes—went perfectly with it. The outfit was nowhere near as dressy as Dot's was going to be, but I thought I looked nice, and I was warm and comfortable. A chill still hung in the March air, but so far the rain had remained trapped in the fat gray clouds above.

"Nah," I finally answered. "I like what I'm wearing, and it's too cold for a dress."

"Fine." She rolled her eyes. "But you know you'll get drunk and start dancing and you'll be way too hot in that later, right?"

"Well, then it's lucky the party is only downstairs, just a short walk away from my closet with all these clothes in it."

In place of an answer, Dot just stared at me with raised brows and pursed lips. Then, slowly, she held her hand out. Squiggles came running out of the hallway, scampered up her side, and dropped a tube of mascara in her palm.

Dot thanked her gray ferret while keeping her eyes on me, then turned to face her. "I know. She's being sassy. I don't like it."

Charlie snorted and flopped the magazine down on the bed, leaning back against my multicolored, geometric-patterned sheets. I flashed him a conspiratorial smile and went over to the side table. It held a cluster of framed pictures: the one of my mother that had survived the crash, one of her with the guys' moms, one of the five of us as kids, and one of Dot, Charlie, and I mugging for the camera. Nestled among the frames was an old, ornately carved jewelry box. It was way too heavy and bulky to have been anything I would've owned before, but Josh had given it to me as a

Christmas gift and then promised to fill it over the next unspeci-fied period of time.

I knew he meant forever—Variant Bonds were unbreakable—but none of us were ready to say that word out loud yet.

Alec had told me he loved me, but I hadn't said it back, and none of the others had broached the subject. I suspected they were giving me space and letting me take the lead—as they had with the sex—but an insecure part of me also wondered if maybe they weren't ready for that level of emotional commitment yet either. I mean, really, we'd only known each other for a year. We may have played together as kids, but I didn't remember that.

The box only had a few items in it—a bracelet Dot had given me that same Christmas, a gold pair of earrings (I was wearing them when the plane crashed, and they were the only piece of jewelry I had from my mom), a silver caffeine molecule necklace I'd bought for myself, a few bits of costume jewelry. I lifted out the simple rod pendant that was also a panic beacon and tucked it under the fabric of my sweater. I wasn't wearing it for protection. It was the first thing they'd given me. It may have been delivered in the worst way possible by Alec, but it was from all of them, and I'd come to love the heavy weight of it around my neck.

"What're you wearing tonight, Dot?" I asked to distract her from further bitching about my outfit. Charlie was in jeans and a shirt-sweater combo, his black hair falling over his forehead.

"Something new." She grinned before she got back to applying her makeup. The look she was going for tonight was heavy and dramatic—exactly her signature style before Charlie went missing. I looked forward to seeing what she came up with, even if I wasn't entirely looking forward to the actual party.

I still hardly knew anyone that well, and with Davis Damari—my psychotic biological father whom my mother had kept us on the run from my entire life, aka the man responsible for kidnap-ping and torturing Charlie and dozens of other Vitals, aka one of the richest men on the planet, aka the biggest asshole to have ever lived—still underground, it felt wrong somehow to celebrate.

But Ethan insisted we had plenty of reasons, and Dot agreed wholeheartedly. My birthday was only a few days away; I'd refused to allow them to make this party all about that—not after the track record I had with birthdays—but they'd waved me off and said it was a multi-celebration. My birthday would be toasted, but so would Charlie's safe return, our win in solving the mystery of the missing Vitals, and Uncle Lucian's recent recovery and release from the hospital.

I wandered over to the window as the song changed to something a little more upbeat. The room I'd moved into in the Zacarias mansion was a little smaller than the others on this wing, but it faced the backyard and caught the afternoon sun beautifully.

Ethan was standing halfway between the house and the pool, completely in his element, dictating the final preparations. He gestured to someone I couldn't see around the corner. In the next moment, the string lights came on, and he clapped his big hands together.

People had already started to arrive—some of Ethan's sports friends and a few other people he and Josh were close with but I didn't know that well. Getting into deep conversations was hard when you were hiding a big secret about yourself. Thankfully we didn't have to worry about that anymore. My identity and my Vital status were public knowledge now.

A few more people streamed out of the house, and Ethan welcomed them enthusiastically, wrapping them all in big hugs, high-fiving, and carrying on.

I couldn't see them from my window, but I knew at least three Melior Group teams were stationed around the perimeter. Every Vital in attendance had their own personal security detail, a very visible team was at the front gates checking vehicles, and another was at the front door, checking each person before they entered the house.

At the first party I'd attended here, security had been nonexistent.

The air was getting brisk as dusk settled in—not that it bothered Ethan. My fire fiend was dressed in his signature jeans and a white T-shirt stretched over his defined, broad chest.

Everyone else, however, would be feeling the cold. Of course, Ethan and Dot had thought of that too.

After saying something to the group that had just arrived, Ethan summoned a ball of blue fire and threw it almost lazily over the still water of the pool. It hit its target—a brazier on the other side—and a bright warm flame rose instantly. He lit two more braziers, then paused and turned to face his audience, a cocky grin on his face. He held his arms out at his sides and lifted them dramatically. The other dozen braziers lining the perimeter of the area, as well as the big firepit opposite the bar, all flared to life.

I couldn't help smirking. His friends were loving the show, shouting and clapping Ethan on the back. He was reminding me of the confident, full-of-life jock I'd first been warned against by the Reds. But that memory was making me think of Beth—poor Beth—and Zara . . .

I couldn't go there. Instead, I focused on the small, pulling ache that had appeared in my chest. It had been a while since I'd transferred any Light to Ethan, and he'd just used up every extra bit he had with his little magic trick. He wasn't depleted to a dangerous level—not by a long shot. I wouldn't have even registered this mild of a pull a few months ago, but our Bond was deepening by the day, and I could sense their needs more and more effortlessly.

I pressed my palm flat against the windowpane and called up the Light, making my skin glow that ethereal white, and remotely transferred just enough to replace what Ethan had used up.

His chest puffed out on a deep breath, and he paused midsentence and looked straight up at my window. Even from this far up, I could see the dimples from his smile—or maybe I just knew them so well I could picture them without having to see them.

I smiled back, shutting off the flow and snuffing out the weird glow with it.

"That is so fucking creepy," Dot murmured, staring at me from her spot on the floor, one hand still holding the mascara wand in midair. "But so fucking cool." She smiled wide, then half turned to Charlie. "Why can't you glow and transfer Light to me remotely? Underachiever. You know how handy that would be?"

He just flipped her off with a sweet smile on his face.

"It's not exactly all sunshine and rainbows," I grumbled. We still didn't fully understand *what* it was. Not to mention the fact that dozens, if not hundreds, of Vitals had been kidnapped, experimented on, and tortured by Davis Damari in his demented search for another like my mom. Like *me*.

"Hey." Charlie's gentle voice drew my attention back to him as he scooted to the edge of the bed. "None of that. I can see you overthinking it again. Blaming yourself."

We'd had several conversations about this—I wasn't hiding how I felt from my friends. They knew all about my guilt, my remorse, my worry.

"None of that was your fault. None of it. *He* did that. You saved me, Eve. You saved us all. If it wasn't for you and your impromptu trip to Australia, I don't know how long they would've taken to try the Lighthunter. I don't know if it might've been too late . . ."

He trailed off, reliving horrors I couldn't even imagine. I sat down next to him. Dot sat on his other side but remained silent.

"I'm really glad you're OK, Charlie," I whispered, resting my head on his shoulder and wrapping my arm around his waist. When I felt Dot's delicate arm over mine, I knew she was mirroring my pose.

Beneath the soft fabric under my cheek was scarring. The day after Alec and I had helped the nurses and doctors manage the pain of the burn victims, the healers had finally arrived. They'd repaired the worst of the damage, made sure the muscle was strong, the bone unaffected, the skin stitched back over it all. But even they weren't miracle workers.

Almost the entire left side of his body had been covered in

burns, some more severe than others. Most of it had returned to smooth skin after the healing, but Charlie still had scars on his hip, his elbow, and over his shoulder and neck. Most of it could be covered by clothing, but he didn't seem to care too much.

He gave us both a squeeze and then extracted himself. "All right, enough of that. This is supposed to be a celebration, no?"

"Yes!" Dot hopped up. "No more moping. Only fun and merriment from now on."

She turned back to the mirror, but I saw her wipe some of the moisture under her eyes before she went back to doing her makeup.

"I'm going to head down and get a drink." Charlie stuffed his hands into his pockets and wandered out of the room with an easy smile.

"Do you think he's OK?" Dot kept her eyes trained on her own face in the mirror but pitched her voice low.

I went to stand behind her, placing a comforting hand on her shoulder. "I think he will be. With time."

It always took time. I could attest to that. But this family I was suddenly a part of was made of tough stuff.

"I can't wait to meet Eduardo." I smiled at her, hoping to lighten the mood.

"Me too. Wish he could've been here in time for the party."

While locked in a cell, Charlie had met the love of his life, his cellmate Eduardo—the only other Vital with a sibling for a Variant that I knew of. The two of them had slowly gotten to know each other, tended each other's wounds, kept each other sane, and eventually, fell in love.

Eduardo and his brother lived in Colombia, and he was due to arrive for a visit in a few days. I'd never seen Charlie—who was sometimes even quieter than Josh—so excited.

We were excited to meet him too. In all the chaos of the rescue, Ed was taken to a different hospital and went home with his family, so none of us even knew how important he was to Charlie until he demanded a laptop so he could track Ed down.

"We'll just throw him another one." I rolled my eyes.

"Brilliant idea!"

I wasn't entirely sure if Dot was joking. I groaned, not eager to repeat this madness again so soon, and she laughed maniacally. Next to the mirror, Squiggles bobbed her upper body up and down and ran around in a few excited circles. I think it was her way of laughing.

"You two are creeping me out. I'm going downstairs." I gave them one last frown and turned for the door.

As I passed Josh's room, I poked my head in. He had music playing—some band I didn't even recognize.

I crossed the room to the bathroom. The light was on inside, and the door was ajar. I nudged it the rest of the way open and smiled.

Josh was standing at the sink, doing his hair. His preppy look was impeccable as always—navy chinos and a cream cashmere sweater, a checked shirt collar peeking out from underneath. I leaned in the doorway and checked out his ass as he put the finishing touches on his now perfectly styled dirty-blond hair.

Just one hour ago he'd been reading a book in sweats with a tear at the knee and a Warrant T-shirt. His favorites were the Metallica, David Bowie, and Linkin Park ones, but other than those, I hadn't seen him wear the same shirt twice.

"Can I ask you a question?" I asked. His beautiful green eyes met my dull blue ones in the mirror.

"Of course." He smiled. We were all making more of an effort to be honest with one another.

"You're obviously more comfortable in jeans and band tees. Why do you dress like an Abercrombie and Fitch model every time you're in public?"

He rinsed the hair product off his hands. "You think I look like a model?"

"Well, yes, but that wasn't my point." I smiled smugly.

He laughed, his eyebrows rising in surprise, then dried his

hands off on a towel and pressed a sweet kiss to the tip of my nose. "Don't you want to go down to the party?"

Not really. "I want to know more about you. I thought we all promised to be more honest, answer each other's questions." I looked at him expectantly.

He grabbed my hand and gently pulled me into his room. "Come on, I'll show you."

He led me to the impressive bookcases on the opposite side of the room and stopped in front of the complicated sound system. The shelving reached almost to the top of the twelve-foot ceilings, and neither one of us could reach the top without a stepladder. He pointed up, and I craned my neck. The entire top shelf was lined with identical brown leather-bound spines without titles.

"Those are my dad's journals. He used to write in one every day." Josh's arms circled around me, his chest pressing into my back. "When our parents died, I was so lost. The only people I would even talk to were the guys. Then I hit puberty, and I was just angry *all the time*. Some of that anger was directed at my parents. I nearly threw all these out. I packed them up and dragged them all the way down that ridiculous driveway"—we both chuckled—"to dump them on the curb. I figured if they weren't going to be around, I didn't want to get to know them any better. But Alec saw and dragged them right back, and then a few years later, he gave them back to me. It was right around the time he and Gabe were getting heavy into the fighting scene. Kid and I started tagging along, getting mixed up with shady people. That's when they got their shit together and Alec pulled these out of his closet. I was so happy he'd saved them I cried like a little baby."

I didn't speak, riveted.

"I started reading them and couldn't stop. It's what started my obsession with books. I inherited all the vinyl from my dad, but all the books were my mom's. It's funny that reading my dad's journals is what got me to start reading at all. Anyway, my dad was dirt poor growing up. He lived in a trailer with his aunt and went hungry more than a few times a month. But he studied hard, stayed out of trouble, and got himself a scholarship to Bradford Hills Institute. That's where he met my mom. But everyone judged him for his worn, old clothes. No one took him seriously. People constantly dropped jokes about how he was punching above his weight with my mom, wondering what the hell she was doing with him."

I frowned, my heart aching for Josh's dad. I knew what it was like to be on the receiving end of derisive comments about who you were dating—I'd been subjected to months of it from Ethan's exes.

"My dad wasn't a vain man, but he firmly believed in making a good impression—that if you presented well, people were less likely to judge you on what you looked like and more likely to listen to what you had to say. He got pretty successful in the music business, made his own money, and dressed in a three-piece suit every day of his life. He was only relaxed and casual with his family."

"Like you," I whispered, and he smiled.

"Yeah. I didn't grow up poor like my dad—they left me a lot of money—but I learned a lot reading his journals, and this place . . . much as I love Bradford Hills and my family, Variants can be judgmental, bitchy, and gossipy. I refuse to give them any reason to say I'm less than, that I don't belong here because my dad was trailer trash. I make an effort with my appearance not because I care too much what people think but because it was important to my dad, and because it makes me feel closer to him."

For a beat, we fell into silence, Josh's revelations sitting heavy between us. I didn't know what to say. On one hand, it seemed like a massive burden—feeling as if you had to look a certain way so your place in society would never be questioned. But on the other, it didn't feel as if Josh was pandering to the stuck-up Variant elites. He was just trying to do his dad proud.

"Plus, have you felt how fucking soft this cashmere sweater is?" Josh grinned, obviously trying to lighten the mood. "It's like butter."

I smiled. "I think your dad would be proud of you."

A wave of emotion crossed his features, and he cleared his throat, looking down. I wrapped my arms around his neck tightly, and he crushed me to him in one of his signature hugs.

When the giant speakers came to life downstairs, the heavy bass of some hip-hop song interrupted the moment. Josh kissed me firmly on the lips, only just teasing me with his tongue before pulling away.

"Let's get down there before Ethan comes looking for us." He took my hand and led me down the stairs. I was worried for a second I'd upset him by unwittingly bringing up his parents, but if anything, he looked a little lighter—as though a burden had been lifted, now shared with me.

But to me, it didn't feel like a burden. I knew more about Josh and his history, and I couldn't wait to hear even more—to learn more about each of them. It felt like a gift. I smiled and squeezed Josh's hand as we descended into the growing chaos of the party.

I was looking forward to seeing Ty. He'd been at work all day but had promised to be at the party. Even Alec had grunted noncommittally when we asked if he'd come. It wasn't a yes, but it wasn't a no either.

I wasn't sure if he'd be there, but I wasn't sure of a lot when it came to Alec. He'd relaxed considerably since all the secrets between us had been laid on the table; he wasn't flinching away from my touch now that we knew his ability could take pain away as well as inflict it. But his unreturned declaration of love sat awkwardly between us. Over the past couple months, he'd become quiet—not necessarily angry or defensive like before, but certainly more thoughtful. Add that to the fact that any time I tried, he found a way to avoid sex with me, and I knew something more was festering in that complicated, broody mind of his.

I was hoping the party would give us all an opportunity to relax a little, but I was also hoping it would allow me to get to the bottom of the Master of Pain's latest issue with me.

TWO

The setting sun cast the vast, open spaces of the Zacarias mansion into shadow. As Josh and I reached the bottom of the stairs, someone flicked the lights on, and the ostentatious chandelier in the foyer tinkled to life.

A maid opened the heavy front door, letting another few partygoers in. I didn't know them, but they waved to Josh as they passed, following the music to the back of the house.

We trailed after them, our hands swinging between us.

"You kids have fun tonight. You've all more than earned it."

We turned to see Uncle Lucian emerge from the corridor leading to the west wing. A black-clad Melior Group agent walked ahead of him, carrying a small piece of luggage toward the garage.

"Thanks, Uncle Luce." Josh leaned down slightly to give Lucian a hand slap–fist bump combo.

Lucian had survived the rescue mission, but not unscathed. He was in a wheelchair, and despite the healer's best efforts, it didn't look as if he would ever walk again. The damage to his hip and spine was just too severe.

"Are you sure you don't want one of . . . the guys to go with you?" I was about to say one of us, but I wasn't entirely comfortable including myself. The guys were incredibly close to their uncle, and I still wasn't sure how I fit into that dynamic.

"I'll be fine." He smiled. Despite being confined to a wheelchair, Lucian Zacarias was all poise and dignity—his clothes impeccably fitted, his salt-and-pepper hair trimmed, his face clean-shaven. "I have a whole Melior Group team for security, and two nurses to tend to my every need."

He was staying in his city apartment for the night. He said it was because he had early appointments with specialists and doctors, but I was pretty sure he was just leaving so we would have his gigantic house to ourselves.

"And me." Olivia, Lucian's sister and Dot and Charlie's mom, came out of the nearest room. She stopped behind her brother and rested her hands on the back of his chair. "What am I? Chopped liver?"

Lucian rolled his eyes, but humor crinkled at the edges. "Yes, Olivia, you're a damn saint. I don't know what my team of well-paid, highly skilled people and I would do without you."

I stifled a laugh.

Olivia whacked him on the back of the head. "Ungrateful little shit. Do you have any idea what you put us all through while you took the world's longest nap?"

"Nap? I was in a coma! And isn't it politically incorrect to hit people in wheelchairs?"

"Whatever. Come on, wheelie, Henry's meeting us for dinner. I don't want to be late." She pushed his chair forward, giving us a stern motherly look as she passed. "Don't get into too much trouble."

Lucian yelled over his shoulder, "Get into as much trouble as you can. In fact, try to trash the place! We have all these contractors around. I wouldn't mind an excuse to keep them longer and get the kitchen remodeled!"

They bickered all the way to the parking garage door, where

two burly Melior Group agents picked Lucian's chair up and carried him down the stairs. The contractors Lucian had mentioned were working on making the mansion more accessible, but most areas still didn't have ramps installed.

"Come on, let's get a drink." Josh tugged me in the direction of the kitchen.

A few hours later, I was sitting on the kitchen bench facing the dance floor, my third cocktail in hand. The bright orange drink perfectly matched Dot's outfit.

She was in tangerine from head to toe. She should've looked like a traffic cone or a Teletubby, but she didn't. The high-waisted pants and crop top fit her small frame so perfectly I had a feeling they were tailored. Paired with bold black jewelry and dangerous black platform heels, they made her look like a supermodel.

She was tearing it up on the dance floor while I chatted with Charlie and a couple of his friends about their theses. We'd gotten into a lively discussion about Variant abilities and how they seemed to evolve with other advancements—like the ability to control electronics.

I spotted Alec moving slowly along the edge of the room but kept my focus on the conversation, animatedly waving my drink in the air to emphasize my point. A tiny bit spilled, and when I looked for a spot to set the drink down, I glimpsed blonde hair near the dining table. Leaning up against the wall was Dana.

She was dressed in all black, no hint of the revealing top she'd looked like sex in the last time, and she was alone, her arms crossed, her gaze focused on something in the crowd of dancers. I glanced in the same direction but couldn't figure out what she was looking at.

"Eve?" Charlie brought my attention back to the conversation.

"Sorry!" I blurted out. "I just have to go do something."

I knocked back the rest of my drink and discarded the empty glass on the counter. It didn't take me long to spot Tyler.

In jeans and a casual shirt—with rolled-up sleeves, of course—he stood at the other end of the island, speaking to a colleague from Bradford Hills Institute's Admissions Department. Where the last party had been mostly college kids, this one had a mix of ages and, according to Dot, fewer attendees. It still looked like a concert crowd to me, but either way, it was definitely mellower.

As I approached, Tyler took a sip of his scotch, and his eyes found mine. He smiled and pulled me into his side. After he introduced me to his colleagues, I excused us and pulled him a few steps away.

"I have a question," I said close to his ear. His intelligent gray eyes looked at me lovingly, but I didn't actually want to voice my question.

I pressed my lips to his cheek, letting the kiss linger for a moment as I transferred a little extra Light. I could've just glowed and done it remotely, but while the Variant crowd was used to Vitals with multiple Variants, and therefore multiple partners, they were still wary of the glowing. No one really knew what to make of that yet. Least of all me.

When I pulled away, Tyler had a knowing look in his eyes and an amused smile playing at his lips. "What's your question, Eve?"

His ability would've immediately filled in the gaps: I wanted to know why Dana was there. I wanted to know who invited her and why she'd come when she looked so miserable.

Tyler looked over my shoulder, but I made sure not to turn. The last thing I needed was for her to think we were talking about her. Even though we were.

"She's on duty." He pulled me closer. "She's security detail for one of the Vitals here. He hasn't spoken to her in months, other than at work."

He watched my face for a reaction. I nodded and smiled, hoping my expression looked relaxed and didn't give away the confusing mess of feelings writhing inside me.

I knew Alec wasn't interested in her anymore. He'd told me so himself. He loved me. He'd told me that too. But he hadn't said it since, and he was once again keeping his distance. My insecurities were getting to me. I hadn't said it back to him—I wasn't sure I felt it yet—but I still didn't like the idea of him being with another woman. Especially her.

The very fact that I was overthinking this shit pissed me off, and I rolled my eyes at myself. I was just letting past hurts and worries get to me. She hadn't said it in so many words, but even Dana had made it clear she was no longer after Alec.

"Thanks, Ty." I pressed another kiss to his cheek and, before he could stop me, pushed through the crowd.

"Hey." I smiled a little too brightly when I reached her.

She frowned, then went back to scanning the crowd. "Hi."

"Um, do you want a drink?" I gestured to the bar outside.

She didn't look at me. "I'm on duty. I can't drink."

"I mean, like, juice or soda or something . . ."

After a few moments of awkward silence, I sighed and turned to go, but at that moment, she spoke. "I could go for a lemonade."

"Coming right up!" I sped away from her, on a mission. Once I'd grabbed her a lemonade at the bar, I wriggled back through the crowd, handed it to her wordlessly, and smiled.

She took a sip. "We don't have to be friends. I don't need your pity."

I crossed my arms. "Trust me, there is no pity. And no, we don't have to be friends. But we don't *not* either."

"What?" She finally looked at me, confused.

"Look, all I'm saying is, what's in the past is over, and we have enough *actual* enemies—people trying to kidnap and maim and kill us—that there's no point being hostile over petty shit."

She sighed. "OK. Fair point."

Even though trying to make peace felt all kinds of awkward, Dana hadn't done anything wrong. She'd fallen for Alec—they'd found solace in each other when the rest of society had shunned them. She hadn't known I was his Vital. I had a feeling Dana, just like Alec, didn't really have any friends. If nothing else, I could understand her on that front. I'd gone my whole life feeling lonely until I came to Bradford Hills.

I'd extended an olive branch, but that was enough for one night. "Anyway, have a good night." I smiled, more genuinely this time, and turned to leave.

"Thanks for the drink," she called after me. I could've sworn it sounded sincere.

I made my way back toward the bar. In my awkwardness with Dana, I'd forgotten to get myself another drink, and after that, I needed one. Ahead of me, people started laughing nervously and jostling each other out of the way. Next thing I knew, I was face-to-face with the Master of Pain himself.

He looked just as calm and unyielding as he always did, at least to the casual observer, but I could see the panic in his slightly wide eyes, his clenched teeth. I flashed him a smile and kept going. Judging by how easy it suddenly was to walk through the crowd, he followed close behind.

He sidled up next to me when I reached the bar. Once I'd placed my order, he spoke. "I didn't invite her. She's here on duty. Just so we're clear, I meant what I said—I only want you."

He kept his voice pitched low, so I answered the same way: "I know."

He frowned, confused. He'd expected drama. I tried not to let the amusement show on my face.

I'd seen him a few times throughout the night, sometimes speaking to someone, sometimes with one of my guys, but always off to the side and always watching me. Which made me wonder . . .

"Are you on duty?" I asked.

"Working? Not tonight. But I'm always on duty when it comes to your safety." He leaned in a little as he said it, making the statement that much more dramatic.

I rolled my eyes. The buzz of the alcohol was making me bolder. "Why do you have to be so fucking intense all the time?" I flashed him a cheeky smile. The bartender slid two Long Island iced teas across to me, and I thanked him.

Alec was frowning so hard the scar in his right eyebrow was puckering. "I'm not—"

"You're pretty fucking intense, bro." Ethan did not keep his voice down as he slapped a big hand on Alec's shoulder, gaining a few nervous laughs from the people nearby.

"Hey, my little pony." He flashed me a dimpled grin. The nicknames were getting ridiculous.

"Hey, care bear." I smiled back and took a long drink.

Alec snatched the other cocktail. It was intended for Dot, but he threw the straw on the ground and gulped the drink in one go, not even flinching at the amount of alcohol. "I am not—" he began again, but Ethan's and my burst of laughter interrupted him. The look in his eyes was just so . . . *intense!*

"Come dance with me!" Ethan demanded and, without waiting for an answer, threw me over his shoulder and headed for the dance floor. I shrieked but managed not to spill too much of my drink. I waved at Alec, who was staring after us, his hands in fists.

I finished my drink as Ethan and I found Dot in the middle of the dance floor. Someone coming past took the empty glass, and I wrapped my hands around Ethan's neck. His hands went to my hips. Every inch of my front was pressed up against the hard muscles of Ethan's body.

After a few songs, I felt the heat of another body at my back, but Ethan smiled mischievously and the touch felt familiar, so I didn't panic. Another pair of hands landed on my waist, just above Ethan's, and when I turned my head to look, my eyes found intelligent gray ones.

I was a little surprised to see Tyler and not Josh, but I wasn't complaining. He caught my lips with his, teasing my mouth with his tongue as he pressed closer. The three of us moved seamlessly in time with the music, and I lost myself in their touch.

To see Tyler, who was always so careful and controlled, with a little bit of glassiness in his eyes—to feel him gripping my waist with his hands, kissing me so passionately in a room full of people —was driving me nuts! I loved to see him let loose a little. It was so rare, but when it happened, I just about went weak at the knees.

As the music changed to a slightly slower, more sultry beat, he broke the kiss and, always the leader, set the pace. It wasn't long before the three of us were pretty much just grinding on each other, and I was loving every second of it.

I glanced around the room. Alec stood near the hallway leading to the front of the house, his stare fixed on me. I didn't care how much he denied it—he was intense in everything he did. But as much as I teased him, I wouldn't change that. Alec didn't do anything by halves, and something about that was intoxicating, even as I got more and more frustrated by his assholeish behavior.

I kept my gaze fixed on his as Ethan and Tyler swayed with me, their hands running up and down my sides, gripping me, stroking me. Having Alec watching added another layer of desire to my already heated state.

The music changed to a loud and fast crowd favorite that had everyone jumping up and down to the beat. It broke our lust haze, and we pulled apart to join in.

My skin was still flushed, and the ache low in my belly wasn't going away. I looked back to where Alec had been standing. He was walking toward the front door, one hand rubbing his closely cropped hair. He must have reached his quota of peopling for the day, if not the week.

"I'm gonna check on Alec," I yelled close to Tyler's ear, and he gave me a look that somehow managed to be both skeptical and knowing.

I rolled my eyes and took off through the crowd.

Alec was being as up-front as the others when it came to our unspoken commitment to brutal honesty, but he was still avoiding deepening our physical connection. He'd relaxed about the extra Light since we'd discovered he could use it to take pain away and not just inflict it, but he was still hesitant, still insisting we needed to train and practice and be controlled about the levels. I couldn't get it into his head that controlling how much I transferred to them was effortless now, that knowing exactly how much they needed was second nature.

Of course, I hadn't crossed that physical barrier with Alec yet as I had with the others, so the Light was pushing me to him, drawing me to connect. On the rare occasion I did slip, it was always with him, and he always used it as ammo to argue we still needed to be careful.

But there was more to it. My mind kept filling in the "why" with the worst-case scenario: He didn't want me like that. He'd given in to the Light and accepted the Bond, but it wasn't what he truly wanted.

I could've asked him, of course, but I was being a coward. Once again, we found ourselves at a standstill, things between us strained.

As I descended the stairs past the front door, I had just enough liquid courage to push the issue, and I knew exactly how I wanted to push it.

The gravel crunched under my boots as I rushed to catch up to him, the light and noise of the party fading behind us. He must've heard me chasing him, but he didn't slow down— unyielding as ever. The tattoos I knew were all over his body peeked out from under the sleeves of his black T-shirt. The fabric stretched over his broad shoulders, tension making the corded muscle even more prominent.

I caught up and slid my hand into his, tugging lightly. He huffed but stopped immediately. "I'm not leaving, Evelyn. I just needed some air."

"I know." I tugged again, and he let me lead him between two of the massive trees lining the driveway. The party was in full swing, no one was around, and we were about halfway between the security at the gate and the security at the front door. We were alone, but I craved more privacy, more darkness. I always did with him.

I could've started a conversation, asked if he'd had enough of the party, made small talk. But I didn't feel like talking. There was more than one way to sort shit out between us.

I faced him, playing with the hem of my red sweater. Without thinking about it too hard, I whipped the soft fabric over my head and dropped it to the ground. The air was cool, but my skin felt as if it were on fire.

His eyes narrowed but stayed glued to mine, refusing to look down at my matching red lace bra. I pushed the pang of rejection aside, placed my hands on his hips, and tilted my face up, practically begging him to kiss me.

He was so still, every muscle in his body strained as if poised for an attack. I couldn't reach his lips if he didn't lower his head, so I pulled the neck of his T-shirt down and kissed his chest. He smelled like smoke from the bonfire and some other fresh, manly smell—probably his aftershave. I darted my tongue out for a tiny lick.

As if my tongue had flipped a switch, he grunted and sprang into motion. He grabbed under my ass with both hands and lifted me. I wrapped my legs around him, and my back slammed into the rough surface of the tree just as Alec's lips slammed into mine.

I groaned and rolled my hips. He was rock hard already. This was that all-consuming intensity I loved so much. I knew it wasn't healthy to avoid talking about our issues, but fuck if my body couldn't care less. When Alec kissed me like that, nothing else existed.

But as suddenly as it started, Alec broke the kiss and stepped away, dropping me to my feet. He leaned one hand on the tree next to my head and dragged the other down his face. We were both breathing hard.

"What are you . . . *why*, Alec?" I hated how desperate, how hurt, I sounded.

"You don't want this," he ground out, his eyes downcast.

"What?" I was not expecting that to be his answer. "You don't get to decide what I do and don't want, you fucking jerk."

His eyes flicked up, now full of defiance, his anger rising to meet mine. "You are so fucking impossible sometimes."

I took a deep breath. I hadn't come after him for this to become another screaming match. "Please explain what you mean, because I'm getting really confused, Alec. I can't keep doing this."

He sighed. "It's just the Light. You've done it with the other three, and the only reason you want me is because of the fucking Bond. It's pushing you to make it even."

I blinked and stared at him. He was keeping his distance because he thought I didn't want to be with him?

I threw my head back and laughed because I didn't know what else to do. The laugh ended on a groan, and I opened my eyes to look at him.

His teeth were grinding, his eyes narrowed, but there was hurt behind the anger.

"I'm not laughing at you," I rushed out. "I'm laughing because I've been having this exact same doubt—worrying that you didn't actually want to be with me. That you resented the Bond. Sometimes it's eerie how similar we are." I ended on a whisper.

"I want you." He ran his thumb over my cheek, and I leaned into the touch. "Don't ever doubt that. But I don't want to do this if it's not for the right reasons. I want you to want me too, and not just because the Light makes you."

"I *do* want you, you idiot," I whispered back, but he just gave me a skeptical look.

I rolled my eyes and swatted his hand away. "*You* can resist the pull of the Bond, have enough self-control to not fuck my brains out while the others are doing exactly that, but you don't believe *I* can decide for myself whether or not I want to be with you? So, what—you're not controlled by the Light but everyone else is? Give me a break."

He opened and closed his mouth a few times, then just sighed, defeated.

"Fine," I declared. "Then I'll prove it to you."

I sank to my knees, keeping my gaze locked on his, and slowly but confidently reached for his pants.

"What are you doing?" he asked, exasperated, as I started undoing the buttons on his jeans.

"Showing you I can control myself." I pushed down his pants, but before I could reach for the underwear, he wrapped his hands around my wrists.

"Get up, Evelyn, you don't know what you're doing."

I gritted my teeth. His assumption was patronizing and just plain mean, but I refused to allow my anger to rise. I had something to prove. I may not have been as experienced as him, but I'd been with enough guys to know how to give a blowjob.

I stayed exactly where I was and stared him down. He'd stopped what I was doing, but he wasn't leaving. That meant he didn't actually want to. I was *so* close to breaking him.

"Alec, remove your shirt, put your hands on the fucking tree, and shut up." I didn't let any frustration leak into my voice. He ground his teeth, his icy eyes glaring at me, his nostrils flared. Then he huffed, released my wrists, and did as he was told.

His shirt joined mine on the ground, and I spared a moment to appreciate his amazing body—the tattoos, the scars, the V at his hips leading right where I needed to focus. As he lifted his head to the dark sky on another sigh, I grinned.

He wasn't leaving, and he was actually listening to me. He was *trusting* me.

By the time his gaze returned to mine, I'd schooled my features into a neutral expression. I placed my hands on his hips, rubbing his hip bones with my thumbs to let him get used to my touch. Before I went any further, I checked in with my Light. The strain of it wasn't unbearable, but it was definitely nudging me to Alec, wanting to bring him into the fold of our Bond. I locked it down tight. I closed the flow in and out of me and bolted that shit.

Then I moved my fingers to the waistband of his briefs and pulled them down, freeing his erection.

As I slowly stroked him up and down, I could feel that pressure building at the base of my spine again, the desire to take more, to demand more from him. But I did my best to lock that down too and focused on the silky-smooth feeling of him in my hand.

I looked up at him. He was looking down, but he wasn't watching my hand; he was watching me, his eyes boring into mine, the emotion swirling there incomprehensible. I kept eye contact as I leaned forward and took him into my mouth.

His eyes narrowed, hooded; his lips parted on a sigh.

I loved every fucking second of it. I loved watching Alec give in, let go of some of that fear and self-loathing and just feel *good*.

It was *my* hands, *my* mouth making him feel good, making him let go.

I took him deeper into my mouth, swirling my tongue around the tip as I pulled away. One hand stayed at the base of his cock, the other at his hip as I set a steady rhythm.

He groaned, his breathing coming in pants. After a while his hips started making little involuntary jerks, and I knew he was close. But I refused to let him have any control.

I released him from my mouth and squeezed his hip to get his attention. He looked down at me, a hint of surprise and a little fear in his gaze.

"Don't move," I whispered, an inch away from his throbbing hardness. My eyes were challenging. "I am in control here. Understand?"

He nodded and bit his bottom lip.

I nearly groaned. I knew what it felt like to have those teeth biting *my* lip.

Once again, I took him into my mouth. He sighed, the sound pure ecstasy. I heard light scraping as he tried to grip the bark.

As Alec dug his nails into the tree, I dug mine into his hip, reminding him I was in charge. His breathing had become completely erratic, moans and groans escaping his mouth more and more often, eliciting my own sounds of pleasure.

My lips were starting to go a little numb from the constant friction, but it wasn't long before he released a guttural sound and came in my mouth. I swallowed it, gagging slightly as I wasn't prepared, then stroked him gently and sat back on my heels.

I rested my head against the tree and sighed. Above me, Alec was shaking lightly through the aftershock of his orgasm.

I stood slowly and pressed a kiss to his chest, letting his trembling arms box me in. When my lips touched his skin, he dropped his arms and wrapped me in a hug.

"Maybe you should sit before you fall down," I whispered into his neck, smiling.

"No." He nuzzled into my hair. "I have a favor to return."

He dragged his rough hands down my sides, then cupped my ass over my jeans.

I leaned away and put that serious look back on my face. "No. I don't want that from you today."

His brow furrowed in clear confusion and hurt. I realized I'd echoed the cruel words he'd left me with in Tyler's study, just after he'd driven me to the brink of ecstasy and not allowed me to return the favor.

"I want *everything* from you, Alec." I injected as much conviction into my voice as I could, saying the exact opposite of what he'd told me back then. "I want you in every way, and I don't know why you think I don't. But this is about me proving to you I have control. *I* have control over my Light and my desire. I'm *aching* for your touch. You have no idea how hard it is to say no, to remove your amazing hands from my body." As I spoke, I grabbed his wrists and took his hands off my ass. "But I'm going to walk away now to prove to you I can. I have just as much self-control as you, Bond be damned."

For a few seconds, I took in the stunned yet hopeful expression on his face, then I kissed him on the lips once, grabbed my sweater, and pulled it back on as I walked away. I made my point and left him there, his dick hanging out, shocked but satisfied and, hopefully, convinced.

The thumping bass from the house reminded me there was a party still in full swing, and I headed in search of my guys. I'd lit a spark with Alec that I hadn't allowed to ignite fully, but the music was pulsing and so was my desire. Someone was getting lucky tonight . . . maybe a few someones.

THREE

I was trying to finish my cereal before Ethan got back from his run. He loved feeding me, and it was always waffles this and poached eggs that. I loved it most of the time, but it was next to impossible to match the enthusiasm he had from the second he woke up. I needed coffee before I could even speak coherently. Sometimes, I just wanted to sit at the bench, eat my Wheaties, and drink my delicious latte.

I'd put the TV on for background noise but soon remembered why we were all avoiding it—except for Tyler, of course. The four TVs in his office were always on, and he scrolled through news sites on his phone as much as he sent messages and emails. I wondered if it was this aspect of his nature—the desire for knowl-edge—that had determined his Variant ability or if it was his ability that made him crave knowledge more and more. It was a chicken-and-egg problem. According to evolutionary biology, eggs in general have been around for roughly 340 million years, whereas chickens evolved some fifty-eight thousand years ago. Science had solved that problem, but I didn't know how to solve it in Tyler's case.

The news for the past month had been all about the events at the lab in Thailand. They were getting some of it wrong and just plain making up the rest, but the Melior Group board had put a gag on any of their staff discussing the events, and they'd encouraged survivors and their families to stay quiet too. They wanted to avoid spreading panic about the kind of experiments that had happened down there, as well as prevent tensions between humans and Variants from escalating.

I shoved another spoonful of cereal into my mouth and frowned at the TV. I hadn't registered the channel when I turned it on, but the remote was so far away, in the living room, I didn't have the energy to get up and change it.

It was on a conservative human news network. They had a rotating stream of politicians and social commentators making wild assumptions and whipping up fear.

". . . and why won't the mighty Melior Group comment on what exactly they found?" demanded a heavily made-up middle-aged woman in a blue pantsuit. The rest of the panel nodded in agreement. "Surely they've finished their investigation by now, but they won't even tell us *that* much. How can we be sure it wasn't actually *them* running these experiments—trying to make themselves stronger or inventing new abilities. I mean, this could be a real threat to national security, Tom." Her face was nearly purple as she finished her tirade.

"What a moron," I mumbled into my cup, taking another sip of my latte.

"Who's a moron?" Tyler came into the kitchen dressed in a white shirt with a tie, his hair the neatest I'd ever seen it.

I pointed at the TV with my spoon. "Some nutbag."

He frowned, went over to the living area, and changed the channel to a breakfast show. "Don't watch that crap, baby. We know the truth. That's all that matters."

I huffed but couldn't help smiling. He'd called me "baby." I'd been having regular sex with him for weeks now, but I still had a massive crush. Any time he flirted or used a pet name, I got butterflies in my stomach.

"Why are you all dressed up?" I asked.

He was standing at the fridge, eating strawberry yogurt from the tub. "I have a meeting." He looked at his watch. "And I'll be late if I don't get going."

He shoved three more giant spoonfuls into his mouth, gathered his messenger bag, kissed me on the lips (butterflies!), and ran off.

I'd just stood up to put my bowl in the dishwasher when Ethan and Josh came into the kitchen. They were both freshly showered after their workout, Ethan's hair slightly damp but Josh's perfectly styled and parted on the side.

"Hey, pumpkin tits!" Ethan grinned at me as Josh wrapped his arms around me from the back, nuzzling his nose into my hair. "Want some breakfast?"

I absentmindedly rested my hands over Josh's. "No thanks. I ate."

I didn't throw a ridiculous nickname back at him—the TV had distracted me again. The cooking segment had given way to a news report. "Protests against Variant-run institutions and businesses have turned violent as tensions between human picketers and frustrated Variant business owners begin to boil over. In Los Angeles, a large group of protesters outside a Variant abilities training studio started breaking windows, and a fight broke out when the business owner—a Variant with a water ability—attempted to disperse the crowd by dousing them with water. Similar incidents have occurred in other cities the world over, with some of the worst violence seen in Moscow, where a riot erupted. The widespread violence resulted in several deaths and many injuries with . . ."

I hardly registered Ethan's protestations about me having fed myself. I waved him off, my full focus on the TV.

Variant Valor were getting louder and more brazen in their discriminatory rhetoric, and more and more Variants were no longer ashamed to say they subscribed to the organization's extremist views. Some had even set up local branches and held meetings. We'd been invited to more than one in Bradford Hills.

Tyler and the administration at the Institute were doing all they could to shut it down, but there wasn't much they could do about people meeting off campus.

The Human Empowerment Network had taken on a life of its own. Melior Group investigations had all but confirmed that the HEN had been started by Variant Valor and Davis Damari himself to create more fear and unrest, making it easier to push the boundaries of what was acceptable in terms of controversial legislation and risky experiments and business ventures. Davis had no qualms about breaking the law when it came to his demented science experiments. He had enough power and influence to build an underground facility in Thailand without anyone knowing or questioning it.

"It's going to turn into World War III at this rate." I groaned and rubbed my forehead as images of the riots in Russia flicked across the screen.

Josh used his ability to press the power button on the remote. "Hey, look at me." He turned me in his arms, and I looked into his kind green eyes. "The news always makes it seem worse than it is. They're fearmongers. That's exactly what Davis wants—more fear —but it doesn't change the facts. There's a whole private security firm, hundreds of highly trained operatives, working against him. All you have to worry about today is focusing on your lectures and your chemistry lab. OK?" He raised his eyebrows.

I nodded and went to get ready for school, but the heavy feeling of dread still sat in the pit of my stomach. I focused instead on the weight of the books I stuffed into my bag and the hint of Josh's cologne as I slipped on his Bradford Hills Institute hoodie.

When I'd grabbed everything I needed, I went back downstairs, sitting on the bottom step to put my boots on. They were a cute black pair of ankle boots that went great with my skinny jeans.

"Has Tyler left already?" Lucian came out of the west wing corridor dressed in a suit and tie, a briefcase on his knees. "I thought we were heading in together."

He looked around and I followed his gaze. Plaster dust covered the marble floor of the foyer, and various piles of building material and tools littered one side of the wide space. Lucian had to navigate slowly around some timber to join me at the staircase, and I frowned at the offending wood. I would have to have a chat with the contractors about being mindful of their client.

"He said something about having an important meeting and ran out about half an hour ago." I shrugged.

"Oh. Must've come up last minute." Lucian shrugged too, not at all put out by the fact that his adopted nephew and righthand man had left him behind.

Boots thudded down the stairs. I turned to see Alec jogging down, dressed in his Melior Group blacks but not armed. His ink was snaking out of the sleeves of the tight long-sleeved T-shirt and crawling up his neck. I wanted to tear the fabric away to see them fully, move my hands down his defined, scarred chest and undo his belt . . .

"You're going in with me and my team, Uncle Luce." Alec's deep voice drew me out of my lascivious thoughts, and I was glad I couldn't blush. "Gabe had to rush in."

"Ready when you are." Lucian smiled and started to wheel himself over to the garage door. "Have a good day, Evie."

"You too!" I yelled after him.

Alec held a hand out, and I took it, letting him pull me up to standing. His jaw tightened as he watched Lucian navigate the new ramp down into the garage.

His focus was on his uncle, but his hand was still wrapped around mine. We'd come so far from the days when he couldn't even stand to be in the same room as me, but every step forward with Alec felt like a step up an impossibly steep incline, and the path was along a cliff with no railings. Shit could turn catastrophic at any moment.

But the blowjob I'd given him at the party had made my point. We hadn't talked about it, but I knew Alec needed to process things in his own silent way. Sometimes that took him a long time.

Meanwhile, every time I laid eyes on him, I wanted to jump him and tear his clothes off. Part of that was the Light pushing me to even the connection to my Bondmates, but part of it was *me.*

I just hoped I'd proven I could control that aspect of our connection. He was more affectionate, slowly thawing out. He was getting there. But would he get there before my ovaries exploded?

I gave his hand a squeeze. "He'll be fine. He's a strong man. He raised your stubborn ass, didn't he?"

Alec looked down at me and blinked in surprise, but his beautiful lips pulled up into a smirk. Rather than acknowledge my assumption about what he was thinking, he pressed those smirking lips against mine, pushing his tongue into my mouth.

I couldn't even remember what I was teasing him about.

"Upstairs . . ." I whispered against his lips. I couldn't even fully form the thought; I just wanted to get him into a locked room. He groaned and ran his teeth over the curve in my neck before placing a gentle kiss in the same spot.

"Duty calls," he growled. He gave my ass one last squeeze and stepped away.

"And we'll be late to class if we don't get going." Josh sounded amused as Ethan grabbed my bag off the bottom step, flashing me a wink and a dimple. When did they even come into the room?

Alec kissed my forehead and disappeared into the garage. I took several deep breaths and made myself think about the chemistry lab I had that afternoon.

Two silent agents drove us to campus in a blacked-out, bullet-proof vehicle, another car following close behind. The bald man in the passenger seat was my security detail for the day. Since I often had Alec or Tyler with me, I didn't have a regular guard, so when they were both busy, it was always someone different.

I stared out the window at the trees swaying in the light wind and soft sunlight. All the snow had melted weeks ago, and despite the lingering chill, it would've been a nice day to walk. But our days of walking to campus were over. Being exposed outside of a safe zone—like the Institute, the mansion, or Charlie and Dot's place—had been deemed too much of a security risk.

Thinking about chemistry, the weather, and the constant threat on my life helped to distract me from Alec's lips and body, and by the time we were pulling through the security checkpoint at the gates, the throbbing between my legs had almost completely stopped.

My bald companion stayed glued to my side the entire morning, opting to sit next to me in the lecture instead of standing in the back of the room with the other agents. Despite his closeness, he refused to engage in conversation, replying with short monotone answers while his eyes constantly scanned our surroundings. I eventually just started to ignore him.

He stayed one step behind me as I walked between classes, got myself a coffee, and picked up a book from the library. He was still half a step behind me as I headed to a café in a quieter part of campus to meet Dot and Charlie for lunch.

It was the same café where Dot had interrogated me about Alec while Charlie watched with careful interest. It seemed fitting it would be the place I would meet yet another new friend. Charlie's boyfriend, Eduardo, had landed late the previous night.

The three of them were already seated at one of the outside tables, coffees steaming in front of them, outdoor heaters keeping the chill at bay. I picked up my pace, my shadow sticking to my side.

"Hey!" I waved as I reached them, slightly winded. "I'm so sorry I'm late. My last class was on the other side of campus."

"Totally fine, girl." Dot jumped up to give me a hug, and I held her tightly for a moment. The horrific shit I was seeing in the news every day made me want to hold all my loved ones a little tighter. "We ordered you a latte."

"I love you!" I was hungry, but I needed coffee just as badly.

"Hey, Beau! Haven't seen you in a while, man. How've you been?" Charlie shared an enthusiastic handshake with my shadow, and the man's seemingly permanent scowl actually relaxed.

"Good to see you up and about, Charlie. I had to take some medical leave after rescuing your ass in Thailand. Had a couple broken ribs and shit."

Charlie laughed. "Well, thanks, man, and good to see you back on the job too. Wanna join us for lunch?"

Beau flicked his gaze to me before straightening his posture. "Thanks, but I'm on duty. Better get back to it." With a nod, he stepped back and positioned himself near the corner of the building, where he could see the whole square and keep me in easy reach.

"Eve!" Charlie didn't miss a beat. He was more animated and talkative than I'd seen him . . . probably ever. "Meet Eduardo."

He reached his arm out. A guy with short curly hair and a tan complexion stepped into Charlie's embrace and smiled at me shyly, his dark eyes meeting mine for only a fraction of a second.

"Hello." His voice was smooth and masculine but soft, almost hard to hear.

"Hi. I'm Evelyn. It's so nice to meet you!" I stuck my hand out and plastered a wide, genuine smile to my face.

He stepped away from Charlie and squared his shoulders, but instead of shaking my hand, he wrapped his arms around my waist and pulled me in for a hug.

"Oh!" He seemed so shy and quiet. The sudden display of familiarity took me aback.

I returned the hug, but he pulled back quickly.

"Thank you, Evelyn." He had a slight Spanish accent. "You saved our lives. More and more Vitals were not coming back from the lab. I don't know how much time we had left before he went too far and . . . I don't know how to repay you."

Now it was me who was unable to keep eye contact. I'd received multiple emails and DMs on social media from grateful Vitals and their families. Many people had approached me at

Bradford Hills with the same depth of gratitude Eduardo was showing now. It always surprised me.

"You're welcome." I smiled, keeping it simple.

"For someone who hounded Alec for months trying to deliver your own 'thanks for saving my life' speech, you sure don't know how to take it," Dot teased, breaking the moment.

"Hey! At least I accepted the thanks." I wagged a finger at her, and we all settled into our seats and ordered.

Once our food arrived, I turned to Charlie's new boyfriend, eager to get to know him. "So, Eduardo—"

"Please," he cut me off, "call me Ed."

"Ed." I smiled. "Your brother is your Variant?"

"Yes." He swallowed his bite of pasta before continuing. "He has a strength ability. It was hard for him to have me leave again, but he couldn't get time off work, and I had to see Charlie."

"I wish you could stay longer." Charlie pouted.

"I'm staying for a whole month!" Ed laughed but rubbed Charlie's knee.

We chatted easily for the next half hour, the sun pleasantly warm on my back. As the waitress cleared our table, a familiar noodle of fluff caught my attention. Squiggles came running out of the trees. She scampered up Dot's leg but then immediately shot across the table straight at Eduardo.

"Hey, girl!" I reached out to give her a little pat—we were becoming friends, despite only being able to communicate through Dot. She usually went straight to me after checking in with her.

Dot groaned, throwing her head back. "She can't even talk to you! How was she supposed to let you know?" She bugged her eyes out at Squiggles, and the ferret gave her a death stare, lifting her little paws onto Ed's chest.

"What's going on?" I chuckled.

"She's upset we didn't tell her we were having lunch. *Really* she's upset she lost sight of Ed for an hour. It's not my fault you don't like the food I buy you and insist on hunting your own." Dot rolled her eyes.

"Squiggles has taken a liking to Ed," Charlie explained as Ed started to scratch her little head.

"It's because I give the best head scratches," Ed cooed at the ferret.

"He does." Charlie nodded seriously, as if we were discussing Ed's qualifications for a high-paying job. "He gives the best head scratches."

Ed just smiled and lifted his other hand to the back of Charlie's head, giving him the same treatment. Both Charlie and Squiggles closed their eyes and melted into his touch.

Dot bugged her eyes at me and shook her head. *Can you believe this shit?*

I laughed silently, my shoulders shaking. *Who cares? I'm happy they're happy.*

I really was. It warmed my heart more than I could describe. Charlie still struggled with what happened to him, but he was seeing a therapist specializing in trauma, and he was safe and happy. That would always make me smile.

My phone vibrated on the table, and I picked it up and opened the email without thinking.

Dear Miss Maynard,

You don't know me, and I hope you don't mind me messaging you out of the blue. But I saw the footage of you where you glowed, and it was so similar to my own experience that I just had to reach out and . . .

The smile fell from my face, and I exited the email without finishing it, dropping my phone on the table a little harder than intended.

"What's the matter?" Dot's voice was heavy with concern. A

split second later, Squiggles leaped into my lap, her little face looking up at me.

I stroked her back, feeling the soft fur under my fingers. "Nothing really. I'm fine. Just keep getting these emails."

"What emails?" Charlie leaned forward. "Is someone bothering you?"

I waved him off. "It's nothing like that. I just keep getting messages from people claiming . . . They're from other Vitals saying they can glow like me."

"Have you been replying?" Charlie reached down for the messenger bag he usually had with him—the one with his computer. He was already going into super-hacker mode, ready to look into it, but he didn't have his computer with him. With a frown, he returned his hand to the table.

"No, I've just been ignoring them. After everything that's happened, how can I trust any of them are genuine? I mean, statistically I know it's improbable that I'm the only one with this . . . quirk. But any one of them could be Davis trying to lure me in. It's too risky and too convenient. Why have none of them come forward before? How is there absolutely no mention of this glowing bullshit anywhere? Like, *none* whatsoever?" I was starting to ramble, frustration leaking into my words as I gestured wildly.

Charlie caught one of my hands and held it on the table between us. I took a deep breath and returned the other to Squiggles's fur.

"You're right to be suspicious, Eve." Charlie gave me a hard look. "But I'm sure some part of you is curious?"

"Of course! But with Davis breathing down our necks, Variants and humans tearing each other to pieces, my GPA needing to be kept up, and Alec's stubborn ass refusing to have sex with me . . ."

I clamped my mouth shut. I couldn't believe I'd just blurted that out. Dot knew most of it anyway, and I didn't mind talking to Charlie about it, but the last thing I wanted to do was make Ed uncomfortable. When I looked in his direction though, his expression was nothing but concerned, if a little amused.

"We can deal with the Master of Pain's sexual hang-ups another day." Dot waved her hand.

"And we can deal with the emails whenever you want." Charlie patted my arm. "I can look into them, do some digging, see if they're at least legit people. But you're entitled to a private life, Eve. You don't have to answer them if you don't want to."

I nodded and let Dot change the topic. I could see Charlie's point; I was under no obligation to reply to any of these people. But the main reason I was avoiding the emails wasn't privacy—it was fear. The idea that this was another way for Davis to suck me into his clutches again—that it could put my Variants, my friends, my family in danger—terrified me.

But my mind was naturally curious. Surely some of them were legitimate, honest calls for help? If these people were telling the truth, they were likely just as scared and confused about their glowing as I was. Maybe getting together could help us solve the riddle of what the glowing was. Was that worth putting us all in potential danger again?

On the other hand, could I live with making decisions out of fear, especially at the expense of truth and knowledge? Did I want to live like that?

FOUR

The morning of my nineteenth birthday, I wasn't entirely sure how to feel. I'd found the answers to questions I'd been living with for years. I had my Bond, and we were getting stronger every day. For the first time in my life, I was introducing myself as Evelyn Maynard. I was even starting to feel as if I was part of a family.

Yet the first thing I thought about was the fact that it had been two years since I lost my mom.

I missed her so much.

I wanted to remember all the good things about her, not the gut-wrenching way her hand had been yanked out of mine as she fell to her death. That was the visual my brain kept replaying in vivid detail.

Regardless of all the positives in my life, bad things always happened around my birthday. Why should that change now?

Shit could go horribly wrong in so many different ways. Maybe this was the day Davis ordered another attack by Variant Valor. Maybe Zara would come for me with Rick's lightning ability. Maybe some other horrific thing would happen—something my mind couldn't even fathom. I was tempted to stay in bed with the curtains drawn.

But I also had people to spend my birthday *with* now. I knew my guys would have something planned, despite my telling them how I felt about birthdays. They would all be downstairs, waiting for me. Tyler and Alec would've taken the day off work. Ethan would be planning an elaborate feast. Josh had probably put an insane amount of thought into a present. I couldn't pass that up.

Ignoring the whispering what-ifs in the back of my head, I got out of bed. I brushed my teeth, stuffed my feet into my astronaut boot slippers, and headed downstairs.

As soon as I reached the bottom, Lucian came out of the corridor leading to the west wing.

"Good morning, Evie." He rolled to a stop in front of me and smiled. "Happy birthday."

I smiled back, but it didn't reach my eyes. "Thank you."

Before I could continue to the kitchen, he spoke again. "I know this day is incredibly difficult for you." He took my hand. I was expecting it to be awkward, but it was comforting. "I was hoping you would let me take you out for breakfast."

"Oh." My eyebrows rose in surprise. "Like, all of us or . . . ?" I could hear the espresso machine working in the kitchen, several male voices chatting.

"Uh, that's not what I had in mind, no. But if that's what you'd prefer . . ." He dropped my hand, gripped the wheels of his chair, and cleared his throat. "When the boys came to live with me, we kind of started a new tradition. On their birthdays I take them out, and we spend some one-on-one time together. Sometimes it's just a meal or a coffee. Other times it's a movie or an entire day. The idea is to have some quality time that's just theirs. You're a part of this family, and I'd very much like to include you in this tradition. Of course you should spend the day with your Bond, but I'd love to at least take you for coffee."

I swallowed around the lump in my throat. "I'd really like that."

I gave him my first genuine smile of the morning. I had a feeling Lucian would've been a great father. Then I realized that's exactly what he was. He was a father to the four orphaned men in the next room.

He was being a father to me.

It was the best birthday present I'd ever received.

"I'll just go get dressed." I turned for the stairs just as Ethan burst out of the kitchen.

"You're up!" He headed straight for me as he yelled over his shoulder, "Guys! She's up!"

Ethan lifted me off the ground with a firm grip around my waist and planted a dramatic kiss on my lips. "Happy birthday, sugarplum." He flashed me his dimples.

"Thanks, honey bear."

He set me back on my feet. Tyler wrapped his arms around me from behind and gave me the sweetest kiss on the cheek, whispering "Happy birthday" in my ear. I melted into his embrace, closing my eyes.

But the next thing I knew, the distinct sensation of Josh's ability tugged along my skin, and I was pulled out of Tyler's arms and straight into Josh's.

A burst of joyful laughter bubbled out of me. Josh's hugs were always a little too firm—as if he thought I'd disappear if he didn't hold on tightly enough—but I loved them.

After a barely there kiss, he whispered "Happy birthday" against my lips and slowly, reluctantly released me.

I looked over his shoulder. Alec stood slightly apart from the group, his hands in his pockets, his bright eyes watching. His strong features were relaxed—not frowning or scowling—as he waited patiently.

He'd spent a long time waiting for me.

He extended his hand, and I stepped forward and took it. As he pulled me to him, a little pang of excited nervousness shot down my spine. Would he kiss me tenderly and whisper in that honey voice? Would he bruise my lips with his intensity? I never knew.

It turned out to be a combination of the two. His sexy smirk appeared, and my honey-voiced stranger told me, "Happy birth-day, Evie." He pulled me against his chest and threaded his hand into the back of my hair. Then Alec Zacarias, Master of Pain himself, kissed me silly. I sighed, my arms brushing against the prickles of his closely cropped hair.

Someone cleared their throat. I froze and extracted myself from Alec's grip, taking a moment to catch my breath before turning back to the rest of my Bond and Uncle Lucian.

Ethan clapped his hands, the booming sound bouncing off the walls. "OK. Pancakes for breakfast?"

"Actually," I said, and they all pulled up short, "I have plans."

"Plans?" Tyler arched a brow, but Josh's eyes flew to the kind man in the wheelchair, and his lips turned up in a smile.

"Yeah. I promise I'll spend the day with you guys, but Uncle Lucian is taking me out for breakfast. Just the two of us."

I couldn't stop the grin. I hadn't intended to call him Uncle Lucian, but now that it was out there, it felt right. If things had turned out differently, I may have grown up calling him Dad, maybe never even knowing he wasn't my birth father. But that title didn't sit right. Calling him what the guys did felt natural.

I ducked my head to hide my goofy grin and made my way back upstairs before anyone could say anything.

Twenty minutes later, my hair was brushed, and I was dressed in jeans and a long, thick cardigan, an oversized scarf wrapped around my neck to ward off the cold. Lucian's driver chauffeured us—in a brand-new, wheelchair-friendly vehicle—to the little café that made the best coffee in town. The waiter seated us at a corner table and handed us some menus.

Two agents sat at a nearby table, but the rest of the security detail remained outside.

After perusing for only a few seconds, Lucian dropped the menu back on the table. "Pancakes," he breathed sadly. I frowned. "Maybe we should've stayed at home, had Ethan make you pancakes. I'm sorry . . . I forgot . . . She kept it going, right? She mentioned it several times, that she still made pancakes for you every year and . . ."

"Yes, she kept it going." I reached out and covered his hand with mine. "You know, come to think of it, I've never missed a year. Even last year, when I was in foster care with this older couple—Marty and Baz—Marty made me pancakes." I smiled fondly, reminding myself to send them an email when I got home. "They weren't Mom's pancakes, and all it did was make me think harder about the fact that she's gone, but I appreciated the gesture."

Lucian opened his mouth to say something just as our waiter walked up to the table.

"Ready to order, folks?"

"I'll have the pancakes and a latte." I didn't hesitate as I handed over my menu.

"I'll have the same." Lucian nodded. "But make mine an English breakfast tea, milk on the side."

The waiter took our menus and moved off.

I made a disgusted face. "English breakfast tea?"

Lucian laughed. "What? I lived in London for years. I picked up some habits. It's pretty good when the tea is high quality."

"I never took you for a tea snob," I teased.

"Look who's talking, miss 'fair-trade, organic espresso or nothing.'"

"At least you don't make your tea in the microwave," I conceded as we both cringed. America was the only country I'd lived in where the concept of a kettle was foreign.

"I have to admit, it's good having those espresso machines at the house and the apartment for when I want a decent coffee. Don't know why I didn't put them in sooner."

"Maybe because you can wave a distinguished hand and someone rushes out to get you one whenever you want."

He rubbed his chin in an exaggerated way. "You might be onto something. Maybe it's the novelty of doing it myself—experiencing how average people do it."

We both laughed. I was happy to see he had a sense of humor about his obscene amount of money. Just like Ethan, he didn't let his privilege go to his head.

We spent the next half hour eating the fluffy, sweet pancakes and sipping our tea and coffee while we chatted, avoiding the heavier topics of my mother and all the tensions in the world. When our plates and cups were empty, a comfortable silence settled between us. I stared out the window at the people strolling past on Bradford Hills' main street.

"Evie, before we head off"—Lucian's expression became solemn—"I wanted to speak to you about something. And if you don't want to discuss this today, just say so. It's totally fine. But I wanted to talk to you about setting up a memorial plaque for Joyce."

"Oh." I didn't know what to say. The idea hadn't even occurred to me. I'd spent the past two years trying to just survive without my mom.

Suddenly I felt as if I was letting her down. She deserved to have something permanent to mark her life. She deserved to be remembered and honored. Tears stung my eyes, and I took a labored swallow around the lump in my throat.

Lucian sighed. "I'm sorry I brought it up. I know this must be an incredibly difficult day for you, and I just wanted to do some-thing to focus on the person she was instead of dwell on the way she died. We can discuss it another time."

I looked at the ceiling, trying to dry up my tears before they fell. "No. It's just a really emotional day for me. To be honest, I'm feeling bad I didn't think of it."

He smiled. "You've had a lot to deal with, and honestly—"

Whatever he was about to say was cut off by a loud whooshing that drowned out all other noise. A wind so strong it overturned tables and chairs exploded through the café, making it difficult to breathe.

I threw my hands up instinctually to protect my head, but

through a gap in my forearms, I saw one of the Melior Group agents get taken out—by *water*.

All the liquid in the area—the teas and coffees, the dishwater in the sink, the water in the small fish tank on a side table—congregated into one ugly, gray, writhing ball of water, which affixed itself to the head and upper body of one of our protectors.

The man pulled his gun but quickly realized it was useless. What good were bullets against a seemingly sentient ball of liquid? He thrashed, bumping into people and furniture still being tossed about by the wind. After a few minutes of frantic scratching and clawing, he fell to his knees, then onto his front, his body convulsing as he drowned.

Once he stopped moving, the water lost its shape and pooled around him. His empty eyes stared upward, wide and unblinking.

The unrelenting wind whipped my hair around my face, making it almost impossible to hear or move. I jumped as someone's hand closed around my wrist, but when I turned, it was only Lucian. His chair had been pushed up against the wall. He pulled on my arm, gesturing for me to get behind him as his eyes flicked to something over my shoulder.

I dropped to my knees, and the chair I'd been sitting on flew into the cyclone. Struggling to keep my balance, I crawled over to lean against Lucian's legs and try to get my bearings.

Most of the people in the café, as well as the furniture, had been pushed to the walls. Some cowered in fear; others appeared to be unconscious or dead. I had no idea where the agents outside were or if they were even alive.

The drowned agent's partner lay half-behind the counter, a snapped-off chair leg sticking out of his chest. Blood dripped from his mouth and the wound, puddling beneath the gun next to his outstretched hand. The wind slowly dragged the weapon across the tiles, marking a crimson streak along the ground as it skittered past a pair of small purple boots. I followed the legs up until I was looking at a young woman. She was the only one in the room standing, not at all affected by the wind. The blonde hair in her messy ponytail didn't even stir.

She was short, maybe a half foot taller than Dot, and dressed in jeans and a black long-sleeved T-shirt. A dirty apron hugged her hips. She looked like one of the kitchen staff—an unassuming twenty-something, maybe even a Bradford Hills student—except for the crazed look in her narrowed eyes and the way her teeth gritted as she arced her hands in wide sweeps.

She was coming straight for me and bringing *fire* with her.

The wind didn't abate, but now she was drawing fire from the grill in the back, pulling it forward, letting it swirl with the wind and ignite everything it touched. Her intense gaze never left me as she approached with small, slow steps.

If the chaos and destruction so far hadn't already scared me stiff, the intention in her look and posture certainly would have. My heart hammered in my chest. Every muscle in my body tensed as my mind went crazy with options, but they flew through my head too fast for me to grab on to an idea and run with it.

I couldn't move, couldn't call for help, couldn't do anything to attack her or defend myself.

Defend. *Block!*

Maybe I couldn't do it, but Lucian could.

I reached a hand up, and his warm grip closed around my wrist. As soon as I had skin contact, I pushed as much Light into him as I could.

Transferring to a Variant outside my Bond always took more time and effort, but I forced the Light to bend to my will quickly. It poured into Lucian almost as fast as it did to my Variants.

Before the woman was halfway to us, Lucian raised his other hand over my shoulder. Finally, I could breathe properly.

I heaved a few gasping breaths, my limbs trembling as the intense pressure of the cyclone released. My hand stayed tightly wrapped around Lucian's wrist to maintain the flow of Light.

He'd thrown up a shield. The wind and fire lashed against it angrily, revealing its invisible domelike shape.

Smoke choked the air. The wind had whipped the flames into a furious blaze. People were coughing and spluttering, trying to move away from the woman and the fire.

Lucian's shield kept growing. I didn't know how far it could expand, but it was the only thing we had at the moment, so I kept pumping him full of Light until we could figure out another way out of this. Several people got encased in his protective ability and scrambled closer to us. Some started trying to open the door, but it wasn't budging.

We only had half the people protected, and some of the others were starting to get burned. Their screams mingled with the deafening roar of the wind.

The woman's voice rang out, loud and clear over it all. "Give her to me!"

If there had been any doubt she was after me, it was just smashed to pieces. People were dead because of me; they were getting hurt, injured, burned. How many more would die? Lucian couldn't seem to make his shield expand farther, couldn't reach the people on the other side of the room.

Fear, desperation, and hopelessness constricted my throat like a noose. I looked around desperately for something, anything . . .

My wide eyes locked on the gun that had slid past her. It was just out of my reach, but I didn't hesitate. I dropped Lucian's hand, hoping he could sustain the barrier for even a few moments, and lunged for it.

It was sticky with the dead man's blood, but I lifted onto my knees and held it with both hands, just as Ty had shown me. I pointed it right at her chest—the easiest target for inexperienced shooters to hit—and pulled the trigger.

The recoil threw me off balance, and I dropped one hand to the ground to steady myself, unable to follow through with another shot. By the time I recovered, the chaos had stopped.

The woman stood in the middle of the café, a stunned look on her face as she clutched a spot just under her right breast. Blood oozed between her fingers.

Moans of pain filled the café. Some people scrambled up and moved toward the door, which was barred with pretty much all the furniture in the building. Others remained frozen, watching the woman warily.

Shouts and barked commands could be heard from outside. They would have access to us in a matter of moments.

I kept my gun on her.

"He's never going to stop coming for you." Her steady, if a little high-pitched, voice was directed to the ground. "Do you understand?" She looked up at me, her eyes wild. "He's *never* going to stop."

I adjusted my grip on the weapon, ignoring the shuffling behind me as people shifted furniture away from the door. I kept my laser focus on her.

"It's better if you just . . ." Her free hand curled into a fist. Blood dripped from her wound onto the floor, and she swayed a little, widening her stance. "It's better for all of us if you just . . . *die.*"

Behind her, fire from the grill rose several feet into the air, then swirled toward me like a striking snake.

The gun was snatched from my grip. Lucian pointed and fired. Unlike me, he knew how to handle a gun. He fired off three shots in quick succession—two to her chest and one to the head.

The fire fizzled out inches from my face as the woman crumpled to the ground, dead.

Despite his messy clothes and tangled hair from the gale-force winds, Lucian's face was calm, determined. He lowered the weapon and looked at me.

Melior Group agents streamed into the space from the newly cleared front door and the back of the building, guns raised, shouting orders.

"Are you hurt?" Lucian's sole focus was still me.

I slumped against the side of his chair. "I don't think so. But I don't think I can walk just yet." My voice was hoarse, and I dropped my head, taking deep breaths.

Lucian's hand went to the tangled mess at the back of my head —I didn't look forward to brushing through that later—but he didn't ask any more questions.

The next few hours both dragged on painfully slowly and were a blur of activity. The guys showed up around the same time as the ambulances. Tyler's black Escalade screeched to a halt at the curb, the doors opening before it had even fully stopped. They flocked to me like birds—big, muscled, tense, angry birds. But their hands were gentle, their kisses soft.

Eventually the EMTs made them back away so they could check me for injuries. Alec lingered the longest, his hands on either side of my head, his forehead pressed to mine. He was in full gear now. I had no idea when he'd had time to put on the vest and strap all the weapons on.

"Alec, I'm OK. Just let them check me so we can go home."

He kissed my forehead and leaned away. "You're going to the hospital for a thorough check-up, but I have to stay here for a while. I . . ." He hesitated, but I could see the *love* in his eyes, could practically feel the words trying to tumble off his lips. "I'll be there as soon as I can."

He turned and walked away, his shoulders stiff. Kyo fell into step beside him, with Marcus and Jamie following close behind.

As the EMTs started checking me for injuries, I turned to Tyler. "I didn't know he was working today."

"He was on call. He'll have to stay until things are finalized here." Tyler cast his eyes over the scene, his brow creasing. The place was crawling with Melior Group operatives, as well as local police. "It's good for us to have someone we trust on the ground anyway."

I wasn't sure what he meant by that. Couldn't we trust anyone employed by Melior Group? Weren't they all under Lucian's orders and at Tyler's beck and call? I kept my mouth shut; this wasn't the best time to raise the issue.

Lucian lost patience with the EMTs before I did, insisting he was fine and wheeling himself over to one of the senior police officers.

Josh sighed. "I'll go talk him into going home."

Law enforcement interviewed everyone while the street was still shut down. Businesses had been evacuated while we were still fighting for our lives inside. No one was permitted to return yet, but a crowd was gathering at both ends of the street, held back by police tape and armed men.

When a news van rolled up, I groaned. Soon after that we left. We managed to convince Lucian to come with us, but he refused to go to the hospital. Despite the guys' arguments, I insisted that if Lucian wasn't going, neither was I. I just wanted a shower, something to eat, and the safety of home.

Grudgingly, and with a cavalcade worthy of a president, Tyler drove us back to the mansion.

"Food or shower first?" Ethan held my hand all the way home, up the stairs from the garage, and through the foyer. I really wanted a shower, but the mention of food had my stomach growling. It was well past lunchtime, and near-death situations really took it out of a girl.

I tried not to dwell on the fact that I'd been in enough near-death situations to know that.

Ethan was all too happy to feed us, whipping up some mac and cheese. We all slumped around the dining table. Lucian wheeled into his spot at the head, and Josh pulled me into his lap, crushing me to his chest.

Tyler was on the phone, demanding updates and answering questions while Lucian threw in his two cents over his shoulder.

As Ethan dropped bowls in front of us, Tyler hung up. "It's confirmed. Our guys raided the woman's apartment in Bradford Hills East and found all kinds of Variant Valor paraphernalia, including propaganda material. On her computer they also found some direct communication between her and some of Davis's higher-ups. They're discreetly telling some of their more zealous followers they need you."

He looked right at me, tired, resigned. Considering what she'd said, it wasn't much of a surprise.

I picked up my fork and started eating. The mac and cheese was delicious, as Ethan's food always was—creamy and rich with little bits of bacon through it. Perfect comfort food.

"Why did she try to kill me?" I asked my empty plate, interrupting whatever it was they were talking about. I'd tuned out, but now my food was gone; I couldn't stop my brain from demanding answers.

I looked into Tyler's calm gray eyes. "At the end, after I shot her and she lost control of her ability, she said something about it being better for everyone if I just died, and then she came straight for me. If Davis needs me, why would she try to kill me?"

Had we read the situation wrong?

Tyler shared a loaded look with Lucian but didn't try to evade the question. He was getting much better about the whole "keeping secrets to protect me" bullshit. "We also found some evidence that Variant Valor was threatening her family. I suspect she realized she was going to fail to capture you, that she was probably going to die, so she decided to kill you"—his eyes darkened and his hands curled into fists, making the roped muscles in his forearms twist—"in order to prevent others from going through what she was going through."

"He's getting desperate." Lucian took a sip of his whiskey.

"He's always been desperate. He's just no longer hiding it as well as he used to," Josh observed.

Davis had been obsessed with my mother's glowing Light for years. That fixation had driven his every decision. And now here I was—capable of even more—and I was just out of reach. There was no doubt in my mind he would do whatever he deemed necessary to get to me. My shoulders slumped. How many people had to die?

I cleared my throat and pushed the despair deep down into a dark, soundless part of myself where I could avoid dealing with it a little longer, right between Zara's betrayal and Alec's undying love.

"What was her ability exactly?" I gave my mind something else to think about. "I've never seen it before."

"It was a rare one," Tyler answered. "She had the ability to control the elements. Not like Kid—she couldn't conjure fire like he can, but she could control existing fire, water, air."

I thought back to how the liquids formed a ball to drown the agent, how the fire only came from the grill in the back.

"It's a bit of an evolutionary throwback." Tyler had answered my question, but he was giving me what I needed—a distraction. "We've found that the types of abilities that manifest in Variants are sometimes affected by environmental factors. A lot of defensive abilities happen during periods of war and unrest, for example. And it's only in the last thirty to forty years that we've started seeing things like being able to control electronics. That woman's ability would've been incredibly useful a couple hundred years ago. Not that it wasn't useful in this day and age, but back then, it could've been the difference between life and death."

"Yeah, I read a paper on this a while back in the *Journal of Variant Studies*. They looked specifically at never before reported abilities throughout history and were able to pinpoint a specific environmental factor that served as a trigger for each one. Doesn't explain things like telekinesis"—I gestured to Josh—"or Alec's pain ability though, so environment is clearly not the only factor."

"Definitely not," Josh agreed. "Some abilities have been around since before recorded history and show no signs of disappearing. Genetics play a factor, but they're still doing research on that."

Tyler, Josh, and I kept talking about Variant abilities and science for a while longer, but when I yawned three times in one sentence, Ethan pushed his chair back.

"Let's get you showered, baby." He pulled me out of Josh's lap, but before I could take two steps, he picked me up and held me to his chest.

"I can walk just fine, big guy." I wrapped my arms around his thick neck and ran my fingers through his black hair. It was getting long, starting to fall over his forehead the way Tyler's did. "I wasn't hurt."

"I know." He kissed me on the cheek and started to climb the stairs. "I just wanna hold you."

Those words in that deep, gruff voice just about melted me. If he wasn't careful, I would trickle right out of his big arms. I buried my head in Ethan's chest and rested in the comfort of his strong hold, all the way to my en suite.

FIVE

Ethan left me alone to shower, and I spent a long time under the hot spray. I scrubbed every inch of my body and painstakingly detangled my hair, using nearly half a bottle of conditioner. Then I just stood there, letting the water soothe my muscles until I no longer felt like a tension wire.

When I started to get wrinkly fingers, I dried off and put on one of my soft cotton sleep shirts. I picked the towel back up off the end of my bed and tried to squeeze more moisture out of my hair.

The thud of boots on carpet was my only warning before the bedroom door burst open and a furious Alec stormed into the room.

The sudden loud noise startled me, and I dropped the towel. "Fucking knock, Alec!"

He just strode inside, still in his full uniform. "Why the fuck aren't you at the hospital?" His voice was hard and unyielding, his hands in fists by his sides.

"Because there's nothing wrong with me, asshole."

"Get your shit. I'm taking you to the hospital."

"No." I took a few steps away from him, stopping near the

open window. The evening breeze had a chill on it. "The EMTs checked me out and I'm fine."

Alec growled. He turned away and ran his hands over his buzzed hair before swinging his furious, wide eyes back to me. "I can't believe those motherfuckers didn't take you to the hospital. I'm gonna kill them."

He stalked forward until we were chest to chest. "Evelyn, I'm not going to say it again. Get your shit and let's go."

I crossed my arms and tilted my chin up. "No."

He pressed his lips together, breathing hard through his nose. Frustration and barely restrained anger laced every exhale. He was practically throwing a temper tantrum, and I refused to pander to his ridiculous demands.

"Alec, would you calm the fuck down? The EMTs said I was fine. I just wanted a hot meal and a hotter shower. What is going on with you?"

He moved so fast it was almost a blur, his hands going to my waist and gripping tight, as if he were about to lift me and just carry me to the hospital kicking and screaming. His hands moved up my ribcage, then back down to my hips as the rage in his face melted away, replaced by . . . fear?

"I just . . ." He closed his eyes and took a deep breath. "I'm fucking terrified of losing you, OK? I need to make sure you're not hurt."

"I'm fine." I covered his hands with mine and pressed my forehead to his. "I'm right here, arguing with you." I smirked and moved one of his hands up to my neck. "I'm standing and breathing. I don't have a concussion or even a scratch on me. A few bruises, but that's it. I'm *safe*, Alec." I squeezed his hands, making him feel my flesh in his fingers. "I'm safe."

For a few moments we just breathed, him holding me, me feeling more and more grounded by his strong hands. Rain started to pitter-patter outside, giving the cool breeze a distinctive fresh smell.

As the rain picked up, Alec pulled me into his arms, making me lift onto my toes.

The rain started hitting my ankles, but I ignored it, waiting until Alec was ready to let go. I was the one who'd nearly been killed, but it was *me* who needed to reassure *him* that everything was OK. Alec was strong in so many ways—formidable even—but he would always have a weakness for those he loved. And he'd told me in no uncertain terms that he loved me.

When he finally loosened his grip, I kissed him but didn't linger long. The rain was going to ruin the carpet, and the cold wind was giving me goosebumps. I turned and pulled the window shut, enjoying the soothing, steady rhythm of the rain hitting the glass.

"Are you sure I can't convince you to go get checked out?"

The stubborn jerk just wasn't dropping it. I rolled my eyes. "If I'm not feeling well in the morning, you can take me. I promise. Now can we drop it?"

He frowned, not liking my compromise, not liking any compromise ever. His eyes raked over my body but not in that lascivious way I loved; he was still looking for injuries.

I was done arguing. Better to give him something else to focus on.

I stepped into his personal space once more, wrapped my arms around his neck, and pulled him into a kiss. Not the gentle reassuring kiss I'd given him moments ago, but that all-consuming, desperate kind we'd perfected—only I wasn't entirely sure who was desperate in this scenario. Was it him? Desperate to make sure I was safe, to feel me in his arms. Or was it me? Desperate to feel alive after coming so close to death.

Reflexively, his hands gripped my hips, almost bruising, then grabbed my ass. He rolled his own hips, rubbing his erection against my front.

Then all at once, his hands and his mouth were gone.

I stumbled as he stepped back, but I leaned into the fall, kept going, refused to let him speak or leave or stop. With a sudden, aggressive move that made his eyes widen, I shoved him in the chest. His back collided with the mirror on the wall next to my bathroom, cracking the glass. He grunted in surprise, but I was already crushing my breasts against his front, clutching two fistfuls of his shirt, and hitching a leg over his hip. He grabbed my thigh with one calloused hand, his other arm banding around my back and pulling me impossibly closer, and then he was kissing me again.

We writhed against each other—teeth scraping, hands roaming—ignoring the destruction, the cracks.

I pulled back slightly and reached for his zipper. His movements stilled and his hands dropped away from my body.

Defeated, I dropped my leg and stepped back, keeping my gaze on his boots. My bare feet looked so small next to them.

He cleared his throat. "The broken glass. I just—"

"Don't," I cut him off and crossed my arms.

He sighed and pushed past me, walking to the door. As his hand reached for the knob, I turned to my dresser and began digging through my underwear drawer. I couldn't stand to watch him walk away again.

After an extended moment of stillness, he huffed, and I heard him moving around behind me.

I paused, my hands running through my damp hair. Alec had never been in my room. He hung out with us in Josh's room more than he used to, and I'd crawled into bed with him a few times— mostly after he got back from some days-long mission and the Light was straining me toward him. Once he'd crawled into bed behind me when I was sleeping with Tyler.

I turned to find him sitting on my bed. He didn't look at me— just started to unlace his boots.

"Are you here to sleep or . . . ?" I wasn't entirely sure how I wanted to end that sentence, but what I'd said at the party still held true. It didn't matter that I'd been attacked, that he was freaked out about it. I wasn't going to allow him into my bed if he wasn't ready to be with me fully.

Just thinking about it had my pulse quickening, and I was suddenly very aware of the fact that I wasn't wearing any underwear. I'd been heading to the dresser to get some when he barged in.

He stared me down for a beat. "Or," he declared, a challenge in his eyes. He was still testing me. Still unsure.

I crossed my arms. "I meant what I said, Alec. You can't stay here if you're unwilling to let go of your martyr crap and be with me. I want to fuck."

It may've been a crude way to put it, but he seemed to respond to me best when I was fired up. I just hoped it didn't backfire. His eyes narrowed, but his lips twitched into an almost smile—something between pleased and amused.

In answer, he pulled his black T-shirt over his head and threw it to the ground, putting his glorious, tattooed, scarred body on display. I raked my eyes over the muscle and the ink, the raised pink scars, and the smooth skin. My lips parted slightly.

I walked over to him and dropped my hands to his shoulders—these shoulders had carried so much. So much pain, so many worries, so much responsibility.

"Are you sure you—"

"Shut the fuck up, Alec," I rushed out before leaning forward and crushing my mouth to his. He responded with a low growl, his hands going to my hips and tugging me closer. I lifted one knee to the mattress and left one foot planted on the floor between his feet. He had to tilt his head up to kiss me, and I liked having the upper hand. I was the one guiding the kiss, controlling the angle.

As we kissed—our tongues battling, our teeth scraping—he dragged his hands down my sides until his palms found skin at my legs. Then he trailed them back up, lifting the cotton hem of my shirt. When he reached my hips, where his fingers should have found my underwear, he broke the kiss and stared at me.

His stunning eyes were hooded with lust, but there was also a hint of surprise, as well as some other, more perplexing emotion.

He didn't let himself get lost in it though. He moved his hands to cup my bare ass and squeezed, kneading the cheeks. His breath washed over my chest, tickling the spot just above the neckline. His mouth was so close to my breasts—I couldn't stop remembering how good his tongue had felt when it circled my nipples.

I yanked my top off and threw it somewhere behind me. I was completely naked, hovering above the Master of Pain as his hot breath washed over my breasts and his hungry eyes took me in. I had a feeling he was hovering too—hovering on the edge of giving in to our relationship, our Bond. If he needed more pushing, I would push, but I knew I nearly had him.

I moved backward to remove his pants, but he stopped me. Apparently he was done letting me take charge.

He held me to him with one strong hand still on my ass. The other moved to the back of my knee, nudging until I was right where he wanted me—both knees planted on the mattress, straddling him. I was spread open, and a shiver crawled up my spine as the cool air hit the heat and wetness between my legs. But he didn't let me lower onto his lap. The hand on my ass kept me upright as he leaned forward to wrap his mouth around my right nipple, just as I'd hoped he would only moments ago. As his teeth bit down lightly, I moaned. He moved to the other breast, giving it the same treatment. My nails dug into his shoulders, one hand going to the back of his head to hold him close. I didn't want him to stop.

But he did, releasing my left breast after one last bite that bordered on painful—if anyone knew how to walk the line between pleasure and pain, it was Alec. His hot tongue licked a trail between my breasts and up to my collarbone; his hands ghosted along the inside of my thighs.

He ran two fingers over my already slick folds before making a circle down, then back up my thighs. His fingers ran over me again, this time with more pressure—feeling how wet I was for him before he'd even touched me there. He groaned and pressed his face into the bend of my neck, kissing, licking, and biting between pants. His chest pressed flush against my front, and all I could do was try to remain upright as he slipped his fingers inside.

He didn't give me a chance to adjust—didn't check if I was ready or if this was how I wanted it. He just held me to him and pumped his fingers in and out, deep and fast, his mouth sending gasping breaths over my neck.

I groaned and pressed my breasts against him, loving the pressure, the extra friction. The orgasm came fast and wild—as everything always did with Alec. It exploded out from his fingers, and I involuntarily rocked my hips.

My knees were weak as he finally let me lower to his lap. I rested my forehead on his shoulder and took a moment to catch my breath. One of his hands rested at my hip while the other stroked my back tenderly. But judging by the straining bulge in his pants, there was nothing too tender about his thoughts.

I sat up and kissed him softly, taking a deep, satisfied breath.

But I wasn't done with him.

To break the kiss, I sucked his bottom lip into my mouth and bit down hard. He grunted in surprise, and his hand slapped my ass. The crack of his palm connecting with my flesh reverberated through the dark room.

I leaned back, surprised—half at the fact that he'd done it and half at the fact that I was kind of enjoying the warmth as the sting faded.

I didn't let either of us overthink it though, quickly moving my hands to his fly.

His fingers wrapped around my wrist, and for a split second, my mind flashed back to that night in Tyler's study when he'd rejected me, made me feel worthless. Uncertainty clawed at me, but I forced those thoughts away and met his gaze.

"Don't," I whispered and narrowed my eyes. My body still craved his. "Don't try to bail again."

He released my wrist and cupped my cheek, but his harsh words contrasted with his gentle touch. "Would you fucking relax? I'm just trying to get the condom out of my pocket before you tear my pants off."

"Oh . . ." I bit my lip and waited for him to pull the foil packet out—then did exactly as he'd said. I ripped his pants and underwear off in one go and settled back over him. We were both completely naked now. Another surge of excitement coursed through me; we were even, and he wasn't leaving.

"The guys told me you're a contraceptive Nazi so . . ." His tone was teasing as he slid the condom down his perfect, erect cock.

"Well, *excuse me* for not wanting to catch some disease from one of you man-whores." I shoved his shoulders, and he flopped down on the mattress with a crooked smirk.

"Ex-man-whores. None of us have been able to so much as fucking look at a woman since we touched you."

Now probably wasn't the best time to bring up Dana, so I went with a simple yet classic retort. "Fuck you, Alec."

He rolled his eyes. "Would you stop talking about it and fucking do it already?" He held his erection by the base and moved it up and down, teasing me, spreading the wetness.

I reached down and covered his fingers with mine, stilling his movements, then started to lower myself onto him.

We both sighed in pleasure. When I was halfway down, enjoying every slow inch of this moment—the moment I'd been dreaming about for so long—he removed both our hands from between us and thrust his hips up mercilessly.

"Ah!" I cried out in surprise and pleasure, but outrage quickly followed. "Fucker!" I frowned at him. *What a dick.*

He just smiled his cruel smile, and despite myself, I smiled back. I couldn't worry about that anymore—Alec was inside me, and it felt fucking amazing.

I started moving up and down in a slow rhythm, trying to draw this experience out as long as possible. I wanted to feel every inch of him as he moved inside me. I wanted to revel in his hands roaming my body. I wanted to commit every lascivious image to memory.

He lay back and let me have my way with him.

For about two minutes.

Then he sat up. With one hand gripping my ass and the other threaded in my hair, he flipped us over as if I weighed nothing. His hand in my hair tugged roughly, almost too painfully, yet it sent a jolt of desire straight to my core. My pussy tightened around him as I gasped. He pressed me into the mattress, still inside me, and kissed me. His hips remained perfectly still as his tongue explored my mouth, the kiss building and building in intensity until we were both breathing hard through our noses. I kept trying to move my hips, roll them, do something to get that friction happening again, but he kept me pinned as his mouth devoured mine.

When he decided he'd had enough, he broke the kiss, lifted himself onto his hands, and started pounding into me—long strokes, nearly all the way out before driving back in. Where I wanted to prolong and savor every moment, apparently Alec had decided we'd waited long enough. He wasn't holding back anymore.

I loved that he was giving in to it, but why did it always have to be a battle of wills with him? Why did it always give me a little thrill to challenge him? To *be* challenged by him? What the fuck was wrong with me?

But I didn't have time to unpack that. Alec's hips were chasing all thought from my mind as he drove in and out of me mercilessly.

He watched me with piercing blue eyes as he fucked me, taking in my flushed face and swollen lips, watching my breasts bounce in response to his movements, watching his cock disappear into me repeatedly. He couldn't get enough.

I could feel another orgasm coming. The tingling heat spread from deep inside, and my core muscles clenched in preparation. I started making incoherent sounds between panting breaths, clawing at his shoulders, trying in vain to bring him closer.

He hissed as I accidentally drew blood with my nails, smearing the crimson over his shoulder. But he didn't stop pounding into me, and I was too far gone to care.

When I closed my eyes and rolled my head back, he growled, "No," and I snapped my eyes open again. "Look at me. I want to watch you come."

"Oh, fuck." His words were the final push that sent me toppling over the edge. I watched Alec watch me come apart under him, the orgasm crashing through me in waves.

He didn't stop or even slow down, didn't give me a moment to recover. He just kept up his merciless pace. I was hypersensitive to his every movement, every nerve ending on fire. His eyes raked up and down my body, and it wasn't long before he found his own release.

With his gaze fixed on mine and his lips parted on an O, he groaned. The soft but guttural sound rumbled from his chest, and I had to admit, I understood why he'd insisted on watching me come. Watching him do the same—seeing him unravel on top of me in pure ecstasy—was mesmerizing.

He dropped to his elbows, and I locked my ankles behind his back, keeping him buried inside me as he caught his breath.

His hands threaded into my hair, much more gently this time. Nuzzling his nose against mine, he kissed me, then drew back just a fraction. I smiled, letting my happiness and satisfaction show— hoping he could see there wasn't even a hint of regret.

He smiled back, a rare genuine smile that almost made his eyes sparkle. Happiness shone in his gaze too, and . . . *love*. He had that same look on his face as when he'd first declared his love to me.

To stop him from voicing it again, I tilted my head up and kissed him. I wasn't ready to hear him say those words again. I wasn't ready to say them back. Alec and I were moving forward in our own stunted, fucked-up way, but I couldn't go that far yet.

He kissed me back, then pulled out and headed into the bathroom to clean up.

Fuck! I mouthed to the ceiling, running my hands through my hair. I went into the bathroom after he'd finished and rushed through my nighttime routine, petrified he'd be gone when I was done. But when I came back out, he was under the covers, staring at the window with one hand under his head.

I flicked off the bathroom light, casting the room into almost complete darkness. The curtains weren't drawn, but rain still pattered outside, and there was no moonlight.

I crawled into the bed next to him, pleased to find he was still as naked as I was. He wrapped himself around me from behind, and I fell asleep in his arms.

The next morning I woke to the sound of birds chirping obnoxiously and bright sunlight streaming through my window. One of my arms was slung over Alec's waist, and when I cracked my eyes open, I found myself staring at his tattooed back. But someone was pressed to *my* back too, sandwiching me between two muscled male bodies.

I rolled over as carefully as I could, but Josh was already wide awake. He smiled when I faced him fully. He was shirtless too, and I wondered how the hell I got so lucky—most mornings I woke up next to at least one Adonis of a man, usually two. If any of our beds were bigger, I'd probably be waking up with even more from time to time.

I smiled back, biting my bottom lip.

"How was it?" he whispered, gripping my hip over the covers.

I didn't know how to answer that—it was way more complicated than my brain could manage before coffee—so I just grinned in response.

He raised his eyebrows, a cheeky smile pulling at his lips. "Shall we wake Alec and ask him?" It was an empty threat, but my eyes widened in warning anyway.

He laughed silently, his smooth shoulders shaking, and leaned forward to kiss me. I kept my mouth shut to his probing tongue though, paranoid about morning breath.

He propped himself up on his elbow just as Alec yawned and rolled over.

"Morning!" Josh grinned at Alec and jumped up. He used my bathroom, put his shirt back on, told us Ethan was making pancakes downstairs, and left.

I chuckled but looked at Alec, a little worried about his reaction.

"I'm not used to sharing." His voice was gritty from sleep, but it didn't sound angry or hard—it sounded like raw honey. "But I'll *get* used to it."

He smiled and pulled me into the crook of his elbow.

"You OK?" I asked. I didn't know what else to say. I wasn't about to offer to be with only him. Not one part of me wanted to— they were all mine equally, and they would all have to share equally.

"I'm fine, precious, I promise. It helps that it's them. That we're already close. That they already know all my dark secrets."

"Do I know all your dark secrets?" I ran my hands over his torso, tracing his scars. They fascinated me. They were like a roadmap of his pain, his history. I wanted to know the story behind each one.

"Not all. But I'm sure I don't know all yours either."

I shrugged. "My biggest secrets were my real name and the fact that I'm your Vital."

We were both silent for a while, him trailing his fingertips up and down my back, me paying special attention to the scar that usually disappeared into the waistband of his pants. I could see now it went over his hip and all the way to the top of his thigh.

"Maybe you could tell me about some of your scars."

"I'll tell you anything you want to know, but not today, OK? I want to just focus on the nice things today—fucking pancakes, and that sickening sunshine and rainbows and unicorns and shit."

"OK." I chuckled and decided to take the focus off him. "You know, I only have one significant scar, and I don't even know how I got it."

I pushed the blanket down, revealing both our naked bodies, and lifted my knee over his belly so I could point to the long scar on the side of my right knee.

"I think it happened when I was little, before my mom took off. She refused to talk about anything in the past. She never mentioned any of you my whole childhood—not even Lucian. That's probably why I don't really remember much."

"I know when you got that."

I propped myself onto my elbow. "What? How'd it happen?"

"I was around twelve, I think. You were three, maybe? I was hanging with some friends after school. I don't even remember what we were doing, but I decided I needed to go home. I had this urge to just . . . go. Then for some reason, I found myself walking to your mom's place. So I get there, and you're crying. Like, at the top of your lungs, hysterical crying, and there's blood trailing down your leg. Your mom couldn't get you into the car, and it wasn't serious enough to call an ambulance, so she'd called a doctor to come out, but this guy couldn't even get close enough to clean the cut. Anyway, I walk in, and you reach your fat little arms out to me, and I take you, and they're finally able to treat it. I don't even remember how you got the cut in the first place. I think that was the day they realized you might be my Vital. Not that anyone said anything to me . . ." His voice took on a note of bitterness.

"I'm so sorry, Alec." I rested my chin on his chest, keeping my eyes on his face. "If I hadn't been a kid, I never would've let anyone take me from you."

"I know." He ran his thumb over the scar on my leg. "It's just that for the longest time, I thought that was the reason she took you. That my ability was so horrid and disgusting the adults decided it would be better if I never had my Vital. That your mom decided I wasn't good enough for her little girl. I know now why they couldn't tell me more at the time, but yeah, my mind filled it in with the worst explanation possible."

I sighed, my heart breaking for him, for me, for all the shit we'd been through because of things beyond our control.

"Anyway"—he planted a kiss on my forehead and sat up, swinging his legs over the edge—"we said we weren't going to talk about heavy shit. Let's go get some fucking pancakes from one of your other boyfriends, the one who happens to be my cousin." He shook his head, but when he turned around, a teasing smile tugged at his lips.

I laughed, letting the conversation drop. We got dressed and headed downstairs, following the smell of freshly ground coffee.

SIX

Tyler drove us into the city early in the morning, our security detail close behind. The butterflies in my belly wouldn't leave me alone; they'd been flapping all night. We'd spent so much time keeping our Bond a secret it was hard to let the paranoia go.

I'd agonized over what to wear the night before. I even called Dot to get her opinion—she said it didn't matter, that I could show up in my underwear. All they were interested in was my status as a Vital. Eventually she took pity on me and told me to look presentable but not too dressy. No jeans but probably not a collared shirt either.

I settled on pale blue woolen tights, a simple long-sleeved dress that fell to my knees, and my favorite cardigan for warmth. Tyler wore one of his endless supply of perfectly fitting shirts and light gray pants. He looked sophisticated and smart.

I fidgeted with the hem of my dress and huffed, regretting not wearing pants.

"You OK?" Tyler placed a gentle hand on my knee, keeping his other firmly on the steering wheel.

"I don't know. I'm obsessing over my outfit. I think it's my brain's helpful way of distracting me from freaking out about this." I played with his fingers instead of the hem.

He squeezed my hand, halting my nervous movements. "It's going to be OK. It's standard protocol to go in and register. They'll sit you down—"

"But you were so adamant it was dangerous. You wanted to keep it a secret."

"When we first realized what you were, yes, that was the biggest threat. Some of the things I've seen in reports, the places Alec's been, the things we've both done in this job . . . The work we do is important, but it's not pretty."

"Not helping."

He turned a bend in the road, and the early spring sunshine streamed in through my window, making me even more hot and uncomfortable.

"Let me finish." He chuckled. "At the time, I was really worried about Ethan and Josh getting recruited. If they decided to join on their own, then so be it, but I wanted them to finish college first, to have a *choice*. Once Melior Group knows a powerful Variant has found a Vital, they put a lot of pressure on. They offer a lot of money, promise travel around the world, put on the guilt trip about using their rare ability for good. It's not how Lucian and I would run things, but the recruitment side of it isn't up to us. I wanted to save them from that, and I wanted to protect you from the kidnappings. Now . . ."

"That's the least of our worries."

He sighed. "Yeah. Now we have a face and a name to put on the threat, and if Ethan and Josh join up with Melior Group, I don't even care anymore. I just want us all to be safe, and we won't be until Davis is rotting in a hole somewhere."

His grip on the steering wheel tightened, his knuckles going white.

"What about the humans?" I asked. Part of this meeting would involve an interview with a representative from the government. All Variants had to be registered—it was the humans' way of feeling in control. They thought if they could list and catalogue all the Variants, everyone would be safe.

"That's just a standard, boring part of the process." Tyler waved his hand dismissively.

I'd asked most of these questions already over the past few days, but he patiently answered them anyway. He knew I felt better if I had all the facts. I'd even badgered Alec to tell me the layout of the building so I would know what areas to avoid. He looked at me as if I was losing it, told me I would never be left unattended, and shut me up with his mouth and hands.

They all seemed to be using sex as a distraction—I'd had more sex in the last few days than I'd had in the few *years* since I'd started having sex. Or maybe that had more to do with Alec *finally* completely being in. The Bond was even, the connection as deep with each one as it was with the others.

Tyler battled the Manhattan traffic, then the next thing I knew, we pulled into an underground garage. Two armed guards checked Tyler's ID—even though they greeted each other by name—and signed me in, and we parked in a spot with a little "Reserved for T. Gabriel" sign above it.

My heart hammered in my throat. I swallowed around the pressure and rubbed my hands on my thighs, but Tyler wasn't about to let me sit there and freak out. He got out of the car, slung his bag over his shoulder, and went to the elevator. I followed him, trying my best not to show my nervousness.

In the elevator, he tapped away at his phone with one hand and threaded his fingers through mine with the other. We got off on a really high floor, stepping out to a stunning view of Manhattan through a floor-to-ceiling window.

"Whoa." My trepidation was momentarily forgotten as I took it in, spotting the Empire State Building and the Chrysler Building and straining to glimpse the Statue of Liberty in the distance.

"Come on." Tyler tugged me along. "I've got the same view from my office."

"Of course you have an office here." I rolled my eyes as I

followed him past the shiny reception area, through another keycard-protected door, and into a vast open-plan office area.

"Hey, kitten."

I turned to see Kyo smiling and coming toward me.

"Hey!" I grinned and gave him a hug.

"Here for your induction?"

"I guess."

"We couldn't put it off any longer," Ty jumped in.

"You'll be fine, Eve. There's nothing to be nervous about." Kyo smiled in his easy, relaxed way.

"Oh, shit, we're really scraping the bottom of the barrel if they're letting you join." Marcus sidled up to us, grinning.

I flipped him off. "You'd be lucky to have me."

"Yeah, we would." Jamie slapped Marcus on the back of the head and also gave me a hug. "Just promise you'll let us be part of your team when you steal our Master of Pain."

"Huh?" I frowned and looked at Tyler.

"When, *if*, a Vital decides to join Melior Group, they're automatically placed in a team with their Variants. It's the easiest arrangement—Bonds naturally work well together. If you join, Alec will automatically be assigned to your team, and I'll probably have less desk time and more field time too."

"Oh." I didn't want to break up Alec's team. I didn't even want to join Melior Group! I wasn't a spy. I was a scientist. "None of you have anything to worry about. The scary, dangerous, brooding thing isn't really up my alley. I'm finishing college and figuring out why the fuck I glow."

Everyone chuckled, but Kyo also surreptitiously looked around the office before leaning in. "Just be careful about what you say. Pretty much everyone here is trained in intelligence gathering. There's always someone listening."

My eyes widened and I gripped Tyler's bicep. All the banter had done a good job of distracting me, but now the nerves came slamming back.

Tyler sighed. "Thanks. That's real helpful, Kyo."

I shot Kyo a dirty look as Tyler led me away to a boardroom, which looked surprisingly mundane. Surrounded by glass windows, it had all the elements you'd expect—comfortable chairs, a projection screen, a conference phone.

Tyler barely had time to deposit his bag on the long table and rub a few soothing passes up and down my arms before other people started arriving. A woman in an ill-fitting suit was one of the first. She introduced herself as Susan from the Variant-Human Relations Department and shook Tyler's hand and mine before taking a seat. The next few were Melior Group employees and greeted Tyler as if they knew him.

"Shall we begin?" At Susan's invitation, we'd just moved to take our seats when the door opened again.

"Victor." Tyler greeted the man in the sharp blue suit, and the others in the room sat up a little straighter.

"Hello, Tyler. I thought I might sit in for this one. Please carry on like I'm not here." He sat at the far end of the table and motioned for us to continue.

Tyler cleared his throat. "Evelyn, this is Victor Flint. He's our recruitment manager and a member of the board."

"Nice to meet you, sir." I was too far away to extend my hand, so I just waved. He returned it with a tight smile. The anxiety twisting my gut doubled down, but I made sure to keep a neutral expression on my face and my hands steady as I laid them gently on the glass tabletop.

"I hope you don't mind if I go first," Susan said. "I have another meeting to get to."

No one objected, so she pulled a small stack of papers from her bag and slid them over to me. She explained the forms were standard and just a way to verify my identity and register me as a Vital in the database. Each one had Evelyn Maynard written on it, and most of my other details were already filled in. I signed in all the marked spots. She handed me a brochure about my responsibilities as a person with abilities in the wider community, said goodbye to everyone else in the room, and left.

"OK, Evelyn," said a short woman who'd been speaking with Tyler but hadn't bothered to introduce herself to me. "I'm Gemma, and it's my job to make sure you understand what it means that you're a Variant and that you're receiving the appropriate training."

I nodded. She handed me pamphlets, then spoke about Variant DNA and how Variant Bonds worked. It was barely scratching the *surface* of stuff I already knew. Between Tyler's tutoring and my own obsessive study, she really couldn't have told me anything new. But protocols had to be followed. She ticked boxes on a tablet screen as she went through each topic.

"Have a glance at this list, and if you agree that I've explained all the items on it, please tick agree." I ticked it without even looking at the list properly. I was getting bored. My focus kept wandering to my periphery where Victor sat, observing me as keenly as I wanted to observe him.

"Now, you're attending Bradford Hills Institute, which means it should be easy to make sure you get the necessary education and training from now on. Tyler here can make sure you're moved into the necessary classes."

"Actually," Tyler interjected, "that won't be necessary. I've been tutoring Evelyn in the relevant Variant studies topics since we first learned of her status as a Vital, and she's already enrolled in several Variant studies units. She's a keen student and her knowledge is not lacking."

"Oh, OK. Perfect. That takes care of that then. I'm done." Gemma smiled at me and pressed some more buttons on the tablet.

Victor shifted in his seat. "Thank you, Gemma." He leaned back and folded his hands casually in his lap, his head tilted to the side. Everyone paused and gave him their full attention.

"Evelyn, there is one last item I'd like to discuss with you." His gaze was relaxed but intent on me.

I cleared my throat, not sure what to say, but Tyler spoke

before I could. "What's this about? I wasn't informed of another item for discussion."

Victor waved his hand dismissively. "Oh, you're free to leave, Mr. Gabriel, if you have something else to attend to. It's a last-minute item that I didn't have a chance to add to the agenda. I only need a few more minutes of Evelyn's time."

No one got up. If anything, they settled into their seats, paying rapt attention to whatever this was.

There was no way in hell Tyler was leaving my side. His shoulders tensed just a fraction, but he managed to keep a neutral look on his face as he leaned his forearms on the table. "I have time."

Victor nodded before turning his full attention to me. "I'm a busy man, so I won't beat around the bush. Evelyn, I'd like to make you an offer. The standard offer that Gemma outlined stands, of course—we're always happy to offer positions to extraordinary Variants and Vitals. You would be an asset. But I'd like to extend an additional, rather unique offer to you also. We all know you're more than an exceptional Vital. Despite your Variants' refusal to discuss the matter, which I completely understand"—he held a hand out to Tyler, giving him a conciliatory look —"I think we've all seen the footage of the unfortunate incident at the senator's residence in Manhattan. The glowing."

I narrowed my eyes and wrapped my arms around my chest before I could stop myself. I had no idea what the glowing meant, and I didn't like being confronted with it.

"What is this about?" Tyler asked.

Victor kept his keen gaze on me. "I'm offering you the opportunity to figure out what it is. How it works, what it can do, what the limitations and dangers are." My eyebrows rose as he continued. "I would like to offer you access to some of our top researchers and scientists, a safe environment in which to test your particular…situation."

"Why was I not consulted on this? Or even informed of it?" A hint of frustration leaked into Tyler's clipped tone. No one else at the table spoke, but they watched the two men verbally sparring with ravenous eyes.

"I didn't have approval to make the offer until earlier this morning. There was nothing to inform you of. And to be quite frank, I wanted to bring this directly to Evelyn. I know you've shut down offers of a similar nature from Bradford Hills Institute."

Bradford Hills Institute had made offers like this?

My immediate reaction was to get pissed off at Tyler. How dare he make such a decision for me? Did the others know too? But I made a conscious effort to keep the irritation from showing on my face. After the initial knee-jerk reaction, I realized exactly why Tyler hadn't entertained the idea. We knew I could use my glowing to kill a Variant—draw the Light right out of them—but the rest of the world didn't. I had enough of a target on my back without exposing me, us, to more suspicion from powerful people.

Tyler looked at me out of the corner of his eye, but this time, I spoke first. "The reasons why we turned down the offer from Bradford Hills Institute are between my Bond and me." I placed my hand lightly on Tyler's forearm, surprised at how calm my voice sounded. "But since you took time out of your day to make this offer to me personally, I'm happy to consider it."

I smiled politely, pushing as much Light to Tyler as I could before removing my hand. Hopefully the extra boost would help him figure out what Victor's angle was, but I also hoped he'd use it to see what I was about to do. We needed help figuring this glowing shit out; Victor Flint had the resources—I just needed to make sure we got as much out of this as possible.

Clasping my hands together, I leaned on my elbows. Tyler moved in the same instant, settling back in his chair and placing a comforting hand low on my back.

He was sending everyone at the table, including me, a clear message—I was taking the lead now.

Victor didn't miss a thing. His calculating gaze flicked between us, and he tilted his head, an amused smile briefly passing over his features.

"Excellent." He leaned forward too, mirroring my position. "A team of researchers would be at your disposal. Ideally, we would have you come in two to three times per week for a few hours. They'll run tests to see if we can identify any anomalies in your blood, your DNA, and your physiology, then they'll observe and measure you in the glowing state both alone and with one or several of your Bonded Variants present so they can observe the transfer. We will leave no stone unturned until we know all modern science can discover about your situation."

I didn't like how he kept referring to it as a "situation," as if it had happened by accident and wasn't permanent. This was part of who I was. Yes, it could be dangerous, but it was pretty fucking extraordinary too. Even so, I was glad to see how hard he was trying to sell me on his offer. "Thank you for not beating around the bush. I'll offer you the same courtesy. I'd like to know what's in this for you?"

"Whatever do you mean?" He smiled, his tone slightly teasing. He knew I'd figured him out; he just wanted to hear me say it.

"Firstly, as you said, you're a busy man—you wouldn't waste your time on something if it wasn't important to you. Second, Bradford Hills Institute is an educational facility. Their primary focus is education, knowledge. Melior Group is a *business*. Your bottom line will always be *the bottom line*. Clearly you believe you can learn something from studying me that will allow you to make money. My best guess would be a new method for delivering Light to your active agents remotely. That would be invaluable in the field."

His smile only widened. "Very clever. I would genuinely like to help you, Miss Maynard." I was no longer Evelyn. That was good—he was treating me with more respect. "But of course, you are correct. This is a business, and my team's secondary purpose would be to develop technology with what we learn from studying you."

Tyler remained reclined. "Victor, you're trying to use my Vital as a prototype for new tech that could make you billions. Can you not see why I would have an issue with this?"

"Of course I understand your reluctance, but—"

"I'd like to be paid," I cut him off. I was done with pleasantries and I was getting hungry. "This is business, and you stand to make a large amount of money. I want an hourly rate and a cut of the profits from whatever prototype comes from these experiments. I want my Variants to be compensated for their time too."

For a beat, Victor watched me with a calculating look. "Fair enough. We can arrange an hourly rate for yourself, Mr. Paul, and Mr. Mason. As Mr. Gabriel and Mr. Zacarias are already employed by us, this will simply be part of their working day. And you can have two percent of the profits for the first five years on the market. In exchange, you make yourself available two times per week for a minimum of three hours."

"Ten percent for the *lifetime* of the product, and Tyler and Alec get extra pay—this is well outside either of their roles." Neither one of them needed the money, they were all rolling in it, but I needed to ask for things so Victor would feel as if he won when I finally agreed. "Three hours, two times per *month*. We all have lives, Mr. Flint. And you leave Josh and Ethan alone. Your recruiters don't go after them. Ever. If they choose to join Melior Group at some point, then so be it, but they will not be pressured into it. No offense." I threw a quick glance at Gemma, barely registering the look of surprised respect on her face. "And I'd like clearance for the three of us. I'd like Tyler and Alec to be able to tell me about their day at work without holding back any details. Those last two points are not negotiable." I leaned away to drive my point home, crossing my legs.

"Five percent for the lifetime of the product, no extra pay for Tyler and Alec, three hours one time per week, and we'll not actively recruit Ethan and Josh for the next five years. I'll have to see what I can do about the clearance—it's not only up to me." He remained leaning on the table, his hands in front of him.

Tyler had told me as much about the clearance level—that it

may be difficult to get, even with him and Lucian pushing for it. It couldn't hurt to have another person arguing for us.

"You leave Josh and Ethan alone for good—as I said, that's not negotiable—and we have a deal."

He pressed his lips together and sighed, then stood and reached a hand over the table. "You have yourself a deal, Miss Maynard."

I stood up and shook his hand firmly.

"I'll have our legal team draw up the paperwork."

"I'll have mine look it over before I sign."

"I would expect nothing less." He laughed as he left the room. Everyone filed out after him, and Tyler led me to his office down the hall.

As soon as the door closed, I collapsed against it and took a massive, shaky breath.

"Holy shit." I laughed and ran my hands through my hair, trying to calm my breathing, stop my heart from hammering in my chest. I had no idea a conversation could result in so much adrenaline.

Tyler tugged my hand from my hair and pulled me into his arms. He kissed me passionately, the hard planes of his chest flush against my body, and then just as suddenly pulled away. His hot breath washed over my face in panting breaths as he leaned his forehead against mine. "That was the hottest fucking thing I've ever seen."

I chuckled and kissed him again, high on the rush of the negotiation and the feeling of Tyler's arousal pressing into my belly.

I stepped out of his arms.

"I'm not happy that you kept the Bradford Hills offer from me." I wagged a finger at him.

"It's not that I was keeping it from you." He adjusted his pants, moving his prominent hard-on. "I just knew we wouldn't be able to take them up on it. I was saving us all some time by cutting the conversation off before it began. And we've had quite a bit on our plate. It just never made it to the top of the list of priorities to discuss. I'm sorry."

"Apology accepted, but please don't turn things down on my behalf again. I agree with your assessment of the situation, but I need to be included in these conversations. We need to make these decisions together, even if it takes up some of your precious time."

"OK. I get it."

"Good. Now take me to lunch so we can discuss this situation I just got us into without speaking to you first."

He laughed and stuffed some papers into his messenger bag before leading the way out of his office. "Alec is going to be so pissed at you."

I chewed my lip as we reached the elevators. He was right. Alec didn't want me anywhere near Melior Group. Now I was about to be there every week, potentially exposing some serious vulnerabilities. "Yeah, he is, but I have boobs to distract him with. And the angry sex is phenomenal."

Tyler groaned. "Now I'm thinking about how to make you angry."

SEVEN

Halfway through my first lecture of the day—Synthetic Organic Chemistry—I had three pages of notes and several new books on my TBR list. My phone vibrating in my backpack was an unwelcome distraction. With a huff, I pulled it out to silence it and saw it was an incoming video call from Harvey. I frowned and waited for it to ring out.

Once it stopped, I tapped out a quick message.

Did you butt dial me? LOL!

I'd kept in contact with him since my impromptu trip down under. We chatted online from time to time, and I'd even reconnected with Mia, Harvey's sister. It was the first time I'd reconnected with anyone from my past. My mother had always forbidden it. Being able to chat with him was really nice—he was my friend first, and that friendship was still there. But we didn't do video chats. I'd mentioned I had an early class when I spoke to him the night before, so the call was a little unusual.

Wasn't a butt dial.

I sat up a little straighter at his reply, confused. The three little dots told me he was typing.

I need to speak with you urgently. Can you call me please?

I chewed on my bottom lip. I didn't really want to get up in a silent lecture theater. I'd had enough of the Variants of Bradford Hills staring at me to last a lifetime.

My lecture finishes in about half an hour. I'll give you a call right after.

His reply was instant.

This really can't wait. Please hurry.

That got my alarm bells ringing. Keeping as quiet as possible, I packed up my books and shuffled to the end of my row. The professor didn't even miss a beat, continuing to educate everyone else on azobisisobutyronitrile and radical initiator mechanisms. I rushed to the doors, my mind full of questions, my gut telling me I may not like the answers.

Alec stood in the hallway, talking to a Melior Group woman I'd never seen before. The black-clad operatives were all over the place. Most of the ones assigned directly to Vitals were in the lecture theater.

Alec was officially assigned to me for the day but preferred to wait outside during my classes; it was less distracting for me and allowed him to get a little work done, making calls and barking orders at Kyo, Marcus, and Jamie. When he saw me come out, his posture straightened, and he excused himself immediately.

"Evie? What is it?" He loomed over me, but before I could answer, my phone started buzzing again. We shared a look and I rushed outside. Alec stayed glued to my side.

I sat down on a bench in the courtyard, under the shade of a maple tree, and answered. Alec remained standing in front of me, his arms crossed.

"Harvey? What's wrong?"

"Hey, Eve." It was way past midnight in Melbourne. His voice sounded hoarse, and heavy bags sagged under his eyes. "I really need to talk to you."

"OK . . ." I waited, but he seemed to be struggling to get the words out.

"Just . . . uh . . . don't freak out or anything."

My spine straightened, and I threw a wary look in Alec's direction.

Another more feminine, more sarcastic voice came through the phone. "For fuck's sake. Just let me talk to her, human boy."

My heart flew into my throat, and I sprang to my feet, gripping my phone tightly. I knew that voice.

"Harvey!" I yelled, my voice shaking. Alec was making a call, keeping his eyes on my screen but staying off camera. "Harvey, listen to me."

At the same time, Harvey replied to Zara, "You asked me to talk to her. What the fuck . . ."

The video feed went shaky, as if they were fighting for the phone. Then a blinding flash of electricity cut across it, and the call cut out.

"Shit!" Hot, panicked tears stung my eyes. Did I just watch another friend die? Did Zara take another person from me, just as I got him back? "No! No no no." I prodded my phone with shaky fingers.

"What do I do?" I turned my panicked gaze to Alec.

He tucked his phone into his pocket before placing both hands on my shoulders. "We're going to call him back. She had him call for a reason, so they'll take the call. I've already arranged for it to be traced. Take a deep breath."

I nodded and tried, but it just made me hyperventilate more.

Before I could calm myself enough to call him back, Harvey's name popped up on my screen again.

Another jolt of cold panic shot up my spine, and I gritted my teeth, making myself answer it. Alec stepped out of the camera's way once more as Harvey's face appeared, Zara's right next to it.

"Harvey!" The panic in my voice was palpable. "Get away from her. She's dangerous, do you hear me? She is *not* my friend. I don't know what she's told you, but—"

"Deep breath, Eve," Harvey interrupted me, his eyes wide, his hand held out in front of him. "I'm OK."

Zara rolled her eyes. "Would you chill the fuck out? What do you think I'm going to do?"

She leaned back heavily in Harvey's computer chair, scowling. As if I was the one being unreasonable.

"Chill the fuck out?" I gritted my teeth, aware of the danger in angering an unhinged person, but my rage was rising fast. "You have Rick's power. The same power that killed Beth. Remember Beth? *Your friend?* And now you're holding *my* friend hostage, so *excuse me* for getting worried."

"Yes, I fucking remember Beth!" she nearly yelled, and Harvey shushed her with a hand on her arm, checking over his shoulder. Why was he trying to hide the fact that a dangerous lunatic was in the house?

Zara took a very deep breath, visibly calming herself. "Eve, I need your help."

I blinked slowly at my screen, waiting for the punch line to the sick joke she was clearly making before killing Harvey in front of my eyes.

She stayed silent, and when her eyes started darting about the room, it sunk in. "Holy shit, you're serious."

"Yes, I'm fucking serious. I made a mistake. I fucked up *real* bad, OK? And now my life's in danger, and things are so much worse than you know."

"I don't care!" I screamed. The lecture I was supposed to be in must've finished. Students were streaming out of the building, a few throwing me curious looks.

"Eve, please, just hear us out." Harvey's voice was calm, and I tried my best to take my cue from him. I couldn't risk her hanging up again.

As if he read my mind, Alec's warm, calloused hand wrapped loosely around my forearm. I glanced over the top of my screen to see him holding up a thumb as he mouthed, *Got her.* I focused back on my phone as Alec pressed his earpiece and listened in.

"Harvey, I'm so sorry you got dragged into this," I said, "but it's going to be OK." I chewed on my bottom lip, wary of revealing too much. Melior Group operatives were on their way, and I didn't want to give her a chance to run.

"You suck at this." Zara rolled her eyes. "I don't know how the fuck you lied about your identity your entire childhood. You can tell whichever Melior Group lackey is standing next to you to come out. I know they've tracked me to Harvey's house. I called to tell you where I am. I need help."

I couldn't help glancing up at Alec again. He wore his signature scowl as he reached a hand out for the phone. I passed it to him and, with shaky legs, lowered myself back to the bench.

"Oh, hey, Ace." Zara's tone was saccharine, and I wondered why she was being so antagonistic if she really wanted our help. This could all be a trap, but Alec knew what he was doing. I had to trust he would take care of it.

When he spoke, his voice was hard but professional. "Zara, if you're serious about handing yourself in, don't struggle. They're under orders to detain you. Do not resist. Do you understand?"

I didn't hear a response before Alec kept speaking. "If you use your ability and any of the men and women coming your way are harmed, you will spend the rest of your life rotting in a windowless cell." Most people wouldn't have picked up on the emotion in his voice, but I detected the hint of anger in the slight growl in his throat, the way his free hand curled into a fist.

"Harvey," he continued, "just stay out of the way, man. And show them your hands so they know you're not a threat."

Without warning, he hung up. I took the phone numbly as he sat down next to me.

"You hung up?" I stared at the phone, then at him as prickles of panic started to poke at me again. "Wait . . . what . . . *why?*"

Alec put an arm around me and spoke in a low, soothing tone. "Our team was thirty seconds out. She can't get away now, and Harvey will be better off if he's not distracted. It's handled. Wanna go grab some lunch?"

"Do I want to . . . *what?*"

I guess he was used to dealing with life-and-death situations, putting it out of his mind once he'd done what he could, trusting the people on the ground. But I wasn't. My mind and heart were still in that dark room in Australia.

"Evie." He nudged my chin until I was facing him, then gently held the side of my neck. "There's nothing more we can do. The team will report as soon as it's done. You need to clear your mind. Focus on me. Look at my eyes, precious."

My mind beat against his words, my thoughts going faster than I could articulate them. But I made myself look into Alec's piercing eyes. His stare had always been arresting, but now when he looked at me, love permeated his gaze, not hostility. My shoulders relaxed slightly as my breathing slowed to match his.

He smiled, then leaned down and placed a gentle kiss on my lips. Pulling away just a fraction, he spoke in almost a whisper. "Feel the cold breeze on your skin."

I listened, feeling the breeze.

"Listen to the voices, the leaves, the cars in the distance."

I listened, remembering where we were. The people, the sounds, the sun streaming through the leaves—everything slowly came back into focus. Alec's honey voice and strong hands calmed me down despite myself.

He leaned away, a faint smile on his face, just as Charlie walked up to join us.

"Good work." Alec fist-bumped him, and Charlie gave a smug smile.

"What was that all about? Or should we not discuss it in public?" Charlie looked around. The courtyard was clearing again as students and staff moved off for their next classes and commitments.

"I think we're safe," Alec answered.

I sat up a little straighter. "Wait, that was you? Tracking the call?"

"Yeah." Charlie shrugged before casually sitting down on my other side. "So why was I tracking a call from your ex-boyfriend to your ex-boyfriend's house?" He raised his eyebrows, his amused gaze moving to Alec. "Interesting use of Melior Group resources."

Alec leaned around me and smacked his cousin on the shoulder. "Smartass. Zara surfaced."

Charlie whistled low. They were both men of few words, and while it was annoying sometimes, it had its benefits when you were discussing sensitive information in public.

"I thought your stalking ways had reignited. But, just for the record, she saved my life, so my allegiance is to her now." Charlie gave me a warm smile.

I smiled back and looked down. "I didn't really do anything. Just helped find you."

"Always so modest," Charlie teased.

"Wait, what do you mean about stalking?" Something clicked in my mind as I remembered what Alec had told me about the year I spent in Idaho. I pushed the residual hurt down as Alec ran his hand over his buzzed hair.

"How you gonna throw me into it like that, man?"

"I told you. I'm on her side now. Besides, what difference does it make? She already knows most of it."

"Yeah, well, maybe it's better not to rehash old—"

"It was you?" I cut Alec off, staring at Charlie. "That year I lived in Nampa? You were the one blocking me from finding Alec."

It made sense now that I knew how Alec's mind worked. He wouldn't have wanted it to be easily traced by Melior Group, nor would he have wanted to justify the use of resources, but he would've needed someone he trusted to do it. Charlie was the obvious choice.

"Yep. Kept you well away from this asshole but kept him informed of your every damn move. Made a good amount of money that year. He *really* wanted to keep you a secret, and he was willing to pay well."

I smacked him on the shoulder too. "Charlie!"

"But!" He leaned out of my reach. "In my defense, I put a stop to it."

"What?" Alec and I both said.

"Why do you think you were offered a scholarship here?"

"I'm gonna fucking kill you," Alec growled, but I was pretty sure he wasn't serious. "I want my money back."

I just gaped, a smile tugging on my lips as Charlie argued, "Technically, you paid me to block her from finding you and to report on her movements and 'anything suspicious.'" He used air quotes. "You never expressly said I couldn't do anything to help her out a little."

"Wait." I finally found my voice. "So I didn't actually earn my scholarship? You just . . . hacked me into the system?"

"Oh, Eve, no!" Charlie waved his hand. "All I did was bring you and your brilliant science mind to the attention of the admissions board, nudge them to get in contact with your school. The rest was all you, babe!"

I let out a relieved sigh. Of course I belonged here. The idea that I didn't get into Bradford Hills Institute on merit should've never crossed my mind. If there was one thing about myself I was sure of, it was my intelligence. I was excelling in all my classes, even despite the constant disruptions and catastrophic, traumatizing events.

I pulled Charlie into a tight hug. My gratitude was threatening to burst out of me—pop open my seams and pour out like the stuffing in a teddy bear. "Thank you, Charlie. You changed my life."

"Well, you saved mine, so we'll call it even."

I chuckled and pulled away, taking a deep breath to ease the persistent pressure of tears behind my eyes. Charlie's eyes looked a bit misty too.

"Are you two *crying?*" Alec sounded perplexed, and we both burst into quiet laughter.

I cleared my throat. "I really appreciate it, Charlie, but why?"

"I didn't know you were Evelyn Maynard, or Alec's Vital, but I knew you were damn important to him. For him to spend that kind of money and insist I keep it confidential under threat of excruciating pain, not to mention that he went out there every chance he got to keep an eye on you himself . . . I knew you were something special. Secrets never last long, and the sooner they come out the less damage they do."

"I was handling it," Alec grumbled.

"No, you were sticking your head in the sand while developing an obsession. I know I meddled, but I did what I thought was best for everyone. I did it because I love you." Alec just grunted, but Charlie kept speaking. "When I saw you two meet for the first time in the square that day, I knew who and what you were."

"Holy shit." Charlie knew I was a Vital before I did. He knew my true identity and kept it to himself. "You knew the whole time? But Dot said she told you."

He chuckled. "She did when she figured it out, but I already knew."

"Oh man, don't tell her she was actually the last one to figure it out. She'll *hate* that."

Charlie cringed. "Yeah, good point."

"Why didn't you say anything?"

"I was a virtual stranger. I may have known a lot about you, but you'd only just met me. What would you've done if I'd walked up to you and announced I knew your real name and oh, by the way, you're a Vital and this asshole is your Variant?"

"Yeah, fair point, I would've disappeared."

"No, you would've *tried.* I was never letting you out of my sight again," Alec declared, and because I'm just a little fucked up, I felt warm and fuzzy at his stalkerish declaration.

"Plus"—Charlie shrugged—"much as I wanted to give Alec a push, there was a good reason he was keeping it all a secret. I may have meddled a little, but once you were in the same place, it was up to you."

Alec and I both scoffed. If it wasn't for Charlie "pushing things," who knows where we would've ended up?

Before we could continue the conversation, both their phones went off. They glanced at the screens and got up.

"What's going on?" I slung my backpack over my shoulder.

"We're being summoned." Alec took my hand and pulled me in the direction of the admin building. "The team in Australia has checked in with an update."

The anxiety Alec and Charlie had so expertly distracted me from flooded back, and I picked up the pace, leading the way to Tyler's office.

EIGHT

I t was unseasonably warm for April, warm enough to be outside in shorts and a tank top while Ethan grilled hamburgers for lunch. Ed, Josh, Tyler, and Charlie played some fast-paced card game on the patio table that had them shouting and laughing while half the cards ended up on the ground.

Dot and I sat by the pool. She flipped through the latest edition of *Modern Variant* while I perused Josh's copy of *God is Dead* by Nietzsche—a welcome break from the complex scientific theories I usually read. It'd been a long, taxing week.

Alec and his team were at work. Zara had landed at a secure private airstrip the day before, and they'd been tasked with getting her safely to Melior Group HQ. Another two teams had assisted, along with Dana. With Dana there, Zara would be as harmless as any other twenty-year-old college student, but they weren't taking any chances.

Alec had checked in a few hours earlier; everything had gone off without a hitch. Zara was secure in a specially built cell, protecting her from abilities outside of it and protecting everyone else from her. Alec wanted to be present for her questioning that afternoon.

I wasn't sure if I was more worried about him or her.

Josh's, Ethan's, and my clearance hadn't come though yet, so he couldn't give us too many details. I suspected Victor was dragging the process out—just to show me he was in charge. I'd mentioned it to Lucian over breakfast, and after raising his brows in surprise, he'd grumbled, "Leave it to me," then disappeared once more behind his newspaper.

I had a feeling the clearance would be sorted out quickly.

But ultimately it didn't matter. Alec would tell me whatever I wanted to know, right after he crawled into my bed in the middle of the night and we had sex. Again. Since our first time together, hardly a day had gone by that I didn't have him inside me.

Even though the intimacy levels with the others remained the same, I still wanted him. I wanted them all. I was insatiable, as if we were making up for lost time—playing catch-up on all the sex we could've been having if it wasn't for the secrets and the pain and the holding back.

"Do you think Zara did it on purpose?" Dot's voice was sad, her eyes downcast but not focused on the magazine.

"What do you mean? It's not like she tripped and accidentally nudged me into a van with people who wanted to kidnap me."

"No, I know." She turned her almost too big eyes on me, and the scowl on my face melted away. "It's just . . . I don't even know what I'm saying. Forget it."

She waved her hand and turned back to the magazine, but she wasn't even remotely reading it. It was upside down.

"Dot. What's going on? Talk to me."

"I know she didn't do anything to me directly." She stared at her lap. "She didn't shove me into a van or stand by while I was experimented on. But after Beth died, I felt like I was getting her back as a friend, you know? Like the three of us were getting really close. It felt almost like old times. It just hurts to know it was all a lie. And I also feel like I should've known. Out of everyone, *I* should've picked up that something wasn't right with her. I guess when I say I wonder if she did it on purpose, I'm hoping maybe it wasn't her. Like maybe Davis had some kind of mind-control Variant or machine that made her do all those things."

I sighed. Zara's actions had affected so many people, in ways I didn't even fully comprehend. The fact that Dot was hurting made me so fucking mad . . . but I breathed through it. I needed to be there for her.

"I wish I could tell you that was the case—that Zara's as much a victim as we are—but we both know there are no recorded cases of Variants with mind-control abilities. And when I spoke to her on the phone, she said, 'I fucked up.' She owned it. I'm sorry, Dot, but she did this, and now she has to pay for it."

"I know. I'm not suggesting she should get away with it. I just . . . I don't know!" She threw her arms up and let them flop back down to her lap. "This whole situation is so fucked up. What happened to Charlie is fucked up. What happened to you is fucked up. What Zara did is fucked up. Her whole childhood was fucked up. I mean, it wasn't a surprise to anyone that her parents were involved with Variant Valor from the start. They're about as elitist and bigoted as you can get. And they were so hard on her. *So* mean. I remember this one time I was at Zara's place—we must've been, like, thirteen—and her mother came right out and said, 'You don't even have an inkling of an ability; you're a disappointment and a waste of space.' It was awful. I can't imagine the kind of shit they said when no one else was around. I just wonder if she would've done all those terrible things if she'd had a better family life."

"Maybe. Maybe not. Zara couldn't choose her parents, and neither could I. But at some point, we have to stop making excuses." Maybe it was a harsh way to look at things, but I just couldn't accept any argument that absolved Zara of the responsibility she had for her own actions. I was simply too angry.

We settled back into silence. I didn't want to argue with Dot or take my anger out on her. None of this was her fault.

She reached a hand between the loungers, and I took it without hesitation, squeezing her fingers. We held hands until the rage in my chest subsided, until she stopped staring into her lap as if the weight of sadness made her head impossible to lift, until the warmth of the sun and the sound of laughter behind us reminded us we had things to be happy about.

The silence once again turned comfortable, and we got back to reading.

After barely ten minutes, Dot let her magazine flop onto her chest and gazed at the glistening pool. "That water looks so inviting."

I dropped my book to the ground beside me. "It really does. I'm just trying to figure out if it's warm enough."

"Food's up!" Ethan yelled, sending a flock of birds flying out of some nearby oaks.

My stomach grumbled.

"Let's test the water after we eat." Dot led the way to the outdoor dining area.

We spent a relaxed few hours eating, drinking, joking around, and decidedly *not* talking about Zara, Variant Valor, the Human Empowerment Network, or Davis.

We did brave the pool in the end, Ed leading the charge as he pulled his shirt off. "I've been dying to get into that pool since I got here, but it's been too damn cold!"

His defined, tanned chest was narrower and more delicate than Charlie's, sprinkled with black chest hair that matched the curls on his head, but the two of them had one distinct thing in common. It wasn't until Ed ran for the pool that I saw his scars. Charlie's burn scars covered his right side, but Ed's were mostly on his back, starting at his shoulder blades and disappearing into the waistband of his shorts.

"I passed out from the smoke, and he shielded me from the fire with his body until they came to get us out. I'm so lucky to have him." Charlie stood next to me as the others stripped down and jumped in after Ed.

I took Charlie's hand. He gave me a squeeze back, and we shared a sad smile. There were so many things I could've said, questions I could've asked. But the best way—the only way—to get Charlie to talk was to just *listen*. I waited patiently, happy to abandon the rest of the afternoon and sit with him as long as he needed.

Instead, his smile widened, and he pulled me toward the pool. He wasn't ready to talk more about it, and that was completely fine. He knew I was there whenever he needed me. We all were.

I followed Dot's lead and stripped down to my simple black bra and underwear, not wanting to waste any time hunting for a bathing suit. I was the last one in . . . and apparently a rotten egg . . . because apparently we were all in elementary school again.

We splashed around and joked and then started getting out one by one.

The sun peeked in and out between fluffy white clouds. The heat that had made it just warm enough to be in the water was fading fast, chased away by a cold breeze.

As everyone else ran for the house, shivering, I huddled under the water. If I stayed there, the cold wind couldn't freeze me to death.

Apart from me, Ethan was the last to pull himself out of the pool, the fire tattoo dancing as his muscles bulged under his weight. Naturally, he didn't seem to feel the cold.

"You coming?" He half turned to check.

I shook my head and crouched farther, dipping my neck and chin into the water.

He laughed, flashing me a dimpled grin, and launched himself back in.

I screamed and jumped up, trying to avoid getting my head drenched from the tsunami he'd caused with his cannonball.

He swam to my side underwater before emerging, his jet-black hair plastered to his head. "What do you feel like for dinner?"

That boy always had food on his mind. I smiled and waded around, trying to ward off the chill. "What do you feel like making?" I rarely got a craving for a particular food. Whatever he chose to make was always delicious.

He flashed me another brilliant smile, leaning his elbows on the edge of the pool. "I found one of my mom's Mediterranean cookbooks, and I've been wanting to try some more stuff. I really want to do the moussaka, but I've never made it before and I'm not sure I have time to experiment, so I was thinking I could do this pasta dish. Now, I know what you're going to say—pasta's not really original, and there's more to Mediterranean food than just Italian, but . . ."

I chuckled as he kept talking. I wasn't going to say that at all, but he was on a roll, and there was no stopping him from geeking out. I slowly treaded water, watching him.

Light reflecting off the water made his amber eyes sparkle, and his hair was dripping, the droplets meandering down his broad chest. His big shoulders were pushed forward, and the fire tattoo contrasted starkly with the blue water and light tiles. He'd started to tan over the last few weeks; his naturally olive skin soaked up even the meager spring sun and had taken on a golden glow.

He was beautiful.

A fuzzy, overpowering feeling bubbled up in my chest, and I froze, transfixed, almost overwhelmed by its intensity. I wanted to hold Ethan close and never let him go. I wanted to kiss him silly until he was laughing and the dimples became permanent. I wanted to see that carefree, happy look on his beautiful face every day for the rest of my life.

As I realized what this feeling was, what I'd been feeling for a long time but hadn't allowed myself to examine, I shot through the water and wrapped my arms around his neck.

". . . the balsamic vinegar can be—" When I plastered myself against his front, he cut himself off, dropping his arms to hold me loosely around the waist.

"Ethan?" I struggled to hold back my smile, a tinge of nervousness mingling with the excitement.

"Yeah, bubble butt?" he half teased, searching my face.

"I love you." I let the grin break out in full force.

He blinked as all the teasing and lightheartedness left his features, replaced by that rare intense gaze. Then his arms tightened around me, and he pulled me against his chest as the most brilliant smile I'd ever seen crossed his face.

"I love you." He said it back without hesitation. "I think I've loved you since I first laid eyes on you."

I chuckled. "So that was an expression of love, was it? Throwing a ball of fire at my face and scaring me half to death?"

He grinned. "You weren't scared. You hardly even flinched. That's what made me want to know you."

He cut off my witty reply with a soft, gentle kiss. I tightened my arms around his neck and wrapped my legs around his waist, drawing him impossibly closer. We made slow circles in the water, moving deeper into the pool as his tongue waded into my mouth and he waded further and further into my very soul.

We broke apart, panting, and I opened my eyes to see beautiful flames covering the entirety of the pool's surface. They licked four feet into the air, banishing the cold wind.

I looked around us in wonder, smiling, warm and fuzzy on the inside *and* outside. It was almost exactly like the day we'd first tested our Bond connection, except this time, the flames weren't raging as high, didn't have that jerky, uncontrolled, volatile energy. Ethan was in perfect control; the fire was only high enough to hide us from view, an even height all over. He was doing this on purpose.

"What—"

My question was cut off when he leaned forward and started kissing and sucking my neck, then moved his hot mouth up to my ear.

"I want you," he whispered, and I groaned at his words, my thighs tightening around him reflexively.

I kissed him again, pushing my tongue into his mouth. With one hand, I undid his swim trunks while he nudged the fabric of my panties out of the way. Our movements weren't jerky or desperate—we knew we had the rest of our lives to spend together —but we weren't taking it painfully slow either. Neither one of us wanted to wait much longer to start that life.

Within minutes of declaring our love, Ethan was inside me, filling me up in every way. We both sighed into the feeling— warm, safe, and so fucking good. It was the first time I'd had him inside me without a condom, feeling every inch of silk-covered steel as he slid in.

We made love in the pool, staring into each other's eyes as his bright flames lit up the water around us. I'd never felt closer, more connected, to him.

We came at the same time, our foreheads together, our soft moans mingling as we watched each other unravel in the sweetest kind of surrender, our souls bare.

I rested my head on his shoulder, and he just held me as the flames flickered out completely. It was now dusk. A gust of wind reminded me we had no business being in a pool at night in April unless we wanted to freeze, but I didn't care. I was safe and warm in my fire fiend's arms.

When we finally got out of the pool, Ethan froze, his back tense as he turned to me, wide-eyed. "Shit! Condom."

I chuckled and took his hand in mine. "It's OK. I got the implant over a week ago, remember? We're safe."

He took an exaggerated sigh of relief. Tyler had used his ability to make sure we were all clean before I had the procedure.

Another chilly gust of wind made my teeth chatter, and Ethan wrapped a big towel around my shoulders. We headed back to the house hand in hand.

"Maybe I'll do the moussaka after all," he mused. "I think I have enough time. I'll have to get more eggplant though."

"Sounds perfect." I smiled up at him.

NINE

I forced myself to sit up straighter in the lecture theater seat. The coffee Josh had brought me after lunch just wasn't cutting it.

It had been nearly two weeks since Zara's capture—or surrender, depending on how you looked at it—and I was trying to maintain a routine, refusing to let her disrupt my life any further. But the Variant history lecture, a compulsory unit for all students with Variant DNA, was not holding my interest. Shaking my head to clear away the fuzziness, I noticed I wasn't the only one having trouble concentrating.

It started with a few whispers, pockets of people shifting in their seats, bending their heads together. Then it spread farther. People were getting louder and looking at their phones.

The professor shushed them, a stern look on her face, but whatever was happening had them ignoring her. People were starting to get downright rowdy.

A pang of worry shot down my spine, and I looked to the back of the room, searching for my security detail. The agent was standing near the door, his finger pressed to his ear as he spoke softly into his unseen mic. He was the only black-clad figure there—apparently I was the only Vital in the lecture today.

Without even meaning to, I reminded myself of the exits. The closest was the one next to my security detail. Two emergency exits were on either wall at the bottom of the room, and I was pretty sure the office behind the professor's lectern had another door leading to a corridor on the other side of the building.

The professor gave up trying to wrangle the crowd and demanded to know what was happening. One of the students in the front row got up and showed her his phone. The professor frowned.

"Surely this is a hoax," said a boy a few rows down.

"How is this possible?" a girl sitting near me asked no one in particular.

"I have to call my mom." A young boy, no more than sixteen, haphazardly gathered his things and rushed out of the room. Others followed, the theater erupting into disorder, the lecture forgotten.

I packed my books and stood just as the crowd parted. Alec came down the few stairs to stand at the end of my row. He was in uniform, a gun strapped to his hip, his tattoos almost completely covered by the long sleeves.

I swung my bag over my shoulder and took his hand. "What's happening?"

"Not here," he growled over his shoulder as he pulled me along.

When we exited the lecture theater, my other bodyguard fell in behind us. Alec marched us across campus, glaring at anyone who got too close. Several other people were rushing in various directions too, while some just stood around talking animatedly or looking at their phones.

I was dying to know what the hell was happening, but clearly it was serious, so I kept my mouth shut.

We jogged up the stairs to the admin building and marched straight past the reception desk, Alec's boots thudding on the polished concrete floor as I struggled to keep up. The receptionists barely spared us a glance. At the elevators, Alec ordered the other

Melior Group agent to stay there, and we headed up to Tyler's office.

Once inside, Alec finally dropped my hand.

". . . you understand? Stand down." Tyler was on the phone, every muscle in his body stiff. "We can't risk turning this into an international incident. We'll just have to deal with it as best we can *quietly*." He was silent for a few moments. "Good. Report as soon as you have something." Then, without saying goodbye, he hung up.

"Guys, I'm starting to freak out here." I found myself shifting closer to Alec, pressing myself into his side.

Alec wrapped one arm around my shoulders as Tyler sighed and leaned on his desk. He picked up the remote, pointed it at the TVs on the wall behind me, and turned up the volume.

Staring back at me from the screen, a charismatic smile pinned to his face, was Davis Damari—my so-called father and the reason for everything that had ever gone wrong in my life. I stiffened, the blood rushing to my ears making it hard to hear. Alec squeezed my shoulder.

Davis was giving some kind of speech in front of a crowd. Cameras and microphones were everywhere.

"This is, we believe, one of the greatest scientific breakthroughs in modern history. Not only can we now isolate Variant abilities, we have developed technology that enables us to give Variants *without* abilities the gift of an ability."

The news program cut to a reporter summarizing the situation. Apparently Davis had given an impressive speech only an hour ago. My eyes flicked around the other three screens. Each one was covering the news; each one had his ugly face plastered all over it.

Tyler stepped around his desk and planted himself at my other side. But even Alec's and Tyler's comforting arms around my shoulders and waist couldn't stop me from feeling as if the world was crumbling around me.

"What the fuck is happening?" I muttered to myself. No one answered.

After the incident in Thailand, Davis, his core group of scientists, and some of his more fanatical Variant Valor supporters had completely disappeared. Melior Group had worked tirelessly to find him, but Davis was rich and well connected. He had friends in high places everywhere to keep him safe.

I'd had several arguments with Tyler over why it *wasn't* all over the news that Davis Damari was behind Variant Valor, the attack on Bradford Hills Institute, the Vital kidnappings. The whole world should know what a piece of scum he was. But Tyler and Alec kept explaining it wasn't that simple.

Much of what happened in Thailand was classified and therefore couldn't be discussed. Plus, apparently Melior Group's board had decided it would be bad for business if it got out that dozens of their best elite operatives had been knocked out in one fell swoop by a single Variant with an impressive ability. They were trying to save face.

Senator Christine Anderson was talking, but she refused to front the media or go on record with human law enforcement for fear of her life.

Zara was cooperating too. She'd told Melior Group about another of Davis's secret labs in Australia, but by the time Melior Group had got a team there, the place was empty, completely cleared of people or any trace of useful information.

While we knew the truth, the rest of the world was left to wonder what the hell had happened in Thailand, and Davis's name was not once mentioned in relation to the incident. This had resulted in more suspicion, fear, and worry in the general public. They were filling in their gaps in knowledge with the worst-case scenarios.

And now the psychopath behind it all stood, untouched, in a three-thousand-dollar suit, announcing a "scientific breakthrough" as if it was just another business day and he had nothing to do with the chaos erupting all over the world.

Davis Damari was winning. It made my blood boil.

He didn't go into detail about how exactly he gave abilities to Variants who hadn't manifested any, but people were losing their minds, reporters clambering over each other to ask questions.

One of the main sound bites they kept repeating was that the technology was nearly ready, but there was one last kink to figure out. They were close, really close, but something stood in their way. At this point, Davis announced he was out of time and walked away from the frenzy of questions.

"It's me," I breathed, stepping out of their embrace. "I'm what's preventing him from figuring it out."

The attack at the café, the woman's declaration that he would never stop coming for me—it made sense now. When he'd captured me in Thailand, he hadn't had enough time to test his process, perfect it, poke, prod and torture me until he understood my glowing Light better. He still needed me to figure out how to not kill people during the procedure, because even *he* couldn't sell *that*.

The door swung open, and Ethan and Josh burst into the office, finally tearing my attention from the four screens.

"Why haven't they arrested him?" Ethan's booming voice bounced off the walls. "Why the fuck was he able to just walk into a car and be driven away?"

Josh remained silent, a deep frown on his face. He crossed his arms and leaned back against the door.

"Keep your voice down." Tyler's commanding tone had an immediate effect on Ethan. He didn't back down completely, his big shoulders still tense, but he did unclench his fists and take a deep breath.

"Sorry." He sighed. "I just don't understand."

"It's OK, Kid." Alec slapped a hand on his cousin's shoulder as Tyler muted the screens.

"He's in fucking Dubai. We have operatives in the area, but we couldn't get them there before the cameras showed up. We couldn't take him into custody with the whole world watching—

not when no one knows all the shit he's done. And now this . . ." Tyler groaned, running his hand through his messy hair and looking out the window. "He planned this perfectly. He disappeared off the face of the earth, forced us to spread ourselves thin looking for him, then reappeared in a location where we couldn't get to him in time. Now with this announcement, the press will be on him like a bad smell, not to mention all his supporters and lackeys. He's basically made himself untouchable."

He was looking out at the campus grounds below, and I knew what he was seeing—people rushing about, some excited, some worried, *everyone* talking about it.

"So what do we do?" I asked. I needed a plan. I always felt better with a plan.

Alec lowered his tall frame into one of the tub chairs.

No one answered.

"Guys!" I nearly yelled, a bit of panic leaking into my voice. "What do we do?"

Tyler squared his shoulders. "We keep an eye on him, and we work on our own strategy."

"Which is what exactly?" Josh spoke for the first time.

"We have to be smarter than him, stay one step ahead. If Eve is right, and I think she is, that he needs her to complete his machine, then we learn everything we can about the glowing Light. Maybe we'll be able to use that against him somehow. We've already agreed to work with Melior Group's research team —may as well use that to our advantage. But let's keep as much to ourselves as we can, OK?"

Ethan frowned and shared a look with me and Josh. "Are you saying we can't trust Melior Group? What's going on?"

"Nothing I can put my finger on yet." He exchanged a loaded look with Alec. "All I'm saying is, we should keep our cards close to our chests. People are scared, and scared people do stupid things. In the meantime, now that he's surfaced, we have eyes on Davis. He's hiding behind powerful men with even more questionable morals than his, but at least we can track him now. As soon as we can take him down discreetly, we will. All we can do now is stay vigilant and gather as much information as we can."

"And above all"—Alec rose to his feet, turning to face me —"we protect Evelyn."

TEN

After ten minutes of focused mindfulness, I opened my eyes. Controlling my Light flow had become second nature, almost instinctual. Our Bond was settling; it was formed, strong, *equal*. No one held back and created an imbalance in the connection, and the Light no longer gushed dangerously out of me in order to solidify our Bond. Transferring Light was just part of my physiology now—almost as effortless as breathing.

But the *glowing* Light required more intention. I'd only glowed in a handful of situations—most of them highly stressful and potentially deadly.

Continuing to take deep breaths, I uncrossed my legs and dropped them to the ground in front of the couch. Ethan and Josh sat in matching armchairs across from me, a heavy stone coffee table between us. The rest of the room was decorated like a modern living space—polished concrete floors, leather furniture, open bookshelves styled meticulously, hints of metallics and marble in the decor—but the heavy white drapes had nothing but thick brick walls behind them, and the giant mirror to my left concealed a team of Melior Group researchers, watching my every move.

This session was meant to be as "natural" as possible, hence the living room setup. They wanted me to do my thing without external influence so they could observe—from behind the safety of the glass, of course. Dana was in the next room on standby in case anything went wrong.

My first session had consisted of a battery of medical tests and basic observations of my Light levels when I let it flow into me unobstructed, when I mentally shut it off, when I transferred to someone in my Bond, then someone outside of it. Those were baseline tests.

This session would be the first time they observed the glowing, and since we couldn't be sure it wasn't dangerous, I had to have my Variants there to transfer to. I didn't want to find out what would happen if I took in that much Light and had no outlet for it.

I sat up a little straighter and focused purely on the Light, letting my instincts take over to an extent. I not only dropped my mental barriers—unlocked the doors, so to speak—but threw them open and shouted, "I'm here."

The Light was all around us, in the air, in every Variant, and in very tiny amounts, in every living thing.

I pulled, imagining the warm white glow on my skin. As if imagining it had made it manifest, I started to glow. It slowly got brighter and stronger.

Ethan and Josh wore matching brilliant grins. Both of them sat forward, their elbows on their knees, their faces full of pride, wonder, *love*.

Before the glow became blinding and made it impossible for anyone to observe anything, I reached my hands out. Neither of my Variants took my hand. They just waited, patiently.

I sent the Light to them; it felt like warm water running over my skin.

After a quick transfer, the glow faded, and I stopped the flow of Light.

We sat in silence for a few moments. The head researcher, Karen, usually used the intercom system to give us instructions, her calm voice filling the room through the built-in speakers.

But after I finished my glowing transfer . . . nothing.

I shared a confused look with Ethan and Josh before turning to the double-sided mirror. My own reflection stared back at me.

Just as I was about to get up, Karen's voice came through the speakers.

"That was incredible!" She sounded more animated, more excited than I'd ever heard her. So did the cacophony of chatter in the background. "Just amazing!" She cleared her throat, shushing some of the other excited nerds before speaking again in a slightly calmer tone. "Now we need to observe the abilities in action—to illustrate that Light has indeed been transferred."

Needing no further instruction, Ethan and Josh got to their feet. Ethan curled his fingers, and a bright blue ball of menacing fire appeared, while Josh lifted the solid stone coffee table up to the ceiling with a flick of the wrist.

They had us repeat the process a few times, measuring the levels of Light and my vital signs, sometimes taking the guys into other testing areas where they could use their abilities to their full potential by basically blowing shit up.

While practicing was good, none of this was new to us. We were almost bored, going through the motions for the sake of the scientific process, to make sure everything was recorded accurately.

It wasn't until toward the end of the session that we learned anything interesting. We were discussing what I'd observed about how the process of drawing Light to me worked, and I explained that I seemed to be able to draw it directly from specific individuals. In the next round of tests, Karen asked me to draw directly from Ethan and transfer to Josh.

Ethan stood at my back, his hand resting lightly on my hip. His other hand gripped mine, and I threaded my fingers through his.

Josh stood several feet away, his hands in the pockets of his chinos, his perfect lips turned up in a slight smile.

I was getting tired, but I inhaled deeply and focused on my

connection to the fire fiend behind me. I took my time, making sure to block all other sources of Light while drawing on Ethan's alone.

As with all things, when it came to my Bondmates, it came easier than anything. I didn't even have to pull—I just opened my arms and his Light charged into my embrace.

As soon as my skin began to glow, I lifted my free arm and sent the Light to Josh. I nearly gasped as the sheer power of Ethan's force flowed through me. For a few seconds, we were all connected. It felt incredible on a soul-deep level—so good I absentmindedly arched my back, a familiar ache in my lower belly building unexpectedly.

Ethan's hand on my hip gripped tighter, and I shut the flow down, the glow fading.

Josh didn't look so casual anymore. His hands were out of his pockets, his smile replaced by a much darker, more heated look.

Karen's voice came through the speakers, throwing cold water on the moment. "Mr. Mason, if you would . . ."

She sounded a little amused, but Josh squared his shoulders and, as he'd done countless times already, lifted the coffee table into the air. The heavy piece of furniture burst into bright blue flames, singeing the ceiling and startling us all.

Josh's panicked eyes flew to us. He was effortlessly keeping the flaming table off the ground and away from other flammable things, but he clearly had no idea what to do about the angry blue flames.

Ethan wrapped one big arm around my waist and reached the other over my shoulder. It took him longer than usual, but he put the fire out, and Josh lowered the charred, smoking mess back to the ground.

"What the fu—"

The door burst open, interrupting Josh's confused utterance, and the entire research team swarmed into the room.

Some threw a barrage of rapid-fire questions at us, furiously writing everything down, while others inspected the coffee table. I was so fascinated myself I didn't even mind the session was going past time. A flurry of theories buzzed through my mind, but I carefully avoided sharing too much of my own thoughts. If there was one thing I'd learned from both my upbringing and my time in Bradford Hills, it was when people knew things about you, they could use them against you.

After a solid half hour of this, and declarations that we had to repeat it in future sessions, they finally allowed us to leave. Everyone trickled out of the room, chatting excitedly. As Josh, Ethan, and I passed the door to the observation room, a man in a navy-blue suit broke off his conversation with Karen and came toward us.

"Miss Maynard." Victor Flint flashed me a grin, all teeth, and shook my hand.

"Mr. Flint." I smiled politely, and he turned to my Variants.

"You must be Mr. Paul." He shook Ethan's hand, then Josh's. "And Mr. Mason. Pleasure to meet you both, and I am deeply sorry you won't be joining Melior Group in any capacity other than as test subjects. But a deal is a deal."

He flashed me that grin again.

"You were watching," Josh stated, stuffing his hands in his pockets. Ethan wrapped a protective arm around my shoulders. Either they didn't trust him or they were picking up on my unease.

"I caught the tail end of the session, yes. I must say, I was very pleased by what I saw. We're learning so much already. I have every confidence we'll be able to give you some clarity about your condition, Miss Maynard."

"I certainly hope so." I resisted the urge to cross my arms—I didn't want to appear rude or standoffish—and settled for clasping my hands.

"Oh, I *know* so." He laughed deep in his chest. "And the process is shedding light on things I didn't even expect, like the events in Thailand. You've just solved a problem that's been plaguing the investigators for months."

"Oh?" I raised my brows but didn't say any more. Sometimes the best way to get people to talk was to just be quiet. But Victor didn't seem at all reluctant to share information.

"Yes, the fire in the parking garage. We determined early on that Davis remotely detonated several explosions as he made his escape." I remembered the booms, the ground shaking. "But those were primarily on the other side of the facility, where the labs and files were. He was destroying evidence, or trying to—we still managed to recover a good deal. Anyway, those explosions resulted in fires, which spread quickly to other areas, including the holding cells where they were keeping most of the Vitals. But they did not spread as far as the garage, where I believe you were . . ." He looked pointedly at Josh and held his hands above his head, miming the way Josh had kept the ceiling from collapsing on us.

Josh nodded and Victor kept speaking. "There really was no discernable reason for that part of the structure to have caught fire. We couldn't work it out. Until today. It seems Mr. Paul's fire ability transferred to Mr. Mason through you, Miss Maynard, just like what happened here today."

I blinked. Of course, it made sense for one of the head honchos of Melior Group to be across the major points in the investigation, but I didn't think he was looking into such minute details.

His assessment seemed accurate. I'd suspected the same thing when I saw Ethan's ability manifest at Josh's command, but I'd been waiting until we were somewhere private to raise it with them.

Josh appeared unfazed, his posture still relaxed, his curious eyes studying the middle-aged man in front of us. Ethan, on the other hand, was suddenly breathing more rapidly, his arm tightening around my shoulders.

"But I see this isn't entirely shocking news to you." Victor kept the smile plastered on his face, but his eyes narrowed. Before any of us could respond, he pulled something out of his pocket.

"In other news, your clearance has been approved and finalized. These passes will give you access to all parts of the building that your clearance level is permitted to enter. Not that you'll need to access other areas, but it will make coming and going to these sessions easier. Pleasure meeting you, gentlemen. Goodbye."

He handed the plastic passes to us, turned on his heel, and disappeared down a corridor.

Ethan backed away from me until his broad back hit a wall. He slid to the floor, threading his hands through his hair.

Josh and I exchanged a worried look and crouched down next to him.

"Baby?" I scratched the back of his neck, my other hand going to his knee. Josh placed a comforting hand on his shoulder.

"It wasn't me," Ethan whispered into his lap. "It wasn't me, you guys. I didn't burn them."

He took a massive, shuddering breath and looked up to the ceiling, relief palpable in every fiber of his being. Ethan had been convinced it was his fault the fires had started. That it was his fault all those people had been burned, even killed. Tyler had explained the investigators' findings, but Ethan couldn't be dissuaded, couldn't forget the distinctive blue tinge of the fire we'd all seen.

Hearing Victor spell it out and seeing for himself how the glowing Light transfer worked had finally made it all click. He wasn't to blame.

He gave me a brilliant smile, dimples on full display, and pulled us both in for a hug. We sat on the floor laughing, shedding a few happy tears, and then Josh got to his feet.

He held his hand out to me. "Come on. I need to get back to my thesis, and you're going to be late for lunch with Dot."

"Shit!" She was probably furious. I was surprised she hadn't sent Squiggles to find me—or a bear.

While I was in the bowels of Melior Group doing my best impression of a lab rat, she'd spent the morning shopping with Kyo, Marcus, and an entourage of security guards. The plan was to have lunch together at one of Dot's favorite cafés in the city. She'd been trying to take me there for ages.

When we finally made it to the lobby of the building, Dot grumbled about my lateness but still gave me a hug. Marcus had some work to get back to in Bradford Hills, so he was getting a lift back with Josh, along with all of Dot's purchases.

Dot kissed Marcus goodbye openly, her short frame plastered to his tall one, then took Kyo's hand and led the way toward the exit.

"I don't know about this." Josh frowned as he held me close. "Maybe we should all head home and Ethan can make you lunch?"

I wrapped my arms around his neck, fiddling with the stiff collar of his shirt. "We have a full Melior Group detail, we have Kyo, and we have my big fire fiend. We'll be fine."

After what had happened at breakfast with Lucian, they were all understandably cautious. I was shaken too. The fact that he could get to us in Bradford Hills—probably the most guarded place on the East Coast—was disconcerting, to say the least. But I refused to live my life in fear. That's what drove the division, the unrest.

"Text me as soon as you're heading home," Josh demanded, holding me almost too tightly.

"I promise." I breathed in his expensive aftershave, resting my cheek on his shoulder.

"Maynard!" Dot yelled, her voice echoing in the cavernous marble-lined lobby. She and Kyo were waiting for us beside the revolving glass doors. "Move it! I'm hungry!"

Josh planted a little kiss on my nose and turned away, taking some of the countless bags off Marcus and heading for the parking garage.

The security detail wanted to take armored cars to our destination, but it was only three blocks away, and Dot and I insisted on walking. It was a beautiful spring day, though a bit chilly in the shade of the tall buildings, and we wanted to enjoy the sunshine and the blossoming trees.

It might've been better to take the cars though—the walk turned out to be less than relaxing.

Seeing high-profile Vitals with a couple of security guards had never been uncommon, but lately, it seemed as though anyone with Variant DNA who could afford it was hiring either Melior Group or another security company to follow them around.

Walking down the street, we saw several people being followed closely by frowning armed guards, but nothing compared to the entourage we had. No fewer than eight Melior Group operatives surrounded us, all of them taking their job very seriously and making the lives of anyone walking in the opposite direction a nightmare.

Dot either was oblivious to it or just didn't care, walking confidently with Kyo just ahead of us. They were downright adorable, hand in hand, leaning into each other, giggling like schoolkids.

I smiled, overjoyed that my friends had found happiness in each other. Ethan squeezed my hand and gave me a knowing look.

"People are staring," I whispered out of the corner of my mouth.

He chuckled and slung an arm over my shoulders. "People always stare at you. You're beautiful. You just never notice."

I huffed and slapped him on the stomach, but I couldn't stop a wide smile from crossing my face.

We came to a stop next to an older Beaux Arts–style building. The café had cute striped awnings, planter boxes hanging off the low windows, and a door angled into the corner.

"I can't wait for you to try the crumpets!" Dot grabbed my hand and bounced on the spot. "They make them from scratch, and they're so good."

"What's a crumpets?" Kyo frowned, but Ethan's face had lit up.

We weren't allowed to go inside yet though. Several of our

guards held their hands out in a halting motion while two headed for the front door to ensure it was safe.

As they reached the door, it swung open, and a furious middle-aged man in a sunflower apron marched out. The guards all reached for their guns, on high alert. Ethan pushed me behind his wide frame as Kyo did the same to Dot.

I couldn't see what threat this man with narrow shoulders and more salt than pepper in his hair could pose. But then, the short young woman who'd tried to kill me hadn't exactly looked like a crazed murderer either. Considering what happened with Zara, I was the worst judge of who could and couldn't be trusted.

"Oh no you don't!" He wagged a finger in our direction, not even slightly intimidated by all the heavily armed men and women giving him warning looks.

One of our guards, his voice calm, tried to keep him back with an extended arm. "Sir, you need to step—"

"This is *my* café, and I'll do whatever the hell I want. You haven't taken that right from me yet, so I'm exercising it. And *you're* not welcome here."

"Excuse me?" Kyo bristled.

"I may be just a Dime, but I still have rights. This is my establishment, my *home*, and I refuse to allow guns inside. I refuse to allow people like you . . ." he sputtered, obviously frustrated. "Variant abilities may as well be weapons. I want my patrons to feel safe. *I* want to feel safe. Leave! You are not welcome here."

For a moment, no one said anything. The man crossed his arms and planted his feet wide, guarding the door with nothing more than a furious glare and sheer determination.

Ethan sighed, his big chest puffing out, and gave me a sad, worried look over his shoulder.

I reached out and took Dot's hand. Her eyes met mine.

"Let's just go," I whispered, and she nodded. It wasn't worth it. We didn't want to make anyone feel more unsafe than they already did. I knew what that felt like, and I refused to add to it.

Kyo was the most frustrated. "It's not right. This is discrimination. He can't just . . ."

Dot took his arm and pulled him along, doing her best to soothe him as our entourage closed in tighter.

We ended up in a diner a few streets over, the four of us seated in a booth. Our protectors spread out, some sitting close by, some posted at the exits.

It was a somber lunch. The food was mediocre; even Ethan didn't finish his BLT. They didn't have an espresso machine, so I went without coffee. I really needed it too, judging by the building headache behind my eyes.

After a long, heavy silence, Dot pushed her plate away. "Everyone is acting weird and doing strange things, and it's scaring me."

Kyo rubbed her back. "Everyone is scared. That's why they're acting weird. I've got your back."

"I know you do, but that's not really what I mean. I'm scared for my immediate safety, yes. It's hard not to be, considering . . ." She looked at me, her perfect brows pulling together.

"Considering the constant attempts on people's lives?" I deadpanned.

"Yeah. But when I say I'm scared, I mean in a bigger sense. I'm scared about what the world is turning into. I'm scared about what all this fear will lead to. I don't want to spend the rest of my life being followed around by an entire team of agents while I get kicked out of my favorite restaurants and shops."

"We got turned away from a lingerie boutique earlier today as well," Kyo explained. "The owner there wasn't quite as dramatic as the guy at the café, but she made herself clear. Variants aren't welcome."

I sighed. "I hate this. And I can see both sides. I mean, I was raised human, never believed there was anything special about me whatsoever. You do kind of feel like Variants get privileges, advantages that we don't. It's worse in some parts of the world, but I can see how it breeds resentment. You fuel that resentment with fear

—suggest that now, not only do human kids have less access to the opportunities Variant kids have, but their lives are in danger too? I wouldn't want my family anywhere around us either."

"But we're not like that!" Dot sounded equally pleading and outraged. "Most Variants are normal, happy people trying to live our lives, just like humans. I'm not interested in blocking anyone from having a better life. I'm certainly not interested in killing little human babies."

"No, and most Variants would agree with you. But then you see more and more of them joining Variant Valor, and not shy about talking about it. You see people using the word *Dime* with abandon. It would be pretty hard not to feel attacked."

"Yeah, I get that." Dot flopped back against the back of the booth.

"Variant Valor aren't the only ones getting louder," Ethan grumbled. "I'm seeing more and more mentions of the Human Empowerment Network too."

"Yeah." Kyo drew Dot to his side. "Both the boutique and that café had big posters in the windows—'Human Safe Space' in big bold letters with HEN's branding all over it. They're taking the safety-in-numbers approach, and they're not being subtle about it."

"It's just creating more division," Ethan agreed.

"The most frustrating thing"—I clenched my hands into fists —"is that none of these people, Variant or human, realize they're pawns and playing right into that asshole's hand. Davis is behind all of this. It's no coincidence that this divisive rhetoric got more intense after he did his press conference. This is what he wants. He *wants* the Variants scared of the humans so they'll spend all their money on his sick invention. He *wants* the humans scared so the division continues to breed."

"I wish we could just hunt him down and lock him in a dark hole where he can't touch or hurt anyone," Ethan muttered. He was such a sweetheart. Davis may have been my biological father, but I wanted him dead, not locked up.

"Do that, and he becomes a martyr. Even harder to fight against a legacy than a man," Kyo argued. "Toppling Dictatorships 101—discredit and besmirch the charismatic leader. *Then* take him out."

I wondered just how many governments Kyo and Alec's team had been involved in tearing down, but I had a feeling even my new clearance level wouldn't be high enough to gain me access to that information.

"I. Hate. Him." My voice was clear and level as my eyes narrowed on the table, not seeing our half-empty plates or the condiment bottles. Only his ugly face.

My friends watched me warily.

ELEVEN

The late afternoon sun bathed the yard in a golden glow. I put in one earring and watched from my window as Ethan got out of the pool, his lean muscles effortlessly lifting his heavy frame out of the water.

The mid-May weather still wasn't warm enough for most of us. Other than that one blissfully hot day a few weeks back, it had been too cold for swimming. But Ethan never felt the cold. As he dried his hair off with a towel, all that muscle glistened in the sun, making me want to go down there and lick the water droplets off his smooth chest.

I shook myself out of it and put my other earring in, then turned and paused.

Josh was at my door, leaning on the frame and watching me as I'd been watching Ethan.

"You are so beautiful," he stated, his boyish face full of sincerity.

"Thanks. This dress is stunning." He was in sweats and a Queen T-shirt, and I was in eveningwear, my feet tucked into bright red heels. The strapless dress tapered in at the waist and stopped at about midcalf. Black tulle surrounded my legs, but a red lace top layer popped against the black. Dot had painstakingly braided my hair into a pattern almost as intricate as the bold design of the lace.

The dress had appeared on my bed a few hours earlier when I emerged from the shower, just as I'd started to panic about what to wear.

When Tyler had first told me about the event, I'd groaned. But he never asked me for anything, and after he explained why he needed the extra Light boost, I agreed quickly.

The formal evening had been organized under a cloak of secrecy; it brought together security, law enforcement, and intelligence bigwigs from all over the world. The situation with Variant Valor and the Human Empowerment Network was continuing to escalate, and some leaders wanted to increase their efforts to work together, hoping more cooperation would help. They were holding a massive meeting, hosted by Melior Group, but it wouldn't take place until the next day. This evening was a welcome cocktail event with a formal dress code. Because we couldn't possibly solve the world's problems in smart casual.

I smiled as I walked toward Josh. "I'll never get over your uncanny ability to choose a dress that's perfect in every way, right down to the fit."

"Actually, Ethan helped this time. We went together."

"When did you two have time to go shopping?" Between our sessions at Melior Group, the continued training with Kane, studying for exams, and preparing for summer classes, we were all busy.

"We invited you to go with us, remember?" Josh raised his brows. When I gave him a blank look, he rolled his eyes and smiled. "But of course, you had your head in a science book, so I should've realized you barely heard a word I said."

I chuckled, wrapping my arms around his neck. "It really is beautiful. Thank you. You guys spoil me."

"Actually we're holding back. You don't know what spoiled looks like. And I wasn't talking about the dress. *You* are beautiful."

He squeezed my sides for emphasis and pulled me fully

against his front. My breath hitched. I stared into Josh's knowing green eyes, my smile falling away. It really hit me once more how much he thought about me, how in tune he was not just with the size of my body when buying me couture but with my thoughts, feelings, wants, and needs. I could've put it down to the Bond, but that wasn't it. The level of attentiveness was uniquely Josh.

"Josh." My voice was low. I bit down on my bottom lip, suddenly a little nervous. The words were at the tip of my tongue, but a tightness squeezed the base of my throat, making it difficult to get them out.

Of course, he knew what I was thinking.

He smiled. His whole face lit up, and his eyes practically sparkled, just as Ethan's had in the pool when I told him.

"I love you too, Eve." He beat me to it.

"You stole my moment." I slapped him lightly on the shoulder, my own matching grin already breaking out on my face.

"I love you, Josh." I said it anyway.

"I know, but it's really nice to hear it." He pressed his lips to mine in a passionate kiss that definitely ruined my lipstick.

We heard footsteps coming up the stairs but didn't break apart. When I felt a hard, warm chest at my back, I knew it was Ethan and I was at risk of ruining more than just my lipstick.

I broke the kiss, but Ethan's lips were at my neck, his breath tickling my skin. "Don't stop," he whispered, breaking up his words with the occasional soft kiss. "I like seeing you all dolled up like this, kissing Josh when he doesn't look even remotely in your league in his ratty clothes."

As Josh started kissing the other side of my neck, all I could do was hum in acknowledgment, although it came out more like a moan.

"What's wrong with what I'm wearing?" Josh whispered before licking a particularly sensitive spot.

"Nothing," Ethan answered, "but it's such a contrast to what *she's* wearing that I can't stop thinking about . . . ruining that dress."

I moaned again. I was just about to ask them to show me exactly how they planned to ruin it when I was suddenly yanked away. Strong, calloused hands pulled me out from between Ethan and Josh so swiftly the two of them nearly bumped into each other. Ethan caught himself on the doorway, and Josh leaned a hand against Ethan's bare abs.

I looked between them, then up and around to Alec, cocking one eyebrow to show my disapproval.

"We're going to be late if you start that now. You two need to make yourselves scarce." He kept my back against his chest, his hands on my bare shoulders.

Josh sighed and hung his head, and Ethan immediately lifted his free hand to the back of Josh's neck. It was a reflex, a comforting gesture, but standing so close, with their hands on each other and Ethan shirtless, they almost looked like . . . lovers.

Their eyes locked for the briefest of moments before they pulled away. As Josh walked past, there was no mistaking the little smirk on his face. Ethan looked more confused, but curiosity definitely gleamed in his eyes too as he headed for his room.

"Why are you always cockblocking me?" I sighed, leaning back against Alec.

"Because we really are going to be late." He ran his hands down my arms slowly and pushed his hips forward, pressing his erection into my ass. "And because I want to ruin that dress myself later."

When he kissed one side of my neck, then the other, I shivered, my lips parting on a heavy exhale.

"Now hurry up." He pulled away, smacked me on the ass, and thumped down the stairs.

Fucking tease. I rolled my eyes before fixing my lipstick and grabbing my clutch off the bed.

Tyler's left hand rested on my leg, playing absentmindedly with the tulle, while his other scrolled through messages on his phone. Alec had a firm, unmoving hand on my other leg as he looked out the car window at the dusky sky.

Apparently taking a limo for just the three of us was overkill, but we couldn't possibly drive ourselves, so we were on our way to Manhattan in an Aston Martin town car driven by the same driver who had taken us to the gala. His name was Joe.

Important people were flying in from all over the world—we couldn't *not* throw a fancy event for them, although this would be much more low-key than the gala. Only about 150 guests were expected.

"So how come they're all coming here?" I asked. "Why aren't we flying off to Geneva or something?"

"It's New York," they both answered at the same time, as if it were obvious. Joe's shoulders shook with silent laughter.

"Americans . . ." I sighed. "You know there are cities just as vibrant and just as important as New York. And probably more convenient to get to for most of these people."

"I'd like to remind you that you're also American." Alec turned to face me. "And there's nowhere in the world like New York."

Tyler gave me a more serious answer. "Melior Group is hosting the event. Our HQ is here. It made sense. Plus, it gives us the chance to make sure it's well protected, allows us some control over who's invited, and puts us in a leadership position before any of the conversations have even started."

He stuffed his phone into his jacket pocket and smiled in a way that reminded me of our study sessions, when he was waiting for me to understand something complex, already believing without a doubt I'd get it.

I nodded. The choice of New York wasn't just arrogance—making everyone come to them; it was strategic. I should've known.

Joe pulled the car into an alley and then . . . stopped. I

frowned, craning my neck to look out the windshield. It was just a dark and dingy alley, complete with trash cans and back entrances.

But the guys both got out of the car. Tyler held his hand out to me, and I let him help me out, still confused.

"Stay close, Joe," Tyler said to our driver as Alec went to a nearby recess in the wall. It was so dark I couldn't tell if a door or a vampire was in the shadows. "It'll be at least two hours before we can leave, but we may want to leave early."

I had no idea why Tyler would want to leave early when we were here to gauge the other leaders, but I'm sure it was part of his master plan.

"Yes, sir." Joe nodded and drove off toward the other side of the alleyway.

"Uh, where exactly are we?" I finally asked.

"Dammit." Tyler huffed and reached into his pocket, pulling out a hundred-dollar bill. He handed it to a smug, smirking Alec, who promptly pocketed it.

I just got more confused and crossed my arms over my chest.

"I bet that you would hold yourself back from asking any questions until we were in the building." Tyler sighed.

"*I* bet that you'd crack before we made it inside. I won!" Alec looked a little too pleased with himself.

I rolled my eyes at them both. Betting money on me. *The nerve.*

As another set of headlights illuminated the dirty alley, Tyler guided me toward the dark recess in the wall, his hand at the small of my back. Alec pulled a heavy steel door open, and we all walked into a brightly lit corridor.

A team of agents stood on the other side, in suits but fully armed. They nodded to Alec and Tyler and waved us past.

Alec took the lead, stopping at a set of elevators and pressing a button. The fabric of his perfectly tailored suit stretched over his muscular shoulders. He was in all black, as usual, but the simple suit and shirt—no tie—fit him perfectly. I was pretty sure it was the same one he'd worn to the gala.

Tyler, on the other hand, was in a beautiful gunmetal gray three-piece suit, the crisp white of his shirt providing a contrast to the dark, smooth fabric. A pale blue tie and pocket square finished off the polished look. The colors went together seamlessly and made his gray eyes pop. Even his messy hair was in a somewhat neat style, held in place by product. I couldn't stop looking at him.

"Well?" I asked again as we waited. I couldn't help myself. I hated not knowing things.

They both chuckled before Tyler took pity on me. "This isn't like the gala. The point isn't to be seen and make a spectacle. This is a private, secure event. It's being held in an event space at the top of an office building with no ties to Melior Group. There are three separate access points through which guests will arrive. Each has a team posted. Plainclothes officers on the street are keeping an eye on it as well."

I nodded as we entered the service elevator.

As we rode up in silence, the butterflies returned. Did I really have any business being here? I was a nineteen-year-old science nerd—what the hell did I have to talk about with leaders of militias and heads of state? I blew out a big breath and straightened the front of my dress.

Alec wrapped an arm around my shoulders, and Tyler took my hand and squeezed.

"You'll be fine, and you look beautiful." Tyler smiled.

"Just let Gabe do the talking," Alec added, "and give him some Light when he signals you. Smile and be polite and don't drink your weight in Dom Perignon like last time."

I glared at him. "That would be my volume, not my weight, as champagne is a liquid. And that's rich coming from you, considering you were the cause of my drinking that night."

Alec groaned and removed his comforting arm. But before we could really get into it, the elevator doors opened, and the distant sound of chatter and clinking glasses reached us.

"We've gone over this. You've got this. And Alec will never be far. He's your personal security detail tonight."

We followed the sounds of people down the plain corridor, then crossed an open foyer area into a stunning, sleek, modern event space that felt as if it were floating above the city.

Along one entire wall, floor-to-ceiling windows jutted out at an angle, making it feel as if you could just walk right off the edge. The furniture was all sharp angles and shiny surfaces. Candles in geometric holders sat on the bar and on the edge of the stage, where a blonde bombshell sang a slow, sultry tune in front of a small band.

I was pretty sure I was the only one in the room with a *teen* on the end of my age. It made me feel even more awkward and self-conscious.

Tyler placed my hand in the crook of his elbow, like a real gentleman, and led me into the room through the dead center of the double doors. He was making an entrance. I wanted to make sure I looked the part, so I plastered a smile on my face and hoped like hell no one saw the slight twitch in my lip. Alec fell back, blending into the crowd while still staying close.

Tyler walked up to a man in an expensive suit and turban. He introduced me as his Vital and then spent a few moments in conversation—mostly just pleasantries. I stood there and nodded and hummed a few times before it was time to move away.

He repeated that process with a handful of other people—all men, most of them middle-aged or older, and each with a beautiful woman on his arm.

"Can we get a drink?" I blurted out before we could get into another conversation with another boring person.

"Sure." Tyler smiled and started to lead the way toward the bar, but halfway there we were intercepted.

Victor Flint stepped into our path.

"Miss Maynard." He nodded and I managed a smile. "Tyler. How's everything going?"

"All to plan so far, Victor. You'll know if there are any issues."

"Good." He flashed us that toothy grin, and I did my best to keep a pleasant, neutral look on my face. I wasn't sure if it was his no-nonsense, borderline rude way of speaking or the fact that I felt he always had an ulterior motive, but I wanted to get away from him. I had to play my part though—be the good little Vital.

"Alec." Victor shifted his gaze to somewhere behind us. "You don't usually attend these events, do you?"

Alec's voice was flat, his face emotionless. "I'm on duty, sir. Protection detail."

Victor's eyes met mine just as Karen joined our group.

"Evelyn." She beamed, and I gave her a greeting and a smile much more genuine than the one I'd given Victor.

"I didn't know you were going to be here, Karen." I was beyond happy to see a familiar face.

"Oh, it was last minute. Lucian wasn't able to attend, and the other board members asked me to step in. I don't usually deal with this side of the organization." She smoothed the front of her blue velvet gown, looking almost as uncertain as I felt.

Lucian was usually the one to attend these events, and more public ones like the gala, but despite returning to work, the pain from his injuries was sometimes too much. Tonight he was home in bed, sedated into a painless sleep while one of his nurses kept an eye on him.

Victor interrupted our conversation. "Let me get you a drink, Karen. We should let Mr. Gabriel focus on his task." He took her by the elbow and was already turning away when he addressed Tyler. "Report to me in the morning, before the meetings, so we can debrief." He walked away, barely giving Karen an opportunity to wave goodbye.

"Dick," I muttered under my breath. I couldn't help it—the man had no manners.

Tyler shushed me, even as he chuckled, and led me the rest of the way to the bar.

"There are ears everywhere." Alec leaned in and tapped the earpiece that allowed him to communicate with the other agents.

"Both electronic and of the Variant kind. Several people here have enhanced hearing."

As if I could know which ones they were by looking at them, my eyes scanned the room. Enhanced hearing was one of the common abilities, often overlooked and easy to hide once the Variant learned to turn it on and off. But it was probably one of the most underrated too, especially in the spy game. I made a mental note to watch my words and accepted the champagne flute Tyler offered me.

I took a sip and was not at all surprised to find it tasted incredible. I looked behind the bar; instead of Dom Perignon, as Alec had insinuated, they were serving Cristal. Just as expensive, and it would be just as much of a shame if it ended up being vomited out in a back alleyway.

My nerves calmed significantly once I realized how little attention most people were paying me, and the next hour crawled by. Tyler and I floated about the room, engaging in brief and seemingly insignificant conversations as I sipped on my champagne and he nursed a scotch. Waiters carried around finger food, and the band kept playing pleasant background music.

We schmoozed with dignitaries, military leaders, and directors of intelligence organizations and other private security firms. None of them were recognizable or particularly famous, but the people in this room, if they chose to work together, could change the world . . . or control it.

Occasionally, I was even included in the conversation.

It seemed like boring chitchat on the surface, and for the most part it was, but Tyler was getting more from it than anyone could possibly know. I kept transferring Light to him in controlled doses as he needed it.

It felt good to know I was doing my part, despite it being a bit boring. Seeing as how I couldn't just glow in the middle of a crowded room, I had to stay right at his side, and because he was wearing a suit, I had to be crafty in how I transferred.

It was a brush of our fingers there, a straightening of his

perfectly straight collar here, a push when his hand came into contact with the bare skin at my back. I was quite literally glued to him.

And Alec was glued to me. He wasn't always in sight, but I could feel him nearby, feel his eyes on me. I would look over my shoulder, and there he was, giving me a slight nod, his blue eyes piercing into mine.

As I finished my second glass of champagne and dropped it on a nearby high table, another couple approached us.

The Japanese couple both looked to be in their late forties. The man wore a perfectly tailored blue suit, and the woman was in a stunning traditional kimono, her black hair in an elaborate updo.

They bowed, and the man spoke in perfect, if slightly accented, English. "Good evening. I am Itsuki Takata. This is my wife and Vital, Yui."

Tyler and I returned the respectful bow.

"Pleased to meet you, Mr. Takata. I'm Tyler Gabriel, and this is my Vital, Evelyn Maynard."

A spark of recognition entered Mr. Takata's expression, but he quickly hid it behind a warm, polite smile.

I thought back to the months my mother and I had spent in Japan and greeted them in their own language. They both looked pleasantly surprised. Mrs. Takata immediately started talking to me, explaining that she didn't speak much English and had been unable to chat with almost anyone. I apologized for how rusty my Japanese was, but we managed to carry a short conversation while Tyler asked Mr. Takata some seemingly innocuous questions.

As they moved off, I seized the opportunity to take a little break.

"I have to go to the bathroom," I whispered to Tyler.

"No problem." He smiled and grabbed my hand. We stood together for just a moment, and I gave him a good dose of Light, making sure he would have enough until I returned.

As I headed across the foyer, Alec silently fell in at my side.

"You know, you can't go into the ladies room with me," I teased, not even looking at him.

He scoffed. "I take my job very seriously."

At that I did turn to look at him, my eyebrows raised. Was he being serious? We couldn't just clear out the ladies room so I could pee. But then he smirked, the glint in his eyes telling me he was teasing, and I slapped him lightly on the stomach. He wasn't in a bulletproof vest, but it still felt as if I were hitting steel.

He positioned himself right outside the door. Just as I entered, he lifted his sleeve to his lips, murmuring something I couldn't hear without taking his eyes off me.

Only two other women were in there, and I didn't have to wait for a stall, so I finished in no time, fixed up my makeup, and headed back out.

I walked straight past Alec—I couldn't resist provoking him a little. As we were about to enter the main room again, his warm hand wrapped gently but firmly around my elbow and pulled me to the side.

"What are you doing?" I asked. My instincts weren't telling me yet that Tyler needed more Light, but I still wanted to be there for him.

"Just following orders from my superior" was Alec's cryptic answer, but his lips twitched, and his voice had turned to honey— the professional, neutral tone gone. It sent shivers of anticipation down my spine, and I let him lead me into a side room that shared a wall with the main function area.

An oval table in the center of the room looked as if it could seat about a dozen people, but at the moment there was only one. Tyler was leaning on the table, his legs crossed at the ankles, his suit jacket hanging over the back of a chair. He looked so fucking sexy in the vest as he rolled his sleeves up and looked at me sideways, as if he were preparing to get his hands dirty.

My breath quickened and I swallowed. "Your superior, eh?" I had no idea why they'd dragged me into this abandoned, dark room—the city lights behind Tyler were the only illumination, casting his face in shadow—but I could take a guess.

"Yes." I could feel Alec's heat at my back. "Tyler is my superior . . . technically. I was following his orders to bring you here."

"Good work, Alec." Tyler's voice was pitched low, and it was doing things to me . . . also somewhere low.

Alec wasn't touching me, and I leaned into him, hoping to get a reaction. But Tyler issued another order.

"Bring her to me."

Alec wrapped an arm around my middle and slowly walked me forward until we were inches away from Tyler.

"You've been exceptional tonight, Evelyn," he whispered, leaning in. My lips parted. "I know this has been a little boring for you, so I thought we might reward you with a little break."

He didn't wait for my response before crushing his lips to mine, pushing his tongue right into my mouth. I moaned and lifted my hands to his neck, returning the kiss eagerly. Alec remained mostly still, but his chest rose and lowered a little faster against my back, his breath tickling my neck.

Just as suddenly as he'd initiated the kiss, Tyler broke it. He stood up to his full height and removed my arms from around his neck.

"Turn her," he demanded, and Alec obeyed. With firm hands on my hips, he pushed until I was facing him.

"I think Alec's getting a little hot," Tyler whispered against the nape of my neck before placing a firm kiss there. "I think you should remove his jacket."

"Yes, sir," I breathed. Tyler froze, his lips on my skin. I felt him smile, and pleasure welled up inside me.

I slowly pushed Alec's jacket off his shoulders, and he let it fall to the floor behind him. As I ran my hands over the hard planes of his chest, then his shoulders and muscular arms, he watched my every move as if he had all night, his lips parted, his breath quickening even more.

I rested my hands on his hips and tilted my face up to kiss

him, but before I could crash my mouth to his, Tyler's hands covered mine. He caressed my fingers until his hands were wrapped around my wrists, and then he tugged my arms to his sides, pulling me flush with his chest and away from Alec.

"Not yet." His voice was deceptively calm—I could feel his arousal pressing into my ass. I leaned my head back on his shoulder, sparing a fleeting thought for my appearance and hoping they didn't ruin my hair and makeup too much. "Alec, remove her underwear. Take your time."

Alec and I both moaned lightly. I was like putty in his hands, loving this side of him, and Alec wasn't arguing either. Maybe he could learn to share after all—maybe he just needed someone to order him to do it. But I would have to puzzle that one out later.

Alec inched forward.

The way Tyler had my arms pulled back made my chest jut out, my breasts rising and falling with every labored breath. I was ready and wanting. When Alec got his hands on my underwear, it would be soaked through.

Alec bent down just slightly, then placed both hands flat over my thighs. He dragged his palms up, bringing the layers of tulle with him. His fingers crawled over the dress bit by bit until the hem was in his hands.

With his fist full of tulle, he pressed the fabric against my belly while his other hand found my hip under the dress. Gently, very slowly, he traced my hip, then once again dragged his palm up my thigh. It took all the willpower I had not to squirm, move to the side, try to get his hand where I wanted it most. When he reached the top of my underwear, he dipped one finger under the fabric and ran it from one hip to the other, his nail scaping lightly just above my pubic bone.

He watched me the whole time, his icy blue eyes boring into mine, his lips parted. He watched as my breath hitched, as my eyes drooped, as my chest heaved and pushed my breasts out.

He snapped the top of my panties against my skin as he removed his fingertip, but he didn't pull away. With the backs of his fingers, he trailed a path over my pubic bone and down to my most sensitive area. As his knuckles grazed my clit through the fabric, I nearly gave in, ready to beg them to end this torture. But the look of pure lust on Alec's face and the impossibly hard erection against my ass kept me quiet. They were enjoying this as much as I was—it was just as exquisitely torturous for them as it was for me.

Alec's fingers found the lower hem of my panties, and he slipped two fingers underneath, hooking the front of my underwear through the leg holes. He held it as if he was about to rip it away from my body. I wished he would. The visual made me moan, and Tyler's hot breath at my neck started to come harder, his hips rolling against me in tiny, slow movements.

Alec just kept doing what he was doing, the picture of control except for his heavy breathing. His knuckles grazed my pubic hair as he dragged his fingers lower—lower, lower, between my legs. When he reached the warm, moist apex of my thighs, with his fingers caught between the wetness of my flesh and the wetness of the fabric, he showed his first sign of weakness. He swallowed hard, his Adam's apple bobbing, and a barely audible "fuck" passed his lips. But he didn't stop. He rubbed his fingers up and down my folds, spreading the wetness.

Nothing escaped Tyler's notice though. "Alec. Report," he demanded, his voice still pitched low but suddenly strained.

Alec cleared his throat. "It seems our girl's more responsive than we anticipated. She's soaked through her underwear."

"Mmm." Tyler hummed his approval and pressed a sensuous kiss to my neck. "Excellent. I want to see the evidence myself. Remove them. No more teasing."

"Yes, sir," Alec answered with a smirk just as I moaned a "yes" of my own.

Tightening his grip on the crotch of the panties, Alec pulled down, but before the fabric was past my hips, he froze. His shoulders tensed, and the hand holding the dress up clenched tight. His gaze fixed loosely on my chin, but I had a feeling he wasn't really paying attention to me anymore.

Even as my skin still burned with lust, a cold chill ran down my spine.

"Alec?" Tyler's voice lost that smoky, sultry quality, and his grip on my arms loosened.

In answer, Alec pulled my underwear back into place and dropped the front of my dress. He straightened to his full height. "Building is breached. We need to go."

TWELVE

"**S**hit." I was anything but calm as Tyler released me and they both put their jackets back on. "Shit, shit, shit."

Not this again. Not more guns and fighting and people trying to hurt us.

I backed away from the door and stumbled against the boardroom table.

Both of them pulled their guns out, and Alec pressed his left hand to his ear. "K, I need an exit." He was quiet for a few moments, listening to whatever Kyo was saying on the other end.

Tyler's face appeared in front of me, and only then did I realize how blurry my vision was. I blinked, and fat tears fell down my cheeks.

"Eve." Tyler held his gun firmly in one hand, but his other cupped my cheek, wiping the tears away with his thumb. "I need you to be strong. We'll get you through this. We'll get you out. But you need to keep your shit together, baby."

I can't do this. Not again. I can't.

"Yes, you can." Alec crowded me in on the other side, his hand squeezing my waist. Apparently the filter between my brain and my mouth had disappeared. "Evie, you're the strongest person I know. It's time to pull those soaked panties up and get the fuck out of here."

He flashed me his cocky, lopsided smirk that immediately made me want to call him an asshole—but it helped. It was dragging me out of my head, pulling me out of my panic, making my back straighten.

"Is this really the best time to make inappropriate jokes?" My voice still shook, but I was getting there. Feeling their touch grounded me. I placed my palms flat against the sides of their necks and pushed Light into them—giving them as much as I could in a short burst.

"There's my girl." Tyler smiled. Alec just nodded and moved to the door.

I took a deep breath, squared my shoulders, and walked to the door by Tyler's side. Music still drifted out of the main event area, along with the sounds of polite conversation and clinking glassware.

"Why aren't we hearing chaos?" I asked, my voice low.

"Wait for it," Tyler replied. A mere two seconds later, the music cut off, and the timbre of the voices changed, growing more intense, more panicked.

"Wait, why aren't you ordering everyone around?" My question was directed at Tyler, but he didn't have a chance to answer.

"Time to go." Alec pulled the door open and stepped through. I followed, staying as close as I could without impeding his range of movement. I could feel Tyler doing the same behind me.

In the foyer, beautifully dressed people were filing out of the function room and, to their credit, calmly if hurriedly making their way toward the exits. Melior Group agents ushered some people down in the service elevator, while others were sent up the few flights of stairs to the roof.

Alec led the way toward the same service elevators but headed past them. "Kyo said there's a large balcony off the eighty-ninth floor—three floors below the roof, where the choppers are being sent. He said it looks abandoned and doesn't appear to be a target. He's sending Jamie up with gear. Is this the best option, Gabe?"

Tyler thought about it for only a few seconds. "Yes. For now. But things are changing fast—it's like they had a plan, but they're changing it as they go. They're either really disorganized or really fucking good."

"We'd better haul ass then." Alec picked up his pace, and I had to jog to keep up.

We climbed up a dingy back staircase. A faulty fluorescent light kept flickering, making my nerves even worse. After the first flight, I made them stop so I could take my heels off, after which we were able to climb faster without making as much noise.

"Who. Is. Doing this?" I asked between panting breaths, not daring to slow down. Tyler was breathing only a little harder than usual—as if he were going for a light jog, not sprinting up stairs with his life in danger. Alec wasn't even breaking a sweat.

"I'm not entirely sure." Tyler's voice echoed off the concrete walls. "It's not my focus right now. We just need to get you out of here."

I was about to argue, demand he give me answers, when the sound of gunfire startled me so badly I flung myself against the wall. Alec didn't even flinch. Tyler grabbed me firmly by the elbow and pulled me forward.

"Move," he ground out, keeping his voice low. I obeyed.

The gunfire sounded way too close. It came in bursts, separated by silence and occasional shouting. Whoever it was had made it to the higher floors of the building, but it wouldn't be an easy win for them. There was a small army of Melior Group agents to get through.

At a door marked with a plain red "89," Alec stopped. I leaned on the railing, trying to catch my breath quietly.

He cracked the door open, peeked through, then swung it wide and stepped into the service corridor of the eighty-ninth floor. We followed close behind, Tyler closing the door soundlessly.

The gunfire and shouting sounded farther away now—as if someone had left an action movie playing on the TV in the next room—but I knew it could catch up with us at any moment. Both my guys crept forward cautiously, guns raised.

Alec led the way down the corridor and back into the nice part of the building. The plush carpet soothed my bare feet after all those rough concrete stairs.

We made it into another bigger boardroom without meeting anyone on the way. The room was just as dark and quiet as the one we'd been in several floors below.

"J. Report," Alec said, his hand pressed to his ear. "Copy that." He moved to the windows and opened the glass door. A cold breeze lifted the light curtains as he stepped out onto the balcony. With a firm hand at my back, Tyler pushed me out after him.

Plants and seating dotted the edges of the enormous balcony, which was twice the size of the boardroom. Manhattan spread out spectacularly far below us, but the wind this high up was biting.

I wrapped my arms around myself. Tyler faced the door, his gun lowered but ready, as Alec pushed a bench up against the glass railing and leaned over. My heart jumped into my throat—he was bent double over the edge, looking as if a light breeze would send him hurtling down eighty-nine floors to the concrete below. But he didn't fall—he holstered his weapon and reached down. The next thing I knew, Jamie was climbing over the railing, dressed in all black with heavy gear strapped to his back.

I rushed forward to help him take the gear off.

"Hey, kitten," he panted out and smiled, as if we'd just bumped into each other in the mall. "Ready to blow this party off?"

"Yes." I nodded emphatically, my eyes wide. I just didn't have it in me to crack jokes.

Within moments, the two of them had secured thick, heavy ropes to the bolted railing, and Alec strapped a harness on. He removed his suit jacket and draped it over my shoulders. "Put this on. The wind is even worse at the side of the building."

"OK." I nodded.

I went to put my arms through the sleeves and realized I still had a death grip on my heels—one beautiful red shoe in each hand. I dropped them and finished putting Alec's jacket on, rolling the sleeves up several times so I could have use of my hands. The jacket reached the middle of my thighs, and it smelled like him.

"Wait." It suddenly dawned on me what they were about to make me do. "No. Fuck. Alec, I can't rappel down the side of a building! I . . . I'm . . . I do *science*."

Eighty-nine floors, at an average of twelve feet per floor—that was 1,068 feet! We were more than a thousand fucking feet off the ground!

It was Tyler who answered, his harness already in place. "You won't be. Alec will carry you down."

"What? How?"

"Does she ever stop asking questions?" Jamie piped in, sounding way too amused. I was starting to think there was something seriously wrong with all the guys in Alec's team—it was probably why they all got along so well. They were all nuts.

"No," Alec and Tyler answered at the same time.

Before I had a chance to defend my curious mind, Tyler was shoving a harness in my face. He made me put it on while I continued to protest the next phase of their crazy exit strategy. They all just ignored me.

The harness was like something you'd expect to wear when bungee jumping—tight around my thighs, making my beautiful dress bunch up, and with straps over my shoulders.

"She's ready," Tyler announced.

"No, I'm not!" I protested, but Alec spoke over me.

"Ready."

"Ready," Jamie parroted.

They all moved in unison, like a well-oiled machine.

While I continued my stream of protests, Alec attached my harness to his, then attached his to the rope. I kept arguing that I couldn't do this, had no idea what I was doing, was scared, all while following their quick instructions. Before long I was holding on to Alec in a piggyback position.

When he swung his leg over the railing, I squeezed my mouth and eyes shut, my heart jumping into my throat. The wind whipped the soft tulle of my skirt around my legs, which were clenched tightly around Alec's middle.

He didn't give me any warning or ask if I was ready. He just pushed off the wall, and we went plummeting. My eyes flew open, and my stomach joined my heart in my throat as I released a high-pitched, breathy scream. Sleek glass sailed up as we went down. The sound of the rope feeding through the device attached to Alec's harness was almost drowned out by the wind.

We jolted to a stop, and Alec propped his booted feet against the building. I took a breath.

"Evie." He spoke just loud enough to be heard over the rush of the wind. "We're trying to get out undetected here. This is a *stealth* mission. I need you to keep your mouth shut."

I was about to snap back at him—even if we were flying down the side of a building in a life-and-death situation, I was not about to let him get away with telling me to keep my mouth shut—but without waiting for a response, he pushed off again.

Again fear wrapped its cold claws around my throat. But I stayed silent. I focused on my dress whipping almost painfully around my naked legs, on the harness digging into my skin, on a little mole on Alec's neck I'd never noticed. I made a mental note to give that a proper look when we weren't running for our lives. Fear of skin cancer never leaves you after you've lived in Australia.

After several excruciating seconds, movement to my left and above us caught my eye.

Jamie and Tyler came sailing down the side of the building, overtaking us in seconds. Alec cursed and picked up speed. At first I thought he was just being competitive, but then I saw Jamie pull out his gun.

Jamie and Tyler took several shots in quick succession at the glass just below them. They holstered their guns, swung out wide, and threw themselves at the glass. It shattered around them as they disappeared into the building.

With one more gut-wrenching drop, Alec lowered us to the same spot, and Jamie and Ty pulled us in.

"What's going on?" I demanded as soon as we were out of the screaming wind.

"They made us," Tyler explained as he detached my harness from Alec's. "They were keeping all the people upstairs hostage, but as soon as someone spotted us coming down the side of the building, they pulled everyone to come after us. We think they're after you. Some of our people made it upstairs, and the hostages are saying they're looking for a girl."

My heart sank. Of course they were looking for me. More people were getting hurt because of *me*.

"We have to move," Alec growled, loosening his harness. I just stood there, trying not to let the despair take over.

"They're trying to get to us, but our guys are heading them off where they can. It's pandemonium out there, and we need to use this opportunity to get out another way."

"There's no clear exit," Jamie announced, as if that wasn't a big deal. "The most lightly guarded one is the east stairwell. They have four on the ground. We can take 'em."

The others didn't answer as they finished taking off their rappel gear. When Tyler started to remove my harness, I jumped, but there was no time for him to try to calm me, comfort me. The others were already walking out the door, guns cocked and at the ready.

Ty pushed me forward, remaining at my back. We rushed down the hallway. My bare feet helped me stay quiet, but my dress still made an obscene amount of noise, the layers of fabric rustling with every step.

We passed the front desk of whatever business had their offices on this floor and exited through the massive glass doors.

There were elevators on our left, another set of giant glass doors on the opposite side, and a corridor with an emergency exit sign above it on our right.

Just as the doors swung closed behind me, several masked men emerged from the corridor, guns raised.

For a split second, everyone froze.

Then one of the men spoke. "Just hand her over, and no one has to die."

I took an involuntary step back. It didn't take a genius to figure out these were Variant Valor dickheads—Davis's thugs.

Alec laughed, a low, menacing sound. "If you want her, you'll have to kill us first."

As if to prove Alec's point, Tyler inched forward, blocking me from their view.

I opened my mouth—to stubbornly declare I'd die too before I was taken—but I never got the chance.

A gun went off. I had no idea whose, but it must've been one of the ones pointed at us, because the door behind me shattered. I hunched my shoulders and covered my head with my hands. Glass shards showered over me, getting stuck in my hair and slicing into my exposed back.

Tyler fired, his precise aim taking out one of the thugs before all the glass had even fallen to the tiled floor.

Everyone started shooting, the sound deafening. The glass behind the assailants exploded too, littering the floor with more glittery particles.

More assailants poured out of the corridor and the office on the opposite side of the building, but at the same time, Melior Group agents stepped off the elevators and appeared behind us too. Even people in formal wear, the important dignitaries from the party, were there—diamonds and tuxedos mixing with the bullets and blood.

After the initial surge of gunfire, both sides took cover—in doorways, in offices, behind desks and chairs.

Alec was at the front of our group. Once the reinforcements

arrived, he gestured to Jamie and Ty. They closed in, and Alec roughly pushed me back the way we'd come.

My mind felt slow, as if I were wading through syrup. I didn't even turn around when Alec started nudging me; I just walked backward, flinching at the shattered glass under my bare feet.

After a moment, Alec simply swept me up with one arm and carried me the remaining few steps. He set me down behind the reception counter, and Tyler tugged me down into a crouch beside him.

Alec remained standing. When I looked up, he was looking down, a somewhat confused expression on his face. Time seemed to slow as he pressed a hand to his chest, then pulled it away and stared at it.

He grabbed the edge of the desk with the same hand, but it slid right off, leaving a trail of red on the white surface.

My eyes widened.

My heart stopped.

My throat constricted, cutting off my air.

Alec dropped to his knees as his gun slipped from his grip. The confused expression melted away, replaced by something else, something harder.

Ty, Jamie, and a few other people who'd taken cover behind the reception desk were focused fully on fighting off the assailants. Gunshots and shouts echoed all around me.

None of them had noticed yet. None of them had seen the blood. *So much blood.* It oozed between the fingers of the hand Alec pressed to his chest.

"NO!" My guttural scream immediately drew everyone's attention. My hands became a blur as they flew to his neck, then his shoulders, then the bloody, slick hand at his chest.

Together, Tyler and I lowered Alec to the ground.

As another person came to help, my mind supplied a list of all the vital organs in the area he was shot—lungs, small intestines, heart . . . *So many ways to die.*

"There's no exit wound," someone declared from his other

side. The lethal piece of metal was still lodged in his body somewhere. Killing him.

Why wasn't he wearing a vest? Was Tyler wearing a vest?

I whipped my head around frantically, but Tyler was right next to me—fine. He looked as panicked as me, his eyes wide, his hair all over the place, but he was upright. He was moving. He wasn't bleeding.

I wasn't losing them both.

But I might lose Alec.

Our guys were administering first aid with speed and precision. Alec was still conscious, but his eyes kept rolling back in his head. His breaths came in short pants, as if he couldn't quite make the air reach his lungs.

Every time he managed to get his eyes to focus, he looked right at me.

"Ev . . . Evie . . . I . . ."

I grabbed his hand, struggling to keep my grip against the slippery blood.

"I love . . . y . . . you."

He said, "I love you," but he meant "goodbye." I heard *goodbye*. And I was not going to accept that.

As Alec's eyes closed and his limp hand slid from my grasp, a heavy steel barrier shuttered over my emotions. All that was left was white hot rage and a determination fiercer than I'd ever felt before.

No one noticed me rise slowly to my feet; they were too focused on saving Alec's life. By the time I was standing, my skin had already begun to glow.

I embraced the Light. I let it flood me, consume me, until it filled every fiber of my being. My glow became so bright that some of the people fighting stopped to shield their eyes.

Several guns pointed right at me, and I barely registered Tyler's panicked yell as the triggers were pulled. I didn't even flinch. I already knew a shielding ability was coming up behind me. The representative from Japan, Mr. Takata, appeared at my side, his hands held out in front of him. The bullets harmlessly bounced away.

I continued to push Light to Alec remotely, as much as he needed. It would by no means save him or heal his wounds, but at least it would assist the healing.

As long as Alec held on, I had something to fight for. And I was *so ready* for a fight.

THIRTEEN

I pushed some Light to Mr. Takata, and as I stepped out from around the reception desk, he stayed beside me, keeping me shielded. Tyler stuck by my other side; he kept his gun raised but didn't fire. I was keeping him juiced up too, and his ability would've told him what I was doing. Soon there would be no need for bullets.

My instincts were taking over. I surrendered to the Light and watched in awe as all the Variants in the room became obvious to me, almost as if I were playing a video game and all the guys on my team were marked.

I held my hands out at my sides and closed my eyes; I could *feel* them. I could feel the ones who were using their abilities most; the ones without Vitals who were getting depleted; Mr. Takata with his shield; a woman with an ability to freeze a person on the spot, trying to get close enough to touch people without getting shot; a man with a fire ability like Ethan's, but instead of throwing fireballs, he had to intensely focus to make an object or person erupt in flames.

I could feel Davis's men too. They had a shield, a man with a water ability thwarting our fire guy, a few others with common speed and strength abilities. I felt the Light inside them, and I *pulled* until they fell to the ground unconscious.

The Light flowed through me with the force of a waterfall—making my skin buzz until it almost went numb—and went straight into the Variants who needed it.

With the Variants on the other side incapacitated and our guys overflowing with Light, we overpowered them in seconds.

Most of the Melior Group operatives moved off immediately to clear the building and neutralize the rest of the assailants. The others started tying up our captives—the ones who still lived.

As my glow faded, I dropped my arms to my sides and opened my eyes. The first thing I saw was Tyler's worried expression.

My chest heaved, and my teeth gritted from exertion. I wanted so badly to fall into his arms, let him hold me and take charge of the situation as he always did. But I wasn't done.

I pointed to a slight woman in a stunning black gown who was helping to tie someone up. She had the freezing ability, able to suspend a person in motion—essentially put them on ice.

Tyler rushed over to her, spoke hurriedly, and ushered her to my side in seconds. She looked nervous, her wide brown eyes darting from mine to his, but she took my hand when I held it out. I was fading, and I needed the contact to transfer to her.

I could see Tyler's lips moving as he spoke to her, hear his voice, but his words weren't registering. I turned and led the way back to the reception desk. Halfway around it, I stumbled, but a firm, warm hand steadied me. Mr. Takata was still by my side. As soon as it was clear I wasn't going to face-plant, he released me, tipping his head forward in a little bow.

By the time I turned back, Tyler and the woman were already kneeling beside Alec, nudging Jamie out of the way.

I lowered myself to my knees on his other side. Taking his hand in mine again—it was sticky now, not slippery—I kept pushing Light at him, but there was no point anymore. No amount of Light could help him now. And I had nothing left to give.

I had nothing left.

My eyes drooped, and my head felt heavy. Even as my mind fought to the last second for consciousness, my muscles ultimately gave in. My vision faded, and I fell in a heap next to Alec, our limp hands stuck together with his drying blood.

I came to just as the paramedics were taking Alec away and discussing having me taken to the hospital in another ambulance. I refused, demanding to stay with Alec. They were stubborn, but so was I, and in the end we tailed Alec's ambulance to the hospital.

Lucian was already there. Josh and Ethan rushed forward as soon as we stepped inside, hugging me tight despite the gore clinging to me. They fired off questions, demanded I see a doctor, spoke over each other while frantically running their hands over me.

During the surgery to remove Alec's bullet, I was checked over by a doctor—not even a concussion, thank you very much—and despite my protests, everyone insisted I should go home, clean up, have something to eat. Alec was stable, but they were keeping him sedated so his body could have some time to heal.

"I won't leave this room, and Olivia is on her way," Lucian reassured me.

Tyler had to go back to the scene and do some damage control, make sure his guys were doing what needed to be done. He ran his hands through his hair, his worried gaze darting to Alec, then me. He pulled me into a hug and held me for a long time. I gripped his filthy suit jacket, my eyes closed.

"Please, Eve. Please go home. I need to know at least one of you is safe and warm." He spoke into the top of my head, his chest reverberating under my cheek.

Grudgingly, I realized he was right. I couldn't do anything more for Alec—he had all the Light he needed and then some.

The hospital, under medical supervision, was the best place for him. But I *could* do something to ease Tyler's worry.

I nodded against his chest.

We peeled apart—the front of my dress had stuck to his suit jacket. That's how much drying blood I was coated in.

I looked down at myself and really took it in for the first time. My arms were smeared with blood. It covered my chest, my shoulders, even my hair. My beautiful dress was ruined, but not in the fun way Ethan and Alec had both hinted at. It felt as if the dress itself were blood, soaking into my skin.

"OK." I lifted my eyes. "I, uh . . . I need to get out of this blood . . . the dress . . ."

Tyler leaned forward and placed a gentle kiss on my forehead. "Kid, Josh, take our girl home. I'll send two teams to meet you in the underground parking garage in the north wing. Uncle Luce . . ." He ran his hand through his hair again as he eyed Alec lying helpless in the hospital bed.

"I'm here." Lucian's tone was calm and firm. "I won't leave his side, and I'll call if there are any changes. Go. All of you, get out of here."

The finality of his words pushed us into action. Knowing he was staying made me feel better. It may've been one of the most fucked-up situations I'd been in, but I couldn't help thinking it was nice having a family.

Tyler marched down the hallway first. Ethan, Josh, and I went a little slower, making our way to the parking garage.

We were driven back to the apartment in an armored vehicle with another following close behind. Both were filled with agents armed to the teeth.

All ten of the agents escorted us up from the underground parking garage, through the lobby—where we got some shocked looks from the doorman—and all the way to the penthouse. They made us stand outside the front door while four of them swept the space. I leaned on Ethan and held Josh's hand while we waited.

When they were finally satisfied, they allowed us to enter.

Josh locked the doors, and we all breathed a sigh of relief. No doubt the agents were positioning themselves around the building to ensure our safety. I wouldn't have been surprised if they were waking up all the other residents and sweeping the entire building top to bottom.

The guys took their shoes off as I stood there, not quite sure what to do. I needed someone else to make the decisions, maybe even move my limbs for me. Plus, I didn't have shoes. My feet were barefoot and bloody.

And my dress felt as if it were squeezing the air out of my lungs.

"Get it off," I whispered to the ground. Tears began to track down my cheeks for the millionth time that night. "Get it off me!" My raised voice sounded more than a little manic as I pulled at the collar of the dress, trying to tear it away from my skin.

Both Ethan and Josh were beside me in an instant. One of them pulled my hands away from the dress while the other undid the zip at the back. They pushed the filthy fabric down over my hips and let it flop to the floor.

My breathing calmed but only slightly as my blurry eyes met Josh's worried ones. Ethan's big, comforting hands rested on my shoulders, lightly caressing, but his clean fingers pulled at my tacky skin. I started rubbing my arms, trying to get the crimson off, but it was nearly completely dry, and I couldn't unzip it like the dress.

"I need to get it all off," I pleaded.

Josh looked over my shoulder, sharing a worried look with Ethan, and then they moved at the same time.

Ethan hurried down the hallway as Josh picked me up. I wrapped my legs around his waist and my arms around his neck as he carried me into the bathroom. Ethan had already started the shower, and steam was billowing from it.

Josh set me down and, once he was sure Ethan had a hand on my shoulder, started undressing. Ethan kneeled before me and gently took my underwear off, letting me use him for balance as I stepped out of it.

I stood before him naked, bare, and bathed in blood. He took my face in his big hands and leaned in, placing a tender kiss on my chapped lips and wiping my tears with his thumbs.

"We got you, baby," he whispered against my lips. His breath was minty, his clothing and hair clean. Not draped in death like mine.

Josh finished undressing and adjusted the water temperature. The shower had limited space, and there was no way we would all fit in there.

Ethan released me and Josh took my hand, pulling gently forward.

"I'll make us something to eat and a warm cup of tea while you get cleaned up." Ethan picked up the discarded clothing and closed the door behind him.

Josh coaxed me into the shower with gentle but sure hands. He pulled me in close, then walked me backward until the almost too hot spray hit my shoulders. I gasped, the water waking me out of my stupor a little. I was pretty sure I was experiencing shock, my reflexes slow, my breathing shallow.

"Is the water too hot?" Josh immediately reached for the tap, but I shook my head.

"No, just . . ." I didn't know how to finish the sentence.

Josh settled his hands on my hips, holding me down to earth so I wouldn't float away into a full-blown panic attack. I tried to focus on his slow, even breathing, the way his chest rose and fell, the very fine bit of blond chest hair between his pecs. Droplets of water sprayed off me to land on his chest, shoulders, and belly, gathering together until they started to trail wet paths down his body.

Within a minute of standing under the hot spray, the droplets started to take on a pink tinge. I furrowed my brow, worried I was starting to hallucinate. Then I remembered—the dried blood was finally melting off me.

I lifted my hands to his chest, covering all the red droplets, and looked down. Mesmerizing swirls of red circled the drain, fed by crimson tracks of water traveling down my legs.

Josh reached behind me for a loofah and a bottle of something that smelled like Tyler. He worked some of the bottle's contents into a lather in his hand, and then with slow, careful movements, he washed me.

He cleaned my neck and shoulders, then reached around to do my back, my ass. My breasts and belly followed. He added more bodywash to do my arms.

I kept my eyes on the drain. The blood mixed with the suds, fluffy pink swirls disappearing into the pipes. For some reason, that made it a bit easier to watch.

Josh moved my hands up from his chest to his shoulders, then slowly kneeled down. He cleaned my legs one by one, lifting one foot, then the other. I'd completely forgotten about the cuts on my feet, which stung as the sudsy water washed over them. Thankfully, Alec had carried me over most of the glass.

When Josh stood up again, I let my hands drop back to his chest. I liked feeling his breaths, the faint thud of his heartbeat. I leaned my forehead on my hands. The water running into the drain was now perfectly clear.

Once again, Josh moved, and then shampoo was in my hair. He lathered it slowly, massaging my scalp and spreading it all the way to the ends.

"Lift your head so I can rinse the shampoo." He didn't raise his voice, but the way it bounced off the tiles made it sound louder than it was.

I tipped my head back into the spray. Josh rinsed the shampoo and wiped it away from my eyes.

I lowered my head to look at him and took my first deep breath. My shoulders were relaxing; I was no longer covered in blood. I couldn't be sure if I was still crying or not as my whole face was wet, but my nose wasn't blocked, so that was a good sign.

Josh's vibrant green eyes fixed on me, and as always, I felt as if he could see right into my soul. The water had turned his dirty-blond hair dark, and he licked the moisture off his full lips.

He reached behind me again. Conditioner this time. As he spread it through my hair with care, I trailed my hands over his shoulders to play with the damp hair at his neck. Then I leaned forward and kissed him gently beneath his ear.

It was meant as a thank you—to show I appreciated how attentive he'd been—but as my lips tasted his skin, my body began to crave more.

Maybe it was fucked up that I wanted sex after the horrific shit I'd just been through, but it was never just sex with them. It was healing and comfort and connections and coming home all at once.

After he'd finished working the conditioner into the ends of my hair, he brought his hands back to my hips and swallowed audibly. "Eve?"

He was waiting to figure out what I needed, but his body was already reacting to mine. He was getting hard.

Maybe now wasn't the time. I looked up at his clever, watchful eyes and thought about getting out of the shower, drying off . . . but then I'd have to deal with the rest of it. I'd be out of this steam-and-tiles cocoon, and I'd have to think about the blood circling the drain, Alec unconscious in the hospital, all the people who'd died. *Because of me.*

My eyes stung, and a relentless, unbearable tightness squeezed my chest.

I wasn't ready.

"Just . . . I need . . ." I struggled to articulate my jumbled thoughts between increasingly erratic breaths. "I don't want to think about the blood . . . I can't . . . make me forget . . . please, just . . . make me forget, Josh."

He pulled me against him and kissed me hard, pushing his tongue into my mouth. I threw my hands around his neck and held on, focusing fully on his perfect lips, on my stiffening nipples, on his wet body plastered against mine, on his hard cock against my belly.

He broke the kiss, his mouth trailing a path over my jaw, then my neck, as his hands kneaded my ass. He sucked up the water with licks and kisses against my skin, but they were much gentler than that first kiss had been.

I tugged on the hair at the back of his neck. "More," I whispered hoarsely.

He looked searchingly into my face. Whatever silent question he was asking, he must've found his answer, because in the next instant, he spun me around so I was facing the wall and pressed into my back, the shower's spray still hitting our shoulders and sides.

He pulled me back against him, one hand on my hip, one on my shoulder.

"Feel my body against yours, Eve." He moved against me, our slick skin making it easy, then ground his erection into my ass. My lips parted. *Yes*, this was exactly what I needed.

"Listen to my voice." It was low and all kinds of sexy. He spoke close to my ear, then bent his head and gently bit my shoulder.

"Feel my hands." He squeezed my hip and shoulder. Then he moved one hand to my breast and the other between my legs.

I gasped, my breaths coming faster and shallower.

I placed my palms flat against the slick tiles, my elbows half-bent as I leaned forward. My ass ground into Josh's rock-hard erection, and he groaned. The sound bounced off the tiles and sent another wave of desire straight between my legs, where his hand started moving against my aching flesh.

Josh's long, artistic fingers were nimble, and it wasn't long before the sound of my heaving breaths filled the bathroom. I closed my eyes.

But that was a mistake.

As soon as I didn't have anything to look at, images assaulted my brain: Alec falling to his knees, the blood pooling around him, the blood swirling around the drain.

I forced my eyes open just as Josh pushed two fingers in. It felt incredible, but I wanted more. I leaned forward until my forehead rested against the tiles, my hands on either side of my head.

"More," I demanded with my words and my body, arching back into him.

He removed his fingers and replaced them with his cock. He wasn't slow or careful. He drove into me in one precise thrust. I was ready for him—his hands had made sure my pussy was as dripping wet as the rest of my body—but the sudden sensation of having him completely inside me, the wonderful fullness, surprised me in the best way.

"Yes," I grunted.

All the bloody images were driven from my mind as Josh started to move. As I knew he would, he figured out exactly what I wanted. What I *needed*. He pounded into me, deep powerful strokes that had my whole body moving, my breasts bouncing.

He squeezed my hip hard with one hand, pulling me back onto him as he drove forward. His other hand went back to where we were joined. This time his fingers weren't so gentle and exploratory. He went straight for the most sensitive spot and started rubbing firmly in time with his thrusts.

I kept my eyes open. I watched his hand moving between my legs, my boobs bouncing, his calves and thighs flexing with every movement. I focused on watching us fuck, listening to our grunts and moans echoing in the hot bathroom, feeling Josh slide in and out of me.

The pressure built low in my belly, and I chased it, let it take over. Pleasure traveled up my spine and spread to my chest, my head. Almost animalistic noises burst past my lips as I completely gave in to the orgasm. Stars burst across my vision, the intense waves of pleasure making me stiffen and press my cheek against the wall.

Both Josh's hands gripped my hips as he continued to push in and out of me, but his movements had lost intensity. Now he was taking it slow, making me feel every inch of him as he slid in and out, careful and gentle as I came down from my orgasm.

As I started to catch my breath, I realized my eyes had closed. Images of blood and violence once again seeped into my mind. Alec falling . . . blood pooling . . . blood circling the drain.

I ground my teeth and grunted in frustration, pushing against the tiles until I was upright again.

"More," I demanded. I wanted him to drive every bad thing from my mind until I couldn't think straight. I wanted him to make me forget.

Josh stilled behind me. "Eve . . ." He sounded unsure, worried.

"I don't need your pity."

"I'm not pitying you. I'm trying to take care of you." His voice was calm and patient as he nudged me around to face him.

I immediately felt bad for snapping at him. "I know. I'm sorry. I just . . . please make me forget."

Without waiting for an answer, I reached between us and started stroking him. He was impossibly hard and covered in the evidence of my orgasm, mingled with the spray of the water.

He let me touch him as he searched my face again. Then he gave me what I wanted.

He pushed me back against the tiles and kissed me forcefully, teeth scraping, tongue battling for dominance. One of his hands slapped the wall next to my head, and the other lifted my leg. He hooked my knee over his elbow and pressed his palm flat against the wall near my hip, keeping my leg angled out. I guided him back inside me, and he pressed his forehead against mine, his breath washing over my wet face.

Then he started to move, driving into me as he had before, his intense eyes watching my face. After a few moments, I felt the nudge of his ability. I lifted my other leg and wrapped it around his hip as he held me up with his mind. The new position allowed me to spread my legs wider, tilt my hips forward. Josh's strokes reached deeper and deeper, and I held on to his shoulders and let my head rest against the tiles.

I watched him as intently as he watched me. He was beautiful —his full lips parted, his soft hair falling over his forehead in a wet mess, his green eyes hooded yet still watching, seeing, *knowing*.

His movements became more erratic as he chased his own release. I could tell he was close. I was too. He was hitting just the right spot with every slap of his hips, and that heady feeling was building again.

"Come with me," he growled out as he drove into me one last time and ground his hips against mine.

Just as he'd obeyed all my demands, I now obeyed his. We both crashed into orgasm the same way our bodies had been crashing into each other—with intensity and urgency.

We cried out but kept our eyes open, our gazes locked.

As our breathing slowed, Josh pulled out and lowered me to my feet. My knees shook, but he kept me steady. He moved me back under the spray and rinsed out the conditioner I'd completely forgotten about. I held his gaze, reading his unspoken message even as he read every expression on my face.

He'd given me what I asked for, but now he was taking care of me.

As the last of the conditioner left my hair and the water washed our sweat away, I leaned forward and kissed him gently.

He sighed against my lips, and his shoulders relaxed under my hands. I hadn't realized how tense they were until I felt the muscles soften.

I pulled back and looked him in the eye, running my nails over his scalp. "Thank you, Josh. I love you."

"I love you too." He gave me a small smile, and I knew we would be OK. I was where I needed to be.

I shut off the water as Josh stepped out of the shower and reached for the towels.

I dressed in a pair of Josh's sweatpants and Alec's T-shirt. It smelled faintly like him, and even though it made my heart ache, it also made me feel closer to him.

We came out to the kitchen just as Ethan dropped the last plate of steaming food onto the counter.

"Creamy pasta with some of last night's leftover roast pumpkin and crispy bacon bits," Ethan explained as he pulled out a stool for me. "Nothing fancy, but it's comfort food."

"Ethan, everything you make is fancy and delicious." I gave him a smile, but it didn't feel like it reached my eyes.

Josh took the chair next to me, and as soon as I started eating, I realized how hungry I was. We both stuffed our faces. Ethan ate half of his, then jumped up and disappeared down the hall. He came back moments later with a hairbrush and positioned himself behind me.

"You don't have to . . ." I trailed off as his warm, comforting hand landed on my shoulder, rubbing lightly.

Silently, I got back to eating as Ethan brushed my damp hair. He was so careful, so gentle, I never felt a painful tug at my roots, never had my head jerked back.

Once we were done, they led me to the bedroom in the back.

My body was ready to give in. All my basic needs were taken care of—food, hygiene, sex. Now it was time to rest. But a faint blue glow was peeking through the curtains, and I made myself stop at the threshold. "It's morning. We should go back to the hospital."

Josh reached out to me. "Eve, you need to rest."

Ethan, on the opposite side of the bed, did the same. "Uncle Luce said he'd call as soon as there was any news."

I looked between them. I couldn't crawl into a warm comfortable bed when Alec was lying in a hospital with a bullet wound—that he'd taken to protect me. "He needs me."

"Yes, he does." Josh didn't argue. "But you're no good to him dead on your feet. You can't pour from an empty cup."

As if to illustrate his point, I swayed and caught myself on the doorway. In two long strides, Ethan reached me and swept me effortlessly into his arms.

"Sleep for a few hours, and then we'll go straight back," Ethan said close to my ear. "The doctors said they were keeping him under for most of today anyway." He didn't give me a chance to argue before he lowered me to the bed and pulled off my pants.

I didn't have any more energy to object. The pillow was really soft, and my limbs felt heavy. My guys climbed in on either side of me, cocooning me with warm, hard bodies and gentle, tender caresses.

FOURTEEN

Alec had a private room at the hospital, but even Lucian's money couldn't buy more space, and it was crowded with all of us in there.

I sat in a chair, holding his hand in both of mine and trying to stay calm. It really wouldn't help if I started crying again. I'd been doing it on and off all morning—when Lucian called to tell us they were going to wake Alec up, as we hurriedly dressed, when we made a quick pit stop for pastries and coffee. I was so over it; I felt as if I had no control over my own tear ducts.

Lucian looked like I felt. He was in the corner by the door, disheveled, his head drooping. He looked as if he might pass out at any moment but was refusing to leave until Alec woke up. *If* he woke up . . .

The doctors had kept Alec in an induced coma overnight. They'd already given him the medication that would wake him up, and we'd spent the past twenty minutes holding our collective breath.

He *had* to be OK. I needed him to wake up and scowl at something, or I was going to lose my mind.

Tyler was asleep by the window, in the only other chair. His head rested against the back, and his legs were splayed out in front of him. It didn't look comfortable at all, but he'd been up all night. Soft snoring sounds drifted from his slightly open mouth.

Ethan and Josh leaned on the wall behind me, too on edge to sit down.

No one spoke. We just breathed and waited.

Dot, Charlie, Olivia, and Henry were in the waiting room just outside. So were Kyo, Marcus, and Jamie, still in their Melior Group uniforms. Dana was there too, along with a handful of other agents I hadn't met. For someone who pushed people away so expertly, Alec sure had a solid group of people who genuinely cared for him. Loved him, even.

There was that word again—*love.*

I could see it in his eyes every time we had sex, every time we shared a moment of tenderness, a deepening of our fraught bond. I'd said it to Ethan and Josh easily. I was so sure of my feelings for them. They were my world, my home. They all were.

I was waiting for the right time to tell Tyler, but when it came to Alec . . .

Did I love him?

I raised my head to look at him. My eyes landed on his strong, stubbled jaw first, then his nose with the slight kink in it. His eyebrows were relaxed as he slept. His beautiful ice-blue eyes— the eyes that had haunted me for a year, watched me with derision, studied me with abandon, then stared directly into my soul with love—were closed. And I was terrified they would never open again, never watch me tell him I loved him. Because I did.

I loved Alec. It was time to let go of the last scrap of a barrier between us. I was barely holding it up as it was, exhausted by the vain attempt to protect myself from further emotional pain.

He loved me. He was committed. Everything he'd done since he'd said those words had only put them into action.

I propped my elbows on the edge of the bed and pressed his limp hand to my forehead, willing him to wake up, to come back to me.

The big hand in my grip twitched. I whipped my head up.

Alec lay still, his face blank, his breathing even. I focused on his hand, inches away from my face.

This time, I saw his fingers move, his hand just barely closing around mine. I gasped and sat forward in the chair, my heart hammering in my chest.

The movement caught everyone's attention. Ethan and Josh were by my side in a heartbeat. Lucian wheeled himself forward, his questioning eyes hopeful.

Kyo appeared in the doorway the same moment I said, "His hand twitched," as if it was the greatest thing to have ever happened.

"I'll get someone." Kyo rushed away without waiting for a response, but his loud voice finally woke Tyler. He sprang to his feet and pulled his gun out, his eyes searching for the threat before they were even fully open.

"Chill, bro." Ethan tried to keep his booming voice low. "There's no one to shoot. We think he might be waking up."

Tyler took another second to survey the room, then put the gun away. Yawning, he leaned one hand on the foot of the bed and rubbed the sleep from his eyes with the other.

Kyo came back with a nurse and doctor in tow, but fitting everyone inside the room was impossible. The medical professionals needed to be there, I refused to leave Alec's side, and the guys refused to leave mine, so Kyo and Lucian were promptly kicked out. The nurse started fiddling with the machines attached to Alec, intermittently jotting things down on a clipboard, while the doctor checked his vital signs.

She turned to me and looked over the rim of her bright orange glasses. "You said he twitched?"

I nodded. "His hand. Twice."

"OK. According to his vitals, he's not showing any signs of coming out of it just yet. Which is fine, it'll happen any moment now. The twitching is perfectly normal. Sometimes—"

Whatever she was about to say was cut off by a grimace of pain. Her mouth opened on a silent scream, and she doubled over, clutching her head. Behind her, the nurse did the same—moaning as she collapsed against the wall and started to slide to the ground.

The smile that pulled at my lips as I took in the all-too-familiar pain was almost manic. A surprised, delighted laugh burst out of me as my wide eyes darted between the people writhing in pain and Alec's face.

Tyler and Josh rushed to the women and tried to keep them upright.

"I'll get Uncle Luce. Maybe he can shield them." Ethan rushed toward the door, but halfway there, the pained groans stopped.

Alec squeezed my hand.

Everyone paused. Tyler and Josh helped the panting, shaking women into chairs while I kept my full focus on my Master of Pain. His fingers were still wrapped loosely around mine, and his brows furrowed, making that scar pucker.

"How is he scowling while passed out?" Josh shook his head. He came to stand next to me and Tyler, and Ethan took up the other side of the bed.

"Not out, dickhead," Alec croaked, slowly opening his eyes. It looked as if it took quite a bit of effort.

We all breathed a massive sigh of relief. Ethan's eyes were definitely misty as he took his cousin's other hand. Tyler leaned on the bed, his head drooping.

I just kept staring into Alec's beautiful, drawn face as he worked to open his eyes fully. As soon as he managed it, he looked directly at me.

A barely there smirk pulled at his lips. "Did I just hear you laughing at someone's pain?"

I shook my head, trying to hold back more tears. I couldn't speak around the lump in my throat.

He squeezed my hand again, and his smirk grew. "My little fucking sadist."

I laughed, throwing my head back as the lump in my throat

began to ease. My hand stayed tightly wrapped around his as I leaned in close. "Thank fuck you're OK."

I kissed him, softly brushing my lips against his and nuzzling his nose.

Pulling back, I stared into those ice-blue eyes, the ones I'd worried about never seeing again. And again, all I saw there was devotion and love. He looked at me as if I was the only person in the room.

I stroked the side of his head, his cheek. The words were on the tip of my tongue—I felt it, and I'd resolved to tell him—but my stupid brain decided to throw up a roadblock.

I didn't want him to think I was only saying it because he'd nearly died—that it was some knee-jerk reaction to fear. I wanted him to know it was genuine and heartfelt.

So instead I held his gaze. Every other time he'd looked at me like that—with love practically bursting out of his pores—I'd turned away, unable to handle the intensity, the pressure. This time, I returned the look. I thought about how much I loved this impossible, frustrating, broken man, and I let it all show on my face.

His smile widened, and he opened his mouth to say something, but the doctor interjected.

"Excuse me. Make room, please. I *do* need to examine him." She nudged her way past Ethan's bulk and made him and Tyler step back. The nurse joined her and got back to recording things on her clipboard. I had to hand it to them, they were handling the whole "struck down by excruciating pain" thing like champs.

I held on to Alec's hand as the doctor poked and prodded him, asked him a bunch of questions, checked the bullet wound before the nurse changed the dressing.

At the end of it all, she said she was very pleased with how he was doing. The bullet had managed to avoid major organs, so the worst damage was the blood loss and the injury to his muscles. He needed rest and another blood transfusion, but he would be fine. "I'd like to keep an eye on you a little longer, so you're staying for another night, but if all goes well, I should be able to discharge you tomorrow."

She gave him an encouraging smile.

Alec frowned. I could tell he was about to argue, demand to be released immediately, but before I had a chance to chastise him, Tyler beat me to it.

"Wipe that look off your face." Tyler wagged a finger at Alec. "You were fucking shot. You're staying here until the medical professionals say you can leave."

"What he said." I had to add my agreement. Ethan stepped up next to Tyler and crossed his arms, adding his support firmly but silently. Josh chuckled, endlessly amused by our dynamics, as usual.

Alec may've been stubborn, but he knew when he was outnumbered. Plus, no one argued with Tyler when he put his authoritative voice on.

"Fine," Alec grumbled. "I could use another nap anyway." He ended on a yawn.

The nurse cleaned up and left the room, but the doctor paused in the doorway. "Honestly, you're lucky I'm letting you go tomorrow." She stuffed her hands in her pockets and looked at Alec reproachfully. "You had *open surgery*. If you were human, you'd be here for at least a week, and you'd be on bed rest for another month after that. We normally keep Variants in the hospital for three to four days, but since you have a Vital, your body has all the extra Light it needs to accelerate healing. So behave for another day, and thank your lucky stars you have *her*." She pointed at me, flashed him another challenging look, and left the room.

He turned back to me and didn't even hesitate. "Thank you."

I looked down and cleared my throat. "I just happen to be a Vital. Your Vital. I didn't do anything."

"Just accept the thanks, Evie." His voice held a hint of teasing, and I rolled my eyes. We really didn't have a good track record with thank yous.

Tyler interjected before I could answer with another smartass comment. "What do you mean you didn't do anything?"

He stepped over to my side of the bed and turned me by the shoulders to face him, frustration evident on his face.

"You literally saved his life. Several others. You transferred Light to every single Variant on our side, and then when we crushed those bastards in a matter of seconds, you immediately made sure the woman with the freezing ability went to Alec. You bought him valuable time. You're fucking incredible, and I'm proud to be in your Bond."

He leaned forward and kissed me, hard. Alec caressed the back of my hand with his thumb as Tyler sighed against my lips.

"All right, what the fuck happened last night?" Ethan looked between the three of us, his hands on his hips.

Josh lowered himself into Tyler's vacated chair. "Yeah, we still don't have the full story. We got a call in the middle of the night and rushed to the hospital. All Kyo told us was that there was an attack on the event? How did anyone even know about it?"

Someone knocked on the door. Dot stood just outside, Charlie behind her with his hands on her shoulders. Olivia and Henry craned their necks to see in.

"They said you were awake . . ." Dot sounded uncertain.

"I'm still getting reports from operatives in the field and the police. Let's talk about it later," Tyler answered Josh, then stepped out of my embrace.

Alec waved to Dot. "Hey, pipsqueak. What's up?"

Dot took that as an invitation and walked into the room, Charlie hot on her heels. "Don't 'pipsqueak' me. And would you all stop nearly dying and shit? You're making me age faster. I'm going to have to start getting Botox!"

"Glad you're OK, man." Charlie stuffed his hands in his pockets—it couldn't have been easy for him to be in a hospital again—but the look he gave his cousin was genuine and warm.

"Are you comfortable, sweetie?" Olivia went into mom mode, fluffing Alec's pillow and pulling the thin blanket up to cover his shoulders. Of course, that made his bare feet poke out. She huffed. "This is ridiculous! There must be more than one measly blanket in this whole hospital. I can't believe . . ." She muttered and fussed, found a spare blanket, and made sure Alec was tucked in as tight as a cinnamon roll. He grumbled and rolled his eyes, but I think he secretly liked the motherly affection.

When Henry came back, wheeling Lucian in front of him, the guys and I left the room. There just wasn't space for everyone, and I knew his work friends would want to see him.

In the hallway, I leaned my forehead on Ethan's chest. He rocked us lightly back and forth as I listened to his steady breathing, his strong heartbeat. After a few minutes, I turned and rested my cheek on him instead.

Farther down the hall, Dana was chatting with another black-clad woman and man as they waited their turn to see Alec. She glanced over, and our eyes met.

Her questioning look held a hint of concern. *Are you OK?*

I gave her a tight smile and shrugged. *Not really. Could be worse.*

She inclined her head, gesturing to Alec's room with another question in her eyes. *And him?*

This time, my smile was more genuine. I nodded and breathed a deep sigh. *He's going to pull through.*

She smiled back, then said something to her companions. As she passed us on the way to Alec's room, she squeezed my shoulder briefly but didn't say anything.

I lifted my head off Ethan's chest and blinked. Did I just have a silent conversation with *Dana?* Did she let her humanity show by giving me a gesture of comfort? This had to be some kind of dream.

Josh's amused chuckle brought me out of my stare, and I craned my neck to look at him.

"I can hardly believe it myself." He shrugged, but his grin was full of mischief.

I rolled my eyes at him as Ethan looked between us. "Can't believe what?"

My big guy hated being out of the loop, but before I could explain, we were interrupted once more.

"Excuse me." A polite accented voice drew our attention to the older Japanese man standing a respectful distance away. It was the same man I'd met the night before, the one with the shield ability who'd refused to leave my side.

I stepped out of Ethan's embrace, but he stayed close. Josh took my other hand, and Tyler boxed me in from behind. Their protective instincts were in overdrive.

"My deepest apologies for interrupting." The distinguished man bowed low. "I am happy to hear your Bondmate is well and will recover."

"Thank you." Tyler spoke for all of us, but his voice was cautious. "And thank you for your assistance last night, Mr. Takata. Has anyone from Melior Group spoken with you?"

"Oh, yes. I have given my statement to the authorities, and your people have debriefed me. I am hoping to speak with you about the . . . Light." He seemed uncertain about the last word.

"Yes?" Tyler prompted him as I frowned.

"My apologies. I am very tired, and my English suffers for it. Uh . . . *kagayaku.*" He said the word in Japanese, and by some miracle, my addled brain remembered its meaning.

"Glow?" I supplied, and his face lit up.

"*Hai.*" He inclined his head. All three of my Bondmates stiffened. I didn't see anything threatening about him, and my Light-driven instincts had put him squarely on our side of the fight last night, so his intentions were pure, or at least they had been then. Still, their hesitancy put me on edge. Now that I thought about it, he had used the term *Bondmates*—not *Bonded Variants* or *Bond members* as most Variants did. Was that just a cultural thing—a quirk of translation? I'd only ever heard one other person use the term—Nina, the Lighthunter. And why did he want to speak to us about my glowing?

"I am honored to meet one such as yourself. I have known only one other with a glow such as yours, and she was extraordinary also."

He smiled as my eyes widened in shock. Did he know what it was? Why I glowed? Was I finally about to get some answers?

Within minutes, Tyler had commandeered a small meeting room at the other end of the corridor and stationed two guards in front of the closed door.

We settled around the small table. Tyler looked downright exhausted as he collapsed into a chair and leaned forward on his elbows. I took his hand and pushed a little Light to him, hoping it would be both a pleasant sensation and a boost to his ability for the conversation we were about to have.

"Thank you for understanding our need to be cautious." I smiled at the man across from me. The guys were still throwing him worried, suspicious glances. If Alec had been here, he probably wouldn't have even let this conversation happen.

I understood their suspicion, but I was more excited than anything. Trying to find any information on this had been one dead end after another.

"Of course." He nodded.

"Please tell me about . . . uh . . ." The Vital? The other glowing chick? What was the correct terminology?

He smiled and leaned forward, wrapping his hands around his plastic cup of water. "When you glowed last night, the way you drew the Light into yourself and were able to transfer it remotely not only to your Bond but to others, to me"—he pressed a hand to his chest—"I had never felt anything like it. But I saw the glow, and I couldn't quite believe what I was witnessing. You truly are extraordinary, Miss Maynard."

"Thanks," I mumbled and fiddled with the rolled-up sleeve of Tyler's shirt. Tyler threaded his fingers through mine, stilling my hand.

The man continued. "When I was a boy, I would spend summers with my grandmother. She was a Vital, and she had three Variants. She would tell me stories of the ones that glowed—their power and potential. On a few occasions, I even witnessed her skin glow as she transferred Light to one of her Bondmates. But as I grew into an adult, I relegated her stories to the stuff of myth and folktales, put the glow I'd seen down to a child's overactive imagination. The few times I raised it with my parents, they dismissed the topic. For forty years, I put it out of my mind. And then last night, I saw you, *felt* you, and it all came back to me. I knew it was real."

"Is your grandmother still alive?" I was hanging on every word, leaning forward over the table. I didn't mean for the question to sound so harsh—I was simply ravenous for more information. "I'm sorry. I don't mean to be insensitive."

He bowed his head but waved my concern away. "It is quite all right. Yes, my grandmother is still alive. She is one hundred and three years old, but she still tends an herb garden and has tea with her friends every day. Or so she tells me in her letters. She lives in the same village, high in the Hida Mountains, but I have not been to see her in many years."

"I'm sorry"—Tyler leaned forward, suddenly all business—"why are you telling us this? Excuse my bluntness, but what do you want?"

Tyler's ability would've alerted him if any of Mr. Takata's story so far had been a lie—the fact that he hadn't raised any alarms yet gave me confidence—but in most situations, Tyler had to ask questions for his ability to give him the answers. I wasn't sure how much Tyler's ability filled in before the man answered, but he kept a straight face and allowed him to speak.

"Mr. Gabriel, I understand your concern, but I am aware of your ability, and I would like to remind you of mine. I have kept my shield down, allowing you to see the truth in my words. I have no agenda other than to offer my support and my services to you." He looked directly at me. "You are proof that the stories my grandmother told are true, and if that is the case, you must be protected. I am at your service."

Again, he bowed.

A little taken aback, I leaned back in my chair, unsure how to respond. I turned to Tyler for guidance. Ethan and Josh were looking at him expectantly too. He gave us all a glance and relaxed his posture. "He's telling the truth. He has a shielding ability, perfectly capable of blocking me, but he's keeping it lowered."

I cleared my throat. "Thank you, sir, but I'm not sure that I really . . . need anything right now?" I sounded unsure and awkward, even to my own ears. I'd never had someone declare their "service" to me. Was I supposed to assign him a task?

Tyler saved me. "Do you know any others who glow, like Evelyn and your grandmother?"

"No. I'm sorry."

"Does your grandmother?"

"I don't know. It's possible."

"Our top priority is to keep Evelyn safe. I'm sure, considering your line of work, you appreciate how valuable information can be in a situation such as this." They shared a look of mutual understanding. "If you'd like to help, then help us learn more about what this is. Could you speak with your grandmother?"

"Of course. It may take some time. There aren't phones in her village, let alone Internet. I will have to travel there and then back down the mountain before I can get in contact, but I will leave at once."

Apparently he wasn't one to waste time, and neither was Ty. They both rose from their seats. I scrambled to follow suit, as did Ethan and Josh.

"I'll organize a secure line and wait to hear from you," Tyler said.

"Perfect."

Tyler and Mr. Takata bowed to each other. Mr. Takata repeated the gesture with Josh and Ethan, then turned to me.

He took a card out of his pocket and held it out with both hands. "Evelyn, this is my private, secure line. I am always reachable on this number. Please don't hesitate to use it."

"Thank you." I took the card with both my hands, as I'd learned to do when I was a child in Japan, and bowed.

He left and closed the door behind him.

"Got any more cult followers waiting to declare their undying devotion, or can we get the fuck out of here?" Tyler wrapped an arm around my shoulders, his tone teasing but tired. "I need sleep."

"Let's get you home." I hugged him around the middle as Josh opened the door for us.

We checked in on Alec, but he was asleep again. Lucian had been ordered home by Olivia, and the only reason I felt comfortable with all of us leaving was because she and Dot promised to stay until we came back. That and the Melior Group guards crawling all over the building.

We left the same way we arrived—inconspicuously and heavily guarded—and headed back to the apartment.

Tyler fell asleep in the car, then again in the elevator, leaning his head back against the mirror. Once we made it inside, he shuffled to the first bedroom, flopped face-first into the bed, and immediately started snoring.

I felt so bad for him. He hadn't slept in over thirty-six hours. He was always cleaning up the messes, taking care of us.

Well, now he had *me* to take care of *him*.

I pulled his shoes off and unbuckled his holster, then managed to roll him over to remove his pants. I grabbed an extra blanket from the next room to cover him and drew the curtains. Lying down beside him, I ran my hand through his messy brown hair.

I was itching to call Mr. Takata on the number he gave me. In the short time since he'd left, my mind had made a shopping list of questions. But I knew it was better to let him go to his grandmother and get more information first. I so badly wanted to go there myself—meet someone else like me.

But for right now, I was exactly where I needed to be.

FIFTEEN

W e spent another night at the Manhattan apartment, then most of the next day at the hospital with Alec. He slept through most of it. The doctors assured us he was in the clear, but I just wanted to be close to him, hold his hand, even lie down in the bed next to him. I wanted to be there for him just as he'd been there for me when my mother died and I thought I was alone in the world. How wrong I'd been.

Much to Alec's ire, the doctor decided to keep him for an extra night. The next morning Tyler headed into work, and Ethan, Josh, and I drove home to Bradford Hills with an entourage of armored vehicles. Alec would be released that afternoon, and we wanted to get home ahead of him to make sure we had everything set up for his recovery.

But we were so spent we ended up piled on the couch, curtains drawn, and spent the morning watching movies and eating takeout.

Around lunchtime, Josh started flicking through live TV channels to see what was on. I was trying to decide if I needed to pee badly enough to move—I was ridiculously comfortable.

Ethan was reclined in the corner of the big, soft couch, his body slightly turned inward, a cushion half over his lap. Josh had his head on the cushion, the rest of his body spread out. I was squished between my blond bombshell boyfriend and the back of the couch. My head rested in the crook of Josh's shoulder, and one of my legs was hitched over his hips.

Ethan was running his hand through my hair absentmindedly. I was so relaxed I couldn't even be bothered to cover my mouth as I yawned. It was a big one, stretching my jaw wide.

Ethan's hand in my hair stopped. As my yawn ended, I unexpectedly closed my teeth and lips around his finger.

My hand flew to his as the two of them cracked up laughing, making me laugh around Ethan's digit too. But I couldn't let him off that easy. Still struggling to contain my giggles, I tightened my grip on his hand and held his finger hostage with my teeth.

I wrapped my lips around Ethan's finger and sucked.

Both their laughter died in their throats, and I felt their full attention on me, on my mouth.

Excruciatingly slowly, I dragged Ethan's finger out, lightly scraping it with my teeth, then swirling my tongue around the tip. He groaned and Josh gripped my thigh, pulling my leg higher over his growing erection.

I sucked Ethan's finger back into my mouth while rolling my hips against Josh.

I had no idea how the energy between us changed so fast, but I was drunk on it. I loved hearing Ethan groan when I was barely touching him. I loved feeling Josh's arousal pressing into my thigh. Witnessing the effect I had on them made me feel powerful. Loved, safe, and powerful.

I drew Ethan's finger all the way out of my mouth and, with Josh's help, drew myself up, straddling him.

That heavy, needy feeling was building deep inside me, and I rubbed myself up against Josh, seeking the friction that would both ease and intensify it. With Josh's hands on my waist, I leaned up. Ethan met me halfway and kissed me passionately, his tongue invading my mouth.

Josh trailed his hands up my sides, pushing my sweater up,

and Ethan broke our kiss to yank it completely off and throw it to the ground. He leaned back in and started kissing and sucking on my neck. I moaned and turned my head to the side, giving him more access as Josh grabbed my ass, his hips rolling under me to meet my movements.

But with my head turned, I caught a glimpse of the TV and froze.

It was turned down, but the rolling script at the bottom said "Live," and Davis Damari's ugly face filled the screen as he walked up to a podium overflowing with microphones. There were those eyes, the same shape as mine; my full lips; a more masculine version of my nose.

"Stop," I murmured, a cold chill dousing my desire. But they were caught up in the moment. Josh's hips were still pitching under me, Ethan's mouth still nibbling on my neck.

"Stop." I put more force behind the word that time, pushing on both their chests.

That time they heard me.

"What's wrong?" Josh sat up.

Ethan spoke at the same time. "You OK?"

I kept my eyes on the TV as their hands and eyes searched my body for injuries, but they caught on pretty quickly. Ethan grabbed the remote and turned the volume up.

". . . mixed news for you all today." Davis flashed his perfect teeth at the cameras, displaying that charismatic smile that made me want to vomit. "Our team of scientists and engineers have been working tirelessly to bring you our latest technology, which I announced recently. As you all know, this will allow us to transfer an ability from a Variant and give it to any person with Variant DNA who happens to not have manifested one naturally. We have worked out the legal and financial side of the process, ensuring that the donating Variant is compensated adequately for their generous decision to part with their Light-given ability. All that's left now is to make sure our technology, our machines, are perfectly optimized and safe for all parties involved. Safety is our number one priority."

Ethan scoffed. "Please. Safety, my ass."

Josh shushed him and turned the volume up even more. Davis launched into all the wonderful things his company was doing to ensure the safety of its customers—all the amazing things this would do for Variants around the world. The spiel was delivered with ease and practice, the touch of a marketing professional clear in the phrasing. He discussed how Variants who disliked their abilities would be able to rid themselves of an unwanted burden. How Variants with common abilities but no clear use for them would be able to make a substantial amount of money by giving them up.

As if his proposed system wasn't rife with opportunities for exploitation. As if it wouldn't turn into another way for the rich to get what they wanted at the expense of the poor and desperate. As if it wouldn't encourage Variant trafficking.

The reporters were eating his words up, asking enthusiastic questions and flashing their cameras. How did they not see that this could turn nasty overnight? That it was just like what the Lightwhores did—Vitals selling off their precious and sacred Light for a couple bucks? Except this was *permanent*.

His blatant lies made me feel sick. I wrapped my arms around myself, and Ethan handed me my sweater. As Davis kept twisting everything with his clever, poisonous words, I pulled the sweater over my head, and Josh held me close to his chest.

"Unfortunately we've had to push back our timeline." The look of disappointment on Davis's face was so exaggerated I almost laughed. "We were hoping to make the procedure available to the public next month; however, we've hit . . . a snag." He sighed. A flurry of questions flew at him from the reporters, who all spoke over one another. He gestured for them to calm down. "I can't go into too many details regarding the process—there is the matter of intellectual property to consider." He flashed that greasy grin. "But the technology is developed from studying Vitals and the process of transferring Light. There is one particular indi-vidual who is very unique in this aspect, and her Light is what allowed us to get this far with these incredible advancements."

I leaned toward the TV even as I gritted my teeth and gripped Josh's T-shirt, my knuckles turning white.

A reporter cut in. "Are you referring to the girl who glows?"

Davis sighed, another exaggerated, fake look of regret crossing his face. "I'm sure most people have seen the footage of the young lady who glowed as she transferred Light. Yes, her talents are more than just a visually impressive display. Yes, she was instru-mental in assisting us with developing the technology. And yes, we still need her assistance."

"He makes it sound like you were working together," Josh ground out, "not like he fucking kidnapped you and nearly killed us all."

My fists, still wrapped around the poor fabric of his T-shirt, started to shake in anger.

Davis just kept spewing his lies. "I'm very saddened to say she is no longer working with us, especially considering . . . but I won't go into sharing private family matters at this time."

But by saying that, that's *exactly* what he'd done. My mouth dropped open. What the fuck was he up to?

Intrigued murmurs rose from the reporters, but they settled down quickly, eager to hear more from Davis.

"It's all about to become public knowledge now, so I won't deny that the Vital in question is my daughter. The only thing I'll add is that my deepest wish is to see her again. Despite the delays with our project, regardless of the wider implications, I only wish to speak with her again." At this, he turned and stared straight into the camera. "Evelyn, you've left me no choice but to implore you, to plead with you in such a public way—please, darling. Come home so we can make up for all those years apart. So we can get back to our important work and change people's lives. So we can make sure you're safe *together*." I wanted to throw something at the TV, at his ugly face. It felt as if he were staring right at me, the fake sincerity infecting the crowd, reporters, and viewers like a disease.

"Is she dangerous?" Someone shouted.

Davis shook his head immediately, but I caught a glimpse of a satisfied smile. He'd been hoping someone would ask this, maybe even planted someone in the crowd. "My daughter would never knowingly harm anyone." He pressed a hand to his chest, his eyes imploring, then paused, sighed, and leveled everyone with a serious look. "Her Light is incredible, and the glowing is merely a visual representation of how formidably powerful she is. It is this particular brand of Vital Light that allowed us to figure out how to draw the ability from a Variant. But the process can be . . . deadly."

The reporters erupted in a hectic hubbub of questions, shouting and elbowing one another to coax more information from Davis. But he just waved them off and turned away, wiping a fake tear from the corner of his eye.

That son of a *bitch*!

"Fuck!" Ethan and Josh cursed at the same time.

This was bad—really bad.

Josh handed me off to Ethan, stood up, and reached for his phone. Ethan's big arms boxed me in as my heart slowly plummeted, hammering in fear all the way down.

The world's journalists had already figured out my identity. My photo and real name appeared on the screen now that the press conference had ended and Davis had walked out.

"Did he see it?" Josh barked down the phone. He paced as he talked. "The press conference. You didn't see it? . . . Good. Make sure he doesn't turn the TV on in his room . . . I know . . . Fucking bribe the nurse to knock him out if you have to . . . I know . . . I *know* . . . Yes. OK, thanks, Kyo."

He was making sure Alec didn't fly into a rage and rip his stitches open. Because that's exactly what he'd do if he saw this shit—tear the hospital down to get to me. Josh hung up, and his phone immediately started ringing again.

"Hey." He rubbed his forehead as he paced. "Yep . . . She's safe. In Ethan's lap as we speak . . . No way in hell. We're never leaving this fucking house again . . . Good. Agreed . . . I know, Gabe . . . I will . . . OK, bye."

As Josh hung up, Lucian wheeled himself into the room. He flicked on the kitchen light. With the heavy curtains drawn, we'd been sitting in the dark, the glow of the TV the only illumination.

Lucian came to a stop next to the couch. "You saw it?"

"Every damn word," Ethan growled, his grip on me tightening. Josh lowered himself onto the coffee table, his expression grim. "How did we not know about this?"

"We were told he was calling a press conference," Lucian said, "but that was only an hour ago. No one, not even the reporters, were given any inside info. We had no way of knowing he would—"

"Paint a target on my back?" I stared at the corner of the coffee table, next to Josh's knee.

Lucian sighed, but none of them contradicted me.

That's exactly what he'd done. He'd named me, outed me, and twisted it to make it sound as if I were the bad guy—the petulant teenager preventing scientific advancements with petty temper tantrums. Meanwhile, he'd all but announced I could kill people with a simple touch and left it to people's imaginations to fill in the horrific details.

Now every person with Variant DNA who'd failed to manifest an ability would see me as the bitch standing in their way. The one person stopping them from getting what they'd wanted their whole lives. The selfish asshole preventing a scientific advancement that would benefit the entire Variant community.

Every human would fear me too. His description of what I could do with the Light was accurate, but the language he'd used made me sound downright dangerous. To the humans, I was now another threat in a world where they already felt scared for their lives, scared for their children's future, scared for their very right to freedom.

I could see it from both sides. Could already see the kinds of things Variant Valor and the Human Empowerment Network would say about this, about *me*. Hell, I could probably write their propaganda for them.

Whatever way you looked at it, I was a fucking monster.

SIXTEEN

The doorbell rang as I was coming down the stairs. Alec stepped out of Tyler's study to answer it, favoring his right side. Whoever was at the door made his shoulders stiffen, his hand tighten around the doorknob.

He really should've been in bed, not rushing to answer doors. He'd only just been discharged from the hospital a few days ago. I hastened to his side, my heart beating a little faster with unease.

Logically, I knew the guards at the gate wouldn't let anyone who was unknown or uninvited step foot on the property. But every time I walked outside, part of me still half expected cameras and microphones shoved in my face, just as they had been the day after Davis made his passive-aggressive announcement. We'd been on our way to class when reporters had swarmed our vehicle, shouting questions and flashing cameras. Our security detail beat them back before they could get very close, but it was still confrontational.

So were the stares I was getting from students and even a few staff. I did my best to grit my teeth and avoided speaking to anyone for fear I'd tell them exactly what I thought of my so-called father.

Thankfully, that had been my last day of classes before

summer. I had a few assignments to finish and one lab exam, and then I'd get a short break before summer classes started. I could stay home and ignore the chaos until it hopefully went away. It was wishful thinking, but it was better than the encroaching panic that gripped my chest whenever I thought about the alternative—that this would probably get worse before it got better.

It didn't help knowing he was still out there—that he could make another grab for me or continue to twist things to the press, and there was nothing we could do about it.

After Davis's press conference, a stealth team had been sent to apprehend him in the dead of night. They'd had eyes on him since his speech, he was in a new location, they had the numbers. But once again, the attempt was unsuccessful; by the time they arrived, the new hideout was abandoned. Tyler said it was almost as if they knew we were coming. He shared a worried look with Alec while Lucian hung his head in his hands, grumbling unintelligible things for a long time.

Feeling confident about anything was hard when the smartest, most competent, most dangerous men I knew were sharing looks tinged with fear. Every passing vehicle, every unfamiliar face, every ring of the doorbell made me cringe.

When I made it to the door, I heaved a sigh of relief.

"... not even here to see you, Alec." Dana stood on the ornate doormat with her arms crossed, glaring at Alec and looking as hot as she always did. "Although I'm mildly pleased you didn't, you know, die and shit."

"Then why are you here?" Alec's low voice grated, a hint of annoyance coming though, just as Dana's eyes met mine.

I smiled at her as Alec took my hand. "Hey."

She smiled back but answered Alec instead of me. "I'm here to see Eve, actually."

"What? Why?" His hand tightened around mine. Having his ex show up at his front door and demand to see his Vital must've been awkward, but in his usual manner, he was handling it like crap.

"Alec." I tugged on his hand and shot him a reproachful look. "You're being rude."

"Yeah, *Alec*." Dana smirked at him as I ushered her in. "Eve and I are, like, totally BFFs now. She's my bae!" She slung an arm over my shoulders and delivered her speech in an exaggerated SoCal accent.

Alec stood in front of us, frowning.

I couldn't help the laughter that bubbled up, and my shoulders started to shake with my efforts to keep it contained.

Dana let out one long guffaw and dropped her arm. If someone had told me on the night of the gala that Dana and I would be laughing *together* at Alec's expense, I would've suggested they get their head checked, but here we were . . .

When Dana spoke again, her tone was more serious. "I'd prefer to have this conversation in private."

"No," Alec answered without hesitation.

Ethan chose that moment to come bounding out of the kitchen wearing nothing but shorts, his impressive muscles glistening with sweat. He'd clearly just come up from the gym. He faltered as he registered the scene, the easy smile falling from his face. His bulk and height made him look even more awkward as he ran a hand through his sweaty hair, then turned on his heel and went back the way he'd come without a word.

I stifled another laugh. "It's OK, Alec. I'll be fine."

"If you're talking about me, I get to listen," he said, his petulant side coming out. He crossed his arms, then winced and immediately dropped them.

"Why are you even out of bed?" I asked reproachfully, but he ignored me.

"Not everything is about you, oh mighty Master of Pain." Dana's voice practically dripped sarcasm.

"What's it about then?"

"Alec. Go." Dana and I spoke at the same time, in the same exasperated tone.

Alec's eyes widened as he looked between us. Finally, with a groan, he dragged his hands over his buzzed hair and down his face, then rushed out of the room as fast as his injuries would allow, muttering, "This is too fucking weird."

"Lie down on the couch, please!" I yelled after him as he disappeared in the direction of the living room. "Before you tear your stitches!"

I bugged my eyes out at Dana and shook my head.

She chuckled. "This one time we were on a mission in Morocco, and he got typhoid. We were just on recon, but instead of taking two fucking days to rest, he kept pushing it and ended up being evacuated and hospitalized for a *week*."

I groaned but laughed darkly as I led Dana toward the formal sitting room. None of that surprised me whatsoever.

"Your problem now," Dana finished as we sat down on the plush velvet couch under the window.

"Yeah . . ." I trailed off, not really sure how to address that. Even though Dana and I were now on good terms, it was still a bit odd to be sitting next to a woman—a very sexy, beautiful woman—who'd had sex with my Variant.

I cleared my throat. "Can I get you anything? Tea? Coffee? We have this ridiculous state-of-the-art espresso machine I've recently learned how to use."

"No thanks. I don't have a ton of time, so I'll get to the point."

"Oh, OK." I angled my body slightly to face her.

She leaned forward, propping her arms on her knees and taking a deep breath. "I'm here to speak to you about going to see Zara."

She looked at me, her expression wary but determined.

My eyes widened even as my brow furrowed. I leaned back against the plush pillows, at a loss for words. "What?"

"There are only two people employed by Melior Group with an ability like mine—blocking other abilities. Zara's held in a cell that blocks Light and scrambles the use of abilities, but any time she's taken out, one of the two of us has to do it. She's too unpredictable, has very little control of her ability. She's dangerous."

"I know she's dangerous," I growled. She'd handed me over to a man who would have happily seen me die to achieve his goals; her actions resulted in countless deaths and put all my Bonded Variants in danger.

"I'm just trying to explain," Dana rushed out, keeping her voice calm. "I spend a lot of time with her, see her almost daily. And every damn day, she asks about you, *begs* to see you, Eve. She pleads with me to get you to come. You have clearance now, so you can just walk in any time you want."

"Why would I?" I couldn't believe she was asking me to do this. My heart pounded in my head; my fists clenched. "Why the fuck would I give that traitorous bitch another second of my time, another scrap of my energy?"

"I get it." Dana held her hands out in front of her. "Trust me, I understand. Which is why I'm not trying to talk you into it. I'm just passing on information."

"I don't care!" My voice got high. "I don't want to hear it."

"Eve, I'm sorry. I really didn't come here to upset you. I just feel like you deserve to know. You of all people deserve to have all the information in this situation."

She kept looking at me with that calm expression, those expertly made-up, understanding eyes. Stupid, beautiful bitch was being all kinds of patient and mature, which was more than I could say for myself.

If I was being completely honest, I'd avoided thinking about Zara—about how she'd betrayed me, about the cold look in her eye as she'd slammed that van door. It was no wonder having it brought up made me explode; it was the only time I ever expressed anything about it.

Sitting on that plush couch with Dana, the mild spring breeze that came through the window tickling the back of my neck, I realized I hadn't processed the situation with Zara. At all. I'd shoved it into a black metal box and slammed the lid shut with a clang.

I stared at the emerald velvet cushion between us, running my hands over the soft fabric and taking a few breaths.

Finally, I lifted my gaze to meet hers. "What does she want, Dana? I can't handle any more of her manipulation. I seriously don't think I can take another . . . " I trailed off, not entirely sure what I was getting at. Another betrayal? Another drama? Another bombshell I didn't see coming?

Dana wrapped her hand around mine. Her fingers were warm and strong, but she didn't linger. She just gave me a squeeze and released my hand. "I get it. That's why I'm not here to plead her case. I'm not trying to get you to forgive her or whatever. I'm just keeping you informed. What you choose to do with the information is completely your call."

Dana was going out of her way to not keep anything from me. She had no obligation to tell me anything, no stake in my happiness, but there she was, doing the right thing and giving me the truth. It couldn't have been easy to raise such a difficult topic with her ex's Vital and girlfriend. She was beautiful *and* gutsy.

I nodded, and she continued.

"She just keeps asking about you. How you are, what you're doing, how you're coping. I never give her any info—it's against policy to give detainees information about the outside world, and I would never share anything without your consent anyway. Still, she never stops trying. More than anything though, she keeps begging me to bring you to see her. She keeps saying she needs to see you. Not wants—*needs*. She's a little manic about it. I mean, she wasn't exactly mentally stable to begin with, but I think the isolation and the removal of autonomy is only pushing her further into madness."

"Am I supposed to feel sorry for her?" I remained calm, but I was defensive too.

"You're not supposed to feel anything. Just sharing the facts," Dana reminded me yet again.

"I know. I'm sorry." I sighed. "This is just really hard for me. What do you think this is? Is she giving you guys intel? Or is she being difficult until she gets her way?"

"Nothing like that. In fact, she's cooperating fully. She's

answered all our questions, even giving us extra information without us having to ask. She genuinely seems to hate Davis and even her own mother, although I don't think there was ever any love lost there. As to what I think this is about—honestly, I have no idea. All I know is that she's desperate to see you." Dana shrugged.

"OK. Thank you for coming here to tell me."

"It's all good. Call me if you have any questions. Gabe has my number, even if Alec has deleted it. I have to get going or I'll be late for work." She got to her feet.

"I will. Thanks, Dana." We shared a genuinely friendly smile.

After seeing her off at the front door, I wandered back into the sitting room and flopped onto the couch with a huff. I didn't appreciate being forced to deal with my feelings around the Zara situation, but it was probably best I did anyway. It was on me that I hadn't talked to anyone about it yet—let alone a mental health professional.

My mind rifled through the implications and possibilities. A big part of me wanted to go see her just to satisfy my curiosity; I never could resist a puzzle. But maybe that was her plan all along —to get me curious and manipulate me into seeing her. Then again, what if I was just being paranoid? Still, Zara had more than proven she could be devious.

As my mind raced, so did my heart—sadness, anger, and frustration all vying for first place.

With a groan, I sat up straight. For the next half hour I tried to meditate—on the couch, the wingback chair, the floor—but my thoughts constantly wandered. I managed to slow my breathing and heart rate somewhat, but after a while, I gave up.

I needed advice—someone to talk it over with. I could've gone to Dot, Charlie, any of my guys. Even Uncle Luce would have been more than happy to give me his sympathetic ear.

But I needed to feel in control of how much I discussed this, how much time and energy I chose to give it. All of them would push me to talk more, would bring it up the next day, would look at me with cautious worry in their eyes.

So I called Harvey.

At the second ring, I realized it was around four in the morning in Australia, but just as I was about to hang up, he answered.

"Hey, Eve." He didn't sound tired or groggy at all.

"Oh, hey, Harvey. I didn't wake you? Sorry."

He chuckled. "No. I couldn't sleep. Been up drawing for a few hours now. What's up? How are you?"

He sounded relaxed, and I could hear music playing softly in the background. I could picture him sitting at his desk with the drawing pad, a lamp illuminating his work while the rest of the room was cast in darkness.

"What're you drawing? Is it for your course? How's that going?"

He told me about his studies and the friends he'd made but didn't tell me what he was working on. He'd always been very secretive about unfinished projects. We talked about my science subjects too, about our families and the crazy stuff happening all over the world. He indulged me for a while, then pushed. "What's going on, Eve?"

"Maybe I just really wanted to catch up. We did promise to stay in touch."

"Eve. What's going on?" His voice was still warm, but it held a hint of firmness this time.

I sighed. I did call him to ask for help with the Zara situation, so why was I avoiding it? "Fine. I need your advice."

"About?"

"Zara."

"What happened?"

"Nothing? I don't know. She's been locked in a cell since they dragged her back here. It's just . . ."

"Dude! Spit it out."

I rolled my eyes—at myself. Why was this so hard? "She reached out to me, kind of. Through Alec's ex Dana."

"Alec . . . he's the tall, scary one? With the pain thing?"

"Yeah, that asshole."

"He has an ex? Like, some chick was ballsy enough to touch him long enough to sleep with him?"

"Harvey! I don't need reminders of that, thanks!"

"Hey, you're the one who brought it up. Clearly as a distraction tactic from talking about what you actually want to talk about. What did Zara want?"

"Why do you have to be right about everything?"

"It's what I do—I draw and I speak the truth. Zara?"

"She wants to see me. Dana has a blocking ability, and because Zara's electric ability is so unstable, Dana is on guard duty with her a lot. She just came over to tell me that Zara won't shut up about me and keeps begging to see me. I don't know what to do."

"Do you want to see her?"

"No. I hate her." I paused, a little taken aback by how intense those words sounded coming out of my mouth. I'd never said I hated Zara, but maybe that was the feeling I'd been stuffing down. Or maybe suppressing all my thoughts and feelings about this had made them fester and turn into hate. Did I really want to be capable of hating another person? Harvey just sat silently on the line, waiting patiently for me to continue.

"I . . . I don't know, Harvey. I don't want anything to do with her, but it all feels so unresolved."

"You say you don't want to see her, but you're calling me for advice on what to do. Dig deeper, Eve. Use that logical mind of yours. Give me the reasons *not* to go and then the reasons why you *should*."

"I don't want to see her. The thought of speaking to her makes my stomach turn. She betrayed me. She keeps asking for me, and I don't want to give her the satisfaction of getting what she wants."

"And the other side?"

"I need to know *why*." I sighed. That was what it came down to—I wanted to understand why she betrayed me. To an extent, I could guess at some of the reasons, like her zealot parents, her need to belong, her desperation to stop feeling like a failure for not having an ability. But I still couldn't understand why she'd done that to me. It felt so personal. "I want to look her in the eye and ask if our friendship ever meant anything to her."

"OK, here's my advice. Forget about this 'giving her what she wants' bullshit. It's petty reasoning, and you're better than that. Think about what *you* want and need. Really think about it, Eve. If you need to protect yourself emotionally from dealing with her again, then don't go. If you think you'll learn something or get some kind of closure from seeing her, then go. Just do what's right for you."

"Yes, but what is right for me? Tell me what to do, Harveyyy." I dragged his name out on a whine. His advice was solid, but I still kind of wanted someone to tell me what to do. Or did I? I knew that if I went to Alec, he'd tell me to stay the fuck away from her, and I really didn't like being ordered around.

"OK. Go talk to your four boyfriends about this. I'm happy to give you some advice, but this is big, and they need to know. Also, I still can't believe you have four fucking boyfriends!"

I laughed. "You get used to it."

"I bet. I could get used to it in a heartbeat."

"Having four boyfriends?"

"What?! No! Clearly I meant girlfriends."

"I don't know if you could handle four women, Harvey."

"You mean they couldn't handle me."

We both laughed.

When I hung up, I felt lighter. Zara had been a strong presence in my life, one of the only friends I'd ever made. She meant a lot to me, but she wasn't my only friend. I had other people I could rely on—other people who had my back and wanted me in their lives. I had their support through this.

I dragged myself off the couch and went in search of my four boyfriends to tell them what was going on in my life. Look at that —I was learning not to keep secrets from my loved ones. All kinds of personal growth was happening today.

SEVENTEEN

My gin and tonic was nearly empty, but I waited for Tyler to take his turn before deciding whether to finish the last of it.

"Come on, man! Say your thing!" Kyo chuckled, taking a swig of his beer. His other hand gently caressed Dot's ankle. She was in Marcus's lap on the couch, and Kyo was sitting on the ground next to them.

We were all in Josh's room—me, my Bond, Alec's team, Dot, and Charlie—keeping Alec company as he recovered. He kept saying he'd be more than happy to just shut himself in his room and . . . scowl at his wound until it went away or something, but I think he secretly liked us all taking care of him.

It had been only a week since his release from the hospital, but he was healing fast. He'd be going back to work the next day—office work only for a while, much to his ire. He was still on pain medication and not allowed to drink, but the rest of us were celebrating for him.

We were also secretly distracting Charlie from the fact that Ed's visit had ended. He'd been moping around for the last two weeks, ever since his boyfriend had gone home.

Josh had put on some music, and "Want You Bad" by The

Offspring was playing. He mouthed the words, his back to the bookshelves. Barefoot, in sweats and a Blondie T-shirt, he looked the epitome of relaxed.

"OK, got one." Tyler leaned forward, casting his eyes over the group. Dot and Marcus were on his right, Alec on his left. One of Alec's arms rested on the couch; the other held a soda casually between his knees.

"Never have I ever . . ." Tyler started, then paused until he had everyone's full attention. Ethan shifted at my back, breaking off his conversation with Jamie about football or something. I don't know—I tuned out any time sports came up. We were both sitting next to the fireplace, me between his legs.

The fire crackled, making the room slightly too hot, despite the cool early summer breeze coming through the open French doors.

Once everyone was paying attention, Tyler finished: " . . . had sex with a man." He leaned back on the couch, his knowing eyes watching us all carefully.

I downed the rest of the gin and tonic. I'd slept with several men, four of them in this very room. That thought made me giggle. Or maybe it was the four gin and tonics in my system making me giggle. I really wasn't much of a giggler. *Giggler*—was that a word?

Ethan gripped my hip, holding me still against him, but his beer remained untouched by his side.

Dot, Charlie, Josh, Kyo, and Marcus each took a healthy swig of their drink, and then we all gave our full attention to Tyler. Playing "Never Have I Ever" with a truth-telling Variant in the room was way more fun than the regular version.

Tyler's eyes scanned the group, dramatically taking his time even though his ability would've pinpointed the lies immediately.

"Jamie." He barely held back his laughter, his eyes dancing as they zeroed in on the tall redheaded man on my left. "Something you want to share with the group?"

Jamie's head snapped up, his eyes wide in what looked like

genuine surprise. "Me?" His pale cheeks started to turn the same color as his hair.

Laughter bubbled up in my chest, and my cheeks ached from the strain of keeping the smile off my face. Dot had given up and was covering her mouth with one hand, her shoulders shaking uncontrollably.

Jamie's brow furrowed. Then, as he looked out into the middle distance, a look of recognition came over his face. "Oh . . . yeah, I guess that counts." He shrugged and took a long drink of his beer.

"You had a penis inside you! It doesn't matter if there was a woman in the bed. I'd say that fucking counts, bro!" Tyler managed to shout before completely doubling over in laughter. Everyone else let loose too, and the room filled with deafening sounds of mirth.

As the noise started to recede, Jamie managed to shout over everyone, "Gabe, you can see that much detail?" He looked a little horrified.

Tyler chuckled. "Not exactly. It's not like there's a porno playing out in my head or anything. I just kind of . . . know the information." He shrugged.

"For a second there"—Josh held his middle, gasping and letting the odd laugh out between words—"I thought he was looking at you, Kid. I thought you were holding out on us." He descended into laughter again. I was right there with him, throwing my head back and letting Ethan steady me.

Ethan lifted me so I was sitting on his lap instead of between his legs. "I've never left a woman unsatisfied." His deep voice rumbled through me, making me shiver. "So you can suck on my big hairy balls."

I had no idea how his answer related to the suggestion he'd slept with a man, and neither did anyone else, because we all erupted into another laughing fit.

When I managed to calm down enough to breathe, I wiped the tears from the corners of my eyes. "To be fair, his balls are pretty fucking big."

Tyler choked on his bourbon and coke, spraying the coffee table with it.

I managed to keep my laughter in check long enough to point at Ethan. "And you be careful what you wish for"—my pointing finger traveled to Josh—"because he just might."

Tyler made the mistake of trying to take another sip just then, because he choked on that one too. Next to him, Alec leaned his head on the back of the couch and ran his hand down his face in exasperation, but when it came away, I saw the amused smirk pulling at his lips.

"Fresh drinks before the next round!" Dot announced, getting up.

"I'll help." Charlie shuffled forward too. "Everyone having the same again?"

"No!" Josh sat bolt upright, halting them and everyone else's conversation. "Sit down. I got this."

He crawled past the coffee table and over to me, his vibrant green eyes intent on mine.

"Uh, Josh," Alec teased, "the door is in the opposite direction."

Josh just flipped him off and leaned into me, kneeling over Ethan's outstretched legs. His perfect, full lips connected with mine, and I caught on to what he was doing. I kissed him back, caressing his tongue with mine in slow, luxurious movements as I gave the Light free rein to flow into him. A groan reverberated through my chest, but it wasn't me—it was Ethan. His hands gripped my hips as I felt him grow hard under me. Josh had more than enough Light to lift an entire liquor store, but he kept kissing me, pressing against me as Ethan reclined further.

We were nearly horizontal when Kyo's voice finally broke the spell. "Unless you want this to turn into a gang bang, you may want to cut that shit out." He chuckled, but there was no denying the hint of lust in his voice.

Josh finally pulled away, flashing me a brilliant smile and a wink. Then he moved back to his spot against the bookshelf, adjusted the bulge in his pants, and closed his eyes. A look of pure concentration fell over his beautiful face.

Not even a minute later, the door to his bedroom opened, and a cooler full of drinks floated into the room. He deposited it near the door, and several beers and other mixed drinks flew straight into the hands of almost everyone seated around the little coffee table. We all clapped, genuinely impressed.

Josh bowed, grinning from ear to ear, his eyes a little glassy. Then he changed the music—"Bring Me the Horizon" came blasting out of the speakers.

"My turn!" I yelled, sitting up straighter on top of Ethan. His hands on my hips tightened, using me to hide his still prominent erection.

"Never have I ever had group sex!" I blurted the statement without letting myself think about it too much. The alcohol had made me brave, and I was deeply curious what my guys' answers would be.

Poor Tyler nearly choked on yet another sip of his drink, but this time, he managed to cough it back between laughs.

Before anyone could answer, Dot held her hands out. "Hold up! I need clarification. What are we classifying as 'group sex'? Like, anything more than just two people doing it?"

Charlie groaned, clearly uncomfortable hearing his sister talk about sex. "Gross."

I laughed at the disgusted look on his face.

"Threesomes?" Marcus pulled her back against his chest. "Three is technically a group."

"No." Tyler laid down the rules. "A threesome is a threesome. Group sex is four or more people."

He gave a definitive nod, and no one argued. After a beat, we all started looking around to see who would drink. My gin and tonic stayed firmly by my side. Charlie's drink remained untouched, as did Ethan's and Alec's.

Dot, Kyo, Marcus, and Jamie all drank while sharing knowing

glances—it didn't take a genius to figure out they'd all had sex at the same time.

I wasn't sure if I was more surprised by Ethan's or Tyler's response. Ethan leaned forward and whispered against my neck, "I'm a one-woman kind of man, and you're all the woman I need."

I melted at his words, but my eyes flew to Tyler. He necked his beer, finishing the bottle in one go. When he was done, he took a deep breath, dropped the bottle down on the table, and grinned wide. That, coupled with his answer to the previous question, had me wondering just how many women he'd slept with. With his ability and his skilled hands, how many women had he given the greatest pleasure they'd ever known? How many bitches did I need to be jealous of? Was Stacey from admissions one of them? Is that why she was skirting the line of propriety every time they were in the same room?

Suddenly I regretted asking that question. I didn't want to think about their whorish pasts. Chatter and joking filled the air around us again, and I dipped my head and took a long sip of my drink, letting the cold, tart liquid cool my racing heart.

Once again, Ethan's hot mouth brushed against my neck, and he placed a soft kiss just below my ear. "You're all the woman *he* needs too, baby."

I chewed my bottom lip, surprised Ethan had picked up on my insecurities. My big guy wasn't always the best with subtlety—usually it was Josh who watched me like a hawk and figured out what I was thinking.

I glanced in Josh's direction and was rewarded with the kind, knowing look I'd expected, laced with more than a little heat. I couldn't make myself look at Tyler, so my eyes naturally moved to my honey-voiced stranger next.

He was slumped in the corner of the couch, his knees wide, his head resting against the back. He looked down his nose at me, wearing that little smirk I both loved and hated—the one that made things tingle low in my belly, sometimes from frustrated anger and sometimes from pure, scorching lust. He was looking at me as if I were the only person in the room.

Slowly, he lifted his hand from the arm of the couch and crooked his finger, beckoning me over. I bristled at being summoned like that even as my body began to respond. Ethan released his hold, pushed me up, even nudged me in Alec's direction. After a few wobbly steps, I stood in front of him.

He wrapped his strong hands around my waist and pulled me between his legs. I had an urge to lift one knee, then the other, and straddle him, but before I could, he lifted me up, wincing slightly at the pain from his wound, and deposited me in Tyler's lap.

Tyler circled his arms around me, drew me into his chest, and with a gentle hand at my cheek, made me look into his serious gray eyes. "Do I need to kick everyone out of this room so I can show you how much I want you and no one else?" he murmured against my lips.

What was I thinking? This was my Bonded Variant. I was his Vital! Nothing could ever compete with that; nothing could break that connection. Alec and I had tried to resist it. It was impossible.

My paranoid insecurity melted away, and I shook my head. "No, let's keep playing."

I smiled and he nodded, his ability confirming the truth of my feelings. He placed a searing kiss on my lips but didn't open his mouth to me when I darted my tongue out. It left me wanting as he raised his voice and asked whose turn it was.

As the night progressed and the game continued, most of us got more and more drunk. At one point, Dot and Charlie ganged up on me, apparently determined to see me get wasted, as they fired off statements like "Never have I ever falsified identification documents," "Never have I ever lied about my identity," and "Never have I ever tried to run away from my Bond because I thought they were out to get me."

I threw them dirty looks over the rim of my glass while fighting giddy laughter.

At some point, well past midnight, we all started to disperse.

Dot and Charlie's plan had worked—I was well and truly drunk off my ass. I only vaguely registered Alec guiding me up the hall toward his room, the sharp pain in my hip as I barreled into a side table, Alec's grunt as he picked me up and carried me the rest of the way.

As he wrangled me out of my clothes, I blabbered on in half-finished sentences. " . . . evil Dot and Charlie ganging up on me . . . I love them. They're so nice. They're like my family now . . . They *are* my family . . . Everyone is my family." I giggled, stumbling backward, but Alec caught me and lowered me to the bed. He kept me sitting upright so he could pull one of his soft T-shirts over my head.

I inhaled. "You smell good. This is a really soft T-shirt. Why are all your things so soft? What was I . . . oh yeah! The whole world is my family. You know, we need more love in all the . . . um . . . in the . . . the world needs more love. I love Dot and Charlie and everyone else. I have *so much* love."

I grabbed on to the front of his shirt and pulled him down to eye level. My vision was swimming, but he looked as if he was smirking at me, amused. I steadied my swaying as best I could, blinked a few times, then said in an intense whisper, "I have so much love in my heart, Alec, for all of you."

His smile fell, but he kept staring at me with those intense eyes of his, dark blue in the low light of the bedside lamp. "So do I," he whispered, pressing his forehead to mine.

I smiled and nuzzled his nose. The last coherent sliver of my brain—the only little bit not swimming in alcohol—managed to stop me from saying, "I love you." I didn't want to say it to him drunk. It felt cheap and fake, and I didn't want to give him any reason to doubt me.

My eyes widened and I leaned away, my hands flying to my stomach as my mouth filled with saliva.

"Oh shit," I managed to get out before my stomach heaved. Alec sprang into action, shuffling me to his en suite.

The last thing I remember before I blacked out is Alec holding my hair as I vomited gin and tonic into his toilet.

I woke with a groan to the sound of a door banging open.

"Gym?" Ethan's booming voice was like a sledgehammer to my already throbbing head.

Heavy curtains slid across the rail to reveal bright sunlight, which sent even more pain stabbing through my skull. The sledgehammer had the back of my head covered, while the stabbing focused on my closed eyes. I buried my head in a pillow, and my forehead bumped into another forehead. We both groaned.

Vaguely I registered I was in Alec's bed, but his voice came from somewhere behind me, where the stabby light was coming from.

"Yep! I'm feeling much better today. The bullet wound's nearly healed completely."

"Sweet, bro!" Skin slapped against skin; I was pretty sure they'd high-fived. Thankfully, the sound of their obnoxiously loud, manly voices soon moved off down the hall. But the assholes had left the curtains open, and a dull thudding was coming from another part of the house. I couldn't be entirely sure if the thudding was hammers and ongoing construction in the west wing or if it was just my head.

Alec hadn't touched alcohol the night before, so it was no surprise he was up, bright eyed and bushy tailed, but I was about 87 percent sure Ethan had downed at least two six-packs of beer. He'd been giggling like a schoolgirl at one point . . . I just couldn't remember what the joke was.

He'd definitely drunk more than me, and yet he was up and ready to do a workout. *Jerk.* Far more annoying, though, was the bright light still stabbing me in the fucking eyes.

I groaned and cracked one eye open. Josh was in the bed with me, his forehead against mine and his mouth slightly open. I nudged him. His eyes flew open, but then he cringed and tried to roll over.

With a grunt of protest, I halted his movements and gestured vaguely in the direction of the windows. Thankfully, his hangover didn't hinder his ability to know exactly what I was thinking. With a lazy flick of his wrist, the curtains drew closed, casting the room into blissful darkness once more. Then, without me even having to grunt at him again, he did the same to the door.

He rolled over, and I snuggled into his back, playing the big spoon.

I'd spent enough time in Alec's and Tyler's rooms to know the afternoon sun streamed in through the windows on this side of the house. It was *early* afternoon, but I'd still slept half the day away. And I was in the bed alone. Why did they all recover faster than me? Didn't we all have Variant DNA? Why did I still have to suffer the dull headache at the back of my head, the sick, empty feeling in my stomach?

I sighed and crawled out of bed, then used Alec's bathroom to shower and brush my teeth. I really needed to buy another four toothbrushes. Because I stayed with them—one or more of them—several times per week, I ended up using their toothbrushes way more than was hygienic. According to the World Health Organization, the mouth is home to more than seven hundred species of bacteria, and each person has their own unique mix of bacteria that don't take kindly to other bacteria being introduced.

I put thoughts of gum disease out of my mind. The shower and tooth brushing had me feeling almost normal, but there was one more need to attend to. My stomach grumbled as if to punctuate my thoughts.

On the ground floor, I had to step around sheets of drywall and several wheelbarrows full of debris. I frowned, cursing myself for not stealing a pair of Alec's socks. What the hell were they doing up there? This renovation was taking forever.

As I walked into the kitchen, the smell of coffee drove all thoughts of swinging hammers and messy demolition from my mind. I inhaled deeply and followed my nose, walking around the corner with my eyes half-closed.

Like a vision of hotness, all my desires incarnate, Tyler stood at the island holding a fresh latte out to me. I took it with both hands, hugging it to my chest and then taking a sip. I moaned and nearly closed my eyes, but I couldn't tear them away from the perfect man in front of me.

It was Sunday—usually the only day I saw Ty in sweats, relaxing—but clearly, he had to do some work. He was in gray slacks, and the rolled-up sleeves of his crisp white shirt cut into his defined forearms. Despite his neat clothing, his messy brown hair stuck up all over the place, that pesky wayward bit hanging over his forehead, and his gray eyes watched me with so much affection, so much . . .

"Mmmm, I love you." Was I talking to the perfect coffee or the perfect man? My brain was still struggling to keep up. He just kept watching me, his face the picture of patience even though he clearly had somewhere to be.

I took another sip, but it wasn't the amazing coffee spreading warmth through my chest. I set the cup down and leaned my hip on the bench, mirroring his posture.

He tilted his head and smiled. "How are you feeling after—"

"Shh." I cut him off with a hand over his perfect mouth. His eyes widened, then crinkled in amusement. He kept one hand flat on the bench next to his hip, but the other went to my waist.

I removed my hand from his mouth and trailed my fingers over his freshly shaved jaw, coming to rest at his neck, just under the crisp collar of his shirt.

"Ask me what I'm thinking about, Ty." I held his gaze, steady and sure as I let my Light flow into him unobstructed.

I love you.

I love you.

I love you.

I repeated the words over and over in my head, waiting for him to ask the question.

"What are you thinking about, Eve?" His voice was low but playful, his eyes still amused.

I watched, mesmerized and awed, as his ability filled him in. I was thinking the words so hard, with so much intention, it must have sounded like someone shouting in his head.

The playfulness left his expression, replaced by something . . . more, deeper. He smiled and licked his lips as he pulled me against his chest.

"Wait!" I stopped him before he could speak. "I want to say it." A thrilling, light giddiness bubbled up in my chest and burst out of my lips. "I love you, Tyler Gabriel."

He grinned, his whole face lighting up. "I love you, Evelyn Maynard."

I returned his grin and leaned up to kiss him. We held each other close, our kisses messy and erratic, punctuated by laughter and broken by toothy smiles.

By the time we pulled out of each other's arms, my latte was going cold.

He made me a fresh one, pouring coffee into his travel mug as he went. Ethan and Josh came into the kitchen, laden with grocery bags, as Tyler slid my second latte over to me.

"Did you two go grocery shopping?" I frowned as they each gave me a kiss on the cheek and deposited the bags on the island. "Don't you have, like . . . people for that?"

"Yes." Josh chuckled. "But we wanted to get out of the house for a bit, and Kid started getting ideas for dinner and . . . ." He gestured to the food.

"But how about some breakfast first?" Ethan flashed me his dimples, twirling a pan in his big hand before setting it on the stove to heat.

"I have to head into the city for a meeting. I may need to stay the night, depending on how late it goes." Tyler gave me a kiss on the top of my head and turned to leave. "Love you."

"Love you." It was amazing how easy it was to fall into those words, how effortlessly they came tumbling out considering we'd only said them for the first time a few moments ago.

As Tyler left, Alec came around the other side of the island in sweats and a hoodie.

My heart sank even as it started to hammer in my chest.

Ethan cracked an egg into the pan, the oil sizzling.

Alec pulled his hood up over his head, avoiding eye contact.

He'd heard. He must have. He was too close *not* to have heard me tell Tyler I loved him as if I'd been saying it my whole life, as if it were just part of our daily repertoire.

I watched him, chewing on my lip, horrified and feeling like shit.

He collected a bottle of mineral water from the fridge and walked out, not saying anything or looking at anyone. I couldn't see the look on his face, but his unhappiness was clear from the tension in his shoulders, his hurried steps, the way his fingers gripped the bottle. I couldn't imagine what was going through his head, what he was feeling.

Was he kicking himself for the way he'd treated me? Or was he mad at me for torturing him like this?

I was mad at me.

I folded my hands on the cool stone and dropped my head onto my forearms. Why couldn't I just say it? I felt it. I knew he felt it. He'd said it to me. So why couldn't I say it to him? Why wasn't I rushing out after him to tell him this instant?

Alec and I had come very far, but I was still worried he'd hurt me. No one had ever been quite as good at tearing my heart out of my chest and stomping on it to make himself feel better. If I went after him now and tried to tell him I loved him, would he throw it back in my face, reject me yet again? That was how Alec reacted when hurt; he pushed people away, hurt them more than they were hurting him. I just couldn't bear the cold look in his eyes, couldn't stand the thought of hearing his hard, detached voice.

Soothing hands rubbed my shoulders as tears pricked my eyes.

"Just tell him, baby," Josh whispered next to my ear.

My silent tears spilled over. If only it were that simple.

EIGHTEEN

I took the bottle of water from Karen gratefully, downing half of it in one go. When I'd first arrived for my session, I regretted wearing a summer dress and sandals. It was a hot day, but the AC inside the building was pumping. It hadn't taken me long to wish for a cardigan.

But once the session got underway, I was hot and sweaty in no time. They hadn't requested any of the guys for this one. Tyler was in his office some thirty floors up, and Alec was somewhere in the building too, so they were on standby if we needed them, but the research team wanted to test my ability to transfer Light to Variants *outside* my Bond.

"You OK?" Karen took a seat on the couch next to me. We were finished for the day, and it had become a bit of a routine for the two of us to sit down and debrief after each session. We mostly used the area they'd set up as a living room—the couches were comfortable.

I stretched. "I'll be fine. It's just a lot more effort outside the Bond."

"It's to be expected. But if at any point you feel like it's too much, you just say so, sweetie." Karen had gone from barking cold, impersonal commands into the speakers to having semi-casual chats with me and calling me sweetie. I must have grown on her.

The session had been grueling. I could transfer Light to other Variants without a problem. Yes, it required more concentration, but I'd done it enough that it wasn't that difficult. But none of that was new; all Vitals could do that. What they wanted was for me to use my glowing Light to transfer to Variants outside my Bond *remotely*.

I'd done it at the Melior Group event about a month earlier, so it *was* possible, but I'd been acting on pure adrenaline and survival instinct, not to mention the feral need to protect my Variants. I tried not to think too hard about that night. Doing so made vivid, disturbing images invade my mind—the blood, Alec falling to the floor . . .

I couldn't stand the thought of losing any of them.

Naturally, Melior Group had footage of the whole thing, so Karen and the team had studied it. I'd tried to watch it myself, but as soon as the armed men appeared on the screen, I panicked. The thought of seeing Alec get shot from a whole new angle made bile rise in my throat, and I raced out of the room.

Karen didn't make me watch the rest of the video, but she did push me to try to replicate the transfer.

I was grateful for the push. My own mind was curious about this development, but I was scared to try it again. Left to my own devices, I might have avoided the issue indefinitely.

By the end, I'd managed to draw the Light, get the glow up, and remotely transfer some to a researcher with super hearing on the other side of the room. He smiled wide and pushed his glasses up his nose when my Light hit him. Then, to prove the transfer was successful, he started answering people on the other side of the reinforced concrete wall.

It had taken the entire session to get to that point, and now I was exhausted, drained, and starving. Karen kept our chat brief and shooed me out, sending me in the direction of the cafeteria on the fifth floor.

The elevator stopped on the ground floor, and I found myself face-to-face with Dana. Her blonde hair was up in a neat ponytail, her curvy physique covered, but not hidden, by the signature black uniform.

"Hey," she mumbled around a mouthful as she stepped in. She had a giant burrito clasped in both hands.

"Hey," I told her burrito and licked my lips. It smelled amazing. The elevator doors closed again, and we started moving up.

"Research sesh?" she asked, taking another giant bite.

My mouth filled with saliva, and I had to swallow before answering. "Yup."

"How was it?"

"OK. Long and draining. I'm fucking starving."

Finally she realized I was giving her burrito looks that would make even Ethan blush, and she paused with it halfway to her mouth.

"You're on your way to the cafeteria, right?" She took another bite, protectively angling her body away from me.

"Mmhmm." We were already passing the third floor. Food was minutes away. But all I wanted was that damn burrito.

Dana sighed and rolled her eyes, then wordlessly handed over the burrito.

I snatched it out of her grasp and took a giant bite. It tasted just as good as it looked and smelled—tender beef, crunchy lettuce and corn, and she'd doused it in guacamole and salsa. I moaned right as the elevator doors opened on the busy fifth floor.

Several people paused and turned toward my decidedly sexual noises. I couldn't care less. I took another delicious bite as we stepped off the elevator.

Marcus and Jamie stood a few feet away, shoulder to shoulder, barely containing their grins. Marcus's black hair and dark skin couldn't have contrasted more with Jamie's red hair and pale complexion, but their posture and the slant to their smiles were so similar it was clear they spent a lot of time together.

"You doing chicks now, Dana?" Marcus teased.

"I might be." She shrugged. "What's it to you?"

They laughed, and Jamie answered, "Nothing at all, but her Bond members might have something to say about it."

I rushed to swallow my bite. "Knock it off, or I'm telling Dot you were making rude jokes." They just grinned wider. They knew she wouldn't care—Dot loved a dirty joke. "And anyway, I'm all about the burrito."

I took an exaggeratedly slow bite, moaning and rolling my eyes into the back of my head.

All three of them laughed, and Dana slung an arm over my shoulders. "Keep the fucking burrito. That was gold!"

They got food from the cafeteria, and the four of us sat together as we ate, chatting. Judging by some of the questions Jamie and Marcus asked Dana, they didn't seem to know her that well, which was odd considering she and Alec had seen each other for some time. But Alec and Dana could both be standoffish.

Dana didn't seem to mind the questions and even joked around with us. I hoped this would be the beginning of some new friendships for her; I had a feeling she was lonely, not that she'd ever admit it.

"OK. Back to the strategy meeting. Kyo will have our asses if we're late." Marcus got to his feet.

Jamie groaned. "Why do we have to go to that again?"

"Because Ace can't, and we're stepping in for him."

"What's Alec doing?" Dana asked, picking up everyone's rubbish and dropping it in a nearby trashcan.

Marcus and Jamie looked at me, wary.

"It's OK." I waved them off and held up my shiny badge. "I have clearance now."

"It's not that." Marcus rubbed the back of his neck.

"Come on. We really can't be late." Jamie tugged him along, and they rushed off.

"That was weird." I frowned after them.

Dana shrugged. "Men."

"You heading up? I think I'll have to wait for Tyler to finish some stuff before we can go home."

We stopped at the elevators, and she pushed the down button. "Nah. Heading down."

She gave me a tight smile. Other than the labs, the only thing below ground level were the holding cells. Dana was on Zara duty.

I'd spoken to the guys at length after my chat with Harvey. None of them particularly wanted me around Zara for fear of my physical and emotional safety, but they were fine with whatever I decided.

So far, though, I was still avoiding it.

I sighed, thinking back to just that morning, when Karen had pushed me to deal with another painful thing I could've easily kept avoiding. I was on the other side of that now and better for it. I knew more about my glowing Light, had better control of it. I'd worked hard, and it felt good. By the end I was glad she'd pushed me.

The situation with Zara wasn't remotely the same, but I could feel it festering deep in that dark hole I'd locked her up in, twisting my insides any time it stirred.

The elevator doors opened, and Dana stepped in. She raised her hand to wave goodbye, but before she could say the words, I stepped in after her. Her eyes widened in surprise for a second, but she recovered quickly and pressed the button.

I took a deep breath and pushed it out loudly. Did I really want to do this?

"Wait. Is this a good time? Are you, like, taking her to . . ." *be interrogated? Have a toilet break?* I didn't really know how these things worked, and I was looking for an out.

Dana shook her head. "Now is fine."

"Shit." I took another deep breath. Why was I so nervous about this?

Dana placed a hand on my shoulder and squeezed. Surprisingly, it helped. Knowing she was there, and not on either my side or Zara's, made my fidgeting stop, and I took a few calmer breaths.

After that, we didn't speak. The elevator doors opened, and Dana led the way to an anteroom with several corridors leading off it. I had no clue what differentiated them or what they contained. The only signs above the doors showed series of letters and numbers completely meaningless to me.

Dana went to a door on the right, swiped her access card, and pushed it open. I followed her down a long, brightly lit corridor with heavy steel doors on either side. About halfway up, she stopped in front of one of the doors and turned to me.

"The cells in this corridor are reinforced steel on all sides." She pointed to the roof and ceiling. "Plus, they have an extra layer of a special material that's impenetrable by any Variant ability. It's like a thin, clear plastic. No one can hear anything while these doors are closed, but we monitor these detainees at all times."

She tapped a tablet-sized screen next to the door, and a view of the room beyond appeared. It was exactly as you'd expect a prison cell to be—small bed, desk and chair in one corner, toilet and sink in another—but more modern and clean, everything in shades of gray and white. Zara was on the bed, reading.

I looked away from the screen as Dana continued. "There are seven detainees in this section, and only two of them are considered nonthreatening enough to have regular time outside their cells."

Clearly Zara was one of them. I wondered who the other person was and what they were in for. And what about the other five? What made them so unstable that even having Dana around to neutralize their abilities wasn't enough to deem them nonthreatening? I also wondered what that ability-blocking material was, how they'd developed it, why it wasn't available widely. I was grateful to Dana for giving me all this information; it provided a much-needed distraction from my nervousness and gave me a sense of control.

"When I open the door"—she gestured to the handle

—"there'll be another one behind it made out of the clear material I mentioned. You have clearance to be here and speak with her, but you don't have the training or permission from management to be in the same room as her. You'll have to speak through the membrane."

"Good." I nodded. I still wasn't entirely sure how I would react.

"Ready?" She held her pass poised over the scanner, waiting for my OK.

I nodded. Dana swiped the pass and pulled the door open.

The sound drew Zara's attention, and she dropped the book and sat up, swinging her legs over the side of the bed.

She opened her mouth to say something, probably sarcastic, but she saw me and froze.

For a beat we just stared each other down. She was in blue pants and a gray T-shirt. Her hair was brushed, but it needed a trim and looked messy at the ends. She had no makeup on—no signature dark eyeliner and bold lipstick.

She looked healthy but . . . bare. Stripped of anything that could exhibit individuality. She probably hated that.

Good . . .

After a moment the shock in her eyes was replaced by something much more complex. Sadness, maybe? A hint of longing and . . . something else? Something messy.

She cleared her throat and slowly stood up. "I'd given up hope that you were going to come."

"Well, I'm here now." I crossed my arms. "So get on with it. Say what you have to say so I can get on with my life and forget you ever existed."

"I deserved that." She nodded, moving to the front of the door.

"You think?"

We were close enough to shake hands, the translucent film of ability-resistant material the only thing separating us. The only sign it was there at all was the slight iridescent quality it had and the fact that Zara's voice sounded just a little muffled.

"How have you been, Eve? How are your guys? Dot and Charlie? I heard they got him out." She looked as if she genuinely cared—as if she genuinely wanted to know how I was.

But I knew how well she could fake it. I'd seen it firsthand—right up until she slammed that van door shut.

"As if you give a shit," I spat.

"I deserved that too, I suppose." She sighed. "But I do. Everything was . . ." She made a circular gesture with her head. ". . . twisted. I fucked up. Big time. Like, *epically*. But I do really care, Eve. I'm so sor—"

"Save it!" I rolled my eyes. "You don't honestly expect me to believe that you spent months plotting against me, pretending to care, yet now, all of a sudden it's real? How fucking stupid do you think I am?"

"I wasn't pretending to care, even then. I love you, Eve, and I was incredibly conflicted about what I was doing, unsure about it until the last minute, but . . ."

I just arched a brow, silently showing her my skepticism.

"I've thought about this for so long—what I would say to you, how I would explain and beg for your forgiveness—but it's all coming out wrong."

"Maybe it's coming out wrong because *you're* wrong. There's got to be something seriously fucked up about you that you could do that to someone you called a *friend*. That you could go and join the very people responsible for Beth's death. Have you ever truly cared about anyone in your life?"

I was being cruel, but I needed to say all the things I'd been refusing to acknowledge for months. I didn't think I'd ever see her again; I had to let it all out.

At the mention of Beth's name, anger flared in her eyes and her fists balled up. For the first time, I saw a glimpse of the Zara I knew—the one I'd called my friend.

My heart clenched.

The biggest thing I'd been avoiding was how much I fucking missed her. It hurt *so much*.

I expected her to throw a cutting remark in my face, but the anger crumpled just as fast as it had come. She hung her head as tears streamed down her face.

Next to me, Dana shuffled and crossed her arms loosely. She wasn't particularly comfortable with emotions, and Zara and I were flinging them around with abandon.

Zara sniffed and swiped at her tears. "You're right." Her voice was strained, but she raised her red-rimmed eyes to mine. "Beth would've hated what I did. What I became. She probably would've stopped being my friend a long time ago."

"No, she wouldn't have." I sighed. "Beth was selfless and kind. She would've stuck by you. She would've stuck by us both and made us make up. Maybe none of this would've even happened if she was still around."

"I miss her so much." Zara sobbed.

"Me too," I croaked. I hated myself for it—I didn't want to show her any weakness.

"She always pushed me to be a better person, you know? Even when we were kids. She would've forgiven Rick right away, probably made really good friends with him too."

I chuckled through my tears. She was right. Making the man who'd killed her a friend was exactly the kind of thing she would've done. I didn't get to know him very well before he died, but I had a feeling Rick would've embraced the friendship— would've embraced any opportunity for redemption.

I guess, in a way, he did redeem himself. He'd tried to warn me to be careful, and in the end, he stood up to his parents and sacrificed himself to save his friend. To save Ethan.

Did Zara deserve the opportunity to redeem herself too?

Beth would've wanted me to be kind, to not hold on to resentment, but I just couldn't get past my hurt and anger. Thinking about Rick and that awful night in Thailand brought it all rushing back, as uncontrollable as a hurricane.

"I know Beth would've wanted me to forgive you, but I can't, Zara. You were one of the closest friends I'd ever had. I loved and trusted you, and you betrayed me. You broke . . ." *my trust? Our friendship? My heart?* ". . . so many things."

I ran my hands through my hair and took a step back. I didn't even know what I was saying anymore.

"Wait!" She stepped as close to the doorway as the clear membrane would allow, her eyes puffy and panicked. "Please don't go."

"What else is there to say, Red?"

"Please, I haven't explained about . . . I want to tell you about my parents and the way I was raised and . . . and how angry I was after Beth, and then Davis . . . He's so good at twisting things. And I know—I *know*—none of it excuses what I did, but I wanted to at least *explain* some of it so you would understand."

"I get it." I spread my arms, then let them drop to my sides. "OK? I know about your childhood and your asshole parents. You told me all about it when we were roomies. I know what a manipulative prick Davis is—I know better than anyone what he's capable of. I know how you must've felt after Beth . . . but you know what I can't get over? Why you didn't come to me. Why you didn't confide in me, let me be there for you. I just . . ." I groaned. The tears were welling up again, and I'd had enough. "I can't do this anymore. Let's go."

Dana nodded, nothing but sympathy in her eyes, although I wasn't sure if it was for me or Zara. Probably a bit of both.

"No!" Zara's voice took on an edge of desperation. "Please! Please, Eve, I know I have no right to ask anything of you, but please, take it. Take it away!"

I paused, mainly out of confusion. What the hell was she talking about? "What?"

"I know you can. Your mom could do it, and you glow, so you can do it too. That's why he wanted you—so he could figure out how you take the abilities away. *Please*, take Rick's ability away again. I don't want it anymore. It's not right. It feels *wrong* in every way."

"You want me to . . ." I was stunned. The last thing I'd

expected was for her to ask me that. "Zara, it could kill you. I've never actually done it, and you know what?" There was that anger again, bubbling up like a geyser. "Where do you get off asking me for anything?"

"I know I don't deserve anything from you, but I don't want it. I don't want to be this . . . this . . . *person*. It doesn't belong to me, and I want to give it back."

"You can't give it back. Rick is dead, remember? And you can't ask me to risk taking your life. I may think you're the scum of the earth, but I don't want to be a killer."

I wasn't entirely sure it would kill her. The electricity wasn't Zara's—it was Rick's. I would technically just be removing something that didn't belong in the first place. But I couldn't be sure. Once it was transplanted, perhaps it fused to her Light, to her very essence.

I had no problem defending myself, but I couldn't stand there and deliberately and calculatingly do something that could end a person's life, no matter how mad I was at that particular person.

"You made your bed, Zara." I nodded at the narrow cot in the corner. "It consists of a thin mattress and a scratchy blanket. Now lie in it."

"I don't care if it kills me." Again, her words floored me. She was no longer yelling and pleading; she was calm now, resigned. "I've got nothing left. I'd be better off dead."

She looked broken. Her shoulders were hunched, and silent tears streamed unhindered down her face and neck.

She shuffled slowly back to the cot.

I turned away before she reached it, and Dana softly closed the door.

I walked to the end of the hall, my steps rushed. I needed to give my body something to do—some other reason for my labored breathing.

Dana caught up to me as I reached the door to the anteroom. She placed a gentle hand on my shoulder. "I'm sorry, Eve. I never would've asked you to come if I knew it would be so . . ."

"Fucked up?" I supplied.

"Yeah." She sighed. "She's been so cooperative and pretty much OK. Honest about the shit she's done but accepting responsibility, you know? Never even hinted at suicidal thoughts . . ."

"Is there anything in that room she can use to . . ."

"No. It's strict policy. They're not allowed much."

"Good. Is she allowed other visitors? Like, maybe a psychiatrist? Maybe I should . . ." I looked back down the hallway. It was so long. Impossibly long.

"No." Dana shook her head. "You didn't even have to come see her. This is not your responsibility. She's in Melior Group custody. I'll make sure she gets some help."

I nodded, taking a few deep breaths, and then Dana surprised the hell out of me by pulling me into a hug. "You've got enough on your plate, Eve. I got this."

I held her tightly, not saying anything—partly because if I started talking about this clusterfuck again, I would start crying, but partly because I was a little speechless.

A year ago, even a few months ago, if someone had told me Dana would one day hug me, be there for me, share her burrito with me, I would've figured one or both of us was certifiably insane.

But there we were. Hugging. In a secret underground prison.

"Thank you, Dana," I whispered as we pulled apart.

"Don't mention it." She smiled, swiping her pass to open the door. "Seriously. If you tell anyone I hugged you, I'll kill you."

I laughed—a loud, full-bellied laugh. It was exactly what I needed to lift the heavy weight sitting on my chest, threatening to suffocate me.

Dana was fast becoming one of my favorite people. Who would've thought?

NINETEEN

D ana pulled the door shut just as the one on the opposite side of the anteroom beeped and opened. Alec stepped out, a deep frown pulling at his brows, his shoulders tense.

When he spotted us, he took a deep breath and blew it out of his nose. "What the fuck?"

"What?" Dana crossed her arms and bristled. "Evelyn asked to see her."

"She's not supposed to have visitors, and *she*"—he pointed at me but didn't look—"is supposed to be upstairs with Gabe."

"Zara can speak with anyone with level four clearance and above." Dana lifted her chin. Considering how stubborn they both were, I wouldn't be entirely surprised if this ended in violence. I took a tentative step back.

Alec threw me an incredulous look before dropping his arms. He rubbed his closely cropped hair and dragged his palms down his face. "Let's go."

He didn't look at either of us, but I knew his words were for me. Without waiting for a response, he walked down the corridor.

I looked at Dana and cringed. "Are you in trouble?"

"Nah." She shrugged. "I followed the rules. He can't do shit to me. You, on the other hand . . ."

I rolled my eyes. "Don't worry. I can take it."

She cocked her head to the side. "You're not at all what I first thought you were, Evelyn Maynard."

"Yeah, I'm a real mystery, wrapped in an enigma, dipped in a glow stick." I waved my hand as I walked away from her, trying not to lose sight of Alec as he rounded the corner.

Behind me Dana laughed, and a door beeped as it unlocked.

I jogged to catch up, but Alec was leaning on the wall around the corner, waiting for me. He didn't spare me a glance before swiping his security pass and opening a door next to the elevator. I followed him into the stairwell and groaned. Kane would be proud of all this extra exercise I was getting in.

Alec took the winding stairs two at a time. I had to jog to keep his tense back within view. His hands were in fists, but his butt looked amazing in the tight black uniform—it stretched over his defined glutes with every unnecessarily large step he took.

I was getting puffed and pissed, and I was done chasing him.

"Alec!" I yelled, but he kept walking.

"Alec, stop!" He reached a landing and froze. I was a little glad to see his shoulders were heaving too. Not as bad as mine, but still.

I climbed the last few stairs to reach him and stood at his elbow, looking at his strong profile. "What the fuck is your problem?"

"Really?" He turned to fix me with a scowl. It reminded me of how he used to treat me at the very start—with disdain. I flinched away, but a lot had happened since then, and I was no longer backing down.

"Yes, really. So I went to see Zara! So—"

"I don't give a shit about that!" His deep voice bounced off the concrete walls. "That's your decision to make, and you were safe with Dana."

"Then what the fuck is your problem?" I threw my hands up and let them flop down at my sides.

"Don't pretend you didn't see—like you don't know what I

was doing in that room." His nostrils flared, his posture and expression radiating anger, but I could see something else in his icy eyes too.

"You're pissed because I saw you doing your job?"

"I'm pissed because you saw what I'm capable of." We were chest to chest now, breathing hard and glaring.

"I know what you're capable of. I'm not a fucking idiot. You have a pain ability. You work for a secretive security company that keeps people detained in the basement of their fancy building in Manhattan."

"Evelyn, I just tortured a man," he ground out, as if I still wasn't getting the point.

I sighed in frustration. "Yes, Alec, I'm aware. Do I like it? No, of course not. Torture has been proven to be an ineffective interrogation strategy. According to several studies, 'rapport-based' interrogation techniques, such as finding common ground and demonstrating kindness and respect, are generally the most effective. But I mostly don't like it because I know you hate doing it. But just like you acknowledge that seeing Zara was *my* choice, I acknowledge that you doing this is *your* choice and part of your job. I don't know what the fuck you're so upset about."

"I've read the fucking torture studies, Evelyn, and it's rare that we use 'enhanced interrogation techniques,' but when it's necessary, guess who they ask to do it? Now stop pretending that you're not repulsed by this. That you don't find me abhorrent for doing it. Everyone else does."

"I'm not everyone else, asshole!" I yelled, right into his face. I couldn't help it. But I did manage to lower my volume, if not the level of intensity, for the next part. "I'm Evie. I'm your Vital. I'm completely and irrevocably tethered to you in every conceivable way. I . . ."

The words were at the tip of my tongue, but I couldn't say them. Not like this. Not through gritted teeth and growling tension.

He was feeling like shit about himself again, as if he didn't deserve my understanding and affection. He'd spent his whole life building that wall. My mind got stuck on those three little words I couldn't say, and what else *could* I say? Would he even hear me anyway?

So I decided to *show* him.

I closed the distance, wrapping my arms around his neck and attacking his lips with mine. He grunted and circled his arms around my middle, pushing his tongue into my mouth. He didn't drive me away with his body as he had with his words. Instead he drew me closer, pouring all his rage and frustration and desperate need into that one frantic kiss. I took it all and gave it right back, our hands pawing at each other, his threading into my hair, mine pulling on his shirt.

The sound of a door slamming echoed through the stairwell, and we broke the kiss but still clutched each other. I held his icy stare as the sound of voices and several footsteps reached us from below. It sounded as if we were right in their path.

I groaned in disappointment. No one could get me going as fast as Alec. More and more often when we got into each other's faces, neither of us willing to let our stubbornness go and concede, it would end in frenzied, passionate sex. I couldn't seem to get enough. It was as if I'd psychologically primed myself to associate our bickering and arguing with sex, like some fucked-up version of Pavlov's dog. Pavlov's cock?

It couldn't have been healthy, but that didn't change the fact that I was so ready to go that my abdominal and vaginal muscles were clenching and relaxing in anticipation. How the hell was I supposed to face people in this state?

Apparently Alec didn't want to wait either.

"Fuck it," he growled and grabbed me by the wrist, climbing the few stairs up to the next level. He swiped his access card and pulled me through the door. Most of the fluorescent lights inside were off. The only light came from the "Exit" sign and the flickering indicators on rows and rows of computers stacked on top of each other in glass cabinets.

As soon as the door clicked shut behind us, Alec picked me up and slammed me against the wall next to the door, crashing his lips to mine once again. I looped one arm around his shoulders and put the other at the back of his head, mushing his face closer to mine. Our teeth knocked. I wrapped my legs around his waist and rolled my hips. He rolled his back, and we found a rhythm, grinding against each other as our tongues fought for dominance.

A few torturous minutes later, his hips stilled, and he pulled his mouth from mine.

I made an incoherent sound of protest and shoved against his shoulder. "Alec, what the f—"

"Shh." His hand clapped over my mouth, and he fixed me with a hard look.

Did he just shush me? I frowned, about to claw my way out of his grip, but then he gestured to the door with his head, and I heard voices. It must've been the same people we'd heard earlier. They were making their way past the door, their voices and footsteps muffled.

I understood now why he'd stopped, but I still thought it was unnecessary to hold a hand over my mouth. So I bit him.

He flinched but only slightly, and instead of giving me a disapproving scowl as I'd expected, he smirked at me. The naughty look, coupled with the lust in his hooded eyes, shot another pang of desire straight to my core. As if he felt the rush, Alec started moving his hips again, his arousal rubbing against me through our clothes.

As the voices moved away, my eyes rolled into the back of my head, and I let my jaw go slack under Alec's hand. I panted, feeling an orgasm building. The excitement of doing this somewhere we really shouldn't only heightened every sensation. With my mouth open, it was easy to dart my tongue out and lick his palm. It tasted just a little salty but smelled like soap—clean.

Alec dragged his fingers across my mouth, pulling my lips to the side, then stuck the tip of his finger into my mouth and let it catch on my bottom teeth. I wrapped my lips around it and sucked it in farther, opening my eyes to watch him. He groaned and leaned forward to bite my neck, then immediately licked and kissed the spot to take away the sting.

He removed his finger and replaced it with his tongue. His big hand held my jaw, keeping my head pinned against the wall.

I loved it when he tried to take charge. It made me want to give in to every demand his body made of mine . . . for about a second. Then it made me want to fight him. In the best way possible.

I pushed hard against his shoulders, and he released me, letting me back down to my feet. My lips were throbbing—both of them—so I didn't waste any time getting more of what I wanted.

I had his belt undone in seconds, freeing his hard length and stroking it.

"I want you inside me," I panted.

He groaned and reached under my dress to pull my panties down. I stepped out of my flats and underwear in one go.

A desk chair in the corner caught my attention. It was an old one, on wheels and without armrests. I twisted out of Alec's arms and took the few steps necessary to grab it and spin it around. "Sit."

His eyes narrowed. "You're in my domain now. You don't get to bark orders."

But he pushed his pants down over his hips and sat in the chair anyway. I smirked as I swung one leg over his lap and hovered above him. With my legs wide, I was completely exposed, and another thrill raced up my spine.

Alec dragged a hand up from my knee, over my thigh, and right to the wetness between my legs. He pushed two fingers inside, and I gasped at the sudden intrusion, nearly losing my balance. I held on to his shoulders as he moved his fingers inside me, making me grind my hips against his hand.

But I didn't want to come on his hand. I wanted to come with his cock buried deep inside me. I shoved his hand away and reached for his rock-hard cock, holding it at the base. I teased myself with the tip, moving it up and down my folds, before sinking down onto him.

He let out a growl that ended in a moan, leaning forward to lick my lips. His big hands held me tight against him, his legs spreading wide under me.

I didn't give either of us a chance to adjust, to get used to the heady sensation of complete connectedness—of feeling, seeing, hearing, breathing nothing but the other person. I started moving on top of him, rolling my hips as I used my legs to push up and down.

I was on top. I was supposed to set the pace, but Alec fought me. His strong hands had a firm grip on my hips, and we once again battled for control. Eventually the battle settled into a dance —a hard, intense dance that had his cock sliding in and out of me, hitting a spot deep inside.

It wasn't long before the orgasm bubbled up again. It had been building since the frenzied kiss on the stairs. I'd been close when he'd had me against the wall, grinding into me. I'd been close when he'd buried his fingers inside me and played me like a stringed instrument. And I was fucking close as I bounced and ground on top of him.

He shoved one of his hands up my dress, pulling my bra out of the way to knead my breast.

The combined sensations, coupled with the knowledge that someone could walk in at any moment, had me crying out as I finally gave in to the climax. It washed over me, making my vision blur as every muscle in my body tensed. I rocked against him and bit his neck, hard, and he responded with a grunt that sounded like a mixture of pain and pleasure. I relaxed some of the pressure of my teeth and licked the skin between them.

Alec's hips were still rocking under me, his movements erratic and desperate. I used his shoulders to balance and, with shaky legs, met his movements with mine, bringing him to release.

He did that sexy as fuck growling moan again as his head dropped back and his chest heaved.

After a few moments, he pulled me against him and buried his head in my neck. I nuzzled his jaw and smiled. This was exactly what we needed. We started out shouting at each other and getting riled up, frustrated, hurt. And we ended up in each other's arms, planting soft kisses all over each other's faces, caressing and holding and showing our devotion.

After one last lingering kiss to my lips, Alec craned his neck, then used his legs to push the wheelie chair over to a side table with a box of tissues. It was only once I had a wad of tissues in my hand that he let me up. We cleaned up as best we could and started fixing our clothes.

"Is there a bathroom on this level? I don't want to get a UTI." I looked around—all I saw were rows and rows of servers.

Alec chuckled as he zipped up his pants. "Don't know. But the level above does."

"Don't laugh, you dick. UTIs hurt like a . . ." I caught sight of a camera near the ceiling, high up in a corner.

"Alec!" I hurriedly pulled my underwear up the rest of the way and fixed my dress.

"What?" His attention was on his phone.

"There's a fucking camera?" I gestured to the item, my tone half question, half chastisement.

He glanced at it and then smirked at me. "We're in the most secure area of the most secure building in Manhattan—except maybe the cells below. Of course there are cameras, precious."

"Fuck. Alec!" How was he so relaxed about this? Yes, the *risk* of getting caught had given me a thrill, but I didn't actually want strangers to watch me having sex. The other guys, maybe . . .

Alec wrapped an arm around my shoulders. "Relax. I'm on it."

He put the phone to his ear, and I covered my face with my hands, leaning into him. I was close enough to hear the ringing on the other end and Charlie's voice as he answered. "What's up, dickhead?"

"Hey, jerk-off." Alec's teasing tone turned serious in the very next word. "I need you to make some security footage disappear."

"Shoot."

"HQ. Main server room on subbasement level 1. The past twenty minutes should do it."

Charlie sighed. "Seriously? Do you have any idea the kind of security I have to get through?"

"You saying you can't do it?"

"No!" Charlie sounded outraged. "Of course I can do it. I'm just saying it won't be easy and you owe me one."

"Good. Also, I need you to do it without looking at the footage."

There was a pause on the other end. "Alec, what's going on?"

At his worried tone, I piped in. "Hey, Charlie."

"Eve?"

"Yeah. Don't stress, OK? He's just trying to prevent some poor Melior Group minion from getting an eyeful of my bare ass."

There was another pause, and then Charlie started laughing, big infectious guffaws that had Alec and I both chuckling despite ourselves.

When he finally calmed down, he spoke between giggles. "You two horny fuckers are lucky I'm in the building. This would be way harder if I was trying to do it remotely, and the fact that . . . hmmm."

Alec stiffened, his arm around me tightening. "Charlie?"

"Meet me in Gabe's office." The line went dead.

"Shit." Alec pocketed the phone and led the way to the elevator.

As we stepped inside, I took his hand and gave him a worried look. "Alec? What's going on?"

"Nothing good. Gabe's office is soundproofed and the only place we can speak freely." He gave me a pointed look, and I pressed my lips together.

As we walked through the halls and past offices and desks, it suddenly felt as if every person was watching us, every wall had someone on the other side listening in.

We reached Tyler's door at the same time Charlie did. He was dressed simply in black jeans and a gray sweater, a laptop tucked under his arm, his expression blank.

We let ourselves in without knocking. Tyler lifted curious eyes at the intrusion, took in our serious expressions, and stood up from his chair.

Alec locked the door as Charlie dropped the laptop on Tyler's desk and propped his hands on his hips.

Tyler didn't speak. Didn't ask unnecessary questions. He just let Charlie talk.

"Something's not right. When I went in to get rid of the server room footage, I noticed something off."

"In what way?" Tyler pressed. He didn't question the fact that Charlie was erasing security footage, which made me wonder how often he did this for them. How many secrets did they have?

"I'm not the only one that's been in the system, which isn't surprising in itself, but I'm the only one that goes in and out undetected. The others I can track. I can see what they've done, changed, erased. With enough digging, I can find out who it was. But I think I just found evidence of someone else—someone as discreet as me."

"What?" Tyler's eyes widened as he leaned on the desk. "Do we have a breach? Should I be initiating protocols?"

"It's not that simple."

"What do you mean?"

"I need to do a little more digging, but so far, from what I can see, they're not taking anything. They're not copying data, trying to access the encrypted files. They're doing the same thing I was doing—deleting security footage, maybe security pass logs as well."

Behind me, Alec cursed under his breath.

"It doesn't make sense. It's like they're trying to cover their tracks, but they haven't actually done anything."

"It makes perfect fucking sense," Alec growled. He and Tyler exchanged a hard look.

Tyler hung his head and sighed. "This is worse than an external attack, a hacking attempt. This sounds like an inside job."

"Fuck." Charlie sank into a chair and dropped his head into his hands. "I wouldn't have even seen it if these two hadn't decided to have a quickie in the server room and needed me to cover it up."

Tyler shot us an amused look before getting back to business. "All right. Charlie, I need you to keep digging—get me as much information as you can. You have complete access to my office. From now on, we work under the assumption that this building is no longer secure. Keep this between us. Stick to the secure channels—text only. And we discuss this in secure rooms. That's this office, my office at Bradford Hills Institute, and my study at the manor. Alec, update Uncle Luce when you get back. I'm going to fill in Ethan and Josh, but Charlie, I think we should keep Dot out of it."

"Agreed." Charlie's focus was already on his screen, his fingers flying across the keyboard.

"I think you can trust Dot, guys. She wouldn't blab about something like this." I crossed my arms. Keeping things from people was kind of a sore spot for me.

"It's not that we don't trust her." Tyler smiled at me warmly. "It's that it's safer if she's kept out of it. For her."

Grudgingly, I nodded. I'd happened to be right next to Alec when this all happened, but would they have told me had I not been? I had the clearance now. Tyler would certainly have discussed it with me had I pressed for information, but they would've probably preferred to keep me out of it, just like Dot. Because it was "safer."

Well, I was there, and I did hear. I couldn't undo that. All I could do was focus on the issue at hand and try to be useful if I could be. All I could do was prove they didn't need to keep hiding things to protect me.

TWENTY

I'd been to Dot and Charlie's house dozens of times. I'd had sleepovers with Dot, been around for dinner, hung out with Olivia and Henry. Yet as we drove in Tyler's Escalade toward their house, a bit of nervousness still twisted my gut.

Josh took my hand. "What's going on?"

I glanced toward the front—Ty and Alec were engaged in a soft conversation as Tyler drove through the leafy streets of Bradford Hills.

"I don't know." I shrugged. "I'm just a little nervous. It feels really . . . formal or something?"

"It's just dinner." Josh squeezed my hand. "There just happens to be more of us tonight."

We were on our way to Sunday dinner. Lucian and Ethan were being driven in the car behind us, a Melior Group vehicle with armed guards led the way, and one brought up the rear. Jamie and Marcus had to work, but Kyo was going to be there too, representing Dot's harem for the night. She'd been referring to each of the men as her "boyfriend," and none of them were seeing other people. It wasn't uncommon for Variants to be in polyamorous relationships, but whenever I asked her how it was going with them, she insisted they "weren't putting a label on it." I called bullshit every time. They worshipped the ground she walked on, and now Kyo was coming to family dinner—shit was getting serious.

When we pulled up, the big metal gates opened to admit the cavalcade of cars, and we drove to the main house.

As the driver of the car behind us lowered Lucian in his wheelchair, we all headed toward the front door. Another pang of nervous uncertainty shot through me—should we knock?

Ethan bounded up the stairs, beating us all there, and let himself straight in. He left the door wide open as he disappeared toward the kitchen, yelling about basting the turkey or something. I chuckled, some of the tension easing. He'd really wanted to do the cooking but had to work on an assignment, and Olivia had ended up having the dinner catered.

We spilled into the large kitchen and dining area, everyone saying hello and hugging. Henry uncorked several bottles of wine, and Alec handed me a glass.

"Thanks." I smiled and brought it to my lips. I'd never really had wine and wasn't sure if I liked it, but as the burgundy liquid hit my tongue, I moaned a little in surprise and appreciation.

Alec smirked at me. "I'm starting to think you have expensive taste."

"Why?" I took another sip.

"That's a Chateau Margaux Merlot." When I gave him a blank look, he elaborated. "It's, on average, one hundred and fifty dollars per bottle, depending on vintage."

"Holy shit." My eyes widened at the unassuming liquid in my glass, and Alec took a slow sip of his own.

After a moment I shrugged and kept drinking. I hadn't grown up with drivers and houses with bedrooms in the double digits, but they *had*, and there was nothing wrong with enjoying the finer things in life. Galileo knows, we'd all had enough shit to deal with —we deserved it.

"We used to do this every Sunday when we were kids." Alec had one hand in his pocket, the other holding his wine glass as he looked out over the room of laughing, talking people—our family.

I frowned. "I thought Olivia and Henry didn't move here until after my mom and I left?"

"They didn't." Alec wrapped an arm around my middle in an uncharacteristically sweet gesture, and I melted into his side.

It was Lucian who answered me. He pulled his wheelchair up beside us and gave me a warm smile. "Your mom was close with my sisters and Josh's and Tyler's mothers. They were all like a big family by the time I moved back here from the UK. The Sunday dinners were a regular occurrence. It was actually at a Sunday dinner that we first met—that we first realized we were connected."

I sat down on the arm of the couch so I could see him better, and Alec's arm moved from my waist to my shoulders.

Lucian kept speaking. "The dinners were a bit more somber after you and your mother left, and then the accident in Japan . . ."

"We stopped doing the dinners after our parents died," Alec finished for him. "It used to be, like, twenty people, massive amounts of food, and all kinds of ruckus. Then all of a sudden, it was just us. It wasn't the same."

"Olivia and Henry moved back a few months after that. The plan was for Alec and Ethan to move in with them, but by that stage all the boys were staying with me, and they didn't want to be separated." Lucian gave Alec the kind of nostalgic look a father might give his son. "But we did pick the Sunday dinners back up. It was more sporadic than it had been before, but even when Alec and Tyler were hanging around The Hole, getting their asses beat, they showed up for the dinners. They sulked and hardly spoke to anyone, but they still showed up."

"Maybe we can make it a more regular thing now," Alec mused.

Olivia and Ethan were in the kitchen, helping the catering

team finish off the food preparation. Josh was deep in conversation with Charlie, and Henry and Dot and Tyler were looking at family pictures on the wall.

It was so . . . domestic—and a little foreign to me. Or maybe it was the entire concept of family that was foreign. Maybe that's why I'd been so nervous in the car. I still wasn't entirely sure how to be part of a family.

"Sorry I'm late!" Kyo rushed into the room, and Dot practically bounced over to him, giving him a kiss hello that was just on the border of too intimate for a family gathering. He greeted everyone just as the food was ready, and we sat down at the big dining table.

As we ate the amazing food and drank more bottles of the delicious, expensive wine, I relaxed. We may have been a large group, but I knew and was comfortable with each and every person at this table. The conversation flowed as easily as the wine.

By the time we were ready for dessert, we were all wiping tears from our faces as Kyo told a story of how a mobster's spoiled daughter fell head over heels in lust with Alec when they were infiltrating the operation. She hadn't even been deterred by the fact that he kept "accidentally" zapping her with pain any time she tried to touch him or go in for a kiss.

"Do you have any idea how hard it was to keep a straight face?" Kyo said between bursts of laughter as Dot leaned her head on his shoulder and completely lost it. "You got this constipated look every time she walked into a room."

Alec scowled through the whole thing, but I could see his shoulders start to shake and his lips twitch from keeping the laughter in.

After everyone's giggles subsided, the conversations became a bit more subdued. Ethan leaned forward, draping an arm over the back of my chair and speaking to Tyler on my other side. "Do you think there'll be time to go to the fish markets in Tokyo? I really want to try some fresh tuna sushi."

Mr. Takata had been in touch. He'd visited with his grandmother, but the older woman had simply smiled and asked to see me. He was extremely apologetic, but he was stuck between his duty to respect his elders and his newly declared fealty to me.

Now we were trying to find time to plan a trip, but between classes, demanding work schedules, and security concerns, it wasn't easy.

Tyler shrugged, spinning his empty wine glass on the spot with his dexterous fingers. "Don't know. We'll have to play it by ear."

"Have you not been to Japan?" I asked, my cheeks still a little flushed from the laughter and the wine. "The food is incredible!"

My big guy surprised me by answering silently, with a sad nod of his head. He started playing with the corner of a cloth napkin, his eyes not meeting mine.

I frowned and turned to Tyler, but he was watching his wine glass with a look very similar to Ethan's. Confused, I searched for answers across the table. Alec's hands were clasped in front of him, his brows furrowed and his eyes fixed on the table. Next to him, Josh was the only one meeting my gaze, understanding in his eyes, as always, but also sadness.

The whole room had fallen silent, but Josh put me out of my misery. He cleared his throat. "Our parents were killed in Japan. In Tokyo."

My heart sank. "I am so sorry for bringing it up."

"You didn't, baby." Ethan's hand went to the back of my neck. "I did."

"A lot of people died that day." Henry spoke up from the head of the table. He held Olivia's hand as she discreetly wiped away a tear. "It was tragic."

"Yeah, it was all over the news, even here," Lucian added. "Joyce had just arrived there and then went radio silent. Those were the worst twenty-four hours of my life, thinking I'd lost half my family *and* both of you too."

I gasped, my eyes going wide. "Holy shit! I remember this. I was only eight years old, and we were in Tokyo for, like, a day, and then this awful *thing* happened, and next thing I know we're on a train out of there. Were you guys all there? Were we mere streets from each other?"

Alec remained silent, his eyes still glued to the table in front of him, but Tyler answered. "We'd crossed the street—the four of us. We were ahead of them and just made the crossing signal, but they had to stop. If they'd called out, made us wait with them . . . or if they'd rushed to catch up with us . . ."

Josh picked up where Ty left off. "We were thrown to the ground and knocked unconscious, but they all . . ." He cleared his throat again. "I don't remember it. I was told all of it when I woke up in the hospital, but they were all killed pretty much instantly."

The room once again descended into tense silence. No one made eye contact with anyone else. Dot and Charlie looked from their parents to Lucian to my guys with just as much curiosity as compassion in their eyes. I had a feeling no one had spoken much about this before, and they probably didn't know all the details.

Before I could make an awkward attempt at changing the subject, Alec spoke. "It was like all the sound was sucked out of the air, and there was a split second of perfect stillness—everyone paused, knowing something wasn't right but not knowing what. Then I felt this . . . surge. Like something crawling over my skin but also *through* me—something intense and powerful. And then the world just . . . exploded. There was fire and shit floating around in the air—like cars and concrete bolsters. Everyone just dropped. Fell to the ground and never got up again. I was thrown down with the others, but I didn't get knocked out. My cheek was pressed into the concrete." He lifted a hand to his face absent-mindedly, ghosting his fingers over his skin. "And I lay there, and I watched the life drain out of my mother's eyes."

Tears pricked at my eyes as my heart broke clean in half for him. For all of them. Images of the last time I'd seen my own mother attacked my mind—her hand slipping out of mine, her terrified yet surprised face. That image would haunt me for the rest of my life. Knowing my guys were dealing with that same pain—that they knew exactly what that felt like—just twisted the knife.

Yet in some perverted way, it also felt good. The fact that all four of them had experienced the same depth of pain and loss I had made me feel even closer to them. It was yet another thing threading us closer together, strengthening our relationship and Bond.

Our Bond . . .

I gasped, my hands flying to my mouth as the tears spilled over, trailing messy, wet paths down my cheeks and over my fingers.

Alec finally broke his stare-off with the table to look at me, Ethan dropped his arm to my shoulders, and Tyler gripped my knee, leaning forward to look into my face.

"Let's stop talking about it for a while." For once Josh hadn't picked up on what was really happening; he assumed the topic of conversation had upset me. He wasn't entirely wrong, but I was also coming to a realization that made bile rise in the back of my throat.

I shook my head. A sob escaped from between my fingers before I finally forced the words out. "You were all there. And I was there. And your abilities can't harm each other because of me. And *I* was there. And . . . and I can transfer Light remotely. But I'm not . . . I don't remember glowing, but maybe I did. What . . ." I couldn't hold back another sob, dropping my head into my hands. "What if I did this? What if I killed . . ."

I couldn't get the word out, couldn't fully voice that I may have been responsible for the deaths of their parents, not to mention all those other people. I couldn't shake the feeling that my proximity to them had resulted in a massive transfer of Light that they couldn't control. What if their abilities going haywire had caused all the destruction . . . and the death?

"Eve. No." Tyler squeezed my knee. "Think this through. Our abilities can't harm each other now—now that we have you and the Bond has formed. Before that we were definitely able to hurt each other with our abilities. Trust me."

"You didn't do this." Josh's hands landed on my shoulders. I hadn't even heard him get up. "It's not likely you were able to glow at such a young age. You said yourself you'd never experienced it before."

"Yes, but it has happened. Even Lucian"—I gestured in his general direction—"told me I'd glowed once or twice as a kid."

Lucian piped in, reminding me we were still in a room full of people—people whose family I may very well have killed. "Evelyn, that was nothing like what you can do now. It was a flicker of a glow at best, enough for us to know what you were but not enough to do anything with it."

"Yeah, but—" My chair was suddenly yanked backward. The guys' hands disappeared from my knee, shoulder, and neck as I was spun around to face Alec's furious gaze. He lowered himself to his knees, putting his face level with mine and planting his hands on either side of the chair's seat.

I stared at him, expecting him to go back to hating me but really just wanting him to take me into his arms. He did neither.

"Evie, I don't know what the fuck happened that day, but I'm sure as fuck not going to blame an eight-year-old kid. It may've taken me a while to get there, but I'm so glad to have you in my life, baby. Please don't do this to yourself."

"How can you live with even the *possibility* that it may've been my fault, Alec? How can I live with that? How long before you start looking at me with that derisive, mean look again. I can't take that again."

"Evie, please . . ." His thumbs rubbed my hips as his eyes flew about the room, looking for help.

"I really didn't want to bring this up yet"—Lucian's resigned yet determined tone drew everyone's attention—"but we may potentially have some new information on that day."

I had to turn in my chair to see him properly. He was leaning back in his wheelchair, a worried expression on his face.

"Luce?" Olivia looked confused, but there was no denying the hint of fear in her wide eyes. "What is this about?"

"We don't have the full picture yet, and I'm technically not meant to reveal this, as it's classified." He eyed Dot and her parents—the only people in the room without clearance. "But I can't let this go on any further. We've all suffered enough at that man's hands."

Alec's arms stiffened around me, and I leaned into him, angling my body so I could see Lucian better.

"Evelyn, that was in no way your fault. It was a complete coincidence that you and Joyce were there. In Sweden, where you were staying previously, you were discovered by one of Davis's men, and your mom had to get you out immediately. She didn't get in touch until the next day to tell me where you were, and I didn't receive the message in time to tell her that the others were in Japan on holiday, that she needed to leave immediately. By the time I saw her message and replied, she was already offline."

"Lucian, what do you know?" To my surprise, Ethan growled the demand, but my big guy was prone to anger when really pushed. I held his hand in both of mine as Lucian got to the point.

"We never knew what happened. The local police got there before we could get any of our people out. They cooperated with us, but we couldn't find anything definitive. It was only after Thailand that we found some evidence on a hard drive . . . Davis has offices all over the world—that's not a secret—and he had a building in Tokyo. Apparently he had a lab in the basement levels. Not much on the drive we recovered was salvageable, but there is enough to suggest he was running experiments even then. We have no way to prove it, but the logical conclusion is that whatever he was doing down there went horribly wrong and resulted in the chaos and death above ground."

"Why haven't you said anything?" Despite his hard tone, Tyler sounded hurt.

"The techs only just delivered their report two days ago," Lucian explained. "They're still trying to get more information from the drive, and we're nowhere near done going through all that we found in Thailand. He did a good job destroying most of it with the explosions, but we were able to recover a decent amount of evidence. Anyway, I was never planning to keep it from any of you. I'm done keeping secrets from my family." He gave me a meaningful look. Memories of the night we'd stood on his balcony drinking scotch flickered through my mind. "I just wanted to give the techs another day or two to see if they could find anything more. I didn't want to bring it up during this evening, but I can't sit here and watch Evie blame herself for something that was not her fault."

"Thank you." I wiped the tears from my cheeks.

Rather than unleash a barrage of questions, the guys had all gone silent and introspective. If they were anything like me when it came to talking about their parents' deaths, I couldn't blame them.

After a few tense moments, a chair scraped loudly and Dot stood up.

"How about some dessert?" She smiled, but it didn't reach her eyes. The others all murmured their agreement, and Alec and Josh returned to their seats.

"I'll help you." Charlie followed Dot into the kitchen.

Henry grabbed the open bottle of wine from the buffet, refilling glasses until it was all gone, then opening another bottle. Dot and Charlie delivered individual servings of tiramisu to everyone, and conversation got back to normal. It wasn't as lively as earlier, but the heavy emotions had lifted.

I sat back and sipped on my third glass of expensive red, my tiramisu half-eaten. Lucian's last few words kept repeating in my mind.

I can't sit here and watch Evie blame herself for something that was not her fault.

No matter how I looked at it, that statement didn't sit right, didn't ring true. I wasn't completely blameless. I couldn't escape the fact that at least some of this was my fault.

I hadn't set out to hurt anyone, hadn't asked to be born this way, with this much Light and connected to such powerful Variants. I would never intentionally hurt anyone.

But at the end of the day, Davis was doing all this precisely because of what I was. He lied, manipulated, and tortured people in his dogged mission to figure out how my Light worked—so he could exploit it for money and power. He'd driven my mother and me from our home and family, from our Vital Bonds. He'd practically started a war between Variants and humans in an attempt to gain more power.

As I sat at the table with my new family, I looked at each one of them. We'd all lost people because of him.

I had two choices.

I could down another bottle of wine, wallow in my self-flagellating misery, and fall deeper into depression.

Or I could fight. I could do whatever I could to show that, despite the fact that my glowing Light could be dangerous, it could be *good* too. Even though I couldn't fully understand it yet, I firmly believed my glowing was a tool. It would only be a negative destructive force if I chose to use it that way.

I couldn't fight Davis with guns and abilities and secrets—Alec, Tyler, and Lucian had that covered. But I could do what I did best: figure out the puzzle. I had to get to the bottom of why I glowed, and I couldn't do it on my own.

It was time to reach out to some of the people who claimed to be able to glow as I did. It was time to put my mind to figuring this shit out.

"We *need* to go to Japan," I announced.

Tyler stopped midsentence to turn to me. His cheeks were a little rosy; the wine was probably getting to him. "Sorry?"

I cleared my throat and raised my voice. "We need to go to Japan. I need to speak to Mr. Takata's grandmother myself. And,

Charlie, I need help determining which of those messages I've been receiving are legit and safe to reply to."

"Done." Charlie nodded, not hesitating or questioning me at all. Most likely he'd secretly already started looking into it.

When I looked across the table, Josh had a little smirk pulling at the corner of his lips, his knowing eyes full of pride.

TWENTY-ONE

As usual I lost track of time at the library. It was nearly dusk when I emerged, but when I checked my phone, I was relieved to see I hadn't missed any calls—*Tyler must still be in his office working late.*

My security detail for the day was a young guy with brown hair and a baby face. He'd reluctantly told me his name early in the day and then resisted any further attempts at conversation, insisting on remaining one step behind me wherever I went. That's exactly what he continued to do as I turned my steps toward the admin building.

I hefted my heavy bag higher on my shoulder. The agent didn't offer to help carry anything, and checking out that last book had probably been a mistake. With a statistics assignment due just before we took off for Japan next week, I wouldn't have time to read about the emergence of technology-related Variant abilities anyway. My yawn turned into a groan and my steps slowed. Despite the sun setting, the temperature remained high and sticky. At least with summer in full swing, there weren't as many people on campus. I'd almost had the library to myself.

The lights lining the leafy walking path came on. Dusk was

beginning to cast a quiet gray light over everything, throwing twisted shadows from the tall trees.

As I made my way past the cafeteria—which was lit up brightly, bustling with students having their dinner—a couple came out, swinging their own bags over their shoulders. I flashed them a polite smile, but they were caught up in their conversation and didn't see me.

The most direct way to the admin building was down another tree-lined path that cut through the grounds and weaved behind some of the residence halls. Readjusting my bag yet again, I threw the agent a withering look. He just stared at me, his face completely blank.

A few feet along the path, I noticed the couple from the cafeteria heading in the same direction. I could hear their chatter, the occasional light laugh. I looked over my shoulder, making sure they had enough room to pass us if they wanted to.

I made eye contact with the girl and gave her another smile. She was wearing a cute scarf with French Bulldogs all over it and a flowy dress. This time, there was no question she saw my smile, but she still didn't return it. She just watched me with a slight frown as the guy continued to speak to her, his voice low. I faced forward and wrapped both hands around the strap of my bag.

What's her problem? She was probably one of Ethan's exes. They'd significantly backed off when it became known I was his Vital, but some of them were still salty.

I tried to put it out of my mind and think about the pasta waiting for me at home, but when their chatter turned to whispers and then complete silence, a cold chill shot down my spine. I attributed it to the sudden gust of wind, which made the branches above dance grotesquely, but still found my steps speeding up. My emotionless shadow matched my pace.

Any fatigue I'd been feeling was chased away by adrenaline. I looked at my agent again, letting my worry and uncertainty show. He kept his stern gaze fixed ahead and didn't even meet my eye. I eyed his gun and told myself this was why he was here—to protect me if anyone tried anything—but the unsettling feeling wouldn't go away.

All my senses were on alert, my ears listening for any little sound, but I dared not turn around again. As my steps almost doubled in speed, I could clearly hear theirs keeping pace behind me.

We rounded a bend, and the brightly lit square and a corner of the admin building came into view past the trees.

"What makes you think you get to decide who can have Variant abilities and who can't?" a deep male voice growled from behind me.

My heart flew into my throat as the female voice added her own hateful words. "You arrogant bitch!"

Instead of telling them to back off or putting himself between us, my supposed protector *chuckled*.

I didn't think, didn't turn around to argue, didn't even falter in my steps. I just dropped my bag and books and took off running.

My sparring may not have been advancing as well as Kane wanted, and my upper body strength still left much to be desired, but I could *run*. I'd been doing it for years, and it was one thing I had confidence in. I took off so fast and so suddenly that I halved the distance to the end of the path in no time.

But just as fast as I'd taken off, I ground to a halt. Something wrapped around my ankle, and I flew forward. My palms and cheek slammed against gravel.

I didn't focus on the pain shooting through my wrists and head or the fact that all the air had been pushed out of my lungs. I immediately started pushing myself up.

But once again I found myself flying—this time up instead of down. Whatever had wrapped itself around my ankle snaked up my leg and banded around my middle, lifting me clear off the ground until my feet hung below me uselessly.

I thrashed and wriggled as a scream tore through my throat.

Desperate, I reached for my distress beacon necklace, but as my hand closed around it, another two branches snatched my wrists and yanked my arms behind me.

I was being restrained by the very grounds of Bradford Hills Institute—tree branches, vines, and shrubs moved like tentacles on a sea monster to hold me hostage.

Tyler's name came out on a screech. He was the closest, in his office in the building I could see *right there*, but I had no idea if he'd be able to hear me.

"Would you shut her up?" the agent growled, his youthful features twisted with hate.

The girl took her scarf off and handed it to the other guy, who rushed up to me. He had to reach up, but his rough hands tied the scarf around my head, the light fabric shoved into my mouth.

The chick wasn't saying much. The muscles in her forearms strained as she held her hands out in front of her, teeth gritted, panting. Clearly, she had some kind of plant-control ability similar to Dot's animal control—the flora to Dot's fauna—but it didn't seem as though either of the guys was her Vital. She looked as if she was using all she had to hold me up. Impressive, to be sure, but I didn't know how long she could maintain it without a Light boost.

The Light!

I gasped. I wasn't completely powerless, despite being bound and gagged.

I dared not close my eyes for fear of missing what their next move might be, but I concentrated as hard as I could, tapping into my own Light deep inside me.

I was going to drain that bitch of every last drop until she released me.

"Shit!" The guy who'd gagged me threaded his hands into his hair, panic evident in his wide eyes. "What the fuck do we do with her now?"

The agent answered. "We get her to Damari so he can fix us."

"How? Do we knock her out? How do we even get her past the guards at the gate? How do we even contact Damari? I don't know him personally, do you? And what about . . ."

"Shut the fuck up!" said the agent. "I'll take care of the guys at the gate, and we can worry about the rest after. Just help me find something to tie her up with. Elena can't hold her forever."

I bit down on the scarf and narrowed my eyes. Just as I began to glow, footsteps came thudding toward us.

I kept my focus on the Variant in front of me, letting my instincts take over and latching on to her distinct energetic signature. Then I *pulled*.

She gasped, her eyes going wide, and wrapped her hands around her middle, as if the action could hold the Light in. But it was at my mercy; she was powerless to stop me now.

The branch around my middle loosened, making it easier to breathe, and the vines circling my wrists were no longer cutting off circulation.

I'd never pulled Light like this before—from a single, direct source that wasn't one of my Bonded Variants. Sure, I'd pulled it from other Variants in Davis's lab and in the gun fight as Alec lay dying at my feet, but those times I'd simply pulled from all directions, letting the Light drain anyone it recognized as a threat.

This was different—it was personal. I wasn't trying to boost my guys' powers, to give us the upper hand in a life-or-death situation. I was using my glowing ability as a *weapon*, homing in on the one person who posed the biggest threat to me and coaxing the Light right out of her.

It was almost too easy.

She fell to her knees and sat back on her heels, folding in on herself. Her arms stayed wrapped around her middle.

As several Melior Group guards ran toward us, she completely lost her grip on her ability. The branches and vines detangled and retreated slowly.

The guards had their guns drawn, yelling at everyone to get

down on the ground, but they didn't seem sure of whom to point the weapons at.

On the one hand, it looked as if I was being attacked, but on the other, I was glowing like fucking plutonium as the plant life lowered me to my feet. Meanwhile, the agent who'd turned on me was yelling that I needed to be restrained, confusing the crap out of his colleagues.

The girl—Elena—wavered and toppled to the ground.

"No!" I shouted, dread crawling up my spine to grip my throat. I shut my glow down immediately and stopped pulling Light from her.

I'd wanted to defend myself—I couldn't just hang there and let them kidnap me. It was never my intention to kill her.

I rushed forward, but a black-clad woman stepped into my path, pointing a gun at my chest. "Do not move!"

I froze and put my hands up, but I shifted from foot to foot, my darting eyes trying to take it all in, trying to see if I'd just killed someone.

One agent had a gun trained on me, and the other was checking to see if Elena was OK. When she coughed and moaned, I breathed a shaky breath of relief as my tears spilled over.

Other people started pouring onto the narrow path from both ends, drawn by the shouts and commotion. The two agents were struggling to maintain control of the situation.

"She's the dangerous one!" Elena's friend gestured to me, his other hand in a fist by his side. "We should be tying her the fuck up. Handing her over to Davis Damari. Don't you assholes want abilities?"

"I'm human, dumbass!" another guy shouted.

People started yelling over one another, ignoring the firm demands of the armed guards to remain calm and step back. Some of the Variants seemed to know the couple, and most of them wanted my head—or my Light, as it were.

As more and more people piled into the tight space between

the trees, it started to feel like the beginnings of a mob. *Someone should really run and get the torches and pitchforks.*

I took tentative steps back, the leaves and twigs crunching under my feet, as the angry, arguing crowd closed in. More guards arrived, but short of firing weapons, there wasn't much they could do to stop what was fast turning into a riot.

A Variant with super speed blurred through the crowd, and I suddenly found myself restrained once again, my wrists in a tight grip and my shoulders pulled back.

People in the crowd cheered, started pushing forward.

The guard pointing a gun at me faltered, looking between me and my captor with uncertainty. "Everyone calm the fuck down and step back!"

But the yells and angry words of the crowd drowned out her voice. Scuffles began to break out.

"Let me go or I'll drain you," I growled, doing my best to look at the asshole holding me. I caught a glimpse of stubble, a sneering mouth. "I'll drain you like I drained her."

He hesitated, the hands around my wrists loosening just a fraction, but then he yanked me back roughly.

Whatever he was about to say was interrupted by a deafening roar behind us. The crowd immediately quieted down, looking around warily and shuffling backward.

The roar came again, louder, closer. But I couldn't turn to see what was making the terrifying sound. My latest captor finally released me, turning to face the new threat.

The sound of snapping twigs and branches mingled with yet another growl as two towering, dark shapes moved through the shadowed trees.

At the same time the grizzly bears came into the light, Dot and Charlie stepped forward between them, their hands clasped. One of the bears reared up on its hind legs, making us all crane our necks, as the other let out another deafening growl, showing its lethal teeth and jaws.

More fearful shuffling and a few terrified shouts came from

behind me, but for the first time, I wasn't scared. These were Dot's animals; there was no way they would hurt me. I looked into my short friend's fierce eyes and gave her a tiny, shaky nod of thanks. She smiled, dropping her death glare, but it was Charlie who spoke.

"Anyone who does not wish to get mauled by a bear tonight should kindly back the fuck away." His voice was calm and even, his free hand in the pocket of his black pants.

Tyler's voice, on the other hand, was full of barely restrained anger. "Why is there a gun pointed at my Vital?"

I turned to see him standing only feet away, his full focus on the agent whose weapon was still trained on me. His jaw was clenched, his hands in tight fists.

I had an intense urge to run to him, feel his comforting arms around me, bury my face in his neck and ignore this whole fucked-up situation. But I stayed back, knowing he needed to take charge and not wanting to distract him.

"I . . . I'm just . . . she was . . ." The agent's wide eyes flicked from me to him uncertainly.

"Agent, lower your weapon. That is a direct order," Tyler barked.

Immediately, she dropped the gun and stood at attention, her lips in a tight line. As Tyler turned his murderous gaze away from her, her eyes narrowed.

There was division in the ranks; Melior Group was falling apart. That sent a shiver down my spine more than anything else—more than the grizzly bears, the people crying for my blood, the guns pointed at my face. When institutions and organizations of that scale and influence began to show cracks, we were all fucked. We were about three weeks away from the Hunger Games. I just wasn't sure if it would be the humans or the Variants killing the other for entertainment.

"I want these four detained." He pointed to my attackers. "Bradford Hills Institute will not tolerate this kind of behavior. We take the safety of *all* our students extremely seriously."

Operatives pushed through the crowd to obey him. He wasn't armed or in a badass black uniform, but Tyler was the most formidable, commanding presence there. I ached to touch him yet again—that authoritative power made me feel safe.

My treacherous bodyguard had remained quiet after failing to immediately convince his colleagues to detain me. He'd shifted farther back into the crowd, but there was no hiding from Tyler. His men brought the man forward as he struggled to get out of their grip.

Tyler looked at him as if he were a sticky piece of shit on the bottom of his shoe. "I'm going to ruin you." His voice was low, menacing, and full of intent. "The rest of you, head back to your residence halls and expect a visit from a Melior Group agent in the next twenty-four hours. Those of you not living on campus, head to the cafeteria for temporary accommodation. The campus is officially on lockdown. No one is to go in or out."

Some people started to move away, warily eyeing Dot's bears, but others grumbled about not being allowed to leave.

"Move!" Tyler bellowed, his patience wearing thin, and the rest of them flinched and scattered.

Once the only people in sight were us and another four agents, Tyler turned to Dot and Charlie. "You can send them home, Dot." He gestured to the bears. "Thank you. Both of you."

"Anything for Eve." Charlie wrapped me up in a hug as Dot shooed the bears away. One of them nuzzled her tiny frame with its giant muzzle as a goodbye.

She shoved her brother out of the way to squeeze her arms around me. "Would you stop trying to get yourself kidnapped?"

We both chuckled, but a cold, heavy weight settled at the bottom of my ribs. It could have been so much worse.

"Kyo and Marcus are at the east gate." Tyler stepped closer. "They'll get you home, but you better hurry before the announcement is blasted through all the speakers."

Dot and Charlie hurried away, and Tyler finally held a hand

out to me, his warm gray eyes full of an emotion I couldn't nail down.

I rushed to him, fully intending to wrap myself around him and never let go, but he took my hand firmly in his and set a fast pace toward the admin building, the four agents closing in around us.

TWENTY-TWO

I gripped Tyler's hand and struggled to keep up, but we reached the brightly lit lobby in no time.

Stacey was behind the reception counter, looking harried as Bradford Hills staff and Melior Group staff rushed around. She saw us but kept speaking to the man beside her.

Tyler bypassed the elevators and ushered me into a small meeting room. He slammed the door shut with his foot and finally pulled me into his arms.

As the announcement that the campus was on lockdown reverberated through every speaker on site, Tyler held me close. I buried my face in his neck, curling my arms around his waist and holding tightly to the fabric of his shirt. An arm around my back almost crushed me, and another pressed against the back of my head.

His heartbeat was erratic, a staccato rhythm hammering under my cheek, and his labored breaths fanned over my hair.

We didn't speak. We just held each other. He was my anchor —something to keep me tethered to this world, to keep away the panic once again clawing at my throat.

I focused on his firm grip, his warm breath, the texture of his cotton shirt in my fists. But I didn't close my eyes. If I closed my eyes, I would start to relive it, along with all the other things that resided in that festering, fucked-up, traumatized part of my brain.

The branches restraining me, making it hard to breathe.

The blood pooling around Alec's still body.

The steel bars of a cage in a basement.

Beth getting knocked off her feet.

My mother's stunned face as her hand slipped out of mine.

I had to keep my eyes open, keep my focus on the here and now. Or I'd completely fall apart.

After a few minutes, or maybe it was days, Tyler's heart rate began to slow down, his breathing became more measured. My own inhalations and exhalations matched up to his instinctually.

"Nowhere is safe, is it?" My voice was flat—just stating a fact, even if I posed it as a question.

He loosened his grip and leaned back. His eyes searched mine as his mouth opened, then snapped shut again. Finally he sighed and pressed a kiss to my forehead.

Tyler couldn't lie to me—not anymore—and there was nothing else to say.

The sound of the door opening made us pull apart, and then I was crushed to another broad, strong chest.

Alec lifted me clear off the ground, both arms around my middle and his face buried in my neck.

I returned the embrace. It felt good to have him holding me up —both physically and metaphorically. His strength made me feel stronger.

The sound of a female voice made me lift my head. Stacey had followed Alec into the room and was speaking with Tyler in hushed tones, their heads bent together. A Bradford Hills Institute staffer and another Melior Group operative joined us too. The black-clad woman closed the door behind her.

Suddenly, I didn't want to be held off the ground like a child anymore. I wanted to stand on my own two adult feet.

I gave Alec a squeeze and pulled back. Instead of setting me down, he lifted his face and mashed his lips to mine. The kiss was desperate—full of the fear and frustration I was feeling myself. Alec didn't give a shit that we had an audience. He needed to feel me, safe and warm in his arms, needed to reassure himself that I was OK.

I held the back of his head, feeling the demanding strokes of his tongue and the prickles of his buzzed hair under my palm.

Tyler cleared his throat loudly, and we pulled apart. Alec's ice-blue eyes stared me down, searching, but I looked away.

"Faculty and students have all been informed of the lockdown. The protocols are being put into place," the Bradford Hills staffer informed the room as Alec slowly lowered me to the ground.

"All the gates are secured," the woman in black reported, "and we have extra men in place along the perimeter. Every twenty feet, as ordered."

"Can we go home?" I kept my voice low, but we were in a small room and everyone heard me. "I wanna go home."

I wanted to take my Bond and just lock us in a room. What I'd do with all four of them in there, I wasn't entirely sure, but my Light instincts had never done me wrong before. I just wanted them close.

I turned to face Tyler, my eyes pleading.

His expression softened. "Soon, baby."

Stacey gave him an odd look, a slight furrowing of the brows that she quickly wiped off her face. I only saw it because she was standing right next to him, because I was hyperaware of her elbow brushing against his arm as she tapped the tablet in her hands. As usual, she looked sophisticated in a pencil skirt and sweater, though her usually sleek bun had a few bits of hair sticking out of it. That seemed to be the only sign she was stressed.

I moved toward Ty again, but Alec pulled me back, holding me against his chest. I covered his hands at my hips with my own and let him ground me. I needed to be touching at least one of them, and there was a distinct possibility I'd growl at Stacey like one of Dot's bears once I got my hands on Ty.

"We knew there was a risk of some kind of violent or disruptive event," Stacey said to the room, "but considering the circumstances, I think we need to discuss Miss Blackburn—"

"Maynard," Alec and I cut her off at the same time, but I explained, "It's Evelyn Maynard. Can we get that changed, please?" Everyone knew my secrets now anyway. My so-called father had laid me bare for the world to see. Weren't parents supposed to protect their children? Shield them? What a joke.

"Yes, very well." A bit of frustration cut into her perfect demeanor. Stacey didn't appreciate being interrupted. "As I was saying, I think we need to consider having Miss Maynard take a break from classes."

I looked at her sharply and frowned. "You're kicking me out? But I have a scholarship . . ." Of course this had nothing to do with my academic performance. It just seemed as if it needed to be said: I had a right to be there. I'd worked hard and earned my spot.

"Oh, no, sweetheart." Stacey reached a hand out to me, her expression sympathetic if a little fake. "No one is kicking you out. Your scholarship is secure. What I'm talking about is taking a break. Just until things calm down."

"Until things calm down." I crossed my arms and looked at my feet.

"The safety of the staff and students has to be our primary concern, Eve," Tyler explained, his expression resigned, sad. "After the way you were attacked tonight, I simply don't believe Bradford Hills Institute is a safe place for you anymore. And as much as it frustrates me to say it, removing you from the situation would make the other students safer too."

"Right." I'd crossed my arms in defiance, but now I was hugging myself more than anything. They were right—I was dangerous. I could drain any Variant to death if they pissed me off enough, and the fact that Davis had basically put a bounty on my head meant that anywhere I went, I was at risk of starting a riot.

An indignant part of me wanted to argue. This may never get resolved. It wasn't fair. How was it *my* fault that idiots were getting dragged into Davis's bullshit? Why should I suffer because Melior Group couldn't do their damn jobs? All I ever wanted was to study science and find a place to settle down.

But another, bigger, more sinister part of me understood how naive my indignation was.

"Maybe I should just leave. Permanently." It would be less of a headache for Tyler, Stacey, and the Bradford Hills Institute board if I just quietly went away. There would be less drama, and they wouldn't be forced to take sides in a war that no one would ultimately win.

If I was being honest with myself, none of this would be happening if it wasn't for me. Davis wouldn't be trying to make his own Frankenstein monsters if my mother's Light hadn't shown him it was possible. He wouldn't have started two extremist organizations in his pursuit for answers. He wouldn't have kidnapped all those Vitals. Rick would still be alive. Beth would still be alive. People wouldn't be starting riots in the streets if Davis wasn't so determined to get *me*.

I could just hand myself over to him, but then he would have exactly what he wanted, and I shuddered to think what the world would look like if a man like him had that much power.

Really, this would all go away if I didn't exist.

"Maybe I should just . . ."

I trailed off, not quite able to say the word. The fact that this thought had even crossed my mind scared the absolute shit out of me. My whole world tilted on its axis as cold dread trickled down my spine.

Tyler propped his hands on his hips. "You should just what, Eve?"

He asked and his ability filled him in. His eyes widened in shock, horror, *fear*.

I looked away, willing myself not to cry even as my eyes started to sting from impending tears.

"Evelyn, no one is suggesting you leave permanently." Stacey was oblivious to what had just gone through my mind, but Tyler cut in.

"Don't," he growled, stalking forward to stand directly in front of me. His hands cupped my cheeks and lifted my face until I was looking directly into his intense gray eyes. "Don't you dare think like that, Evelyn."

Panicked, I glanced around as much as his grip would allow, worried he would expose to the whole room the single darkest thought I'd ever had.

But he just said what I needed to hear. "You are mine and I love you. You are the most important thing to me. I won't stand for it. Do you understand?"

I nodded weakly, and Tyler closed the distance, placing a searing kiss on my lips. I wrapped my arms around him, and he didn't stop at what would've been proper in a room full of people. He darted his tongue out and I met it with mine.

Alec had no idea what we were talking about, and he wasn't asking—although I was sure there would be questions later—but he could clearly tell something was wrong. Instead of giving us space, he closed in and pressed his front against my back. Tyler continued to assault my mouth, driving any depressing thoughts right out of my mind for those blissful few moments. I was exactly where I wanted and needed to be—with them.

Tyler broke the kiss and touched his forehead to mine. "I love you," he whispered against my lips. "Please don't leave me."

I took a shuddering breath. He'd gotten to the crux of the matter. If any one of them was taken from me, left me, I would be a mess. A broken twisted mess. How could I possibly do that to them?

When Tyler finally stepped away, giving me some room to breathe, the first person I made eye contact with was Stacey. The other two were averting their gazes, but her full, stunned attention was on me—on us.

I think that was the first time Stacey had seen Tyler and me together—*really* together—the first time she'd glimpsed what it meant to be in a Bond. On some level, I felt a little bad for her; she clearly had a crush on Ty, and I knew what that was like. I was still crushing on him too. But as a human, she could never fully appreciate the level of devotion and connection we shared. We were tethered in every way imaginable and in one way even science couldn't explain—by the Light.

She'd finally seen for herself that she truly had no chance with him. He was mine, always was, and always would be.

With a little cough, she looked down at her tablet. To her credit, she didn't give much away, didn't throw me any jealous looks or childish sneers. She simply fixed one of the many stray hairs that had fallen out of her bun, smoothed down her skirt, and got back to business. I had to admire her strength and professionalism.

Before she could speak again, Tyler did. "Can we finish this conversation tomorrow, Stacey? You have the lockdown under control, and Melior Group are all in place with additional agents called in for backup—all bases are covered. I'll speak with Evelyn about her classes at home, and we can finalize the details tomorrow."

"Of course." She smiled politely. "You should get her home. I have a free hour at eleven tomorrow morning?" She tapped at her tablet, and Ty took out his phone.

"That works. Lock it in."

They set the meeting, Tyler made sure everyone was clear on their orders, and we headed into the underground parking garage.

It wasn't until we were safely inside the house that any of us spoke again.

"Hey! That was a late study session." Ethan flashed me his dimples, meandering out of the living room in sweats. He gave me a quick peck on the lips, then paused, his smile faltering.

Josh appeared in the doorway, also in sweats and a band T-shirt. "What happened?"

He rushed over and gave me a kiss too, holding on to my hand.

Alec was the first to speak, but he didn't answer their questions; he just posed another one.

"What the fuck was that in there?" He looked between Tyler and me, his mouth set in a firm line but his eyes full of fear.

"We have a lot to discuss, but I think we should do it on the plane." Tyler ran his hands through his messy hair—a sure sign of stress.

"Plane?" I asked. Josh, Ethan, and I all turned confused looks on him. "What plane? Didn't you just set a meeting with Stacey?"

"We couldn't risk anyone getting suspicious," Alec answered for him.

"You all know there's a mole in Melior Group." Tyler sighed. "Well, considering tonight's events, things are worse than we thought."

"How?" Josh kept his questions simple and to the point.

"We had agents disobeying direct orders. Some are outright siding with Davis. There's a faction within the organization that believes we should align with him—that his goals for Variants are in line with Melior Group's. It's a load of shit, but it goes as high as management. We can't trust Melior Group anymore. We have to go dark," Tyler explained.

"Dark? What does that mean?" I thought I was being somewhat dramatic when I said nowhere was safe anymore, but it looked as if I was more right than I thought.

"We're gonna run." Alec took my other hand and gave me a sad smile.

"We were planning a trip to Japan anyway." Tyler shrugged. "We just have to move it up from next week to, well, right now. And we'll have to take a roundabout way to get there."

"Get packing, you three," Alec barked.

Instead of obeying, Ethan crossed his arms over his big chest. "Is someone going to tell us what the fuck happened?"

Alec's eyes narrowed, but I stepped between them. "I'll fill them in while they pack. My go-bag is ready anyway."

"Of course it is." Alec chuckled darkly as I led the way up the stairs. It felt good to have a task, something to keep my mind off the dark thoughts threatening to creep back in at any moment.

I gave the guys the abridged version of the evening's events, sticking to the facts and leaving out my insidious thoughts. After several bone-crushing hugs and my repeated assurances that I was fine—something I wasn't entirely convinced of myself—they reluctantly left my side to go pack.

I rushed through a quick shower, washing off the heat of the day and the mess of the evening. Meticulously and precisely, I tied my damp hair back, dressed in simple dark clothing, and grabbed my go-bag from the bottom of my wardrobe. I didn't give myself time to slow down and think. Our best chance to get away undetected would be under the cover of darkness, and we had to hurry.

I rushed downstairs, worried I was holding everyone up because of my shower, but I still beat Ethan and Josh. They came jogging down the stairs just as I reached the bottom.

Once we'd all converged in the foyer, I unzipped the front pocket of my backpack and handed each of them a new passport with a new identity.

"Oh, right." Ethan took his wallet out of his pocket, stared at it as if he didn't know what it was for a second, then dropped it onto the side table.

"Jonathon MacLaine?" Alec scoffed, but his eyes danced with amusement.

I gave him a smile and shrugged. I'd toyed with the idea of giving them all action hero–adjacent names but decided against it. This was serious, and I took it seriously. Unfortunately, Alec's *Die Hard* identity was already created by the time I came to that conclusion.

"These are really good, Eve. Thank you." Josh tucked his new passport into his pocket just as Lucian came rolling out of his wing.

"OK, you're all set." He came to a stop before us. "The more stops you make, the better, but you're leaving at night and when no one expects it, so that'll help. Evelyn, do you have those new passports you've been working on?"

"Yes, Uncle Luce."

Everyone held up their new documents, but Lucian was already barreling on. "Just keep your heads down, and don't draw attention to yourselves."

"We know." I went to stand in front of him.

"Crowds are good if you need to lose a tail and—"

"Uncle Lucian," I cut him off, taking his hand in mine. "We know."

I'd spent my entire childhood doing this. Alec and Tyler were highly trained. Ethan and Josh weren't idiots.

He took my hand in both of his and sighed. "Please just . . . be careful. I can't lose any more family."

He gave us all a pointed look, and I leaned down to hug him. He held me close before finally letting go.

Tyler cleared his throat. "I've informed Mr. Takata, through a secure channel, that we're on our way. The only decision left to make is how we actually get off the property."

"Well, then you're lucky I'm here." Olivia strode out of the back of the house, purse over her shoulder, wearing a tracksuit and a determined expression.

"Olivia came to make sure I eat a decent meal for dinner." Lucian rolled his eyes, but I could tell he was happy to have his sister around more. "We're lucky the garage was open when she showed up. No one will see you all getting into her SUV, and no one will question her leaving now."

Once again, Olivia ended up playing my getaway driver. She was much calmer about it this time—no nervousness or second thoughts, no muttering to herself or questioning her decision. She just kept her eyes on the road, and we all crouched in the back.

When the car finally stopped, she paused, pretending to rifle through her purse. "Take care of my boys, Evie."

Then she got out of the car and walked away.

They didn't need taking care of. They were the ones with

incredible, dangerous abilities. She was just telling me in her own way to be strong—that she believed in me.

We waited for ten minutes, then slunk out of the car into a sprawling department store parking lot. There weren't many people around but plenty of cars.

By the time I'd gotten my bearings, Alec had already disappeared without a sound, and Ethan and Josh were making their way over to the next row of cars.

Tyler tugged on my arm, two helmets held in his other hand. He led me to a motorbike parked in a dark corner and swung his leg over. If there was any doubt in my mind that we were about to steal a motorcycle, it was wiped away once he started to hotwire it.

I settled in behind him as the engine came to life.

He grabbed my arms and wrapped them tightly around his waist as he turned to flash me a grin. "This time I don't have to pretend I don't want your hands all over me."

Despite the tense situation, I laughed. "This time I don't have to feel bad about groping you."

I reached between his legs and gave him a gentle yet confident squeeze. He chuckled and pulled his helmet on, forcing me to abandon my grip on the growing hardness to do the same, and we were off.

We drove to Boston, switching vehicles several times, sometimes splitting up into different groups. Josh booked tickets on a flight to Japan as we drove, and we arrived at the airport with plenty of time to clear customs and passport control without a hitch. My fakes were damn good.

TWENTY-THREE

When we got to the gate, most of the passengers still hadn't been called for boarding. Business class was being given priority, so we got in line behind half a dozen other business-class people and waited.

Ethan had his face in a cooking magazine, his bicep bulging. I smiled at him indulgently and leaned into Josh, but when I rested my head against his shoulder, it felt tense. I looked up at him. The expression on his face was one of careful concentration, his full attention on something over his shoulder.

I followed his gaze to the reception desk. In front of the counter stood a woman with short black hair, dressed impeccably in slacks and a white business shirt. She was saying something to the young woman behind the counter, gesturing with her hands. She looked upset, and even though I couldn't make out what she was saying, I had a feeling it wouldn't be long before everyone could.

"Shit." I gripped Josh's arm a little tighter, glancing around the busy terminal, clocking the exits.

Without tearing his gaze away from the unfolding scene—as predicted, the woman was beginning to raise her voice—Josh inclined his head and called out quietly, "Gabe?"

"I see it." Tyler sounded as if he was close behind me, which made me feel a bit safer.

"What?" Ethan whipped his head up, the magazine still clutched in both hands.

The woman's voice finally raised to an audible volume, answering Ethan's question.

". . . not be that difficult!" She huffed, slapping her hand on the counter and propping the other on her hip.

Around us, conversations hushed as others started to take notice, making the flight assistant's response easy to hear.

"Ma'am, as I already explained, the economy section of the flight is full. I simply can't move you. You're welcome to book another flight, but we are under no obligation to accommodate your request."

"This is ridiculous." Again she huffed, her voice more high-pitched. "You have a duty of care to your passengers. I have a *right* to feel safe. How can you expect me to sit next to a . . . *person*"— she spat the word—"like that?"

"We do not ask people if they are human or Variant when they buy their tickets, and we certainly don't segregate our flights as such. That would be against the law. Now, you can either lower your voice and board the flight or you can purchase another ticket, but if you continue to behave in an aggressive manner—"

"Don't you threaten me!" The woman wagged her finger in the young girl's face.

"Motherfucker," Alec growled. He was standing on my other side, watching the scene unfold with a scowl.

An older woman joined the young girl behind the counter. The boarding was getting delayed, and people were becoming fidgety.

"I demand to be moved to a seat that's not next to a *Dime*, or I want a full refund!"

Several people gasped at the derogatory term, but a few exchanged sympathetic looks. One person even nodded.

Fear jolted down my spine.

The fact that seemingly normal businesswomen felt it was acceptable to say that word and demand to be kept away from humans in such a public way was downright terrifying. People were losing their fucking minds.

"If you don't lower your voice, you will not be permitted to board this flight." The older worker's tone was firm, her mouth set in a hard line.

Before the woman could go on another rant, a man stepped up to the counter. He was middle-aged, his hair more salt than pepper, and dressed casually in jeans and sneakers. A backpack was slung over his shoulder.

"Excuse me." He leaned forward, extending a hand to get their attention but keeping a safe distance. "I'm happy to take a later flight, if that's possible. I really don't want any trouble."

Tyler grumbled something under his breath as he stepped around us and went to the other end of the counter.

"Don't touch me." The woman flinched away from the man dramatically, disgust all over her face. He took a step back, his hands out in front of him, and sighed in frustration.

The ground staff started talking again, explaining that the circumstances wouldn't allow them to move either person to another seat or flight—it was outside the airline's guidelines. The younger woman looked as if she was calling security on a walkie-talkie as the other staff began boarding the business-class passengers.

Meanwhile, Tyler stood tall and confident at the other end of the counter, speaking calmly to the man at the computer. Within minutes, he was handing the attendant a wad of cash. When he had his change, Tyler took two steps to reach the commotion.

"Excuse me." His loud, authoritative voice demanded every-one's attention. "I'd like to assist. I don't believe anyone should be subjected to sitting next to such an abhorrent person for any period of time, let alone a long-haul international flight. I've taken the liberty of purchasing a business-class ticket."

He spoke to no one in particular, addressing the group with

one hand in his pocket. He was casual but commanding. Calm but intense.

The woman crossed her arms and threw a smug look at the human man and the ground staff. "I'm glad some people understand what—"

She was cut off by the younger flight assistant stepping up to the counter and addressing the casually dressed man. "Here is your new boarding pass, sir. Your section is now boarding. We apologize for the inconvenience." She smiled professionally as he slowly took the boarding pass, a stunned look on his face.

He looked at Tyler and smiled tentatively. "Th . . . thank you."

"My pleasure." Ty smiled, and they walked back to us together, getting in line just as it moved forward.

The woman snapped out of her shock and *lost her shit* just as four security personnel rushed to the scene. They dragged her away kicking and screaming as several people clapped and cheered.

I beamed at my man, so proud. As he rejoined us, I took his hand and gave him a kiss on the cheek. "You're a good man, Tyler Gabriel," I whispered in his ear.

"I'm just sick of watching this shit get worse and worse." He frowned as his fingers tightened around mine. "We need to start standing up for one another. If ignorant people are going to get more brazen in their bigotry and hatred, we need to get more bold in the way we stand up for what's right."

***

Thankfully, the flight was completely uneventful, even free from turbulence. It wasn't as luxurious as the flight we took in Melior Group's private jet on the way back from Australia, but it was still better than most of the flights I'd been on. Being able to stretch out and lie down was pure heaven.

We landed in Tokyo in the middle of the night. I wanted to

call Mr. Takata and head to his grandmother's village immediately, but the guys insisted on petty things like showers and sleep.

In order to avoid drawing any more attention to ourselves, we decided not to book a suite, opting instead to go with three regular rooms in a hotel. They were pretty small—we were in Japan after all.

After several rounds of aggressive rock-paper-scissors, Ethan won the privilege of sharing a room with me. He threw me over his shoulder and carried me into it along with all our luggage, making me laugh too loudly for a hotel hallway late at night.

His feet hung off the end of the mattress, but he snuggled into my side and fell asleep quickly. Unfortunately, finding my own sleep was more difficult. My mind raced: Were we careful enough getting here? What would tomorrow hold? I slept in fits and starts, and when the gray morning light peeked in through the curtains, I got out of bed.

After a shower, I called room service and ordered enough food for all of us in a whisper, trying to let Ethan sleep as long as possible. Then I called the others and told them to meet us in our room. Tyler grunted, and I heard him call Josh's name as he hung up. Alec had already been up for an hour and been to the gym.

The food arrived just before the rest of my guys did, and for the first time, I was the one delivering breakfast in bed to Ethan. I may not have made it myself, but I ordered the fuck out of it like a pro. It totally counted.

He somehow managed to sleep through the room service being delivered and the others filing into the cramped space. Alec took the desk chair, Josh made himself comfortable on the ground, and Tyler leaned on the headboard next to Ethan, each of them holding a plate of eggs and pastries.

With a warm, delicious-smelling chocolate croissant in hand, I climbed on top of Ethan, straddling his hips. I waved the croissant under his nose as I kissed the stubble on his jaw.

He took a deep breath and groaned lightly. Lazily, his hands went to my hips, and he shifted me just a little lower—until I was settled over his morning wood.

I chuckled, and his mouth and eyes opened at the same time. He took a quick bite of the pastry before leaning up and planting a kiss on my lips.

"Delicious." His voice was croaky and deep—all kinds of sexy.

"Me or the croissant?" I teased.

"Hmm. Not sure. I think I need another taste." He took another bite of the croissant, but instead of kissing me, he pulled at the hem of my shorts, giving me that cheeky grin that made his dimples appear—and usually made my clothes *disappear*.

"We have company," I informed him.

He looked around the room and shrugged. "They can watch. Or join in."

His hands traveled up my sides, cupping my breasts.

"If you don't eat these eggs, I'm going to," Alec announced.

I climbed off Ethan. He groaned in protest, but Alec's mention of eggs reminded me I was hungry too. One basic need at a time.

We polished off all the food and ordered more.

Ethan went to shower while we waited, and I planted myself on Alec's lap, studying the tourist map and pointing things out past the window.

"The Imperial Palace is that way, and just past that is Tokyo Tower." I consulted the map again. "And just a few blocks that way is Shibuya Crossing." I knew they hadn't been back since the accident, but I wanted them to know I was there for them. "We can go there if you guys want to. We can make time."

"No." Alec didn't hesitate. His voice wasn't hard or angry, just sure. "You guys can go if you want to, but I won't. I want to remember them for how they lived. Not how they died."

I stared at his profile as he looked out the window. My Master of Pain could be really poetic when he wanted to be.

"I have no interest in seeing it again," Tyler agreed.

"Me neither," Josh murmured before taking another sip of coffee.

"Yeah, fuck that!" Ethan yelled from the bathroom, proving how thin the walls were in this tiny room.

I hugged Alec and gave him a kiss on the cheek.

"Evie, are you OK?" he murmured against my cheek.

Tyler had filled them in on my dark thoughts after I was attacked. They'd all chastised, pleaded, and questioned me every chance they got while we traveled. I'd been brushing them off, trying to tell them I was fine, but they just weren't dropping it. I sighed and looked away. Tyler and Josh were both staring at me; Ethan was leaning in the doorway to the bathroom, a towel wrapped around his hips.

"Not really," I finally answered, deciding to be honest. "But I'm going to be, and I'm already feeling better than I was last night. Can we just focus on why we're here? One crisis at a time." Being around them, seeing the concern in their eyes, really had made me feel better.

Reluctantly, Alec nodded and gave me another gentle kiss.

More food arrived, and we talked about lighter topics until I received a text message from Mr. Takata; he was waiting for us in the lobby.

We packed up and headed down, dressed in comfortable clothing light enough for a walk in the Japanese wilderness in the middle of summer. I wasn't entirely sure where his grandmother lived, but he'd mentioned it was remote.

In the lobby, Mr. Takata greeted us with the same level of respect and reverence as when we first met, bowing low.

I returned the gesture.

"How was your flight?" he asked as Alec went to reception to check us out.

"There was some drama at the gate—a loud-mouthed, entitled Variant—but the flight itself was fine, and we've had most of the night to rest. I'm excited to get going. I can't wait to meet your grandmother."

He smiled. "She is very eager to meet you also."

"Careful what we discuss in public." Tyler leaned in, giving us meaningful looks.

"Naturally." Mr. Takata inclined his head. "And just so you're aware, my security team will be accompanying us most of the way."

Tyler frowned, clearly not too happy about men with guns being in our general vicinity, but Mr. Takata waved him off. "It is a small team of three men whom I trust implicitly. They have been with me for over twenty years, and one of them is a cousin. I have not told them of your situation, but they have been briefed to defend your life as they would mine, Evelyn—with their own lives."

"Thank you. I really appreciate that."

"Yes." Tyler finally nodded decisively, satisfied with whatever extra information his ability had provided. "Thank you."

Mr. Takata led us out front to a black van with tinted windows. We all piled into the back, with two of Mr. Takata's men in the front. The third man was to follow behind discreetly.

We drove west for hours until the city disappeared, replaced by low buildings and residential streets, then verdant green hills and traditional dwellings. The road continued to narrow, going from a six-lane freeway to, eventually, rough gravel and dirt.

We stopped once for a toilet break and once for lunch at a small ramen restaurant on the side of the road. The owner spoke no English, but the ramen was amazing. Ethan had two bowls.

Around three in the afternoon, just as the road was becoming unbearably bumpy and slow, the van came to a stop.

"From here, we walk." Mr. Takata got out of the van and strapped on his backpack. We followed suit. Two of his men took off into the trees, following a narrow path, while the third waited patiently to bring up the rear.

Mr. Takata took the lead. Tyler shot everyone a stern look I wasn't sure how to interpret, but they arranged themselves so I was surrounded as we hiked. Tyler walked with Mr. Takata,

Ethan kept pace with me, and Alec and Josh stayed close behind us.

No one spoke, all of them on high alert, and Mr. Takata abandoned his attempts at small talk quickly. I understood why they were cautious—we were in the middle of nowhere, in an unfamiliar place. This would be the perfect opportunity for an ambush or a double-cross. But I trusted Mr. Takata, and Tyler's ability would certainly warn us of any danger.

I was really excited to meet another Vital like me—one that had more Variants than was supposed to be possible and glowed like a nightlight. Nothing was going to ruin my mood. I took in the tall trees, listened to the birds singing, breathed the fresh air. Despite the heat, it was invigorating, especially after sitting in a van most of the day.

The uphill path was wide and clear—wide enough for a small horse and cart but way too narrow and uneven for a car. Maybe an ATV could've worked?

I'd never had even a passing interest in ATVs, but an hour into the trek, that was all I could think about through my panting and sweating. Training with Kane was no joke, but this kind of prolonged, long-distance style of exercise—*up a hill*—was way more than I was used to.

Ethan was fine, even with both our packs slung over his broad shoulders, and Alec hadn't even broken a sweat. Tyler and Josh were starting to breathe heavily, and Mr. Takata was struggling about as much as I was.

Still, none of us seemed willing to stop for a break. A heavy tension had settled over our group, probably due to how suspicious my guys were, how leery they were being. I couldn't blame Mr. Takata for wanting to get to our destination as soon as possible, and I couldn't blame them for wanting to determine whether we were really safe here or not.

My legs burned, but the promise of what awaited me on the other side pushed me forward.

After nearly two hours of walking, the trees thinned. Mr.

Takata's pace slowed considerably, and we all had long drinks of water.

Voices and the sounds of life started to reach my ears, and I couldn't stop the smile from breaking over my face.

In my excitement, I tried to rush forward, but Ethan caught me by the hand and held me firmly in place, in the middle of their protective circle.

"Welcome to Urahidaka," Mr. Takata announced. We emerged onto the outskirts of the most picturesque place I'd ever seen.

The houses were mostly wooden, built close together near the center of the village and more sparsely at the edges. Smoke rose from several chimneys, which jutted up from thatched and tiled roofs. Goats and geese wandered as freely as the villagers along cobblestone streets. The village was set into the side of a hill over-looking a valley. A few fat white clouds floated by lazily, but the afternoon sun cast a golden glow over the whole scene.

The air was crisp and fresh, tinged with that light hint of smoke and animal smell that was so unmistakably "countryside." The faint, steady sound of running water indicated a nearby stream we couldn't see.

It was like a postcard!

"It's so beautiful," I breathed. Standing there, looking at the calm valley, the Japanese maples swaying in the light breeze, I could almost pretend all the horrible things happening in the rest of the world weren't real. How could they be when this valley and this village sat here so peacefully?

A middle-aged woman rushed up to us. Her hair was tied back neatly, and she wore a plain yukata.

"*Konnichiwa. Youkoso,*" she greeted us and bowed to each person individually.

"*Konnichiwa.*" My Japanese was rusty, but I still remembered the basics. I bowed a little lower than she did as a sign of respect.

"This is Youko, my cousin. Our grandmother lives with her

and her family. She will take us to her home now," Mr. Takata explained in English.

She gestured politely down the cobbled path toward the squat buildings, and we followed. We passed through the village's main square, which was centered around what looked like a few teahouses and one small grocery store. A large cherry blossom tree grew in the very middle.

After passing down several winding lanes, we stopped at a house. It was similar to all the others in the area—slightly raised and mostly constructed of wood with a tiled roof. A front garden displayed an array of brightly colored, artfully arranged plants.

After we all took our shoes off, Youko led us inside. Most of our group had to duck their heads in order to pass through the doorway.

The home was as traditional inside as it was outside—tatami mats, low tables, and cushions to sit on. As we rounded the corner into the main living space, I froze, my eyes going wide.

If any doubt lingered in my mind about Mr. Takata's story or motives, one look at the elderly woman in front of me instantly dispelled it.

Her face was creased, her white, almost translucent hair tied into a knot. She hunched slightly over the gnarled hands she'd folded neatly in her lap.

She looked like any number of dignified, old Japanese women, but what made her remarkable—what had me gasping—was her glow.

It wasn't nuclear. It wasn't the warm white that emanated from my skin when I was under extreme pressure or, lately, when I called it up intentionally. No, this was a very subtle, almost hazy luminescence that seemed to hover around her.

I didn't have to check with everyone else in the room—I was pretty certain I was the only one who could see it. I felt drawn to her, inexplicably connected in a way that was bigger than both of us, bigger than *all* of us. In a way we weren't capable of understanding yet, no matter how hard we studied or how rigorous our scientific process was.

This was *pure Light.*

I knew she could do what I could do, because I felt it in every fiber of my being.

I moved forward. Her eyes fixed on me as mine did her, completely ignoring everyone else in the room. They all had the presence of mind to remain silent.

I dropped to my knees in front of her and bowed low. "*Konnichiwa. Watashi wa* Evelyn *desu.*" Fumblingly, I expressed my gratitude for her time and for welcoming us into her home.

A light touch brushed the back of my head, and I rose into a sitting position, resting my butt on my heels.

Her hand dropped to my shoulder—a very familiar, even *familial* gesture. She had tears in her eyes as she looked at me for a long moment.

I must've had the same hazy luminescence she did. How long had it been since she'd seen another glowing Vital? I'd never come across another my whole life, and I'd traveled the world. She'd lived most of her life in this remote village. Had she *ever* seen one?

"My name is Tomoko Takata. It is a pleasure and an honor to meet another *azayakana* again. You bring an old lady much joy."

She spoke in Japanese, but I understood most of it, only tripping up on a few words.

"*Azayakana?*" I turned to Mr. Takata, frowning. "I'm sorry. My Japanese is mediocre at best."

He smiled and stepped forward. "The best translation into English is 'Vivid.' It is the word that is used to describe Vitals who glow, such as you."

"Vivid." I smiled to myself. It was kind of appropriate.

I turned back to Mrs. Takata. I had so many questions, and for the first time, I was in front of someone who could actually answer them.

TWENTY-FOUR

Before I could start barraging the old lady with questions, her granddaughter insisted she show us to the bathrooms to freshen up.

"It is nearly dinner time. By the time you finish in the bathroom, I will have dinner on the table."

Dutifully, we all followed her to the small bathroom in the back of the house and took turns. It was basic, but it had running water—an impressive feat considering how remote the village was.

I changed out of my sweaty clothes, splashed some water on myself, and tied my hair back into a braid.

The living space was abuzz with chatter when I came back. Several low tables were laden with food. There was room for everyone, including Youko's husband and daughter and Mr. Takata's three bodyguards.

Mrs. Takata was at the head of the table. She waved me over and patted a cushion next to her, so I settled myself down between her and Tyler. The rest of the guys spread themselves out among our gracious hosts.

The delicious spread contained a plethora of traditional Japanese dishes, such as noodle soup with vegetables, steamed trout, marinated duck, and of course, plenty of steamed rice. As the plates emptied, several carafes of sake appeared. I clinked glasses with Mr. Takata and took a drink, doing my best not to wince at the strong alcohol.

I managed to fumble through some chitchat with his family and grandmother in Japanese, but my knowledge of the language was far too lacking to have the kind of conversation I wanted to have with her.

"Would you mind translating for me?" I asked Mr. Takata.

He nodded and waited for me to speak.

I chewed on my lip, suddenly unsure where to start. I had so many questions; they were all trying to elbow to the forefront of my mind, creating a bottleneck.

Something had been bugging me since I first laid eyes on her, so I decided to start there. "Can you please ask her why I could tell she was Vivid—why I could see luminescence around her, but I couldn't see it on my mother? She was like us too."

Dutifully, Mr. Takata translated the discussion I'd been waiting to have since that day on the empty train platform.

"Your mother has not been around since you met your Bond?"

Technically, we'd "met" as kids, but I was pretty sure that wasn't what she meant. "My mother died before I knew what I was."

She nodded and patted my hand. "You did not see your mother's glow because you had not yet formed your Bond. The Bond makes us stronger in all things, especially our connection to the Light."

"Does she know what it is? The glow? What am I?"

"You are a Vital. There is no question about that. You have the Light and you have a Bond. Your Light shines brighter than others'. It is Vivid. You are Vivid."

"Are there others like us? Has she met others? Why does no one know about this?"

"I knew two others—many years ago—a woman from a village nearby and a man from very far away. They told me of others but not very many. Both of them died in World War II. There have been no other Vivids in younger generations that I know of. In my time, it was something that was not understood, but it was respected. It was said that the glow was sent to us by God, his way of shining his light on our village and sending us strength. It was said that the birth of a Vivid heralded both a great blessing and a grave warning. Death and danger were sure to come, but God had sent us a Vivid to protect us. And indeed, my Bond and I had to do many things to protect our families, our village, our country. But when there is peace, there is no need for the Vivids. We have had a great many years of peace."

I nodded, my mind whirling with the practical applications of what she was saying. What was the most probable scientific explanation?

I turned to Tyler. "Evolution? Could it be as basic as the idea that nature is compensating for the loss of life by providing a line of defense?"

"It makes sense." He nodded, leaning his elbows on the table. "This could be a Variant DNA quirk. When certain levels of cortisol are in the pregnant mother's system, indicating high levels of stress, it could result in the baby being born Vivid. But that doesn't account for all the stresses of life. Why aren't women in domestic violence situations giving birth to Vivids?"

"Maybe there needs to be more at play? I mean, we don't really fully understand the Light. Maybe it has a better sense of what's happening in the world than we do? But I'm not sure if that adds up either. While most of the Western world has had relative peace for decades, how do you explain the fact that there haven't been any reports of Vivids popping up in the Middle East, for example?"

"Maybe there have been," Josh jumped in. "But the number of Variants relative to humans is much lower in that part of the world, thanks to the discriminatory laws during the sixties and seventies. A lot of Variants flee that area. And if it's dangerous to even have a common ability like super speed, I doubt anyone would be shouting from the rooftops that they can *glow*."

"True." I nodded and turned back to Mrs. Takata. "Do you know why the world is so oblivious to our existence? Why there aren't even any mentions in history books?"

"The Lighthunters." She smiled and took a sip of her sake.

Lighthunters? The time we'd spent with Nina a few months prior had certainly confirmed they were real, but any time I'd tried to question her more deeply about her nature, she'd managed to artfully change the topic.

She'd told me all I wanted to know about Variant Bonds, my own Bond and the connections within it, how to follow my instincts when it came to the Light, even about her own Lighthunter abilities. She was a well of knowledge, but sitting there, I realized just how well she'd avoided my questions about other Lighthunters and why the world thought they were a myth.

"I'm sorry. I don't understand." I frowned. "What do the Lighthunters have to do with it?"

"They are called Lighthunters because they are most well-known for finding the threads, connecting the Bonds. But they are also our protectors. Or they were. They shielded us from those who thought Vivids were dangerous, who thought it wasn't natural to have that much Light. They did a very good job hiding us, and we were so rare already. Then there were fewer and fewer Vivids being born. I hadn't heard of a single other like me until my grandson came with news of an extraordinary American girl." She smiled at him, then at me, the deep laugh lines around her eyes and mouth crinkling. By this stage, the whole table had fallen silent, their full attention on the matriarch and her wisdom.

"It is not surprising to me that between how rare we are and the Lighthunters' work, the world simply . . . forgot."

"I remembered." Mr. Takata spoke in Japanese, but the words were simple enough that I understood them. "I remembered your stories, grandmother."

She patted him on the hand, pride in her eyes.

"Please excuse me if this is rude, but where are your Variants?" I asked before I could stop myself. I had a feeling I knew the answer, since none of them were by her side.

"Passed. All four of them. Two were killed a very long time ago, one died in an accident, and one about fifteen years ago from old age."

I looked down the table at my Bondmates—my strong, beautiful, fiercely protective men. I couldn't imagine losing any of them. The mere thought sent pain shooting through my chest, and I involuntarily rubbed the spot. When I turned back to face the old woman, she was watching the hand at my breastbone.

"Yes, it is painful. Your connection is strong. You would not be Vivid without it." She stared into my eyes as though she could see right into my soul. I remained silent.

"You were made to make them strong." She gestured down the table with a swoop of her hand. "But they make you strong too. They cannot do what they do without your Light, but you cannot do what you do without *them*. That is why Vivids have more Variants in their Bonds than regular Vitals do. With practice, you may have learned to draw and transfer Light without a Bond, but it would have required an extreme amount of focus, would have been very taxing on your body. I have not glowed since my Variants died. I am old and weak and no longer have their strength to make it possible. Your Bond is the same. You can take not only from them but from all sources of Light around you because they give so freely. It is the ultimate symbiotic relationship."

"I make them strong, but they make me strong too." I parroted her words, and she nodded. I'd never thought of it like that, but it made sense.

In a regular Bond, the Vital channeled the Light and transferred it to their Variants; the Vital made the Variants strong. But in a Vivid Bond—in our Bond—they also made me strong. I could take from one and transfer to another. I could draw Light into me simply by willing it to come, and I could push it out to them without moving a muscle. The longer I'd been with them, the stronger our connection had grown, the easier it had become.

Yes, training helped, but my Light undeniably became more a part of me the more I used it. Every time my Bond and I got closer physically, mentally, emotionally, spiritually, *I* got stronger.

I brought us all together, tied us irrevocably to each other. I made them stronger than they ever could've been alone.

But they provided the foundation on which our collective strength was built. Each one of them was a solid, unwavering pillar in his own way.

Ethan always craved family, and when we found each other, he was immediately all in. I represented what he'd lost and all that he could have in the future. I was family, and he was devoted heart and soul.

Josh observed everything quietly from behind his clean-cut look and his books. It was his way of feeling in control in a chaotic world that had taken his parents away. But I saw the real him. From the start, I saw who he truly was, and I loved him for it. We showed each other that letting go of control could be freeing.

No one exercised greater control than Tyler. He'd resisted the pull from the first moment, before he even knew what it was. He'd continued resisting after he knew everything, even the things I didn't, even when it required him to sacrifice his own wants and needs. Because that was what was best for me, best for all of us. We'd needed time, and Tyler had made sure we'd had it.

Alec had been there from the start. And I don't mean that day in the hospital after the crash; I mean the *very start*, when we were all kids and had no idea of the hurdles we'd have to jump in order to be together. He was the one who'd made this possible. Because he never gave up on me, even when he knew it would make him more the monster he believed himself to be. Even when he resented it, he kept looking for me. He yearned for me and what I represented.

And he yearns still.

He was engaged in a conversation with Mr. Takata's cousin, but as though he felt my gaze on him, he looked up and met my eyes.

He'd been an asshole—a jerk of epic proportions. We'd both made mistakes, and he'd hurt me more than I thought possible. But he'd also changed. He'd worked his ass off to let me in, to embrace our Bond. He'd told me he loved me, and he'd been showing it every day since. Even as I continued to push him away. Even as I told the others I loved them.

Even as *I* continued to hurt *him*.

"You all must be exhausted." Mr. Takata's cousin started clearing the table. "Let me show you where you will sleep."

Youko and her family were staying with her husband's family, giving up their entire home so my Bond, Mr. Takata, and his security guys could have somewhere to sleep. We were set up in the biggest room in the back, on futon mattresses. A paper screen provided the only privacy.

All five of us were to sleep in the same room together. We'd never done that before—not intentionally. I'd shared a bed with more than one of them on numerous occasions, and there had been those few times, usually after someone tried to kill one of us, that we'd all ended up in the same room. Some of them usually wound up squished on a couch or making do with a pillow on the floor.

But this was the first time we were essentially all sleeping in the same bed.

We were strangely quiet as we got ready for sleep, taking turns in the bathroom, undressing, getting under the covers. Maybe it was because we were so tired, or because the walls were literally paper thin and we could hear Mr. Takata snoring lightly in the main living area.

I wasn't sure where the silence was coming from, but it didn't feel uncomfortable, and I couldn't stop smiling.

Naturally, I ended up in the middle, with Tyler on one side and Josh on the other. Ethan was behind Josh; Alec on the other side of Tyler. The others fell asleep quickly, but I lay on my back, feeling safe and *right* between them but unable to sleep despite how tired I was.

Yes, the new information was running through my mind, making a million new questions pop up. But mostly, I couldn't stop thinking about Alec.

He was just on the other side of Tyler, but he felt so far away. That was my fault.

I felt it, so why couldn't I say it? It had come so easily with the others, so why was it so damn hard with him to wrap my mouth around those words?

Careful not to wake the others, I lifted myself onto my elbows. I just wanted a glimpse of his face, the strong jaw, the scar through the eyebrow, the tiny kink in his nose.

But when I looked over, his stunning ice-blue eyes were staring right back at me. Alec was on his back, one arm propped behind his head, the blanket pushed down around his hips. He was just as wide awake as me.

At the same time, we smiled, an exchange that wordlessly said both "Why aren't you sleeping?" and "You can't sleep either?"

I sighed lightly and inclined my head toward the door, raising my brows.

He nodded and, with lithe, completely soundless movements, managed to get up without jostling the three sleeping men jammed into bed with us. I knew he was highly trained in how to be super stealthy and shit, but that was seriously impressive. I'd have to get him to teach me how to do that.

I crawled over Tyler much less gracefully while Alec silently laughed at me. I flipped him off as I grabbed a light cardigan off the top of my bag and he pulled on a pair of pants.

I led the way through the house, past the sleeping men in the main room, and out the front door. Alec closed it softly.

He was in nothing but a black pair of pants; I was in a tank, shorts, and my loose cardigan. Thankfully, the cobblestones were still warm on my toes from the hot summer sun, and it was a mild night.

We threaded our fingers together and slowly wandered down the curving lane. There were no streetlights, and half the houses probably didn't even have electricity, but the light of the moon was more than enough to light our way. At the end of the lane, warm stones gave way to soft grass as we reached the edge of a wide grassy knoll, the beginning of the steep hill into the valley.

Darkness stretched below us in the valley, but above, billions of stars shone down from a magnificent, cloudless sky, taking my breath away.

For all my travel, I'd never been in a place with so little light pollution. I knew how vast the universe was—how many stars, planets, and other celestial bodies were visible in our night sky— but I'd never seen it so clearly.

The curve of the Milky Way started behind the blue-black outline of the mountains across the valley, then curved above us to disappear somewhere to our backs and to the left. I craned my neck to follow it, my mouth hanging open in awe. Alec wrapped his arms around me from behind, and I rested my head on his chest, just staring up.

I picked out several constellations and planets: Ursa Major, Pegasus, and the brightly glowing, slightly reddish spot that was Mars, some 33.9 million miles away.

If the lifetime of the universe were put into the span of a day, humans would have only existed for the past four seconds. Thinking about that made all the drama and conflict around us feel somehow lighter. When all this was over and no one even remembered our names, the universe would still be shining bright; the Earth would still be here. Life would go on.

The longer I stared, the closer the night sky seemed. Eventually it almost felt as if I were among the stars, as if I could reach out and touch them and they would feel like smooth velvet under my fingers.

Without realizing, I reached a hand out toward the sky. Alec chuckled, his warm chest jostling my back, and I lowered my arm, smiling to myself.

Neither of us had spoken a word. This place was almost magic in its peace.

It was time for me to break the silence.

There was one pressing thing that still mattered, even though we were barely a speck in the dust that was the universe.

I turned in his arms, putting my back to the most amazing view I'd ever seen.

He'd kept a long-sleeved shirt on at all times since we'd arrived in the more remote areas, where tattoos didn't have positive connotations. But now his ink and scars were on full display—his art and pain worn like armor. I ran my hands over his chest and shoulders, feeling the strong muscle under the soft skin.

The blue in his eyes was almost silvery—reflecting the stars. He smiled at me, no sign of the frowning, brooding, tense asshole I'd first met. This was the real Alec. This was *my* Alec, my honey-voiced stranger who was a stranger no more.

This was the man I loved.

"I love you, Alec." I looked right into those mesmerizing eyes as I told him.

He blinked, his eyes widening just a little, and then so many emotions passed over his face that I couldn't have named them if I tried. There was surprise, for sure, happiness in the tentative curve of his lips, even relief in the way he sighed.

I hated that one. I hated that I'd waited this long to tell him, that I'd given him reason to doubt.

But I didn't dwell on it, because the most dominant emotion of all, the one that shone most clearly from his eyes, was *love*.

"I love you, Evie." There was that honey voice I lived to hear. And then he was kissing me.

Alec drew me up against his chest, making me lift onto my toes as I wrapped my arms around his neck and held on. I was never letting go again.

He kissed me deeply—as if we had all the time in the universe. As if the billions of stars shining down on us would just have to wait until we were done expressing our love.

The next morning, I slept in. Alec and I had thrown caution to the wind—or the light summer breeze, as it were—and made love under the stars.

Love! Because he loved me and I loved him and I'd told him. Finally!

We'd crawled back into bed in the wee hours of the morning and told each other again before falling asleep.

I woke up with a smile on my face, alone on the futons with bright sunlight streaming in.

Ethan was in the kitchen with Mr. Takata's cousin, getting a lesson in traditional Japanese cookery. He looked even more giant in the small space but managed not to knock anything over. As he delivered a traditional breakfast of rice, miso soup, and grilled fish, Alec and Josh wandered into the main room.

"Morning!" Josh gave me a kiss on the top of my head and kept heading for the door. "We're going for a run."

I mumbled around a mouthful of food, gesturing for them to wait. I wanted to go for a run too.

Tyler plopped down next to me. "Just eat, baby. I'll go with you later."

I grumbled but kept eating.

Alec kissed the same spot Josh had. "We won't be long. Love you."

"Love you too!" I called after him, smiling like an idiot over my food as he walked out.

Tyler kissed me on the cheek softly and gave me a wide smile, but he didn't comment.

I spent most of the day with Mr. Takata and his grandmother, asking all the questions I could think to ask. Her answers were rooted in myth and tradition. She couldn't give me scientific explanations for how my glowing Light worked and why I had it, but she told me all the stories her mother and grandmother had told her.

She impressed upon me the significance of this "gift." Through both her stories and her straightforward explanations, she told me what I was capable of—the immense amounts of Light I could channel; the remote transfers; the ability to draw from one Variant and give to another, temporarily giving them the other's ability.

She also explained the responsibility that came with having this gift. She spoke candidly about her own experiences of draining the Light from a Variant, taking their ability and killing them in the process.

"There is a reason we have this ability," she explained. "It would not be possible for us to do this if there was no purpose for it, but it must not be taken lightly. You have great power, Evelyn, but you must wield it wisely."

Practically speaking, she didn't give me any new information about what I could do. I'd experienced this all for myself, short of actually killing someone by draining them dry. But she confirmed many of my theories, and talking with someone who truly understood what I was going through was beyond satisfying.

She also told me the glow was a visual representation of my power, a beacon to draw people to my side.

I'd already seen evidence of that: the way Mr. Takata had devoted himself to me without even knowing me, the way strangers had come to my defense on countless occasions—when I was attacked at Bradford Hills, when I glowed the night of the formal evening in Manhattan, even when Rick had risked his life to warn me of the danger I was in from Davis's plans. And that wasn't even counting all the emails and private messages I'd received from Variants and Vitals all over the world.

Yes, the likelihood of a lot of those being fake was high, but I could feel in my gut that plenty of them were genuine too. That's why I'd asked Charlie to wade through them to check which ones might be legit.

People were scared and were looking for a spark of light in the darkness. Maybe it was time they had something to turn to besides the twisted views of Variant Valor and the Human Empowerment Network.

After lunch we wandered into the town square and sat outside a charming traditional teahouse, sipping on sencha as we continued our chats. It wasn't long, though, before we were interrupted by a buzz of excitement—kids rushing through the square, women chattering.

I frowned. "What's going on?"

Mr. Takata sat up straighter, craning his neck to look around. "It seems there is another visitor approaching the village on the path."

Alec and Tyler strode into the square, both of them clearly on alert.

TWENTY-FIVE

"There's someone approaching." Alec told us what we already knew while Tyler simply extended his hand to me.

I took it and pushed Light to him reflexively. He turned toward the path to the village, not visible past the low buildings and winding lanes. His eyes lost focus, but instead of sharing what his ability was telling him, he just frowned and cocked his head to the side.

"Ty?" I tugged on his hand. "Who is it?"

He shrugged. "The most I can sense is that they're not a threat."

I scratched my head. Even with all that extra Light, Ty couldn't tell who it was?

Before I had a chance to think about it too much, the person in question walked around the corner, solving the mystery of why Tyler's ability seemed to be malfunctioning.

Nina was in linen shorts and a loose white shirt, stark against her dark skin. Her hair was once again cropped close to her scalp, and she carried only a large backpack, which no doubt contained several weapons and countless secrets.

"Nina?" Alec and I said at the same time. What was the statistical probability of us meeting up in such a remote place? Maybe she knew we were here? But if she'd found us, did that mean others could too?

When she was about halfway across the square, she spotted me.

"Evelyn?" She smiled and rushed over.

"Fancy meeting you here." I laughed as we hugged. I'd missed her, and I held on for a long moment.

She greeted Tyler and Alec just as warmly and, to our surprise, seemed to know Mr. Takata's grandmother very well. Her French accent was as thick as I remembered, but she spoke to the old woman in Japanese.

Nina pulled up a chair and joined us. "How have you all been? I have seen some things on the news, but I am taking most of it with a large dose of salt."

"How have *we* been? Nina, how have *you* been? Seems you left a few things out the last time we met." I folded my arms, jokingly scolding her but unable to wipe the smile off my face.

"And I see someone has filled you in on it?" She threw Mrs. Takata a look, to which the old lady just chuckled, no remorse on her face whatsoever. "There wasn't exactly complete trust between us when we first met." She eyed Alec, and he looked down, rubbing the back of his neck. He'd been a jerk to her.

"Sorry," he mumbled and stole a sip of my tea. Mr. Takata motioned for the proprietor and ordered more tea for everyone.

"It is quite all right. You were being cautious. I understand. But I was also limited in what I was permitted to tell you at the time. There are some Lighthunters who have been pushing for us to remove ourselves from Variant society fully." She sighed.

"What? Why?" Tyler questioned.

"It is complicated, but it seems that it is proving impossible regardless. That is why I have come here. You were going to be my next stop. You've saved me a flight to America. Thank you!"

"Nina, what's going on?" I leaned forward.

"We are . . . I suppose you could say, investigating? The Lighthunters are visiting Vitals we know, the most powerful ones

—even the few Vivids we are aware of. We are trying to get some understanding around what is happening with the Light."

"What's happening with the Light?" I asked. That sounded ominous.

"It is difficult to explain." She sighed. "Remember how a Lighthunter's connection to the Light is different? How we do not have the abilities or the access that Variants and Vitals have, but we do have a different—in some ways, a deeper—understanding?"

I nodded.

"Sometimes, I see the Bond connections. Like tendrils, tethering individuals together. Your Bond is much more settled, by the way." She smiled. "No more tension. Whatever you've been doing, keep doing it."

I looked between Alec and Tyler. Our commitment to be more honest and open had no doubt played a big part in that, but ultimately, I was convinced it was our love that had made us stronger.

"Please go on," Mr. Takata prompted. He looked just as worried as Alec and Tyler.

"Right. Yes. Lighthunters have a sense of Bonds, connections. We can tell what state a Bond might be in. We can point people in the direction of their potential Variants or Vitals. We can track Bonded Variants and Vitals, like I did to help you find Charlie. How is he doing?"

"Really well. He was hurt badly in the rescue. A lot of people were, but we managed to get a healer to the hospital. He has some scarring from the burns. Lucian will probably have to be in a wheelchair for the rest of his life though."

"Oh no. I am so sorry."

"We're just happy he made it out alive."

"Nina, please." Alec's knee bounced impatiently. "We'll catch you up on everyone later. What's happening with the Light?"

"Right! Sorry. Part of why we're able to see individual connections is because we have a deeper link to the Light. It is like a constant presence—both in me and all around me. A tapestry or a mist hanging over everything. Most of the time it is just a part of how I experience the world, another sense, like sight or smell. But when I need to use it, I become more aware of it. Like when you're looking for an item in a messy room, you use your sense of sight with more intention. When I am looking for a particular Variant, I am more acutely aware of my connection to the Light.

"On the other hand, sometimes it makes itself known to me. Like when a loud noise startles you, you are suddenly more aware of your sense of hearing. When something is significant, it's hard to ignore—sitting here with you, for instance. Your access to the Light is immense, Evelyn, your threads to your Variants solid and strong. It is not something I can avoid noticing." She sighed and threaded her fingers in front of her.

"The same is true when there is something not so positive in the Light. I can tell when there are . . . I believe you call them *Lightwhores* completing a transaction—selling their Light like it's a cheap thing. The Light feels heavy, tainted, in these moments.

"Over the past few months, the Light has been feeling more and more . . . off. It is not a particular incident or location we can pinpoint. It is more like a general sense of it being tainted some-how, strained, tense. It has us all on edge. We have never experi-enced a sense of wrongness of this magnitude. We are worried—worried enough to set aside our internal politics and try to figure it out. That is why we are visiting some of the more powerful Vitals we know. We are hoping by being near you, studying the way the Light is behaving, we may get a clue as to what is happening."

I shared a worried glance with Alec and Tyler. "Nina, it's probably Davis—what he's doing with his machines."

It was bad enough he was causing political and social unrest all over the world. I hadn't considered that his fucked-up experi-ments could have an impact on the very thing fueling Variant abil-ities, the very thing that made us what we were. He was rotting everything he touched.

"Yes." She nodded solemnly. "That is what I and most of my fellow Lighthunters believe also, but we thought it prudent to rule out any other potential issues. Plus, visiting with the Vitals allows us to explain the precarious situation, to urge them not to support this lunatic in any way. Maybe even to fight."

Alec perked up. "Fight? How?"

"We do not have all the answers, but we do feel strongly that he cannot be permitted to continue unresisted."

"Agreed." Tyler took a sip of his tea and crossed his legs. "But if fighting is even an option, and you have the kind of resources you seem to be hinting at, why haven't you done anything yet?"

"It is complicated." Nina sighed. "There is a reason we have managed to remain secret. We rarely get involved in any way that's not discreet. I am hoping that will change very soon."

Mr. Takata sat up even straighter, his expression serious. "Knowing what I know due to my work, and knowing what I know due to my connection to two Vivids, I can't in good conscience sit by and do nothing. Regardless of what the Lighthunters decide to do, I am prepared to take whatever action is necessary to put a stop to this. I am at your service, Evelyn."

"Thank you." I smiled, still a little uncomfortable at the intensity of his devotion.

His grandmother patted his hand and smiled, the lines in her face deepening. He'd spoken in English, but she'd gleaned the gist of it.

"I don't know what the answers are." Alec took a sip of his own tea, scowling at the little cup as if he wished it were something stronger. "I'm not even sure what the right questions to ask are. But one thing I know for certain is we have to keep Evie safe."

No one disagreed with him. Nina started to chat with Mr. Takata and his formidable mother in Japanese while Alec continued to scowl into his tea.

Tyler was leaning back against the wall of the teahouse, frowning, his unfocused gaze pointed at his feet.

I was just about to ask him where he'd gone when his shoulders tensed. The change in posture was barely discernible—something I wouldn't have even noticed if I hadn't been staring at him.

His eyes remained unfocused but started to dart around, as if he were looking for something the rest of us couldn't see.

I moved without thinking, my Light reacting to his body's need for it. My hand covered his, and after only a few moments, he whipped his head up.

He flipped his hand so he could hold mine in a firm grip. "We need to leave. They found us."

"What? How?" I demanded at the same time Alec shot to his feet with a growled, "Fuck." He looked ready to throw me over his shoulder and just run down into the valley.

"We have about an hour until they reach us. They've been watching you since we met in New York." Tyler nodded at Mr. Takata, and the older man frowned in confusion.

"It's not possible. I've taken every precaution."

"Your countermeasures were excellent, but some footage from the hotel lobby slipped through. It took them a while to put it together, but now we have a team of six, disguised as tourists, coming up the main path." He pointed across the square.

"Are there any other ways in or out of the village?" Alec asked as everyone else got to their feet.

"No," Tyler and Mr. Takata answered at the same time. The latter elaborated, "Climbing the peak of the mountains is too treacherous, and the descent into the valley can only be managed if you're a goat."

Alec cursed again, but Mrs. Takata cut in with a gentle touch to her grandson's arm. She spoke in rapid Japanese, impossible for me to follow, but he translated for us.

"There is a young man in the village with an invisibility gift. He does not have a Vital, but if you are willing to share your Light, Evelyn, he can hide you all."

"But what about you? What about the village? These men are dangerous." I took Mrs. Takata's hand. Her skin was paper thin, her hand fragile, but her grip was strong. I'd only just met her, yet I'd already learned so much. Now I was about to leave just as I'd brought danger to her doorstep.

A heavy, twisted feeling settled in the pit of my stomach. Destruction followed me everywhere I went.

"If they are claiming to be tourists, there should be no issues." Mr. Takata waved his hand. "If they ask questions, well, I am simply here visiting my grandmother. And if they get violent, we are more than capable of defending ourselves."

He was such a calm, pleasant man I sometimes forgot Mr. Takata was in the same line of work as Alec and Tyler. I nodded reluctantly.

"We have a way off the mountain, but then what?" Alec asked. "We can't trust any of our Melior Group contacts on the ground here. Not anymore. What's our next move?"

"You come with me." Nina crossed her arms, nothing but determination on her face. "I can get you out and somewhere safe, and it may be just what we need to convince the rest of the Lighthunters to take action."

Alec looked to Tyler. We had no other ideas, and it sounded good to me, but Alec was letting him make the final call.

Tyler propped his hands on his hips and sighed. "I can't tell if what you're proposing is safe—your immunity to my ability is irritating, to say the least—but I think it's the best chance we have. The Lighthunters have managed to evade discovery by the entire world for hundreds of years. Can't think of a better group of people to keep us hidden, keep Eve safe."

He shrugged, and it was decided.

Nina nodded and turned to Mrs. Takata, expressing her disappointment that their visit had to be cut so short. In my broken Japanese, I expressed the same sentiment, giving the old lady a low bow. She pulled me into a hug and patted my cheeks.

"We will meet again." She nodded with a tranquil smile.

Ethan and Josh wandered into the square, chatting and joking as they strolled. As they approached us, Josh noticed something was off first, his easy smile falling.

"Pack your shit," Alec barked before they even had a chance

to greet anyone. "We've been made. We have twenty minutes to get out of here."

"Nina?" Josh ignored him and came forward to say hi.

"Oh man." Ethan groaned. "I was just about to get something to eat." His shoulders slumped as he turned to follow a marching Alec back to the house.

I took his hand. "Yeah, but you're always about to get something to eat."

"True." He grinned at me.

Within fifteen minutes we were packed and at the start of the path. We said our goodbyes, and the villagers all went about their daily lives as if we'd never been there.

The young man with the invisibility—he didn't look older than seventeen—was so excited to put his ability to use he was practically bouncing on the spot. He needed contact to keep us hidden, but as I reached for his hand, Nina grabbed my wrist and stepped between us. Without any thought for personal space, she placed her hand on the man's chest and cocked her head. After a few moments, she smiled.

"When you can, head east," she told him. "Your Vital is in Africa, somewhere south of Ethiopia."

"Thank you!" The young man beamed, bowing repeatedly and grinning.

Nina stepped away, and I took the man's hand, pushing Light to him in a steady stream. The others made a chain behind us, and we stood at the side of the path and waited.

It was almost too easy. The six men came walking up the path, barely breathing hard after the long, difficult climb. They were casually dressed, like tourists, but their expressions were hard, their eyes searching, and they barely talked.

They passed us without so much as a glance. Once they were well on their way to the center of the village, we moved down the path.

At the bottom of the mountain, we said our goodbyes to the youth who'd probably just saved our lives. He grinned, clearly happy to have been useful, as well as overjoyed at the knowledge Nina had shared about his Vital.

A beat-up old van pulled up next to us, and we piled in. The driver said a few short words to Nina but generally ignored us until he deposited us at a small airstrip.

We rushed from the van into a small plane, the engines already firing up as the door was pulled shut. The pilot was as quiet as the driver, not asking any questions and not sharing anything either.

As we settled into our seats, I finally took a few full breaths.

Ethan took my hand in his big one and promptly fell asleep. I smiled at him affectionately even as I cursed him out of envy. He really could sleep anywhere.

Just as fast as we'd arrived, we were leaving Japan, this time, hopefully, completely undetected.

I leaned my head on my fire fiend's big shoulder and closed my eyes, hoping to get some sleep too.

TWENTY-SIX

Nina unbuckled her seatbelt and stood in the aisle, hands on her hips and an excited look on her face. "Time to go."

She started pulling bags down from the overhead lockers.

"Time to go?" I shared a worried glance with Ethan. "Uh, in case you haven't noticed, we're in the *fucking air*."

"We're somewhere over the Mediterranean, right?" Tyler questioned, picking up one of the bags and starting to strap it to his body.

Holy fucking Heisenberg! They were going to make me jump out of this plane.

"Extraction?" Alec asked.

"Naturally." Nina had her parachute in place and was adjusting a pair of goggles. "I have a boat coming to get us."

Alec nodded, a smile pulling at his lips as he started to strap his parachute on. "Nice."

"*Nice?*" I screeched. Ethan and I stood, holding on to the backs of our seats. He looked wary but not panicked like me. Josh remained in his seat, unfazed, still reading his book. "Not nice! No one said anything about jumping out of a plane! I'm not jumping out of a *fucking plane!*"

Alec grabbed my wrist and pulled me into the aisle. He

planted both hands on my shoulders, piercing me with his blue-eyed stare. "Bailing out now while the pilot keeps going and lands somewhere far away means we evade anyone who might be tracking our flight on radar. We have all the equipment. This is the best move."

I fisted my hands in his shirt, as if I could stop him from hurling me out of a plane. "Jumping out of a fucking plane is the best move? I don't fucking think so!" My voice sounded frantic as my heart hammered in my chest.

"You get so sweary when you're stressed." Alec chuckled. "It's cute."

Tyler handed Ethan a harness. "You and Alec are closest in height—you can tandem jump with him."

"Cool!" Ethan started putting the harness on. He looked more excited than scared now, as if this were an adrenaline experience and not a life-or-death situation.

We were twenty thousand feet in the air. Tyler said we were over the Mediterranean. We'd be landing in water. I quickly calculated terminal velocity—we would be falling somewhere between 120 and 150 miles per hour. Water is incompressible fluid, so hitting it at terminal velocity would be like hitting concrete. The likelihood of surviving a fall like that was . . . practically nonexistent.

My body screamed at me to sit back down and strap on my seatbelt. My mouth just started screaming. "No no no no no! Don't make me do this! I'm not fucking doing this! We're all going to die! Oh my god!"

"Did she just say *god*?" Ethan chuckled, leaning over Alec's shoulder to look at me.

"Fuck, she's really freaking out." Tyler leaned over Alec's other shoulder, frowning.

"Evie." Alec shook my shoulders lightly, his voice firm. "Calm down."

"Calm down?" I finally released his shirt and pulled myself up to my full height. "Calm down?! Never in the history of calming down has being told to calm down resulted in a person. *Calming. Down. Alec!*" I screamed into his face, letting all my fear and frustration loose.

Instead of getting pissed off or yelling back, he smirked as if I was amusing him. Then, before I could start yelling again, he leaned forward and kissed me. With one hand on the back of my neck and the other at the base of my spine, he pinned me against him and devoured my mouth with his. Involuntarily, I wrapped my arms around him and closed my eyes. It was one of those searing, all-consuming Alec kisses I loved so much.

Logically I knew this was a distraction—he was using physiology to override psychology. The tactic annoyed me slightly, but damn, if it wasn't working.

After a few dizzying moments, he pulled back. "You're safe. We've got you. Tyler and I have done this hundreds of times. Josh has a skydiving license. We know what we're doing."

Reluctantly, I nodded.

"Better?" he pressed.

"Better." I nodded again, breathing him in. He made me feel strong, but I'd made it a point to avoid planes since . . . and now I was about to jump out of one, into water no less. Talk about triggering trauma. "I'm still scared, Alec."

"I know. This isn't like that night." He knew where my freak-out was coming from. "We're not crashing. You're safe. You have to trust us, precious. We'd never let anything happen to you."

I closed my eyes and took a deep breath. If there was one thing I could be sure of, that was it. They put my safety above all else. I had to trust this was the best move.

"Two minutes!" Nina yelled from her spot near the door, one hand on the handle.

"Alec, Kid, get in position," Tyler ordered. Alec dropped one last kiss to my forehead and went to stand next to Nina.

Ethan let him pass before pulling me into a hug. "Love you, baby. You're gonna be fine." He kissed me on the cheek and followed Alec. They attached their harnesses together, and Alec started giving Ethan instructions.

"Eve, you're with me. Josh, gear up." Tyler handed me a harness, not dissimilar to the one they'd forced me into just before we rappelled down a building in Manhattan.

"Actually"—Josh closed his book and stood, the picture of calm—"I think Eve should go with me."

I looked between them. Did Josh have more skydiving experience? Alec said he had a license, whatever that meant.

"One minute!" Nina called.

"Good thinking!" Tyler slapped him on the back. "I still want you strapped together though."

Josh nodded, already putting his harness on. It didn't seem to be attached to a large backpack containing a parachute though . . .

"See you down there." Tyler gave me a brief kiss on the lips and moved toward the door, taking his position in line to jump out of a *fucking plane*.

I couldn't believe we were doing this.

"Nina's about to open the door." Josh pulled me to him. "It's going to be windy and loud." As I tied my hair back, he explained the best way to skydive, what to expect, how to hold my arms and legs out.

He flashed me his perfect teeth in a grin just as Nina turned the lever and the door went flying.

Frigid wind whipped all around us with a deafening roar.

I gripped the back of the seat. Nina waved and flashed me a smile as if she were popping out to grab us some coffee, then she stepped out and disappeared. My stomach dropped.

Alec and Ethan shuffled forward, Ethan's back strapped to Alec's front. They leaned forward in the door, and Ethan whooped as they went plummeting.

Tyler checked his straps one last time and stepped out without hesitation.

Josh nudged me to face the aisle, and I felt him attach my

harness to his. "It's our turn," he yelled over the noise. "Now, juice me up, babe!"

I turned my wide eyes over my shoulder, and he caught my lips in a kiss. I pushed Light to him as if my life depended on it, focusing on the feeling of his perfect lips on mine, the tingling, warm sensation of the Light transferring.

As he kissed me, Josh walked us forward, down the aisle and toward the open door.

He broke the kiss and smiled. "Ready?"

I faced forward. We were already at the door, Josh's hands gripping the sides of the opening, bright sunshine and a few fluffy clouds visible beyond.

I dared not look down.

"No." I shook my head. Every instinct I had, every scrap of self-preservation in me, screamed to *step the fuck back!*

But Josh shoved forward, and we were officially jumping out of a plane.

My heart lodged in my throat and stopped beating.

I tried to scream, but the intense rush of air whipping at my face took my breath away.

We don't have a parachute!

My mind reminded me of this little fact now that we were already free-falling.

Somehow, some part of my brain was with it enough to follow Josh's instruction. I held my arms out loosely at my sides, my knees bent slightly, and tucked my chin against my chest, creating a little pocket of air so I could breathe before I passed out.

My eyes watered, and my face felt numb from the frigid air.

Josh's arms banded around my middle, and he reminded me why jumping without a parachute wasn't a fatal mistake.

Our plummet toward certain death slowed. After a few moments, I felt the unmistakable nudge of Josh's ability.

He was using his telekinesis to fly.

In a moment of panic, I slammed more Light into him. I had to make sure he had enough! I knew how draining it was for him to do the flying thing, how hard he'd had to train to get it, how much Light and concentration he needed to do it for any length of time.

He grunted, and his arms tightened around me. Then he chuckled. "Ease up, Eve. I've got plenty. I won't drop us."

He didn't have to shout at all for me to hear him. Actually, all the overwhelming noise had ended. I stopped the Light flow, leaving the connection open in case he needed more, and looked around.

We'd come to a complete stop and were floating among fluffy white clouds.

My shoulders relaxed just a fraction, and I took a deep breath of the fresh air. I hugged Josh's arms around myself, feeling the muscles and tendons in his forearms as I craned my neck to look at him.

He smiled, relaxed, confident in his ability and my Light needed to fuel it. I smiled back, some of the fear finally dissipating. I couldn't even feel the harness tugging me or cutting into my legs; Josh held me in his arms and with his ability with no extra help needed.

I looked down just in time to see one, then two, then three parachutes unfurl and slow the others' descent.

The bright sun sparkled off the water below, and coastline and islands gleamed green and gold in the distance. It was beautiful.

Josh started floating us down toward the water. Unlike the pace we'd been rocking only moments before, his speed now was closer to a rollercoaster than a missile. Much more enjoyable.

"This is like the coolest ride at the fair!" I told him through a smile.

He laughed, but instead of replying, he sent us sailing through the air in a perfectly smooth loop.

I couldn't contain my laughter. I'd gone from abject terror to giddy glee within a matter of minutes. I decided not to consider the implications for my mental state too closely. That was just what being in a Bond meant. They could make me feel incredible no matter how bad things seemed.

As we continued our easy glide toward the glittering turquoise water, I relaxed into Josh's embrace. He was so good at this, as if he'd been born with wings and had been flying his whole life.

As if to illustrate my point, he planted a soft, lazy kiss to the curve of my neck, not even paying full attention to keeping us both airborne. I smiled and wriggled against him, which made me think about how closely he was holding me. His front was against my back, not a breath of space between us, our feet tangling playfully.

"Hey, Josh?" I half turned my head so he could hear me.

"Hmm?" he hummed, his lips still at my neck.

"How long do you think you could keep us both in the air? Theoretically? And how hard would you need to concentrate for the duration of . . ."

He smiled against my neck, making me bite my bottom lip. I had no doubt he knew exactly what I was insinuating, but he decided to tease me anyway.

"For the duration of what? What exactly do you have on that fucking dirty mind of yours?"

I shivered against him. I loved it when he cursed. It gave me a glimpse of his freaky side—a side only *I* got to see . . . and sometimes the others.

"I think you know exactly what I have in mind." I arched my back, pressing my ass into his groin. I wasn't at all surprised to feel his erection.

He chuckled but put a tiny amount of space between us. "I think that can be arranged, but not right now, unless you want an audience?"

I looked back down. We were barely twenty feet away from the surface. The others had all landed and disconnected their parachutes, the colorful fabric floating in the water. A speedboat pulled up next to Nina, and a person reached down to help her over the side.

Ten feet. We were close enough to hear their voices but not make out what they were saying.

Ethan went next, Nina and the other man pulling him up while Alec and Tyler helped from the water.

Five feet.

It was Tyler's turn. He was light and agile, only needing a hand over the edge from Ethan. Alec lifted himself into the boat before anyone could offer him help.

"Shit!" We were about to hit the water. I'd been too distracted watching them all climb to safety to notice. "Josh! I don't want to go in the water, Josh. Josh!"

Our toes only just touched the surface, then he spun us around and farther up, away from the boat.

"It's OK. It's OK, Eve. I've got you." He tightened his grip around my middle, and I realized I was digging my fingers into his forearms. I released my grip immediately and rubbed over the nail marks I'd left in his skin.

"Sorry. Shit, I hurt you."

"No, you didn't. You OK? What's going on?"

"I . . ." I wasn't sure how to articulate it. I couldn't remember hitting the water when the plane crashed, but apparently my body could. Approaching it from the sky made me panic in a way that was hard to explain. "I just *really* don't wanna go in the water."

"We don't have to." He was already steering us back toward the boat, coming in slower and slower. "Tuck your legs up."

I wrapped my arms loosely around my knees. Josh approached the boat with such control I barely even felt us land. His feet touched down on the wooden boards, and the sensation of his ability disappeared.

Alec was at our side instantly, holding me in his arms as Tyler disconnected my harness from Josh's, then set me on my feet. He watched me with a question in his eyes while his hands roamed, looking for injury. Tyler and Ethan eyed me warily too, clearly on edge.

"I'd love to meet you all properly, but it's probably best if we don't linger here too long." The man at the front of the boat drew our attention, speaking in a thick Greek accent.

Working as a team, we pulled the soaking, thin fabric of the parachutes out of the water and dumped them in a corner. Everyone took a seat. Ethan pulled me down between him and Alec, and the speedboat took off.

It was a pretty smooth ride. The hot summer sun beat down from above, and the salty air whipped past our faces as the Greek man pushed the boat faster and faster. There weren't any massive waves or bumpy bits; we just glided along the waters of the Mediterranean . . . for hours.

The noise made it hard to talk, so we spent most of the ride in silence, watching the water and the occasional bit of land in the distance. By the time the roar of the engine started to calm down, I was starving, a little seasick, and completely over the novelty of being in a speedboat.

We pulled up to a small dock jutting out of the side of a cliff face. There was no beach or easy approach to speak of, but three other boats identical to ours were docked there. We got out of the boat and took some time to stretch and look around as the man tied the boat to the dock.

"I'm Stavros." He smiled at us—crooked teeth and deep laugh lines on a tanned face. "Pleased to meet you all."

Nina introduced us one by one. "Stavros is a Lighthunter, like me."

"It's a pleasure to meet you." I smiled, but I couldn't stop my eyes from wandering up the cliff. I had to lean back to see the top. "Um, where are we, exactly?"

"If I told you, I'd have to kill you," Stavros deadpanned, his voice low and gravelly. My eyes widened. Alec stiffened and stepped between the man and me. He couldn't use his ability— none of them could on the Lighthunters—but Alec was deadly for more than one reason.

Nina slapped Stavros on the shoulder and rolled her eyes. "Not funny, old man."

His serious mask dropped, and they both laughed. "It was a little funny."

The scowl on Alec's face suggested he disagreed.

"Come on." Stavros picked up his backpack and waved for us to follow him.

Alec grudgingly brought up the rear. At the end of the dock, stairs zigzagged all the way to the top of the cliff. Most of them were carved directly into the rock, but every once in a while, timber ones filled in gaps.

"We are in the Greek islands." Stavros puffed his chest out. "This island is called Naxonnos, and as far as the authorities are concerned, it is barren and unlivable with no wildlife or plant life of note. It is remote, about three hundred kilometers past the nearest island frequented by tourists or locals. It is also Lighthunter HQ."

He delivered the last line as we crested the top of the cliff. This island definitely wasn't barren or abandoned. Before us was an entire city! Or what I imagined a city would look like without really tall skyscrapers.

Paved streets and low buildings stretched out in front of us. People were milling about; ATVs and golf carts zipped past. I could even see a helicopter on a landing pad to our right. I couldn't believe an operation like this had managed to go undetected by all the world's authorities and operations, including Melior Group.

Ethan echoed my thoughts. "Man, Lucian's gonna be pissed he didn't know about this."

Nina leaned forward, sticking her head between ours to stage-whisper, "Wait until you see what's underground." She winked and grinned at us. "Let's get you settled and fed."

She pushed past us and led the way down the main street. Stavros waved goodbye and wandered off.

A few people threw us curious glances, but for the most part, people just went about their business. I was a little surprised to see so many children running around among the adults.

"Nina, what's with all the kids? I thought this was, like, a secret lair or something."

She burst out laughing, then cocked her head and hummed. "Yes, I suppose it kind of is. A lot of our work happens from here and a few other sites like it across the world, but it is also a settlement of sorts. Lighthunters call this place home. It is a sanctuary as much as it is a lair."

The hot summer sun was beating down on us, and I was grateful when she gestured us toward a shaded table outside a café. She ordered food and drinks for everyone in Greek as we settled in.

"How many languages do you speak?" Josh asked as Ethan fanned himself with the menu. Alec and Tyler sat back, looking relaxed, but I knew they were watching everything closely.

"Twelve," Nina answered as if it were no big deal.

My eyes bugged out. "Fluently?"

"Yes. French is my native tongue, and my accent is stubborn, but I speak, read, and write the other eleven languages fluently."

Before we could ask more, the food was delivered. We all dug in, Ethan the most enthusiastically.

After half his meal was gone, Tyler leaned forward. "You said there was something underground?"

"Yes, about twice as much as you see above ground. Most of the dwellings and everyday life is above ground—cafés, shops, the school, the library, and so on. Below is a large bunker, offices, a server room, surveillance, our secret texts and teachings. Our work is below ground, safe."

Tyler abandoned his food, his full focus on Nina. "What's with all the secrecy? How is this even possible?"

It was killing him that there was something he didn't know—that an entire organization managed to exist without his knowledge.

"At the start, it was about protecting ourselves." She waved her hand dismissively, speaking around mouthfuls of food. "We're talking about hundreds of years ago, when it was believed the Light was a gift from God and Lighthunters were kind of like prophets. We had a connection that no other mortal being did. We understood it, saw it like no one else could. Eventually, some assholes figured out they could make money from this. Between the snake oil salesmen—the ones pretending to be Lighthunters and charging a fortune to send hopeful young Variants on veritable goose chases—and the more sinister practice of capturing, torturing, imprisoning, and exploiting Lighthunters . . . yeah, we decided to go to ground.

"At the time, we were led by a charismatic man named Father Lightwood. He believed we were truly God's prophets, sent here to guide the masses to better live according to how God wanted us to live. He convinced us the best way to do that was silently—that our work was too sacred to risk having it perverted. We withdrew from society, disappeared from the villages and emerging cities, took all our texts and any other texts we could with us.

"Over the years, we continued to erase any trace of ourselves from history. We worked in secret, orchestrating the meetings of Variants and Vitals by setting up scholarships, overseas exchange programs, and job offers to bring them into proximity with one another. We only stepped in where we felt we needed to—like the incident in Thailand."

"I'm amazed you've managed to keep this a secret for so long." Tyler shook his head.

"What happens when a Lighthunter is born? Do you take them from their family?" I questioned.

Nina smiled. "That is not necessary. We are not like Variants and humans. A Variant can be born to entirely human parents and vice versa. A Lighthunter can only be born to Lighthunter parents—our gift is hereditary. Not every child is born with the sight, but no child *outside* a Lighthunter family is ever born with it. There are one hundred recorded bloodlines of Lighthunter families. Sixty-six remain to this day. It is frowned upon and very rare for us to marry outside the community."

I nodded. "I guess not living among the rest of the world would help with keeping the secret." All the kids running around made much more sense now. This wasn't just a hippie commune on steroids or a headquarters for a secret society; this was an entire civilization, living in secret.

Nina smiled sadly. "You have to understand, for us, this secret and the work we do is sacred. We have evolved with the rest of the world—hell, some of the technology widely available now we developed first and then leaked—but our traditions are strong and lasting. The fact that we are even having discussions about getting more involved is momentous. People are scared, but it is time for change. We have the resources to help, and we *should*."

"Why are you telling us all this now?" Josh asked one of the things I'd been wondering too. "You were so secretive when we brought you in to find Eve, then Charlie. Why lay it all out now? Why even bring us here?"

"I trust you." She shrugged. "I think our goals are aligned, and I think it is time. We know more about the outside world than your Melior Group does, but we are still isolated from it. I am hoping that by bringing you here, the reality of what is happening beyond those cliffs will become more concrete for those who rarely leave."

She was helping us, keeping us safe from Davis's greedy clutches, but she was also trying to effect change—in her own community and in the wider world. I admired her for that.

"Nina!" The exclamation was half reproach, half disbelief.

We all turned to look down the street. A small group of people were marching in our direction, varying degrees of anger and confusion on their faces.

Nina groaned. "If they don't excommunicate me first," she mumbled before standing to face the group.

The man who'd shouted, the one in the lead, was tall, his full head of white-gray hair a contrast to his dark olive complexion.

"What were you thinking?" he demanded as he reached us. "You brought non-enlightened here? Have you gone completely mad?"

"I understand this goes against our traditions, but I felt I had no choice." Nina spoke in a low voice, her head bowed, her hands crossed in front of her. "Elders"—she raised her head, looking at them all before turning slightly to us—"this is Evelyn Maynard, a Vivid with great power. She is in danger, and she may just be what we need to help us come to a decision. These are her Bondmates."

A dozen sets of eyes focused on me. I resisted the urge to hunch my shoulders and sink into the chair, opting instead to wave and smile awkwardly.

TWENTY-SEVEN

The first few days with the Lighthunters were like a holiday. They freezed us out of most of their discussions while they decided what to do with us, and we were placed in a cottage on the quiet side of the island. There were no beaches, but the hill was slightly less steep—not like the sheer drop we'd had to climb up on the way in. It was still impossible to walk down, although the goats didn't seem to have any issues.

Our cottage was nestled in among about a dozen others. They were temporary accommodation for Lighthunters who didn't live on the island. As most of them were currently out visiting Vitals and Vivids, all the other cottages were empty.

Ours had a kitchenette, a dining table with four chairs, and a living area with a couch. At the back was a small bathroom and a decent-sized bedroom with two queen beds. Once we'd pushed the beds together and Josh had dragged an extra chair over from the cottage next door, we were actually quite comfortable. A little patio with chairs overlooked the cliff and the stunning view beyond, and farther down, there was even a pool and a traditional Turkish hammam.

We spent the days exploring the island; the perimeter could be walked in under two hours, and we were banned from some areas, so it didn't take long. Josh found a library in one of the main buildings, so he ended up doing a lot of reading. Alec and Ethan exercised frequently, and I joined them for daily runs.

Tyler struggled the most. He was so used to being in control, calling the shots, and knowing everything. Now, suddenly, he was supposed to just stay out of it. There were no newspaper deliveries on the island and no TV in our cottage. We'd all left our phones behind, and he immediately started having major tech withdrawals.

The sun hadn't even set on the first day by the time Tyler talked someone into giving him a laptop with a secure connection. He was able to keep an eye on the news; speak with Lucian, Kyo, and Charlie for short periods of time; and with Charlie's help, even keep an eye on restricted intelligence channels. He didn't share the info unless someone asked, but he was looking more and more worried each day. It wasn't a surprise to any of us that things were going downhill.

We spent the evenings eating slow dinners on the patio and sipping Mediterranean wine. We played truth or dare, laughed, and had conversations that started with statements like "Remember that time we snuck out to follow Alec and Gabe to The Hole?" (Josh) and "OK, real talk, I actually hate mushrooms, and I wish you'd stop putting them in the stir fry" (Tyler) and "I'll kill you all if you ever tell anyone, but . . ." (Alec).

I learned more about Alec and Ty's bad-boy stage, their time hanging with the rough crowd from The Hole.

"Alec did it for many reasons, not least of all for the sense of control it gave him," Tyler mused, swirling his pinot grigio. The corded muscle in his forearms danced with every movement. "But for me it was more about the challenge. My ability is passive. I never had to control it or rein it in. I just had to learn to keep my mouth shut when I accidentally learned something private. But other than that, I was free to use it all day and at any time. Fighting at The Hole made me learn how to control it, how to turn it off. I loved the mental challenge of figuring out how to do that more than learning how to fight, although that was fun too."

"Eventually." Alec smirked. "You got your ass handed to you the first few times."

"Not the first time." Tyler laughed. "The first time I didn't even last two minutes before that fucking light went off telling everyone I'd used my ability. It was second nature. It took me ages to learn how to turn it off. *Then* I started getting my ass handed to me."

Later that night we got onto the topic of food, and Ethan told us he really didn't want to play pro sports. He had the talent and natural affinity for it, could probably have his pick of football, baseball, and ice hockey teams if he chose to really focus and train. "But honestly, all I want to do is cook." He shrugged his big shoulders and looked around at the guys sheepishly.

"Bro, if you wanna cook"—Alec leaned forward, resting his elbows on his knees—"then fucking cook. Who cares?"

Josh jumped in. "Life's too short, man, filled with bad shit, pain, and loss. Follow your fucking dream."

"You can totally do it. I know." Tyler tapped the side of his head, half joking about his ability in an attempt to lighten the mood. It worked, and we all laughed.

I took Ethan's big hand in mine and squeezed. I had no doubts at all he could do whatever he set his mind to. All of them could. And with each other's support, we would be unstoppable. If we managed to survive the clusterfuck our lives had turned into. If the *world* managed to survive.

It seemed none of us really wanted to talk about that though—it was too heavy and bitter a subject for the sweet, warm night. It was too hard to talk about the future when we were precariously balanced on the tip of a sharp knife, unsure if we were about to slide down the smooth side, unharmed, or go plummeting down the sharp edge, leaving streaks of red behind.

Despite the way Tyler frowned at the laptop every day, his shoulders sagging under the weight of his worry, we managed to ignore the world for a few days and just enjoy one another. If my mother had taught me anything, it was to find joy in these moments—to seize the times of laughter and positivity, hold them tight, and let yourself embrace them. Because you never know when the next threat will come.

So I enjoyed the fresh food, the wonderful wine, the honest conversation with my Bond. I reveled in the warm sun on my shoulders during the day, in their embrace at night as I made love to one or sometimes more than one of them.

For a few blissful days, I let the rest of the world fade into the background as I lost myself in their stories, their smiles, their affectionate yet possessive touches. I knew I was sticking my head in the sand, but I couldn't bring myself to care. For the first time since I'd met them, there were no secrets—not from everyone else and not from one another—and no immediate threats to our lives.

So fuck it! I was treating it like a Greek holiday and enjoying every minute.

The morning of the fourth day, we all had a slight hangover from the wine, and we lounged around the cottage and the patio. After days of summer heat, the sky was finally a little overcast, the air blessedly breezy.

By the early evening, it was cool enough for me to go in search of a cardigan. The sun peeked out from behind the clouds for the first time that day, just in time to disappear into the azure water in a stunning sunset.

"I'm gonna go give that steam room a try," Josh announced, dropping the third novel he'd finished in as many days and stretching his arms over his head.

"Great idea." I abandoned my search for warmer clothing and took Josh's hand instead.

"Talked me into it!" Ethan flashed his dimples and followed us out.

Tyler grunted, still buried in his laptop at the table. Alec was napping in the bedroom.

The three of us took a slow, lazy walk in the post-sunset glow, following a cobbled path to a building near the back of the cottages. A couple of outdoor showers stood in the building's little courtyard, just outside a spacious changing room and bathroom. Past that, a glass door led to the steam room.

Josh fiddled with the controls on the wall, and it started to fill with steam.

"Shit." I grimaced. "We don't have bathing suits."

"Who cares? There's no one around." Ethan shrugged, whipping his T-shirt over his head and pushing his shorts and underwear down in one go. Every large, defined muscle was on display; his fire tattoo curved tantalizingly over his shoulder, making me want to lean forward and lick the flames.

"This is a Turkish hammam," Josh mused as he too stripped down to nothing. "Traditionally, they were used in the nude, the men and women having separate facilities or times of the day to visit."

Now there were *two* glorious specimens of male beauty before me—all that corded muscle, masculine spatterings of hair, smooth skin, and abs . . . so many abs.

Josh startled me out of my trance by stepping around me to grab three thin Turkish towels from a shelf. "They did, however, use towels from time to time." He handed one to Ethan and one to me, then secured one around his own hips before giving me a light kiss on the cheek.

He opened the glass door and walked into the steam that billowed out, his ass looking incredible even in a light pink towel. Ethan flashed me another mischievous grin and followed Josh, not bothering to wrap the towel around himself. I could've sworn he put a little extra swagger into his gait, and I stared at his bare ass unashamedly. It was *my* ass after all.

They were right. We hadn't seen anyone else in the cottages. It was unlikely anyone else would be coming to use the steam room any time soon.

I still wrapped the towel around myself after undressing, just in case.

I walked into the steam room and took a deep breath, letting the warm, moist air envelop me and drain some of the tension from my shoulders.

The room was an octagon; each side, apart from the glass-doored entrance, had tiled bench seating. Two of them, on opposite sides of the room, had a little sink on the bench with a beautiful mosaic pattern over it.

The entire room was tiled in dark gray and teal marble, including the pitched ceiling, which met in a point in the middle of the room, like a tent. Everything was very symmetrical and oozed opulence.

Ethan and Josh sat on the bench opposite the door, leaning back against the wall, their towels haphazardly resting over their laps.

In the center of the room was an octagonal, low platform, about the height of a coffee table. I wasn't sure what its purpose was, so I stepped around it and sat between Josh and one of the little sinks.

Steam had already filled the room and warmed the tiles. Even the light fabric of the towel felt heavy and sticky on my skin. Just as I reached to undo it, the door opened, and I paused just shy of exposing my boobs to the newcomer.

"This was a great idea, Josh." Tyler's voice echoed around the room. Alec closed the glass door behind them. They both had matching towels around their hips, which—except for one corner covering their crotches—they removed as they sat down. Tyler settled in on the other side of the little sink, and Alec sat on the opposite side of the room.

Once I was sure no one else was following them, I let my towel drop at my sides and leaned my head back against the tiles, closing my eyes. For a few moments we just sat in silence, breathing the steamy air and letting the heat warm us from the inside out.

I cracked one eye open and laughed. All four of them were staring at me, lips parted, gazes hungry. As if they didn't see my boobs on the daily. As if I hadn't had a threesome with Alec and Josh the night before. As if Ethan hadn't woken me that morning with his fingers sliding inside me. As if Tyler hadn't joined me in the cramped little shower afterward.

It was as if they couldn't get enough. I couldn't get enough of them either.

"I'm getting lightheaded." Ethan kept his deep voice low, but it echoed anyway.

"That's because you're freakishly tall." Tyler chuckled. "Your head is higher and therefore hotter."

"No." Josh's eyes hadn't left my body. "It's because Eve is sitting there completely fucking naked like the goddess she is."

I smiled but didn't reply, instead closing my eyes again. I wasn't embarrassed or self-conscious—I had nothing to hide from them anymore—but I wasn't exactly used to receiving constant compliments either.

"Maybe you should step outside," Alec suggested.

"Nah . . ." Ethan didn't elaborate.

"Then here, cool down a bit." Josh leaned over me to turn on the little tap, his arm brushing against my breasts in what was clearly a deliberate move.

I rolled my head to the side, curious. The sink didn't have a drain, and Josh turned the tap off once it was full. Then he picked up a little metal bowl sitting next to it, scooped up some water, and flung it at Ethan.

Ethan didn't even flinch, but his shoulders shook in silent laughter. "Refreshing."

The sound of splashing in the opposite sink pulled my gaze to Alec. He shut the water off and dipped his hands into it instead of using the bowl, sloshing some onto his forehead.

He dragged his hands down his face and pinned me with his icy stare, leaning forward and resting his elbows on his knees. The movement made the towel slide down, exposing dark hair and just a glimpse of silky-smooth skin lower still.

I turned to the side and copied him, scooping some cool water into my hands and splashing my face with it. Refreshing droplets trickled down my neck, dripped off my chin, ran down my chest. Alec's gaze followed their progress, his eyes drinking in every detail of my body. I could practically feel the caress of his eyes even from the opposite side of the room.

"What's the stage thing for?" I gestured to the tiled octagon in the middle of the room, looking for something to distract me from Alec's lascivious stare.

"Traditionally, bathing was a ritual as much as it was a part of daily routine," Josh explained. "People would take their time in a hammam. Usually an attendant or masseuse would provide an olive oil scrub and use a Kese mitt to exfoliate. That platform in the middle—the *göbektaşı*—is where most of the bathing, scrubbing, and massaging takes place."

"Why do you know so much about this?" Tyler chuckled, scooping some water with the bowl and splashing himself with it. Now it was me watching droplets cascade down his chest, following their path down his abs and past the tantalizing V at his hips, and seeing them get absorbed into the towel that would come away completely at the lightest tug. My fingers twitched, but I kept them on the bench by my side.

"It's history." Josh shrugged. "I find it interesting, and the library had a book about the cultural and historical significance of bathing houses, so . . ."

Tyler smiled, a glint entering his gray eyes. "Why don't you give us a demonstration then?"

He nodded at the platform, then swiped his hair off his forehead. Even wet from the water he'd been throwing on himself, it still managed to get in his face.

The grin Josh flashed him was downright wicked. "Great idea."

But it was Ethan who stood first, not even trying to grab at the towel. "If we're spending more time in here, I need a drink of water, and I need to turn the steam down or I'll pass out."

"Good thinking." Josh nodded as he stood too, coming to stand directly in front of me. Apparently we were all abandoning our towels now, because suddenly I had a half-erect dick in my face. Not that I was complaining. I licked the moisture off my lips and looked up at him.

The sound of the door closing behind Ethan mingled with the echo of Josh's voice.

"Come on, let me worship your body." He held his hand out, and I took it without hesitation, letting him guide me to the platform in the middle.

I sat on the edge, and Josh sat down next to me, nudging my shoulders until I turned my back to him. He started massaging my neck. His nimble fingers worked at the muscles in firm but gentle movements, slowly moving to my shoulders and my upper back.

My skin was damp with steam and sweat, and Josh's hands glided over me with ease, as if he'd used massage oil. I closed my eyes and rolled my head from side to side, giving his fingers room to move and stretching into the pressure.

The sound of the door opening again made me lift my eyes. Ethan waltzed back in, handed us each a bottle of water, and sat down in front of me. We drank deeply.

I knew it was dangerous to remain in a steam room or sauna for too long—you could get lightheaded or even pass out. But the water was helping us rehydrate, and Ethan must've turned the steam down very low. It was still hot and steamy, but it wasn't oppressive and difficult to breathe.

Besides, there was nothing that could tear me away from Josh's hands at the moment. If I passed out, so be it.

"Lie down on your front," he instructed, and I climbed farther onto the platform, my head near Alec's spot on the bench, my feet hanging off the end. The smooth, slick marble surface was almost too hot but pleasant against my skin.

Splashes echoed around me, and then Josh's hand was at my ankle, massaging gently before gliding up my leg. His touch was followed closely by the exquisite shock of cool water, trickling along my ankle and up to the top of my thigh. With my eyes closed, I felt every droplet as it caressed my skin.

He repeated the motions on my other leg—the gentle touch followed by the cool trickle of water up my calf, the back of my knee, my thigh.

Metal clanged against the stone bench, echoing in the dimly lit space. Then two sets of hands appeared at my feet. Judging by the size difference, Ethan had joined Josh in massaging my legs.

They started at my feet, moved up my ankles, calves, the backs of my thighs. They worked in perfect synchronicity, as they always did. It was both perfect—ideal pressure, exact amount of time spent on each muscle—and nowhere near enough.

As they paid special attention to the spot just under my ass, their fingers passing lower and lower between my thighs, the tap came on again. I kept my eyes closed as it turned off, and then a trickle of water started at my neck and traveled painfully slowly down the center of my spine. The droplets tickled a little along my ribs, but I was so lost in all the other sensations that it wasn't unpleasant.

Whoever it was repeated the action, using a little more water this time, covering my shoulders and then continuing past the base of my spine and between my butt cheeks.

Cool, velvety water trickled down between my thighs, adding even more moisture to my already wet folds, teasing my most sensitive parts in the most delicious way. I gasped, the sound startling in the heavy silence.

The air had already been thick with steam; now it became even heavier with taut, breathless anticipation.

TWENTY-EIGHT

As soon as the gasp left my lips, the hands at my thighs moved up and over my ass. They glided up my back, then separated over my shoulders. Ethan and Josh took my wrists and stretched my arms out to either side. Then the two of them started a slow, sensual massage, giving my arms the same treatment as my legs. The water appeared again, trickling over my wrists, up my arms, and to my shoulders.

The third set of hands picked up where they'd left off at my thighs, zeroing in on my ass. Immediately I knew it was Tyler. His hands were strong, firm, but smooth. Alec had rough, calloused hands, despite how tenderly they touched me.

Tyler kneaded my butt with slow, deliberate movements. His outspread hands ran all the way up and over, then caressed down my sides and hips, dipping into the crease before circling back up.

Every time he passed the underside of my ass, his fingers came within a hair's breadth of where I craved their touch the most. The teasing was maddening, and since this was Tyler, I was positive he knew exactly what he was doing.

After hours of this torture—OK, it was probably just a few minutes—his thumbs finally passed over my aching lips, pausing to massage the area for just a moment before moving away again.

I groaned, mostly in protest. I wanted *more*.

But they remained silent. Josh and Ethan's caresses had nearly reached my shoulders, and Tyler started massaging my back in long, slow strokes.

They worked together until every inch of my back was given the same treatment. Finally, Tyler's lips pressed between my shoulder blades, and he gently trailed kisses all the way down my spine. Once his mouth reached the sensitive area of my lower back, he kissed, nipped, and licked my skin as he moved his fingers up the inside of my thigh, up to my core, and slid two fingers inside in one smooth, slick movement.

I arched my back and moaned.

As Tyler moved his fingers, sliding them in and out painfully slowly, more water was poured down the length of my spine. Tyler removed his fingers and licked all the way back up my body, his tongue gliding over each little bump of vertebrae. He kept his body low over mine, his heavy breaths loud in my ear, his hot chest trapping me against the hot tiles.

"Turn over," he commanded, his voice thick with lust. And then he was gone. All their touch was gone.

I was at their mercy, ready to do whatever they asked, and I moved to obey immediately. I lifted onto my elbows but paused.

Alec was still in the same spot, his shoulders propped against the wall, his head leaning back.

Sharing me didn't come naturally to him, and he'd worked to get used to the idea. I'd had sex with more than one of them before, even with Alec involved, but we'd never done *this* before. I'd never had them all in the same room during sex, let alone have them all at the same time.

And that's exactly what I wanted. I hadn't been thinking about it—or much of anything really, I was so lost in the sensations —but now I realized that was *exactly* how I wanted it to play out. I wanted them all, at the same time, equally. As in all other things.

Alec met my gaze unflinchingly. He wasn't paying a lick of attention to the other guys or what they were doing. His full focus was on me, the lust in my eyes, the anticipation in my face, the way my boobs pressed into the tiles every time I took a breath. He was here for me and nothing else, and he wasn't leaving.

In fact, I was pretty sure he was enjoying himself. His lips parted as his hooded eyes took me in. The towel was still in the same spot, just barely covering his crotch, but now the tip of his erect cock was visible over the top of the fabric.

But I still needed to make sure. I focused on his eyes and mouthed, *OK?*

He smirked in that delicious, intense way that could equally mean he was about to hurt me or kiss me. I'd take either at this point. I'd take everything Alec had to give and politely ask for more.

He gave me one nod and pulled the towel away. I couldn't have stopped my gaze from wandering down if I'd wanted to. He wrapped his hand around his shaft and took one long, slow stroke that made me want to crawl over there and help him out.

But the others were getting impatient. Working together, they gently nudged and eased me onto my back.

Now that I was facing up, my back pressing into the warm tiles, I couldn't bring myself to close my eyes. Not with three such amazingly hot men leaning over me. So much glistening skin and corded muscle, the broad shoulders, the tight abs, the erect, proud cocks. They were all hard. For me.

It was intoxicating.

But their eyes, despite looking at me as if they each wanted to take a bite, were full of love. I felt safe, adored, *worshipped.*

The metal bowls were refilled once more, and Ethan and Josh poured refreshing water over my neck, my sensitive, hard nipples, and down my belly. As they reached the apex of my thighs, Tyler pushed my knees apart and let the water sluice down. The sensation was a little weird, almost as if I were about to pee, but it was pleasant. The bowls were set aside, and then their hands were back—*all* their hands, kneading my body all over.

Ethan and Josh concentrated on my top half, massaging my

arms, shoulders, and chest; teasing me by avoiding my breasts; and moving down to caress my stomach. Meanwhile, Tyler settled himself between my legs and worked on my thighs, his fingers pushing harder and firmer, his movements sliding closer and closer to where I wanted him most. His ability would've been telling him exactly where I wanted those hands. Any of those hands, all of them.

Usually when we made love, he blew my mind, picking up on every little thing I wanted and doing it before I could even voice the desire. But this time, he was deliberately denying me, teasing me. They all were, and I was starting to unashamedly writhe under their touch, looking for more friction, more . . . *anything* to satisfy this ache.

As Ethan and Josh finally stepped it up, their hands caressing my breasts, Tyler followed through and swiped his thumbs over my folds, rubbing in an up-and-down motion but still avoiding the most sensitive spot. The frustration was becoming unbearable.

"Please." The word came out on a desperate whisper.

"Enough." Alec spoke for the first time, his voice low but commanding. "Make her come."

Tyler paused and looked up, one eyebrow arched, his lips quirked into an amused little smile. I couldn't see Alec's face behind me, but I could picture the challenge in his gaze.

Tyler was the leader. It came naturally to him, and the others followed his lead because they trusted him. But every once in a while, Josh would step in to point out another option, and Alec would go completely off-script.

I had a feeling we were going to have a lot of fun exploring this power dynamic between them. Little did they know, I was the one truly in charge. If I demanded something with enough serious-ness, they would all willingly give it to me. That's why I loved letting Tyler take the lead, take control of my pleasure—I trusted him without question and knew he would do as I asked if it came down to it.

So I kept my mouth shut, waiting to see who would win this tug of war . . . this time.

"Why don't you come and do it yourself?" Tyler resumed his movements, making me moan, but kept his gaze locked on Alec.

"I'd prefer to watch for now. I want to see the look on her face when she shatters."

Tyler chuckled. "All right."

He slid his hands down my legs, shuffling back as he went. Before I could wonder where he was going, he lowered his head between my legs, wrapped his hands around my thighs, and stopped teasing. He didn't nip and lick and ease me into it. He stuck his tongue out and licked me firmly and decidedly.

I moaned in both relief and desperation. Tyler alternated between licking and sucking my clit and working the other areas with perfect pressure. His hands held my hips down, at his mercy.

Josh wrapped his hand around the front of my neck and, before I could think about whether it made me more turned on or less, dragged his hand down my chest and took a firm hold of my left breast. His perfect mouth closed over my nipple and made me cry out again.

Ethan laced his fingers through my right hand and kissed and licked his way to my other breast. His mouth was gentle, his tongue moving in wide, languorous swoops; Josh was a little rougher, raking his teeth over my sensitive flesh.

I was moaning with every breath, the sounds echoing off the tiles. My entire body was a ball of sensation, pleasure, *sex*. The amount of build-up I'd had to endure meant I was close to climax within just a few moments of having their mouths on me. Every swipe of a tongue on my aching flesh sent me closer and closer to the edge.

I gripped Ethan's fingers and threaded my free hand into my hair, rolling my head back. As soon as my eyes connected with Alec's, he moved toward me. He dropped to his knees, his cock inches from my face. I wanted it in my mouth, but I didn't think

I'd be able to give him a proper blow job—I was moaning and writhing too much, too lost in my own pleasure.

But Alec surprised me anyway. He sat back on his heels and pulled my hand out of my hair with rough fingers. His other hand held my jaw as he kissed me.

The stubble on his chin brushed against my nose as he kissed me upside down, his tongue claiming my mouth.

I had all their mouths on me, all their tongues working to give me the greatest pleasure I could ever imagine. Just as Alec pulled away and licked my lips, I came.

He watched me, just as he said he wanted to. His eyes took in every detail of my face and body as I came undone beneath them, wave after wave of pleasure washing through me; I moaned into Alec's face, and he panted above me.

Tyler slowed down as I rode it out. Ethan and Josh did the same, giving me little kisses.

They all backed up and stood around me, watching with heavy eyes and heaving chests as I slowly melted into a puddle on the platform. I liked having their eyes on me, their undivided attention. It made me feel powerful. Strong.

As my breathing calmed, I struggled up onto my elbows. Alec rushed forward to support me, so I gave up trying to sit up and leaned on him instead.

"Water." I reached my hand out, and Ethan placed a bottle of water in it immediately. I drank half the bottle and handed it back.

Alec was rock hard—he was pressing into my back, his hands starting to roam my body—and I could see how hard the others were too. Seeing and feeling the evidence of their desire had my body responding again already. Alec's touch was becoming more demanding, his hips rocking lightly behind me. Ethan sat on the edge of the platform and leaned in to kiss me, gentle at first but more insistent with every second.

Tyler sat down on the bench and drank his water as his eyes drank in what we were doing on the platform.

He'd started this, probably orchestrated the whole thing, and now he was sitting back to watch it play out. He looked so fucking cocky, with that knowing smile on his face, my favorite little bit of hair falling over his forehead.

I pulled away from Ethan's kiss, and he started kissing my jaw, moving down to my neck as his hand gripped my hip.

Josh walked around the platform until he stood before me, then gave me a brilliant, lust-filled smile. I just loved how freely they moved while completely nude, not even a little shy about the raging erections standing to glorious attention.

Untangling myself from the hands and mouths that already had me ready to go again, I lifted onto my knees and pulled Josh in for a kiss. He groaned into my mouth, grabbing my ass firmly and rubbing himself all over me. The steam made everything slick and slippery.

I pulled out of his embrace, turning to the other two.

"On your back." I didn't specify which one of them I wanted to lie down. I just pointed to the platform. Ethan obeyed immediately, flashing me a dimpled grin. He spread out on one side of the platform, one leg stretched out, the other hanging off the edge with his foot planted on the ground, his thigh muscle bulging. Who was I kidding? All of Ethan's muscles were bulging. All the damn time. He stared at me with adoration, patiently waiting for me to do whatever I wished to his body.

Alec, on the other hand, looked as if he was contemplating scooping me up and running out of there to find somewhere dark he could fuck me hard and fast against a wall, all to himself. I was all for that, but not today.

He was breathing hard, his eyes narrowed, his shoulders tight. He didn't like me telling him what to do. It was always a battle of wills with us. I kept my gaze steady, resolute, and eventually, his eyes still glued to mine, he lowered himself to his hands and knees and spread himself out on his back for me. Because while he didn't like me telling him what to do, he also fucking loved it when I told him what to do. It was fucked up and confusing, but I understood it perfectly. Because it was exactly how I felt about *him* telling *me* what to do.

I wanted Alec first. He'd been first in so many ways—my first Variant; the first one I saw after being kept away for years; the first one to bring me to orgasm, despite the less than ideal circumstances. I wanted him to be the first one inside me now.

I straddled his legs and gripped his cock, giving it a few slow strokes. His breathing got shallower at my touch, but he kept his hands by his sides.

I leaned down and kissed the jagged scars curving around his side. Crawling up his body, I let my breasts drag over his cock, his belly, his chest. He still didn't touch me.

Ethan watched my every move, lying patiently next to us, and all I had to do was lift my eyes to see Tyler staring at us too. Josh leaned down on one elbow on Alec's other side, his eyes appreciatively raking over both my body and Alec's.

Gripping the base of his cock again, I put all my focus on Alec. He was looking only at me.

As I sank down onto him, inch by excruciating inch, we both moaned. Those intense eyes, still fixed on me, threatened to close, roll into the back of his head. Getting that implant was the best decision I'd ever made. Feeling them inside me, skin on smooth skin—there was no better feeling in the world.

His hips bucked up to meet mine, and I splayed my hands on his stomach for balance. Finally, he lifted his hands off the tiles, but instead of touching me, he reached over his head and gripped the edge of the platform. His abdominal muscles stretched under my fingers, and I gave them a less than gentle scratch. I dragged my hands up his chest, then raked my nails back down as I moved my hips. The tile was slippery under my knees, and I couldn't get a good grip, but it just meant I ended up riding him deep, his hips rolling to meet mine in a delicious grind.

He grunted and finally gave in to the need to close his eyes, rolling his head back. His neck muscles pulled taut as his hands gripped the edge even tighter.

I gave up trying to lift my hips up and down and reveled in the feeling of him deep inside me. He was holding himself back from touching me, letting me take control.

Tyler's moan drew my attention. He was stroking himself slowly. I could tell by the tension in his shoulders and the unhinged, hungry look in his eyes that he wanted to finish himself off. But he was holding back, holding out for me, once again showing me how much discipline he had.

Looking at Tyler broke my Alec tunnel vision. Ethan and Josh were still in the same positions on either side of us, Josh's eyes roaming our bodies, Ethan's gaze stuck to my bouncing tits.

I wanted to kiss them, touch them, hold them.

I curled my hand around the back of Josh's neck, and he leaned up to meet me halfway in a searing kiss. With one hand, he kept himself propped up while he dragged the other over the curve of my ass and up my back. My damp hair was sticking to my neck, and he pulled it away with gentle fingers before gently dropping his mouth to my moist skin.

I turned my head to Ethan, and he was halfway up before I even had a chance to reach out to him. He mirrored Josh's pose, leaning his weight on one hand, and let me pull him to me. I kissed him hard, our teeth bumping, our breath mingling as we panted and licked and sucked.

I pulled away for some air, and he immediately bent down to take my breast into his mouth.

With one hand around each of them and Alec under me—surrendered to my touch, letting me use him however I saw fit—I *felt* like a fucking goddess.

My second orgasm tore through me like a dam bursting, a rush of sensation making me forget everything but this single moment in time. I cried out but kept my eyes open and locked on Tyler's lust-filled ones, holding him with my gaze just as surely as I held the others with my body.

Ethan and Josh supported me as I started to relax against them, strong hands at my back. But Alec had other ideas.

Finally, he touched me, tearing me out of their grasp and pulling me down on top of him. One hand gripped my hip possessively; the other grabbed a fistful of my hair as his hips pumped mercilessly. I met his fast, erratic movements as best I could and wrapped my arms around his shoulders, kissing his face, his chin, his neck.

He came with a guttural roar, gripping me even tighter and then collapsing under me. I rested my forehead against his, then gave him a soft kiss, pouring all my love into it, letting my lips linger even though I was breathing hard through my nose. When I pulled away, he smiled and kissed me on the tip of my nose.

As I lifted my hips, his cock slid out of me, and his cum dripped down the inside of my thigh. One of the Turkish towels, sopping wet and ready, slapped down on the tiles next to me. I looked up, and Ty gave me a wink.

I wiped up the mess between my legs and got off Alec.

I didn't want a break, didn't need my body telling me I'd had enough, that I should pause. I was on a mission to have them all.

Ethan helped me crawl into his lap and straddle him, then he kissed me tenderly.

I appreciated his soft touch, his patience and willingness to take it easy, but I didn't need it. I deepened the kiss, rubbing my breasts against his chest, massaging his tongue with mine.

Alec scooted to the edge of the platform and took a few breaths before getting up. I heard the tap behind me running and then water splashing, but I was already consumed with Ethan's touch, his big, gentle hands caressing my body as I started to rock against him. I slid up and down his impressive length, spreading my moisture all over him without actually taking him inside me.

My body was so wired, every nerve ending at attention; it was as if I was constantly on the verge of another orgasm. Judging by Ethan's erratic breathing, the soft moans escaping his lips, he was pretty close too. Not wanting to wait another minute, I pulled back.

Ethan still had one foot planted on the ground next to the platform, and my leg was draped over his thick thigh. With a hand on my ass, he helped me rise up and impale myself on him. I slid down his length and paused, letting myself adjust. Ethan was the biggest in every way, and despite the fact that we'd been having sex for months, it still took me a moment to adjust to his size—to adjust to the stretching, the almost too full feeling. But as soon as I relaxed, it felt amazing.

I rolled my hips and wrapped my arms around his neck. He kept one hand planted on the tiles for balance as the other pushed the sticky hair out of my face. With his big, gentle hand, he caressed my brow, his thumb swiping across my cheek, the tips of his fingers caressing my jaw. All the while, his amber eyes watched me with awe.

My heart felt as if it were bursting as I stared back at him, my sweet, loving, gentle man.

He threaded his hand into the hair at the back of my head and pressed his forehead against mine. We only needed to rock slightly for his big cock to caress every inch of the sensitive nerves inside me.

My hands glided over his shoulders and chest, caressing him as gently as he caressed me, and I kissed him.

Keeping my mouth trapped against his, Ethan leaned back slowly until he was flat on his back and I was riding him. My breasts rubbed against him with every thrust as his hands dragged down my back to hold my ass firmly.

As another orgasm built—heat spreading up my chest and down to my fingers and toes, like molten lava—I kept kissing him. I came, shuddering on top of him and moaning into his mouth as I panted and licked and sucked.

His grip on my ass tightened, and he came with me, his release only a few seconds behind mine. He grunted and moaned but was just as unwilling to break our kiss, his tongue caressing mine, his lips just as greedy.

Panting, I finally pulled away and collapsed on top of him. My cheek pressed against his slick chest as he lazily ran his fingers through my hair.

I'd had three orgasms so far—the most I'd ever had in a single session—and as much as I wanted to have them all, I wasn't sure my body was capable of it.

But Josh wasn't going to let me be a quitter. As if he could sense my doubt, he appeared at my back, his mouth at my ear.

"You like feeling his big cock inside you? Filling you up?" His whisper was hoarse, but his words still bounced off the tiles, making my pussy clench around Ethan's cock.

"Yes," I hissed. Josh gripped my hips and lifted me until I was on my knees hovering over Ethan. Immediately I missed the feeling of him inside me, and just like that, I was ready to keep going, all doubts about my body's limits driven out by Josh's dirty words. I was so lost in my lust I barely registered Ethan cleaning up his hot seed with gentle hands and the wet towel.

"You want me inside you?"

"Yes." I was panting again, or still. I wasn't sure I'd ever stopped. Ethan was trying to catch his breath too, his eyes raking my body.

"You want us both inside you?" Josh nipped my ear, and I shivered. He reached between my legs from behind and stroked me, his fingers gliding easily over the slick flesh. I was so sensitive I nearly came again. Ethan grinned and started playing with my breasts.

"Fuck. Yes." I moaned.

"Who?" Josh dragged his fingers back farther, between my ass cheeks. "Tell me who you want inside you."

"You." I arched my back, desperate for more now.

"I'll take your ass." He pushed the tip of one finger just inside. "I'll be the first one to stick my cock here. But who do you want inside your pussy at the same time?"

"Any of you. All of you." I was incoherent, drunk on sex. I had no idea what I was even saying. I did want them all, and logically,

I knew it was physically impossible, but Josh was making me crazy with his dirty talk.

We'd discussed anal sex. I couldn't stop fantasizing about having two of them at the same time, so I'd sat Josh and Tyler down and told them what I wanted. A brand-new butt plug had appeared in my drawer the next day, and we'd started experimenting, working up to it.

"Next time, you can have whoever you want. But right now you'll have me." Josh put a second finger into my ass, his breath still hot on my neck. At the same time, he finally pushed his cock into me—slowly, so I could feel every inch of him sliding in as he pulled his fingers out of my other hole at the same time. It was such an intense sensation, a unique kind of friction.

My arms started to shake as I struggled to stay upright, and I let myself collapse on top of Ethan's chest. Ethan stroked my shoulders with his gentle hands while Josh kept my hips angled up with a firm grip.

After starting things slowly, taking a few deliberate, languorous strokes, he set a fast pace, his hips slamming against me as though he couldn't seem to keep himself from chasing his release.

His breathing became erratic, but in between moans he managed to make another demand. "Come with me. Fuck. I'm so close."

"Don't know if I can," I panted. It was almost too sensitive, too much. Maybe my body topped out at three.

"Yes, you can." He sounded so sure. His chest pressed against my back as his arms slapped down on either side of Ethan's shoulders. "Ethan, give us a hand here."

His hips never stopped pounding into me as Ethan dragged his hand down my side, then pushed it between us.

"With pleasure." I could hear the grin in his voice as he found my clit and rubbed in rhythm with Josh's fast pace.

"Fuck!" Josh sounded as frustrated as he did satisfied; he

couldn't hold it back any longer. He slammed into me one last time and spilled inside me.

The way his hips ground into me through his release pushed him deeper, hitting the sweet spot. Combined with Ethan's unrelenting fingers on my clit, it was enough to send me over the edge yet again.

"Yes!" I cried out. Josh's tendency to verbalize everything made me more vocal too. I shuddered through my release, pressed between two hot, chiseled chests.

Josh pulled out and collapsed onto his back next to us.

"Just in time." He smiled at me. His wet hair looked almost as dark as Tyler's brown locks, and I ran my hand through it.

Josh kissed me tenderly on the lips, the forehead, and the tip of my nose, then leaned back and closed his eyes as his breathing evened out.

Over the steady rise and fall of his chest, my eyes locked with serious gray ones. Tyler was still in his spot on the bench, slowly stroking himself with one hand. I couldn't believe he'd been touching himself this whole time and managed not to come. The man was the epitome of control.

As he rose to his feet and came around the platform, I had the distinct feeling I was about to see that control shatter.

I rolled off Ethan, onto my back, and propped myself up on my elbows. The movement made Josh's semen come dripping out of me. Ethan was there in a flash, towel at the ready.

Ethan and Josh pushed themselves up off the platform and went to the sinks to freshen up. Behind me, Alec was lying down on the narrow bench, one foot planted on the ground for balance and an arm slung over his eyes.

My attention snapped back to Tyler when he firmly grabbed my ankles. His touch was searing, demanding, and jolts of excitement and desire shot up my legs.

The muscles in his arms and shoulders contracted as he dragged me toward himself, and I dropped to my back, my messy wet hair trailing behind me. When my ass was at the edge of the platform, he let me go, and I lowered my feet to the ground and sat up.

He straightened to his full height and gripped my shoulders as if to push me back down, but my hand was already wrapped around the base of his cock, and I took it into my mouth.

The hot tiles felt good against my pussy, and I rocked my hips back and forth as I sucked Tyler's cock.

"Fuck." His voice was unsteady, strained. He dug his fingers into my shoulders as I took him as deep into my mouth as I could. I swirled my tongue around the head, tasting the salty precum, but before I could repeat the motion, he threaded his hands into my hair and pulled my head back.

I looked up at him and waited. His dick twitched inches away from my mouth, and I licked my lips. Tyler shuddered, the look in his eyes wild as his gaze darted over my face, my body, the proximity of his cock to my lips. His hands in my hair tightened as he breathed through his mouth.

"I . . ." He trailed off without giving me even a hint of what he wanted to say. I'd never seen Tyler so flustered, so out of control. He may have orchestrated this whole thing, but watching it play out was making him unravel.

"Her mouth feels incredible." Josh appeared at his side, caressing my cheek with the back of his hand. "But you want to come inside her."

Finally, Tyler snapped out of it and released my hair. Ethan leaned in, his mouth suddenly devouring mine, and gently pushed me back until I was lying down again.

Ethan and Josh backed away as Tyler dropped to his knees. The low platform put me at the perfect level for him. He pushed my knees wide apart and then entered me in one smooth thrust, burying himself balls deep. I was so wet, slick all over from the steam and multiple orgasms, he slid in with ease, igniting all those nerve endings once again.

I was nearly spent, my body pushed to its limit. But I still wanted him, still craved him, still started to roll my hips against him, begging him with my body to move against me.

His eyes were closed, his hands gripping my thighs with more and more pressure as he struggled to take deep, even breaths. He was trying not to come, not yet, but knowing he was *that close*, I just wanted to push him.

I reached for his hands, intending to pull him on top of me, but something halted my movements.

Alec appeared over me and grabbed my hands with his rough ones. He kneeled on the other side of the platform and pulled my arms over my head, giving me a devious smirk.

With Alec firmly holding my wrists and Tyler gripping my thighs, I was at their mercy once again. I allowed them to take control, too spent to fight them even if I wanted to.

Tyler finally opened his eyes, took me in, and gave Alec a little nod of thanks.

Only when he was positive he was once again in control—of the situation, of his own pleasure and mine—did he finally start to move.

He fucked me deep and hard, barely pulling out before sliding back in. Every time his hips connected with mine, bursts of electric sensation shot from my core through my body, an orgasm building *again*.

Tyler repeatedly dragged his hands over my hips, up my body, over my breasts and back down. His palms slid over my skin like silk.

When his damp hair fell over his eyes, I ached to brush it away, feel the soft locks between my fingers. I tugged against Alec's grip, but he only tightened it, pulling my arms tighter above my head, making my torso stretch like a lazy cat.

Tyler picked up the pace, and on his next pass, squeezed my breasts in his hands, making my back arch. He pinched my nipples lightly just as he ground into me and leaned forward, putting firm pressure on my clit.

I threw my head back and cried out as I came, my vision going blurry, my body writhing under his.

With another few deep thrusts, Tyler groaned, his gravelly voice echoing around our chamber of sex and depravity. He came deep inside me, his fingers digging into the flesh of my hips.

As my vision cleared, ice-blue eyes and a sultry smile came into focus—Alec leaning over me.

"I fucking love watching you come." He released my wrists and moved away to make room for Tyler. Still buried inside me, Tyler lowered himself until his chest was flush with mine. I wrapped one arm around his shoulders and finally ran my fingers through his hair, pushing it off his forehead as he leaned in to kiss me.

We kissed for a long time, lazy and slow, our tongues caressing. Then he finally pulled out and struggled to his feet.

I couldn't even fathom trying to sit up. My eyes were already drooping closed. I could totally sleep here for the night—it was warm enough.

Luckily, I had four Variants to take care of me. Water was once again sluiced over my body, a wet cloth and gentle hands cleaning me all over. Then I was wrapped up in dry towels and lifted into strong arms.

Someone cracked a joke about making sure the steam room was thoroughly cleaned and disinfected before someone else used it, but I was already relaxing against a strong chest.

I was asleep before we made it back to our cottage.

TWENTY-NINE

A warm breeze caressed my naked body as the soothing sound of crashing waves drifted in through the open window. It was still nighttime, the only light coming from the partially obscured moon.

So what had woken me?

I snuggled closer into Ethan's side and closed my eyes.

Murmuring voices made me open them again. I recognized the deep honey quality of Alec's voice and the firm, calm response coming from Tyler, but I couldn't make out the words.

As safe and comfortable as I was boxed in by Ethan and Josh, my curiosity wouldn't allow me to go back to sleep.

With careful movements, I shimmied to the edge of the bed and managed to slip out of the room, grabbing the abandoned sheet off the ground as I passed.

I was sore, every movement reminding me of what we'd done in the steam room only hours prior. But the aches in my arms, legs, and abdominal muscles were nothing to be alarmed about—if anything, they made me smile.

I wrapped the sheet around myself and padded through the little cottage, following their voices toward the front door.

"I just feel so impotent." Tyler's frustrated voice rose, and

Alec shushed him. I paused halfway to the door and clutched the sheet to my chest.

"I know, man. I just want to go out there and . . . punch something," Alec growled, "but it's starting to feel insurmountable. What are we supposed to do?"

"I don't know. That's the problem. I have all the relevant information. I have so much of her Light coursing through me I hardly even need to focus to draw out the truth. It just comes to me. But I don't know what the next move is. Every possible scenario puts her in danger."

Alec sighed.

My days of eavesdropping on conversations and coming to erroneous conclusions were over, and I didn't feel the need to hide from them. So I walked to the door and out onto the patio.

Neither of them so much as raised an eyebrow. They'd probably heard me coming. They sat side by side, their chairs facing the edge of the cliff. The moon, half-hidden behind a cloud, reflected off the inky water in the distance. It was eerily beautiful.

I sank into Tyler's lap, and he wrapped his arms around my middle and kissed the back of my neck. Reaching out, I threaded my fingers with Alec's, and he kissed the back of my hand before dropping it into his lap.

"I'm sorry." I wasn't entirely sure what I was sorry about. So many warring feelings writhed inside me it was difficult to decipher them.

"You have nothing to apologize for," Tyler said firmly,

"None of this is your fault," Alec agreed.

"I hate how messed up everything has gotten." Neither of them replied. What was there to say?

We sat like that for a while, just holding each other and staring out at the moon, listening to the water crash rhythmically against the cliffs.

Eventually, we went back to bed, but I couldn't get to sleep.

I kept staring into space, thinking about all the things I'd avoided thinking about for days, if not weeks. Then I'd stare at their beautiful faces and feel my chest tighten at the mere thought of losing one of them.

As soon as the first rays of sun streamed into the room, I got up —careful not to wake them—got dressed, and went for a run. I pushed my body despite the soreness, letting the burn in my lungs distract me, letting the crisp morning air clear my head. I went around the island twice, waving to some of the Lighthunters we'd met.

By the time I got back, the sun was casting bright rays over the kitchen, where Ethan was cooking eggs. The others sat around the dining table, sipping coffee.

"Hey," I panted, pouring myself a big glass of water and chugging it at the sink.

A chorus of "mornings" accompanied tired, lazy smiles. Ethan kissed my sweaty cheek.

After a hot shower gave me an extra dose of determination, I came back to the dining area and pulled Tyler's borrowed laptop toward myself. He looked up from his coffee with raised brows.

I sighed. "I need to know what's happening out there. I can't pretend anymore."

They all paused and watched me warily.

"Breakfast first." Ethan dropped a plate of eggs and bacon in front of me. His smile didn't reach his eyes.

"Breakfast during," I stated, picking up the fork and opening the laptop at the same time.

Tyler draped an arm over the back of my chair and leaned in, bringing up news articles, intelligence reports, and updates from people we trusted.

"I'm not gonna lie." He sounded resigned. "It's not good."

For the next hour, he updated me on what was happening past the azure waters at the bottom of the cliffs.

The protests and violence had escalated. Some countries had been forced to declare a state of emergency; in other places, curfews and security checkpoints were coming into effect. Variant Valor had branches everywhere. They were well funded by the generally better-off Variants, and their propaganda was all over billboards and the media. The Human Empowerment Network was taking a more grassroots approach—graffiti, human-only areas, Molotov cocktails, and radicalization through social media.

Davis's face and voice were all over the reports—both news and top-secret intelligence.

So was mine.

He was holding press conferences to tell the world I was the key to everything, making it sound as if the technology he was creating would solve everyone's problems.

According to Lucian and Kyo, Melior Group was struggling to keep up with him. They were stretched thin. Part of the forces were tasked with assisting human law enforcement, trying to make the streets safe, but some of the elite teams were still hunting Davis, trying to take him down discreetly.

Lucian happened to connect while we were going over the reports. He explained, "Part of the problem is that he keeps moving and he's well protected by his own lackeys, some of them with dangerous abilities. Then there's the issue of discretion. We need to take him quietly, if possible. We can't just tackle him to the ground in front of a dozen cameras. But by far the biggest problem is the mole we have. Whenever we get a solid lead and set up an operation, he disappears. We suspected it before, but now it's undeniable that someone high up, maybe even someone on the board, is leaking information to Davis." He sounded tired and far away on the other end of the line, and I felt bad we'd abandoned him. Tyler was his righthand man, and he was here with both hands tied behind his back. "There is serious division in the management here, and it's starting to trickle down the ranks. The number of people I can trust is woefully small. Charlie is doing all he can to weed out who the problem is, but they're covering their tracks very well. I don't know how much longer it'll be before I lose complete control over any aspect of operations."

He had to get off the phone then, and Josh made more coffee as we kept going over everything.

Bradford Hills Institute was on partial lockdown. Scared parents were pulling their kids out of school, and even some faculty had stopped showing up. Classes continued amid tight security, but the situation was tense and tenuous. Schools all over the country were in a similar situation.

An encrypted message from Charlie described the mood: "People are terrified. It's like they're all hunkering down and preparing for Armageddon. The US isn't in a state of emergency, nor do we have any curfews in place, but there are outbreaks of violence from time to time. The streets are deserted, half the businesses closed. It's eerie."

"Who can we trust?" I looked between them all. I needed to know where we stood when push came to shove.

Alec leaned forward on the table. "Uncle Lucian. Aunt Olivia and Uncle Henry. Dot and Charlie. Ed and his brother, maybe. Kyo, Marcus, and Jamie, definitely. A handful of other agents you haven't met. I know they're loyal. Other than that . . ."

It was a short list.

"Dana." I nodded firmly. "She may be jaded and frustrated with the way she's been treated her whole life, but deep down she's a good person. She's shown me that more than once. Plus, she likes me. We're practically best friends now. Also Mr. Takata and his men. He's more than proven himself. What about the Lighthunters?" I questioned just as one of them walked through our front door.

Nina had clearly heard the tail end of our conversation, but she didn't seem offended by it.

"Yes." She nodded, perching on the arm of the couch. "You can trust the Lighthunters."

"Are you positive? They were pretty pissed you brought us here." Josh made a good point.

Nina nodded. "They were, but mostly at me for not informing them. We take the security and secrecy of this facility very seriously. Honestly, we are all horrified at what Davis is doing, the way he is perverting the Light for his own sick reasons, the division it is causing all over the world. We can feel it more than anyone. It is painful. We want to help, but we have stayed silent and secret for so long. Honestly, we just don't know where to start."

Nina ran her hands over her cropped hair and stood, starting to pace. "A lot of the meetings recently have been about what our next step needs to be. The more reports that come in from our people on the ground, the more helpless we feel." She huffed.

I folded my arms and leaned forward. If a super-secret, mega-rich society of badasses was at a loss, what hope did the rest of us have?

Nina kept ranting. I had a feeling she needed to get it all off her chest. "There are some advocating for gathering up as many Vitals as we can, especially the Vivids, and bringing them to our secure locations. They want to bunker down and ride it out from the sidelines, just as we have for centuries. But that is ridiculous! We can't continue to ignore the tension in the Light, not to mention all the humans! Who is supposed to protect the humans? Granted, some of them need protecting from *themselves*—I mean, who runs at a Variant with a paralyzing ability armed with nothing more than a baseball bat and their convictions?" She bugged her eyes out incredulously as she referred to footage of one of the riots in Russia that had gone viral.

"Others are arguing we should get involved—come out to the world and tell them of our existence, fight to bring back peace. But people are scared of that too. There is a reason we went underground. I am just not so sure those reasons hold up any longer."

"Something that unifies people could go a long way. A revelation like this—that Lighthunters are real—could bring real hope to Variants," Josh mused.

"Yeah, but what about the humans?" Tyler argued. "They could see this as just another advantage the Variants have."

"Not if you present it in a good light," Ethan argued. "I mean, shit's bad, but there are places managing to stay peaceful—look at Iceland, Canada, New Zealand. They're all managing to keep their shit together. Their governments are pushing messages of unity, and people are following through on the ground, working together and refusing to get whipped up into . . ."

We were all staring at him, struggling to keep the slight shock off our faces. Ethan wasn't usually this vocal in these discussions. He listened and made sure he knew the important parts, but he left the questioning and arguing to Tyler, Josh, and me.

"What?" He frowned. "I read the news. I just prefer to read about the good bits." He folded his arms and looked down into his lap.

"No." Nina stopped pacing. "That is brilliant!"

"It is?" Ethan looked at her, surprised, a smile pulling at his lips.

"It is! And it is so simple. Marketing makes the world go round, does it not? Isn't that what Davis is doing—just really clever, aggressive marketing? If we are careful about the message we send . . ." She muttered to herself in French. "This could make all the difference. If someone can take Davis out, and then we go public with a message of peace and equality . . . We would need to put action behind our words, maybe pick both a human and a Variant organization to support. . . Yes, that might just work. I have to go!"

She ran out of the cottage, probably on her way to convince her leaders that all they needed was a good marketing plan. I hoped they still planned to provide support with their impressive resources—not the least of which were weapons and people highly trained to use them.

Yes, changing public perception and getting people to work together once more would go a long way. But sometimes, it was necessary to fight.

"None of it will make a difference as long as Davis is out there," I declared.

Tyler gripped my knee. "They're trying, baby."

They.

The people we'd left behind were doing all they could to bring down the pathetic excuse for a man I had the displeasure of calling my biological father. While we took a holiday in the Greek islands.

I stood, sending my chair scraping back.

"We need to help. We need to stop hiding and take out the root of the problem or . . ." *die trying*. I couldn't bring myself to say it. The thought of a world without the four of them in it was more than I could bear, but this was so much bigger than us, so much bigger than me.

Yet, somehow, I was the key. I was the only one who could get to Davis. Because I was the only one he wanted.

"What we need to do is keep you safe." Alec leveled a hard stare at me.

I knew that look, the tension in his shoulders. He was gearing up for a fight, but I didn't want to waste any more time fighting him.

I gave him a sad smile. "I know. That's why we ran. That's why we've been staying hidden. I get it. Trust me, I do. My mom made every argument you could possibly think of in support of the whole 'running for safety' thing. But the thing is, much as I love her and believe wholeheartedly she was just trying to protect me, *she was wrong*. And we're wrong by continuing to hide now. The longer we run from this, the worse it'll get."

"What exactly are you suggesting?" Josh raised his voice—so unlike him.

They all started speaking over one another, arguing with points I hadn't even made. They were scared. I let them get it all out, patiently standing at the table and keeping my mouth shut.

When they finally quietened down, they all stared at me with sad, resigned looks.

"You're determined to do this." Tyler had already figured out the gist of my plan.

I nodded. "I am."

"Eve, think about this." Josh looked defeated.

"Please . . ." Ethan's eyes just about broke my heart. I didn't think even he knew what he was pleading for.

"I can't lose you again, Evie." I'd never seen Alec cry, but he was close in that moment, his jaw trembling. "This isn't on you. It's not fair."

I so badly wanted to give in, to let them talk me into staying in hiding and maintaining the illusion of safety. But I had to be strong.

"Life's not fair." I shrugged. "The five of us know that better than anyone. And no, this shouldn't be on me—I don't want this responsibility. But that doesn't change the fact that I'm the best chance we have of drawing him out. He wants me. He's not even hiding it anymore. He's practically obsessed."

"What are we supposed to do?" Josh was really struggling with this. "Just knock on the door to one of his secret facilities? He'll see us coming a mile away. We'll be outnumbered and unprepared. What's the point?"

"No. We make him come to us," Tyler explained, and I knew I had him. We were moving from whether to do this or not to the practicalities of it. "We level the playing field and draw him out."

"How?" Ethan growled.

"I stop running." I moved to my bag in the corner of the room and dug around in one of the pockets for my stash of passports. It took only a moment of flicking through them to find the one I was looking for.

I slapped my Evelyn Maynard passport down on the table—the only legitimate passport I'd ever had, the one I'd applied for as soon as my true identity became known.

"How do we know this will draw him out? How do we know it'll work? How can you just put yourself in danger like this?" Alec continued to argue. I understood why. I didn't want them anywhere near danger either, but it was time for us to do what we'd been working so hard to do since we met. It was time to be brave and honest and work together as a Bond.

"I don't know the answers to any of those questions." I

looked around at them, squaring my shoulders. "But I know without a shadow of a doubt that I can't keep sitting here, hiding and doing nothing, while the world burns. And I know you can't either. I know in my soul that this is the right thing to do, and I know I have the strength to do it. Because I'm not alone anymore."

We took a day to prepare.

Whatever Nina's impassioned speech had been to her leaders, it worked. The Lighthunters were going public. They hoped to burst onto the world stage with a message of hope and unity to distract from Davis's hateful crap.

They were also putting the full weight of their support behind any organization focused on peacekeeping around the world.

Tyler and Alec reached out to the few people we trusted and filled them in on the plan. Every call met with resistance and arguments, but once we'd made a decision together as a Bond, we were united. My guys may not have liked what we were about to do, but they supported me one-hundred-percent.

We packed our meager possessions and went over the plan repeatedly. Alec's team and a handful of other agents would be with us, prepared to go rogue and defy orders if necessary. A few other players in the Variant world were behind us too, including a good number of Mr. Takata's trusted contacts.

When I spoke to Dana, however, she was so quiet on the line, her answers so short and reserved, by the end of it I was questioning my faith in her.

"Look, I know it's a lot to ask—this is really fucking dangerous —so I completely understand if you can't be there to back us up, but please, at least don't tell anyone about it. Give us a fighting chance."

"Yeah . . . I gotta go." She ended the call without even waiting for a response.

"Shit." I dropped the phone and dropped my head into my hands. "Shit fuck fucking tits."

Ethan chuckled as he leaned over the back of the couch to massage my shoulders. "Nothing you can do about it now, baby. You had faith in her humanity—you trusted her. I, for one, am glad you haven't lost the ability to trust altogether after all the shit you've been through."

His words were comforting, as were his strong hands on my shoulders, but I still worried I'd made a colossal mistake.

Once we'd spoken to everyone we could trust, we fell into silence, sitting about the room lost in our own thoughts.

Tyler's computer pinged, and he shook himself out of his contemplation to look at it. "It's Charlie again," he announced, then smiled as he kept reading. "He's asking if the phone is free to set up a secure line? Dot's demanding to speak to you, Eve."

He typed as he spoke, and a few moments later, the phone next to me on the couch rang.

I took a deep breath and answered. "Hey, girl."

"Don't 'hey, girl' me! If you fucking die pulling this shit, I'm gonna be so mad at you. *So mad!* I mean, I know when we did that whole 'go rogue to Australia,' that was a stupid move, but this is some next-level shit. Didn't you all run off so you could be *safe?* And now you're gonna walk right into the lion's fucking mouth! Girrrrl, you *better* not fucking die!" She ranted on about how her friends kept dropping like flies, then went on a tangent about how I'm not even a friend, I'm family. That last bit made me choke up, but I let her get it all out of her system.

When the sounds coming down the phone were more heavy breathing than shouted threats, I asked, "You done?"

"No!" She huffed, then after a pause: "Yes . . . I'm scared, Eve. I don't want to lose any of you."

"I'm scared too. But this is the right thing to do."

"Eve?"

"Yeah?"

"I'm really fucking proud of you."

I had to swallow around a lump in my throat, and even then, my answer still sounded choked. "Thanks, Dot. Love you."

"Love you."

I cleared my throat and wiped the tears off my cheeks. "What's been going on with you? I've only been gone a week, but it feels like a year."

"I know what you mean. So much has changed. I've stopped going to class. Mom and Dad are too freaked out, and the guys are on their side." I could practically hear her rolling her eyes. "I'm still doing a few classes by correspondence, but I'm starting to get cabin fever. I haven't left the house in, like, three days. But I have had a ton of extra Internet time. At least that's still up and running—we haven't gone full *Walking Dead* yet."

I chuckled. Only Dot would be excited about still being able to check social media during a time of crisis. "Been doing some online shopping to fill the time?"

"As if! I'd have nowhere to wear my new clothes. No, I'm using my uncanny digital communication skills to do some good. There's a resistance happening, and it's taking off. Eve, our generation, most of the young people I speak to, want nothing to do with this conflict, and we're sick of being ignored. I started to see these groups pop up all over the world, independent of one another—people using social media to organize peaceful protests and sit-ins, that kind of thing. So I thought, why not connect them? Make a global network of resistance?"

"Holy shit, Dot, that's amazing."

"Yeah, Charlie helped me set some stuff up, secure webpages and shit, and even connected me with some of his hacker buddies. Anyway, we're all working together to spread more messages of unity. There's gonna be a worldwide peaceful protest next week. Oh! And we're getting T-shirts printed!"

I had to laugh at that. Of course she was getting T-shirts printed. I'd been gone a week and my best friend had managed to set up a global resistance movement. "I'm gonna make sure you speak to some of the Lighthunters. What they have planned is really in line with what you're doing too. After . . ."

I had no idea how to finish that sentence.

Nina walked into the cottage, backpack slung over her shoulder. "Ready? The boats are waiting."

The guys started to gather up our last few things while my heart jumped into my throat. I gripped the couch cushion. "I have to go."

"Shit! OK, um . . ."

"I'll see you tomorrow, Dot." Considering how fucking terrified I was, I was surprised at how even my voice sounded. I didn't want to say goodbye to her. I didn't want to say goodbye to anyone.

"Yeah . . ." She was crying again. "Yep. I'll see you then."

I hung up and stood. Immediately, Josh took my hand, giving it a comforting squeeze. Ethan waited by the door. Alec and Tyler were just outside, watching.

I squared my shoulders and walked toward what I knew would be a defining moment of my life—if it didn't kill me.

And my Bondmates would be with me every step of the way.

Three speedboats carried us and a delegation of Lighthunters to the mainland. No one spoke much, and in Athens, we split up. The Lighthunters headed off on various assignments to prepare for what they were about to reveal to the world, and the five of us headed straight for the airport.

I gave the airport worker a weak smile as he checked my passport. In all my years of using fake documentation, I'd never been as nervous as I was to hand over my actual, legitimate passport. The man scanned it, stamped it, and handed it over.

It was done. Evelyn Maynard was officially checked in to the international airport in Athens. I could just imagine some warning system in one of Davis's buildings going off, alerting them I'd surfaced.

I made room for Ethan, then Alec, behind me. Josh and Ty waited just past the little booths. As I moved to join them, I gripped the strap of my backpack, my knuckles going white, and looked up for the security camera. I spotted it in the corner, near the ceiling.

Davis would get access to it.

With every bit of determination and anger I possessed permeating my gaze, I stared it down as if it were the devil himself perched in the corner and not an inanimate object. Just for good measure, I mouthed, *Come and get me.*

Then I turned and marched to our boarding gate.

THIRTY

We had fifteen hours—the time it took to travel from Athens to Washington DC—to mentally prepare for what was to come. I'd expected to find it impossible to sit still, expected to fight against the adrenaline, but as we reached cruising altitude, a kind of calm fell over me.

Alec and Tyler slept most of the way, conserving energy while they could. Ethan dozed too, but he found it difficult to get comfortable in the tight seats, which were definitely not designed for someone his size. Josh and I didn't sleep a wink, both of us lost in our thoughts.

We needed to give our people on the ground time to prepare, but I still wished the flight wasn't so long. We'd debated taking a shorter one, just going somewhere in Europe or even waiting for him in Athens, but in the end, we'd decided to go home.

According to intelligence reports, Davis was somewhere on the West Coast, and I wanted to make sure he came for me himself. Mostly, I wanted to send him a message—I was done running. He was not going to keep me from my home any longer, stop me from being where I belonged. While we weren't flying into New York, it was close enough. Besides, DC was a smaller airport and would be easier to evacuate.

We landed in late afternoon, the hot sun casting golden light over the vast planes of the airport, but when we parked on the tarmac and didn't move for a long time, it became clear something was wrong. Passengers were getting restless by the time the pilot finally made an announcement. "Folks, we have an emergency situation, and I've been instructed by ground control not to approach the airport terminal. We're going to deploy the emergency slides and disembark. I've been assured we're safe here, but we do need to evacuate the aircraft in a calm and timely manner. Please pay close attention to what your flight attendants are saying. Thank you for your cooperation."

The level of chatter rose among the passengers as they started to get a bit panicked, but the flight attendants were professional and efficient, deploying the slides and ushering people down.

Once on the ground, all the passengers were herded onto waiting buses. Men clad in black and holding automatic weapons stood by, watching everything carefully. As we approached the bus, one of the armed men stepped forward and gestured for the five of us to follow him to the side. I could feel the eyes of the other curious passengers burning a hole in the back of my head.

The buses drove off, leaving us with the four armed men on the deserted tarmac. As soon as the other passengers were out of sight, the men relaxed their tense stances and greeted Alec and Tyler.

"Everything's in place. Airport buildings should be cleared within the next ten minutes," the man who'd stopped us in line reported.

"I don't know if this is brilliance or pure fucking madness," another said to Tyler, but his eyes kept darting to me. I must've looked like a mess after the long-haul flight, my hair crazy, my clothes wrinkled, my skin drenched in sweat from the summer sun. It must've been ninety degrees out there.

"We're not paying you to wonder about the merits of missions," Tyler said with a teasing grin.

"Man, you ain't paying any of us for *shit*. I don't even know if we'll have jobs after this, if we even make it out alive. Anyone from Melior Group that's here today is going rogue, acting against direct orders from the board and siding with Lucian Zacarias and you fuckers."

People were putting their jobs, their lives, on the line to help us. Some of the resigned calm that had fallen over me on the plane was chased away by uncertainty.

In place of a reply, Alec clasped the man's hand, and they patted each other on the back. He repeated the gesture with the other three, and I had a feeling they'd known each other a long time.

We parted ways, and a short golf buggy ride later, we walked into the terminal building.

I sighed, glad to be in air conditioning after the oppressive heat. Or maybe it was the situation itself that was oppressive.

Walking through an abandoned airport was kind of surreal, like something from a post-apocalyptic movie. Stores were still lit up and wide open while plates with half-eaten meals and still steaming mugs of coffee littered the tables of restaurants.

We settled in near a wall of windows overlooking the tarmac. Ty and Alec sat calmly on either side of me at one end of a heavy wooden table. Ethan leaned against the window, his feet crossed at the ankles. Josh paced slowly, looking down the wide corridor every once in a while. Really, we had no idea where any potential threat could come from. It could crash through the ceiling for all we knew.

None of us spoke.

Should I be more nervous? I was waiting to face head-on the threat my mother had been running from my entire childhood. But I was eerily calm, as calm as the abandoned airport. I'd made peace with whatever happened next. If I was to die, I was taking him down with me.

The sharp sound of glass shattering in the distance was the first sign we were no longer alone.

We all rose to our feet, and the guys positioned themselves in front of me. Tyler and Alec pulled their guns, and Ethan conjured an angry blue fireball. I'd already transferred all the extra Light I could to them. We were as prepared as we could be, so I just planted my feet wide and waited, craning my neck to see through the gap between Alec and Tyler's broad shoulders.

Davis's men barely made a sound as they approached. The breaking glass had likely been a distraction to get us all looking down the wide corridor, because when they appeared, they converged on us from all directions.

A shadow caught my eye, dancing jerkily on the concrete floor to my left, and I turned just in time to see several masked men rappel down the tall windows and shoot the glass. It all happened so fast, their movements so precise and practiced that I barely had time to blink before one of them landed mere feet from me.

The guys tightened their position around me, boxing me in, as the masked men approached. Despite the assailants' dramatic entrance, they weren't shooting or moving to attack. They just surrounded us, guns pointed.

One of them stepped forward and spoke, his voice muffled through the mask. "Hand over the girl, and we'll kill you quickly."

For a moment, no one spoke. My heart battered against my chest, and my breathing sounded obnoxiously loud.

I couldn't see Tyler's face, but I could see the way his cotton shirt pulled taut over his tense muscles; I could imagine the way his gray eyes narrowed on the piece of shit threatening to kill them. When he spoke, his voice was firm and loud. "No."

As soon as the word left his lips, Tyler and Alec both fired in rapid succession, taking out two men each with clean headshots before anyone else could react. Ethan threw the fireball, the blue flames engulfing his victim faster than any fire I'd ever seen; he threw more as fast as he could conjure them.

Josh simply backed up, his back connecting with my right arm, and watched everything with a look of intense concentration.

Davis's men started firing.

Every bullet came within a foot of us and then dropped to the ground. The tinkling sound of ammo piling up at our feet mingled with the deafening gunfire.

"Take out the blond one!" someone shouted.

So far, only bullets had been flying at us, but when more assailants started running up, it became apparent Davis had sent in his Variants too.

Unnaturally fierce wind started to lift anything in the area that wasn't tied down. At the same time, several machines—transport buggies, vacuum cleaners, anything electronic and on wheels—started careening straight for Josh.

Alec isolated the Variant with the wind ability and the one with the tech ability and took them both out, their screams of pain audible even over the rest of the cacophony.

As Alec defended Josh, Ethan paused throwing fireballs. Instead, he lifted his arms over his head and sent wave after wave of bright golden fire in every direction: the signal for our own backup to come charging in. From every back room, storage area, and hidden location, our people burst out to join the fight.

The Lighthunters—being impervious to Variant abilities, highly trained in combat, and as yet unknown to the rest of the world—were the biggest secret weapon. With deadly proficiency, they incapacitated the confused Variants, who couldn't figure out why their abilities had suddenly stopped working.

My heart skipped a beat when I caught sight of Dot and Charlie, walking slowly hand in hand at the edge of the fighting. I ducked as all manner of winged creatures came flying through the now wide-open space where the glass used to be. Several wings clipped my head and shoulders as pigeons, woodpeckers, kites, hawks, and eagles swooped down on our enemies.

Even Olivia and Henry were there, not that I should've been surprised—they'd both worked for Melior Group at one time. They stuck close to Dot and Charlie, shooting anyone who came close with lethal accuracy.

Lucian had stayed behind, even though doing so had probably pissed him off. But we needed him on the outside. He was managing communications and organizing all he could between the different groups that had come together.

Ed and his brother were there too. Ed was keeping one hand on his brother's shoulder, transferring Light to him, as the bigger man used his strength ability to barrel through assailants, knock people unconscious with a single punch, and throw tables as if they weighed no more than a sheet of paper.

Kyo, Marcus, and Jamie were leading the Melior Group agents who had gone rogue to join this fight. They were in their element, working perfectly as a team, almost every gunshot meeting its target.

Mr. Takata's people were at the same level—highly efficient, deadly, precise. Mr. Takata himself was in a room in the basement, near where they sorted the luggage, with his wife and Vital. His sole focus was on keeping everyone shielded from another potential threat like Sarah, the Variant whose ability could cause unconsciousness on a large scale. We couldn't risk something like that happening again. Mr. Takata couldn't isolate this many specific people to shield—there were simply too many of us to keep track of—but he could, with the help of his Vital, throw a large shield over the whole area to defend against any such remote attacks.

My eyes darted about the room. I wasn't a fighter; I still struggled in the sparring sessions, and I hated guns, so I'd only learned the basics at Tyler's insistence. But I was a *survivor*, and I wasn't completely helpless.

I let my glowing Light surge through me and tipped my head back. Replicating what I'd done on the night Alec nearly died, I drew Light from those meaning to do us harm and pushed it to those fighting on our side. But I couldn't keep that up too long. Davis still hadn't shown himself, and I had to conserve my energy.

As prepared and well armed as we were, we still weren't fighting children. We were up against trained killers and people with formidable, dangerous abilities.

A man with a water ability was throwing massive sprays at

Dot's birds, making it difficult for them to fly and attack. Another person with a speed ability was blurring about the room so fast it was impossible to distinguish their appearance, but every once in a while one of our people dropped, blood gushing from a slit throat, after the person whizzed past.

Both cool water and warm blood splashed me, making me wince as if I'd been slapped. I wiped the mess off my cheek but refused to look at my palm as I rubbed it against a dry spot on my shorts.

A middle-aged woman took slow, careful steps through the chaos, her hands clasped in front of her. Every time someone went for her, she cocked her head to the side, and her attacker dropped to their knees, whimpering in terror. I wasn't entirely sure what her ability was, but I didn't want to find out.

Both sides were taking heavy losses.

We couldn't keep going like this.

"Alec!" I yelled, even though he was standing only a few feet away.

"I know!" he growled as he reloaded his weapon.

"We got you covered." Tyler stepped to the side, and Ethan and Josh shifted to cover the gap Alec created as he turned to face me.

One second my head was spinning from all the chaos, all the violence around me. The next my head was spinning because Alec was kissing me. His mouth devoured mine, intense and urgent. One of his hands gripped my hip while the other still held on to his gun. For few blissful seconds, there was nothing but Alec.

I let the Light gush through our connection. He really didn't need to kiss me to get it. I could've given him all he needed with a simple touch. I could've done it without touching him at all. No, Alec was kissing me so intensely because he needed it—needed the comfort before doing the one thing he hated most: using his ability.

But we didn't have time for this. After only a few moments, I pulled away and gave him a firm nod.

He squared his shoulders and turned, blocking me from most of the action. With a deep breath, he lowered his head and clenched his fists, every muscle in his body tensing as he unleashed the full force of his pain.

We'd been practicing as much as we could, but it was more difficult to do that safely with Alec; someone always had to volunteer to be exposed to excruciating pain in order for us to test his limits. But he'd managed to work out how to isolate specific individuals when sending out a massive blast of his power. Still, his technique was far from perfect, especially in such a hectic environment.

I felt the sheer force of Alec's ability as it blasted out of him. Some people screamed, clutching their heads or stomachs before falling to the ground. Most just crumpled immediately, unconscious, their brains incapable of processing that much pain.

All the noise of people killing one another ceased. Bullets stopped sailing through the air. Things stopped crashing and smashing. People stopped barreling into each other. All was silent as I breathed heavily, my chest rising and falling in an unsteady rhythm.

As soon as bodies hit the floor, Tyler reloaded both his guns. "Regroup! Assume there are more coming! Let's get the wounded to a safe distance and restrain the enemy operatives!"

I lifted my head, letting my surroundings soak in. Smoke billowed from the corridor to our left, which was choked with debris. Most of the furniture—tables and chairs, lounges belonging to various airport cafés—was strewn about or pulverized. But the worst of it were the bodies. A lot of them were just passed out, taken down by Alec's ability, but many more were surely dead. A heavy metallic smell mingled with the smoke—blood.

Blood was everywhere. It wasn't as obvious on the black clothing of the Melior Group operatives or Davis's men, but it was stark against skin. It dripped off the counter near where we stood, giving Jackson Pollock a run for his money with how far and wide it had splattered.

Bile rose to my throat and saliva filled my mouth; I struggled to take a deep breath. Everywhere I looked there was blood. With every breath, I could smell it. My eyes started to water as I clenched my jaw, willing myself not to lose it. Not yet.

"Jamie!" Dot's shrill scream echoed in the now silent, cavernous space.

Just a few yards in front of me, Dot sprinted over bodies and dropped to her knees in a slide, Kyo and Charlie hot on her heels. Her frantic hands ran all over the body of a man dressed in black. Jamie's bright red hair stood out among the dusty gray debris.

Marcus rushed over from the opposite direction, holstering his gun. I rushed forward too but stopped just short of them. What could I possibly do?

"Was it Alec?" Dot sounded frantic as Kyo hurriedly checked Jamie. "Please tell me it was just Alec. He'll wake up. He'll be fine. He just needs to sleep it off."

I hadn't even realized Ethan and Josh had followed me or taken my hands in theirs, but I squeezed them tightly, dreading what Kyo would say next. I could see the devastated look on his face.

Kyo closed his eyes and swallowed slowly before straightening up.

"No." Dot shook her head, her expression something between angry and broken. "No, no, no, no . . ." She kept repeating the little two-letter word as if it would bring him back, as if the rapidly widening puddle of blood around him would magically retreat, as if his chest would start rising and falling once more.

As Dot fell apart, cradled between Kyo and Marcus, another layer of steel shuttered down over my heart.

I couldn't afford to fall apart.

Not yet.

I needed something to focus on, so I took deep, measured

breaths and counted off the people Alec had managed to keep safe from his ability.

Dot and Charlie. *Don't look.*

Olivia and Henry. Bloody and dirty but still standing. *Don't linger.*

Kyo and Marcus. *Don't think about Jamie.*

Ed and his brother. Helping to carry all the unconscious enemies to a secure room in the back. *Don't focus on the smell. Just breathe.*

Several of the rogue Melior Group agents. Is that Kane? Our ruthless trainer didn't look injured at all as he methodically reloaded his weapons, standing tall in a sea of bodies. *Don't think about it.*

And all the impervious Lighthunters, of course.

"Eve?" Josh turned to me, reaching up as if to cup my cheek. I dropped their hands and stepped back, out of his reach.

"I'm fine," I rushed out. If I let them touch me, comfort me, draw me into their arms and hold me, I would fall apart.

Not yet. Don't think about it.

"We need to get all our wounded to a safe place." It was a pointless statement. We were already doing that. The more bodies we moved, the more the concrete floor was revealed. It used to be gray; now it was bathed in crimson.

Thankfully, Josh knew I needed to stay strong. He nodded and moved off, helping to carry the injured and unconscious with his ability. Ethan stayed by my side. I wasn't sure if having one of them always beside me was a good or bad thing. They gave me strength, made me feel as if I could handle this, but at the same time, I was a giant glowing target, and anyone close to me could die at any moment. I couldn't stand the thought of any of my beautiful, loving, kind men . . . *Don't think about it.*

Not yet.

I looked around and spotted a camera near the table we'd sat at when we first arrived. The heavy timber table was the only piece of furniture still standing. I marched over, tilting my head to stare directly into the camera.

"Come and get me yourself, you fucking coward!" I yelled, imagining his face. I knew he'd be watching. I would be if I were him.

Keeping my eyes on the camera, I bent down, picked up a chair, and took a seat at the table, finally looking away to stare straight ahead.

With every steadying breath I took, I reminded myself why we were here, what I had come here to achieve. That strange calm slowly settled over me as the room was cleared of bodies. One by one, my Variants came back to my side.

Ethan leaned on the end of the table opposite me, his big arms crossed. Alec stood tall near him, his feet planted, his gun drawn. Josh was at my right shoulder, his hand resting on the back of my chair, with Ty at my left.

Dot and Charlie, Ed and his brother, Kyo and Marcus, and Nina and the Lighthunters were scattered about the room, catching their breath but on the alert.

Dot's tear-streaked face was set in a hard, steely mask. Her men were one down, but they stood at her back, supporting her just as mine were.

Our eyes met across the room. All my deeply buried pain and worry, all my determination and barely contained rage, I saw reflected in her eyes. We didn't get up and go to each other for a hug.

Not yet.

We didn't say anything or even nod. We simply held each other's gaze for a few long seconds—a moment of pure solidarity.

I understood the look on her face perfectly. And I intended to do something about it.

I wasn't leaving here until Davis Damari showed his face. Until I did all I possibly could to remove his toxic influence from the world.

As the sun set behind me, taking the last bits of natural light with it, I looked away from Dot and narrowed my eyes on the vast open space before me. Half the lights had been busted in the battle, casting the area in an uneven, eerie light, but it was still enough for me to see my so-called father as he approached.

The sound of several footsteps preceded his arrival. He wasn't alone.

THIRTY-ONE

As Davis came around the corner, his expensive shirt and pristine tailored pants a stark contrast to the destruction and gore around him, I knew one thing without a shadow of a doubt.

One of us would not be leaving alive.

"Such heavy thoughts, daughter," he called out, pretending to frown before his face split into a disturbing grin.

I stayed silent. I had nothing to say to this monster. This was another distraction technique, another attempt to get a rise out of one of us. Just like the way he'd made us all wait. It was just another stupid power play.

"Oh, got me all figured out now, do you?" His mind-reading ability was something we guarded against carefully. Lucian had been successfully avoiding it for years, but it didn't matter anymore. I didn't care what he knew. The games, the planning and plotting, the chasing and running—it was all over now. We had no secret twists to throw at him. We'd deliberately gone into this without a concrete plan. We were betting on our Bond connection and our ability to work well together under pressure, hoping beyond hope it would be enough.

"So sorry to keep you waiting. My last meeting ran late." He walked forward confidently, unperturbed by the death stares and the several guns pointed at him. He was arrogant, but he wasn't stupid, and I never expected him to waltz into this alone and unprotected. He had his own entourage.

Several heavily armed people walked ahead and behind him, guns raised. Zara's mom was keeping close to his left side, hardly able to keep her eyes off his profile, and the short, stocky woman from Thailand, Gina, was with them too. I recognized her immediately—I didn't think I'd forget anything from that day as long as I lived.

Rick's mother, who'd had the ability to render people unconscious, was dead—killed by her own son—and his father had been captured and was still imprisoned by Melior Group. Gina, the other Variant from that day, had a shielding ability. She may not have been able to shield as far or as well without her Vital, but I had no doubt she was keeping Davis covered.

A few other people I didn't recognize trailed behind Davis as well.

We were at an impasse. Both sides had guns pointed; both sides were protected by formidable Variants. I didn't think he gave a shit about his people, but I didn't want any more of mine to die. Everyone was on alert, tense, silent.

He stopped just feet away from Alec and Ethan. I could imagine the looks they were giving him, but I kept my face neutral, my breathing calm and even.

"You wanted me here." He spread his arms wide. "I'm here. What now?"

The smile didn't falter, the little gleam in his eye suggesting he had something up his sleeve. That was his advantage—we had no idea what he had planned, while he could read all our minds.

But we had something he didn't have too—we had *me.*

"Don't even fucking think about it," he growled, his amused mask slipping for the first time. "I see even a hint of illumination on your perfect skin, and my men will fire. Your telekinetic may be able to stop bullets, but can he stop them all at once?"

Without needing to hear the order, his goons pointed their weapons at my Variants—more than a dozen guns, trained directly at the people I loved most in the world. I thought Josh could stop them, but I wasn't entirely sure. Those were automatic weapons. I had no doubt he would keep me protected, but could he keep the others safe too? For how long?

Davis gave a satisfied nod and smoothed the front of his shirt. "Good. Now, let's negotiate."

"Negotiate?" Tyler spoke for us all. "You have nothing we want, and there isn't a person in this room willing to bend to your will."

"Everyone wants *something*, and I promise you, I can make it happen. Money? Fame? Power? Everyone has a price."

"And what is it you expect in return?" I knew the answer, but I wanted to hear him say it. For once in my entire existence, I wanted to look at this despicable man and hear him speak the truth.

He cocked his head to the side, watching me for a few moments. Then, for some reason, he decided to give me what I wanted.

"I want you, Evelyn." He folded his hands. "I think we all know why. I've gone as far as I can with my research and engineering team, and they can't figure out how to keep the donor Variant alive. I need to study you to fix it." He held his hand up, stopping any questions before they could be asked. "Because I want to rule the world. I want to walk into any room on the face of the planet and be the most powerful man there. Everyone wants power, *everyone*. Anyone that says they don't is either resigned to the fact they'll never have it or lying to themselves. I'm just willing to do whatever is necessary to get it."

"Why me?" It was the one thing I couldn't work out. "There are other Vivids. You could use any one of them to achieve the same thing." There had been so many people sending me messages; surely some of them had tried to go public with their own ability to glow, despite the unrest and the fear. Davis was surely aware of each and every one.

The look that twisted his features then was so grotesque and full of rage that I wondered how far gone his mind was.

"Because you dare to defy me!" Spittle flew from his mouth as he roared, his hands clenched into fists. Some of the people around him shifted uncomfortably. Zara's mom took a tiny step away.

"Pay attention, Evelyn." His breathing quickened as he visibly tried to calm himself. "You're supposed to be a smart girl. You get that from me, you know. I just told you what my ultimate goal was. I intend to be the most powerful man alive, but what's the point if I don't have you? I can't very well say I am if you continue to defy me. You get *that* from your mother." He wagged his finger at me, eyebrows raised, as if he were telling me off for kicking a ball inside the house.

"Don't you see? It all started with her. Joyce made me what I am—made it possible for me to do what I do. She gave me the greatest gift, my ability. Then the bitch ran off on me!"

"Because you threatened her. Threatened me!" For the first time, I let him get to me, my own anger rising. He smirked, just a tiny twist of his mouth. Josh's hand landed on my shoulder, giving it a squeeze that was both comforting and restraining.

"I simply explained to her what needed to happen next. She could've been by my side, my queen, as I built my empire. You could've been my princess. But that bitch chose to run. So this is how it has to be. She started it, and you're going to end it. Kind of poetic, don't you think?"

"You delayed finishing your masterpiece of machinery for poetry?" I scoffed.

He didn't like being mocked; his hands curled into fists. "You are the fruit of my loins. How could I move forward without your submission? I mean to have *supreme* power over *all* things, Evelyn! Including you! It has to be *you*!"

When he was done with his little tantrum, we all fell into

silence for a few moments. Davis's entourage shuffled farther away from him; even his armed guards threw cautious looks over their shoulders. With them all spread out a bit more, I noticed another familiar face.

"Karen?" My eyes widened, and I slapped my palms on the table and pushed myself up. The woman who was in charge of my training and testing at Melior Group, the one who was as excited as me about the science side of Variants, the one who'd been kind to me—she was right there, standing at Davis's side. Was she there against her will? Had he kidnapped her in an attempt to get to me? Maybe he was blackmailing her?

Karen smiled at me, her lips a thin line, but it was Davis who answered my unspoken questions. "I assure you, Karen is here of her own free will. We've been working together for a long time. You see, we have the same goals when it comes to empowering the Variant community. She's been quite the useful resource."

He smiled at her, and she beamed, wide-eyed, as if she were a puppy and he was dangling a piece of chicken in front of her.

I couldn't believe it. I'd been half-convinced Victor Flint was the mole in Melior Group, but Karen had the highest level of clearance too. She could just as easily have gained access to all the information that was leaked.

I'd been fooled again. Was I so desperate for friendship, human connection of any kind, that I blindly trusted anyone who showed me any kindness?

"What do you want, Damari? How exactly do you think this is going to end?" Tyler still had his gun pointed, as did Alec and everyone else in the room. You could cut the tension with a hacksaw. But why was Tyler pushing him? To break the stalemate?

Davis spread his arms wide. "You summoned me here. What is it *you* want?"

"I want you to die," I declared without even thinking.

Davis chuckled. "So dramatic. But since we're on the topic, here's how this is going to go. You summoned me here, dear daughter, and here I am to collect you. You will come with me, you will cooperate, and you will help me complete my machine. In exchange, I'll let your Variants live."

"I'm not going anywhere with you."

"Well, then everyone dies."

"In case you haven't noticed, we have just as many guns pointed at you as you have at us. What makes you think you'd be able to walk out unscathed?"

"I think I can help with that." Dana sauntered in from around the corner. She was in jeans and a skin-tight tank top, all her curves accentuated, her silky blonde hair tamed in a braid.

Walking in step with her, their hands clasped, was Zara.

I took an involuntary step back. It felt as if someone had stabbed me just under the ribs and twisted the knife. I could understand Dana not wanting to be involved in this fight, wanting to steer clear of trouble, but to go out of her way to thwart us? To work with Davis? To break Zara out and bring her here to betray me *again*? It was just so cruel.

Davis gave her a wide smile and waited patiently until they were standing next to him.

"Fucking bitch," Alec growled, tightening his grip on his gun. I knew he wanted to shoot her in the face, but he was smart enough to resist the impulse. If he started firing, *everyone* would start firing.

"Why?" I hated how hurt I sounded.

"Aww, poor naive little Eve," Dana cooed, a cruel tilt to her mouth. "Haven't you learned by now not to trust everyone who says they're your friend? I thought you were supposed to be smart."

Zara snorted and picked at her nails.

"I'm gonna kill you both!" Dot launched forward, but she'd barely taken a step before Charlie wrapped his arms around her middle and picked her clean off the floor, her feet kicking. Kyo and Marcus stepped in, placing themselves between her and Davis.

Everyone tensed, but thankfully, no one fired. With Dana

neutralizing everyone's abilities, we were all equally vulnerable. Josh wouldn't be stopping *any* bullets, let alone all of them.

"Thank you for bringing her back to us, Dana." Davis lifted his hand and caressed Zara's cheek with the backs of his fingers.

"Yes, I'm so glad you're OK, darling," Zara's mom rushed out. Apparently now that Davis had welcomed her daughter back into the fold, it was OK for her to do the same. Twisted bitch.

For the first time since they walked in, I saw a crack in Zara's sarcastic mask. She covered it quickly, but her free hand started to twitch—little, jerky movements, just like when I was in a cage begging her to help me save Josh's life. When had she slipped back into her delusions? Had she ever truly turned against Davis, or was it all an elaborate lie?

Zara ignored her mom, practically speaking over her. "I'm sorry I ran away. I was . . . confused."

"Water under the bridge." Davis's focus was still on her. "You were my first creation. You're more of a daughter to me than Evelyn ever was."

I rolled my eyes. Was that supposed to make me feel jealous?

"You're about to make up for it, aren't you?" The smile Davis gave her then was nothing short of deranged, and the one she gave him back was just as unhinged. "But first things first. Dana."

"Right." Dana dropped Zara's hand. "I'll wait in the car or something," she deadpanned, then walked off at a leisurely pace.

The exact moment Dana was far enough away to no longer be blocking anyone's ability, electricity started to flitter along Zara's skin, every twitch of her hand eliciting a little spark. Everyone took a collective breath. Her ability was volatile, and she'd had little to no training with it. Josh's telekinesis wouldn't do shit to stop Zara's electricity. If she could focus enough to direct it at any of us, we were fucked.

Davis had the upper hand. Again. Because despite my impressive IQ, I'd done something colossally stupid. *Again.*

"I meant what I said, Eve." The crazy look disappeared from Zara's eyes, replaced with sincerity and determination. The twitching stopped, and electricity that had flickered over her a moment ago now rushed with purpose to her still hand. "I fucked up. But I learn from my mistakes."

"No!" Davis roared, raising his arm as if to punch her. He'd read what she was about to do, but he was too late to stop it.

Zara turned to face him fully and, before he could land his punch, lunged forward, pressing her electrified hand against his chest.

He roared in pain, every muscle in his body tense as the electricity coursed through him.

His goons hesitated, confused by the fact that none of the people they were pointing guns at had done anything. Half of them turned to check what Davis was screaming about, losing sight of their targets.

It was enough for us to act. Tyler and Alec fired off several shots in rapid succession, as did Kyo and Marcus.

Zara's mom lunged, clamping her arms around her daughter's waist and tackling her to the ground. Once the electricity released Davis, he swayed, his eyes droopy, but managed to stay upright.

In the same instant, my legs moved, my instincts carrying me forward. I stepped onto the chair, then onto the table, took two running strides, and launched myself into the air, aiming straight for Davis.

As I sailed through the air, my skin started to glow, filling me with Light and confidence and illuminating the dark space. Almost immediately, the sensation of Josh's ability tugged on my body, and my heart sank. Of course they wouldn't want me anywhere near that maniac! But instead of yanking me back into his strong embrace, it gave me an extra push.

I would've landed short, but with Josh's help, I barreled directly into Davis. We fell hard, my left elbow crunching against the concrete and making me cry out in pain. But I didn't stop, didn't pause to cradle my aching limb. I found exposed skin on his right forearm, wrapped my hands around it, and pulled.

I'd never pulled Light so forcefully before. All my focus was on the pure, unadulterated power surging into me, the Light-fueled instincts telling me to *just hold on.*

"No! Stop! How is this possible?" A frantic voice drew my attention. Gina stood a few feet away, staring at me intently. Karen and a few other Variants huddled around her, seeking the protection of her shielding ability.

"She's not using an ability." Dot took measured steps forward, Charlie and Kyo close behind her with guns pointed. Dot's eyes were narrowed, looking for someone to hurt. "You can't block her."

Before Gina could answer, Dot sprang forward and landed a punch right to her nose. As blood started to pour down Gina's front, the birds returned, lifting messy wisps of Dot's black hair as they sailed past her, straight for Gina. The woman screamed but was completely engulfed.

With Gina eliminated, the other Variants were left vulnerable, but of course, Davis always had another plan.

More people poured into the area, guns raised, abilities ready. I couldn't focus on them enough to know if they were ours or theirs. The last bits of Davis's stolen Light streamed easily into me. It felt like a relief, as if the Light had been waiting for someone to beckon it away from its usurper.

When the last tendrils left Davis's body, I gasped and let go of his arm. The power surging through me was terrifying—it was difficult to stand under its weight. I looked around for help, but my throat felt tight, and I couldn't seem to unclench my teeth. My skin was glowing so brightly some people were shielding their eyes.

But it wasn't just me creating so much light. Ethan stood with his broad back to me, his arms raised, commanding a *wall of fire.* Rising twenty feet into the air and burning a furious blue, it encased the three of us, protecting us from whatever chaos was happening out there.

There was a massive tear in the back of Ethan's T-shirt, and the exposed corded muscle strained with the effort of keeping the wall up. He was burning through Light quickly, but I couldn't transfer to him. Not yet, not alone. Instinctively I knew that if I transferred to any of them, they would end up with Davis's mind-reading ability.

I followed the blue flames up, taking in the sheer scale of what he was capable of. Above us, Josh was flying, hovering close by while making throwing movements with his hands. Crashing and banging followed the gestures.

Failing to get to my feet, I finally looked down at my father.

I had no idea if draining his stolen ability would kill him, and I'd done it without a moment's hesitation. It was time to find out if I'd just committed patricide.

He was prone on his back, his eyes closed, his head to one side. I couldn't tell if he was breathing or not. I leaned forward, reaching out to check for a pulse.

Before my hand connected with his neck, he took a giant breath, his eyes flying open as he shot up into a sitting position. He breathed hard for a few seconds, his eyes darting about and then, finally, landing on me.

"No," he breathed, pressing his hand to his chest. "What did you do?" he roared into my face. "Give it back! Give it back to me *now*, you stupid bitch!"

He lunged for me, and I didn't have the strength to fight him. My back hit the floor hard, knocking the air out of me, and we slid back dangerously close to Ethan's fire wall.

Davis started slapping and hitting me, his movements jerky and messy as he shouted incoherent things into my face. I barely had enough strength to lift my arms and protect my head from some of his blows, but I refused to let my hold on the Light slip. To come this far and then end up accidentally transferring his ability back to him would be tragic.

He smelled like sweat and desperation, the foul odor mixing with the metallic tang of blood in the air.

Searing pain exploded in my side, my shoulder, my neck, my temple. My vision blurred. I was vaguely conscious of several voices calling my name.

I searched for a way out—something, anything to make the blows stop.

But I had no chance. I could hardly move as he kept taking all his madness, all his fear and anger and inadequacy, out on me. He'd been doing that my whole life in one way or another.

He reared back onto his knees, one on either side of my torso, and backhanded me. My cheek burned and my ears started to ring.

With my head turned, I could see Ethan frantically looking between me and something in front of him, his arms still raised to hold up the fire wall as protection from whatever was the bigger threat on the other side. Josh hovered just over Ethan's left shoulder, bullets coming within inches of his face before falling to the ground. So many bullets.

I couldn't hear it over the ringing in my ears, but I could see Ethan yelling, his eyes wide.

Was he calling for help? Telling me to hold on? I supposed it didn't matter anymore.

Davis's hands circled my neck and squeezed.

I doubled my own chokehold on the ability I refused to let him have again. Even if he killed me, I'd die knowing I took from him what was never his to begin with. I'd die knowing I'd crippled him.

I refused to look at Davis. I didn't want my last image of this world to be his ugly, hateful face as he choked the life out of me.

Instead, I kept my gaze on the beautiful rage of the blue flames.

THIRTY-TWO

As though I'd summoned him, Alec burst through the fire. He ran at full speed, taking the scene in and reacting with precision. He raised his gun and pulled the trigger, but it was empty. Without missing a step, he threw it aside, dropped a shoulder, and tackled Davis off me.

They crashed into some furniture beyond the fire wall, and Davis's screams filled the air.

I took spluttering, excruciating breaths, my lungs burning as they filled once again with air.

Tyler burst through the flames a second later, gun raised, the look on his face feral. Blood was running down one side of his face, and his right shirtsleeve had completely ripped off. He lowered the gun and rushed straight to me just as Josh landed at his side.

I managed to lift myself onto my elbow and hold my other arm out. "Stop," I croaked, the word sending a hundred razor blades down my throat. They both paused inches from me and crouched down. Their eyes raked over my body, but they kept their hands back as I coughed and spluttered through the pain. "Need to touch you all at once."

Tyler nodded, but an abrupt escalation in noise distracted all of us. We couldn't really see past the blue fire wall, but it sounded as if more people had joined the fight.

"What's going on out there?" Tyler checked how many bullets he had left, then slammed the magazine back into the gun.

"A bunch of humans just showed up," Josh answered. "I saw them coming and flew down to get to Eve."

"Humans? As in, civilians?" Tyler looked aghast as Josh nodded. We had some humans with us, but they were trained and knew how to handle themselves. A bunch of civilians would get slaughtered.

I'm not sure if Ethan had the same thought or if he'd just had enough of not being able to get to me, but he roared and threw his hands out. The blue wall of fire separated into a thousand fireballs and shot out in every direction.

The fire was so intense that Ethan's targets didn't even have a chance to scream before they dropped to the ground in a smoking, charred mess. He'd executed the maneuver perfectly; only Davis's men had been hit. Everyone else in the room stopped to catch their breath.

The only sound now came from Davis, his screams of pain echoing in the vast space.

Ethan turned to me but swayed. His big body toppled to the ground. He reached for me, eyes drooping, then passed out.

Pain instantly tore into my chest. They were all running low. Now that I was paying attention, I could tell they'd all just about reached their limits, but that last stunt had pushed Ethan over the edge. He needed Light. *Now.*

"Eth . . . Ethan . . ." The massive burden of the Light inside me weighted me down so much I could hardly speak. It was begging, *demanding* to be released. I reached out to him, but I couldn't risk touching him, not without touching them all.

We needed Alec.

But Alec was still pummeling my father, lost in his rage.

Josh rushed to Ethan's side, checking for injuries. I looked up at Tyler, gritting my teeth with the effort of controlling all the

Light, and hoped the pleading look in my eyes was enough to convey what I needed.

Tyler looked in Alec's direction, shouting his name.

Alec was kneeling over Davis, landing punch after punch to his face, ribs, anywhere his fists could connect. Fountains of blood sprayed in gruesome bursts every time Alec's fists connected. I couldn't be sure how much was my father's and how much belonged to the Master of Pain.

By some miracle, Davis was still conscious, screaming between blows. That's how Alec must've been keeping him awake —just enough pain inflicted by his ability to keep his adrenaline pumping and his mind still connected to his body.

Or maybe he was screaming from the pain of the burns. Being pushed through Ethan's fire wall had left half of Davis's face a gruesome, charred mess, with a black hole where his eye used to be. The right side of his body was almost as bad. The smoking flesh seemed to be fused with the fabric of his clothing.

Alec was determined to make him suffer, fully embracing all he hated about himself to hurt the man who had ruined our lives. His expression was feral, his teeth bared, his eyes wild. Blood dripped down his face, and his muscles bunched with every movement.

I knew he'd hate himself for getting lost in the pain later, but I couldn't worry about that yet.

Alec wanted Davis to suffer, but I just wanted this to end.

"Ty!" I managed to yell. Tears of frustration streamed down my face, mingling with the blood and dust in my hair. He was refusing to leave my side, but he saw the desperate look in my face, knew Ethan didn't have much time.

"Josh!" he yelled as he rose to his feet, raising his gun.

Josh whipped his head around, figured out what was needed in under a second, and lifted his arm. Using his ability, he yanked Davis out from under Alec and lifted him into the air.

Davis stopped screaming. His one good eye rolled into the back of his head before it focused on me. Somehow, he managed to smile, the good side of his face pulling up in a twisted, horrific way. "You're all—"

Tyler pulled the trigger, shooting him through his good eye and finally ending his life. Josh released his hold, and Davis fell to the ground next to a slightly confused, panting Alec.

With the screams and the sound of punches gone, my weak voice carried. "Alec."

He finally looked at me, the violent haze clearing from his eyes.

"Need you," I panted. He was rushing to me before the words were even out of my mouth.

Josh's ability lifted me so gently that not a joint was bent, not an injury jostled. He lowered me next to Ethan just as Alec and Tyler dropped to their knees on my other side.

I reached for Ethan, knowing they'd follow my lead. As I grabbed Ethan's cold hand—his hands were never cold—Josh wrapped a hand around my ankle, Alec took my other hand, and Tyler cupped my cheek.

I hoped to the vastness of the universe, to whatever divine power was behind the Light and all that was made possible because of it, that this would work.

I let my hold on the Light go.

My skin lit up, glowing brightly for a few intense seconds before fading once again. My Bondmates grunted and steadied themselves as the force of the Light slammed into them.

I sighed in relief—finally, I could breathe.

Ethan groaned, stirred, then sat up, looking disoriented. It should've taken him at least a day or two to recover from being depleted of Light to the point of unconsciousness. He looked down at our joined hands, and his eyes widened.

"Eve." My name on his lips was a combination of question, plea, and sigh of relief.

I sat up, and Ethan pulled me into his arms. "You scared me, big guy."

"You scared me too, baby."

Ethan would've held on to me for days if he could have, but within moments, I was pulled out of his embrace and into another set of strong arms. Then another and another. We held on, making sure we were all there, all still breathing.

We weren't unscathed by any means. Ethan had nearly died overusing his ability, Josh was limping, the gash on Tyler's head was still oozing blood, and Alec was so covered in gore I wasn't sure what his injuries were. My own body ached all over. Muscles I didn't even know I had were burning, my elbow still throbbed, and I could feel the bruises and scrapes from Davis's bashing.

But we were all still there. We were alive and he was dead.

Once I was sure of the most crucial things to my existence— the functionality of my own vital organs and the survival of the loves of my life—other things started to come into focus.

The airport was trashed. Debris and damage covered everything. Holes in the walls, charred furniture, lights hanging half off the ceiling, bodies everywhere.

I'd never seen so many dead people.

Most of the survivors were either sitting on the ground or leaning on things, catching their breath and evaluating their own injuries. They were all watching us. I looked around at their faces as I rose to my feet. I didn't recognize most of them, but no one was looking at me with hostility or hatred or fear. Mostly it was curiosity and awe, even a few uncertain smiles.

Dot stood nearby, leaning on Kyo.

As soon as our eyes connected, we moved toward each other, wading through the debris and gore to finally wrap each other in a big hug.

"I'm so glad you're OK," she whispered into my neck as I said at the same time, "I'm so sorry about Jamie."

We took shaky, uneven breaths, fighting tears. As we pulled apart, we looked into each other's faces. I wondered if she saw as much strength and determination in my eyes as I saw in hers.

She would survive this. I had no doubt.

When she stepped back, her knees gave out. I lunged for her, but Marcus caught her, sweeping her up into his arms and planting a gentle kiss on her cheek.

"Let's get you some water." Kyo led the way to the heavy timber table that was somehow still standing. He found a few chairs, righted them, and the three of them settled in.

A sob drew my attention back to where Kyo and Marcus had been standing a moment earlier.

Charlie held Ed in a tight hug, his eyes red from crying as his boyfriend fell apart in his arms. Josh took my hand, and I followed his gaze to one of countless bodies near the couple's feet. Ed's brother lay on the ground, a knife sticking out of his chest, his eyes wide but unseeing.

Once again, I fought tears, my lip trembling. I didn't even get to meet him.

I felt frozen. Simultaneously I wanted to turn my face into Ethan's broad chest and forget it all, and I wanted to rush around and look into every single dead face to know exactly who we'd lost.

More and more sniffles and sobs started to fill the air as people took stock of the aftermath.

Olivia and Henry, Mr. Takata, and a handful of other people who'd been hidden away came out of a back corridor. Olivia and Henry went straight to their children as others started to help tend to the wounded.

A spark of electricity drew my eyes to a spot nearby, near where I'd tackled Davis to the ground.

Zara was on her back, her left leg twisted at an unnatural angle, her face scrunched up in pain as sparks flitted over her skin. I stumbled over to her, the guys sticking close by, and dropped to my knees.

"Eve." Her eyes widened, then scrunched up in pain as another flash of electricity skittered over her body. "Are you . . . is he . . . did we win?"

I nodded, swallowing around the ever-present lump in my throat. "He's dead."

She smiled, showing teeth covered in blood. She moaned in pain, and the electricity came more suddenly this time, a violent bolt shooting out of her chest and connecting with the high ceiling above.

"I can't . . . hold . . . you have to . . . Eve, you have to . . ." She was struggling to control Rick's ability. With all the pain she was in and how weak she was, I was surprised she hadn't fried us all already.

"Someone find Dana!" Tyler roared, and several agents dropped what they were doing to rush in various directions. But they didn't get far before Dana came running up.

"I'm here." She sprinted directly for us, a big group of paramedics rushing up behind her. The electricity stopped sparking as Dana approached, and Zara sighed in relief.

Dana skidded to a stop and took Zara's hand. "I told you not to die, you bitch."

Zara laughed, then coughed, the sound wet and dangerous sounding. "Fuck you."

A paramedic appeared next to her, and we backed up so they could work. I wasn't sure if Zara would make it. The blood she was coughing up indicated internal bleeding, and that was pretty fucking serious. But with paramedics here, she had a fighting chance. That was more than I could say for her mom, whose body lay lifeless several feet away.

Had Zara killed her own mother, just as Rick had? Or was she felled by another's hand? Was it Zara's own mother who'd inflicted such damage on her body? It was beyond disturbing to think about, but then, my own father had been beating me only minutes earlier. Had it only been minutes?

"Where the fuck did all these humans come from?" Tyler scratched his head and winced when he accidentally scraped the gash in his forehead. The paramedics were moving through the wounded quickly, prioritizing the worst cases.

"Oh, that was me." Dana waved a hand dismissively, her worried gaze fixed on Zara. "I've been working with some HEN groups in the area. I took a chance and told them what was happening, and most of them decided they wanted to help."

"Why didn't you say something when I called you?" I asked. I'd been so worried after our talk.

"Couldn't. I was about to go into a meeting with Variant Valor —too many of Davis's people around."

The sneaky bitch had been playing both sides, biding her time to make the best move.

"I'm really fucking glad you're not a treacherous bitch," I told her.

As the paramedics lifted Zara's body up on the stretcher, Dana finally looked at me and smiled. "Had you going."

"Yes, you did." I pulled her into a hug.

"And I'm glad you're not, like, dead and shit. I guess." She shrugged, but it didn't escape my notice how tightly she was returning my hug.

"This will never not be weird." Alec sounded disturbed, and we pulled apart. I couldn't believe I was able to smile so soon, but if we were to have any chance of getting through this, we had to hold on to these moments of positivity.

Dana rushed off with Zara and the paramedics as they evacuated the worst of the injured. The few people on Davis's side who'd managed to survive were being led away in handcuffs. Karen was one of them. She was cuffed to a stretcher, her head wrapped in bandages, blood seeping through the crisp, white fabric already.

"Eve." Tyler pulled on my good elbow, his voice laced with urgency.

I turned to look behind us.

Near what used to be the windows and was now a big gaping hole in the wall, a group of people were gathered around something.

I didn't want to know, wasn't sure I could handle losing another person, but I made myself ask. "Who?"

"Nina." Tyler was already pulling me along. I wasn't sure I could've made my feet move otherwise.

I had no idea what time it was, but it was night, and the giant hole just looked like a black pit of darkness and despair. Nina was lying close to the edge of it, the other Lighthunters surrounding her.

"Why didn't the paramedics take her?" I said angrily as we got close enough to see her broken body. They were supposed to be taking the worst of the injured.

Tyler's ability answered the question better than anyone could've. "Her injuries are too extensive. She's got minutes if she's lucky."

The anger evaporated, replaced by a heavy longing feeling it was hard to put my finger on. Nina was a friend, but she was so much more. She'd been there when we needed her most. She was the reason we'd been able to save Charlie. She was the one who'd explained my nature to me better than anyone. She was wise and kind and selfless. The world would be worse off without her. *I* would be worse off without her.

I went to kneel next to her, but she rose into the air, as though floating on a cloud. Her body was lifted upright, her feet hovering above the floor.

Frowning, I turned to Josh, but he looked just as confused.

The other Lighthunters made a semicircle around us, facing the black night.

"Evelyn." Nina's voice sounded weak but calm. Her features were smooth, not at all creased with pain, her eyes tired but relaxed.

"Nina." Tears trailed down my cheeks, but I managed not to sob. I reached up to touch her, but I hesitated, scared I would hurt her. She caught my hand in hers and held it.

I squeezed her fingers, as though if I held on tightly enough, she'd stay.

"Please . . ." I knew it was silly, that it was way beyond anyone's control, but I couldn't stop my plea. "Don't leave me."

So many people had left me, abandoned me, betrayed me.

She smiled. She was dying, her clothes filthy, her umber skin covered in gray dust that only made the blood appear brighter. Her other arm hung limply by her side, the shoulder angled down in a sickening way, but she managed a smile.

"But you are not alone." Her French accent seemed thicker as she glanced behind me to my Bondmates. "You will never be alone again. Just remember to lean into the Light. Let it guide you. Trust your instincts."

She started to glow in much the same way I did when I used my Vivid Light. Her hand felt tingly in mine, and when I looked down, it started to disintegrate before my eyes.

I gasped in shock and looked back into her face just in time to see her close her eyes and smile. She looked at peace as she faded. It was as if she was absorbed by the glowing Light and as if the Light came from within her all at once.

Slowly, softly, she disappeared. Eventually I stood with my hand held out in front of me, staring into the darkness.

As the last few sparks dimmed, the Lighthunters sighed in unison. They held hands for another moment, then all at once, let go.

I couldn't quite believe what I'd seen. It was some kind of molecular disintegration, the very fiber of her being coming apart on a microscopic level and transforming into pure Light.

I filed it away to wonder about later.

"Does that happen every time?" Josh asked. "I mean, do all of you . . ."

"Yes," one of the Lighthunters answered, a stocky man with dull brown eyes. "The Light takes us at the end. Death is never painful or unpleasant for us. We die knowing we continue to serve that which we dedicated our lives to."

The Light absorbed them back into itself, and they lived on in anyone with Variant DNA.

I took a deep breath and leaned back, knowing Alec was there to wrap his arms around me. He always had my back.

The Lighthunters started to clear out, and the five of us gravitated toward the big timber table where Dot sat in Marcus's lap, her feet in Kyo's. Ed and Charlie were with them. Ed had stopped sobbing, but silent tears still streamed down his cheeks as he stared into the middle distance. Charlie was rubbing soothing circles into his back.

Ed had lost his brother and his Variant. My chest felt too tight to breathe at the mere thought of losing one of my Bondmates. I couldn't imagine the pain he felt.

As Josh righted some more mismatched chairs with his ability, I paused at what used to be a bar. Half of it was disintegrated, still smoldering from Ethan's fire, and glass covered every surface. My attention snagged on a few bottles that had miraculously survived the violence. Just as we had.

I stepped past the debris to reach them. Two were some kind of liqueur that looked like it contained more sugar than alcohol. I grabbed the third, a bottle of tequila.

Alec searched the cupboards and found a tray of glasses.

Everyone settled into chairs and stared into nothing, trying to process in their own way. I stood at the table and looked around at all the people I *hadn't* lost. I looked at each one of them in turn and thanked the Light they were still here, still breathing, still living and loving . . . and grieving.

As I opened the bottle, I turned my thoughts to those I'd lost. I poured a bit into each glass and then lifted one.

"To Nina." I slammed it back and immediately reached for the bottle again.

Everyone else watched me, either with blank expressions or as if I were crazy. Then Ethan reached forward and grabbed a glass.

"To Nina." He downed it. Slowly, one by one, they all reached for glasses and toasted the Lighthunter.

I refilled them and raised mine again.

"To Jamie."

We drank. Dot had to take a few deep breaths before she could down the strong alcohol.

We toasted Ed's brother next, then name after name as we remembered the fallen.

As I poured the last drops of the bottle into the last glass, Tyler stood and raised his.

"To everyone we've lost. Their deaths will not be in vain. We will fight to make this world a better place."

As one, we drank.

As I dropped the glass back to the table, I swayed a little. I wasn't sure if it was from exhaustion, the alcohol, or a combination of the two, but just like always, my Bond was there to catch me.

Ethan pulled me into his lap, and I relaxed into his embrace.

Everyone fell into silence. All the injured had been tended to or taken away to hospitals. Those who hadn't needed medical attention had left. Where had they gone? What do people do after an epic battle? Just . . . go home? Have a shower and go to bed?

I could use a shower, and my body already seemed to be shutting down, ready for oblivion. But I wasn't sure if I'd be able to sleep—if I'd be able to close my eyes without seeing crimson.

Ethan's booming voice broke the silence. "Can't believe he called you 'the fruit of his loins.' Who the fuck talks like that?"

For a beat, everyone remained silent. And then we all burst into laughter. We laughed for a solid minute, bent over the table, wiping tears of both mirth and grief from the corners of our eyes.

It was exactly what we needed to break some of the thick tension. As our laughter receded, we slowly got up and started making our way home.

THIRTY-THREE

I stood at the foot of my bed in my underwear, my hair falling down my back in waves, my makeup done, staring at what I'd decided to wear.

It was only a dress, but this felt important, momentous even.

The black fabric and bright poppy prints contrasted starkly with the creamy white linen sheets.

I ran my hand reverently over my mother's dress, the only piece of her I had left. I'd saved it like the precious artifact it was, hardly even touching it where it hung in my closet for over two years.

It was time to honor her memory by wearing it. It was time to remember all the times I'd seen her in it, smiling and happy. It was time to remember all the good and, instead of feeling sad about what we'd lost, feel happy about all we had to look forward to.

It was what she fought for—my future.

I slipped the dress over my head and did up the zip on the side. It was a little loose around the middle, but the top fit perfectly, and the understated A-line shape reached just below the knee. I remembered us being the same height, but I was sure it used to reach midcalf on her.

I smiled and took a deep breath, squaring my shoulders.

At the last moment, I decided to grab a cardigan. I picked a red one, the color almost a perfect match for some of the poppies on the dress. I slipped my feet into black flats and came out of my massive walk-in wardrobe, pausing in the doorway.

I would never get enough of the view from our bedroom. And I would never forget the day they showed it to me.

Ethan had practically been jumping up and down from excitement. Josh had hung back, a smug, knowing look on his face. Tyler had led the way up the stairs, and Alec had held my hand and walked by my side, his posture more relaxed than I'd ever seen it.

They guided me into the newly renovated section of the third floor and paused in front of an ornate set of double doors.

"Ready? Ready?" Ethan's grin was wide, his dimples prominent.

I chuckled. "Ready."

Josh flicked a wrist and the doors flung open.

I gasped, my eyes darting about the room. I'd had no idea what was taking the contractors so long, but it had never crossed my mind that they were converting the space into a giant-ass bedroom for me. For *us*.

I couldn't decide if I wanted to jump on the massive bed first or run past the light, gauzy curtains and take in the view from the balcony.

"The bed is big enough to fit us all." Ethan rushed over to it, then buzzed around the room, showing me all the different features. "My feet don't even hang off the end! But this is *your* room, really. The bed is just for when we all want to be together, you know. There are four bedrooms just off the hallway, two on either side, so we're close, but you still have your privacy. I know how you like your alone time. Oh, and there's a walk-in closet! Look! Josh and I have been buying some things and filling it up already. I hope you like them. And on the other side—I mean, there are bathrooms off the hall too, but this is the main one." He grabbed my hand and dragged me over to another set of double doors.

"We already have a steam room in the pool house." I laughed. The en suite was insane! Massive shower with two showerheads, two sinks—it was the size of the bedroom I'd been using, and half of it was taken up by a steam room. It wasn't as big as the one on the secret Greek island, but it would fit us all comfortably, and the tiles were almost identical. There was even a little sink with a modern mosaic pattern behind it.

"Yeah, but this one's more private." Alec's breath fanned over my neck, making me want to test it out immediately.

"And it has the best view of any room in the house." Ethan was already leading us back out.

A pair of cushy armchairs and a little side table sat in front of the windows. Ethan rushed around the furniture, flapping at the curtain to reveal the stunning view.

"Do you like it?" Finally he stilled and clasped his hands in front of him. I realized he was nervous.

Ignoring the view, I wrapped my hands around his neck and drew his face down to mine. "I love it, big guy!" I gave him a brilliant smile and a soft kiss. "Thank you."

Pulling out of Ethan's arms, I went to each of them in turn, giving them kisses and thanks and appreciation. Then I rushed out of the room, the giddy excitement infecting me.

"Where are you going?" Josh called after me, but I could hear his footsteps following.

"I have to get something!" I knew exactly what I wanted to add to this room first.

I rushed into my old bedroom and over to my dresser, Josh and Ethan only a step behind me. I grabbed the jewelry box they'd given me and handed it to Josh as I gathered up the framed photos —my friends and family cradled in my arms. Needing something to do, Ethan threw my closet open and scooped up a bunch of hangers, then led the way back to my new, magnificent room.

Ethan set to putting the clothes away as Josh and I arranged the photos on the side table near the door. I'd added a photo of Lucian with my mom, my three-year-old self cuddled between them.

"I want more photos on this. We need to take more photos together."

"You got it, precious." Alec, surprisingly, was the first to agree.

"Where do you want this?" Josh held up the jewelry box.

Before I could answer, a piece of paper I'd forgotten I was keeping under the box dislodged itself and fluttered to the floor. I reached for it, but Tyler got there first.

I chewed on my lip as he opened it, his slight frown of curiosity slowly giving way to amusement as he realized what it was.

He smiled at me. "You kept this?"

"What is it?" Josh leaned over, and Alec stepped around to get a better look. Ethan came back out of the walk-in to peer over all their heads.

I was once again grateful I couldn't blush. I had no secrets from them—I loved them more than I loved my own life—but I was still a little embarrassed.

"It's a note I wrote to Eve when she first got to Bradford Hills," Tyler answered as Ethan gently took the piece of paper and they all looked at me.

I rolled my eyes and huffed; it was silly to be embarrassed. I mean, I'd been having sex with the man. We lived together. So what if I'd kept a silly note about school supplies?

"I had a crush on you from the first second I saw you, OK? You were a hot older guy, and you did something really thoughtful for me." I shrugged.

They all looked as if they were trying really hard to hold back laughter, even Ty. He wrapped his arms around my waist and kissed me through our chuckles while the others descended into full-on guffaws.

"It was wildly inappropriate at the time." Tyler pulled away just far enough to look into my eyes. "But I was attracted to you too. I couldn't stop thinking about leaning forward and just closing the distance between us. And then you showed up in my damn office wearing that fucking schoolgirl outfit."

"Oh man, that skirt." Alec groaned.

"You know I spent that whole session with a raging boner?"

"That's why you didn't move from behind your desk." I slapped him on the chest.

We spent the afternoon reminiscing about the way I met them all, teasing each other and laughing as we wandered between my old room and my new one. I was fully moved in before dinner.

The view from the balcony that day had been a bit different. Summer had been ending; the leaves on the oaks lining the drive had only just started to turn.

Now, we'd come through another harsh winter. Summer was just starting. Trees budded with new growth as the morning sun streamed over the manicured grounds. The balcony was smack-dab in the middle of the mansion, and the view overlooked the massive driveway, the top of the iron gates just visible over the trees. Beyond, some of the taller buildings of the Institute peeked over the lush trees littering all of Bradford Hills.

I grabbed my bag off the bed and made my way downstairs.

They were waiting for me in the foyer, reminding me of the day of the gala when I'd come down these same stairs, feeling sexy and confused at Alec's lascivious stares.

This time, there was nothing but love in their eyes as they looked up at me one by one.

I'd asked that people not wear black—I didn't want it to feel like a funeral. Ethan was in jeans, a white short-sleeved shirt stretching over his broad chest. Josh was in chinos and a green polo shirt that made his eyes pop. Tyler wore gray slacks and a crisp blue shirt, the sleeves rolled up. Alec had been wearing more color lately—lifting the blackness from his heart had opened him up to all the vibrancy of life in other areas. His jeans were black, but his shirt was an electric blue.

"You look beautiful." Tyler took my hand as I reached the

bottom. I could hear it in his voice—he was speaking for all of them.

Lucian joined us, stopping his wheelchair near the ramp to the garage.

"Ready?" He looked as distinguished and dapper as ever in slacks and a light sweater.

"Ready." I nodded, and he looked at me properly for the first time. His eyes widened a fraction as they flicked up and down my body, his gaze more disbelieving than anything.

I knew it was the dress giving him pause. He would've seen her wearing it before we left—I'd seen pictures of her in it from before I was born. But I was surprised at how much emotion he seemed to be feeling. His chest rose and fell a little faster, and his eyes were even getting misty.

"Uncle Luce?" I took a step closer to him, worried.

"That dress . . ." His voice was choked, and he cleared this throat before taking my hand in his. "She was wearing that dress when we met. I had no idea she still had it—that you still had it."

"It was one of the only things that survived the crash. She wore it a lot, always on happy days."

"For a second you looked exactly like her. You have the same eyes, the same hair—she had it long like yours when we met."

"I can change if this is too much—"

"No." He shook his head and smiled. "It looks beautiful on you. It's a nice reminder of her. It just took me by surprise, that's all."

"We should get going," Tyler gently reminded us.

We piled into two cars and headed off to a memorial that Lucian and I had organized for my mother.

This was not another funeral. This was a way to acknowledge the past and focus on the future.

In the weeks after the confrontation with Davis, we went to *so many* funerals, sometimes more than one in a day. There were a few days where all we did was eat, sleep, and go to funerals. I almost felt numb to it by the end, but then I'd hear the loved ones start to cry, and it would all come flooding back, my own emotion, my own tears bubbling up.

I cried at every single one.

I bawled uncontrollably at Jamie's, Dot's grief amplifying my own.

The reprieve was brief. We took some time to say goodbye to the fallen, but there was a lot of work to do. We'd taken Davis out —we'd removed the cancer—but we had to make sure his poison didn't keep spreading. Our cuts and bruises were fading, the broken bones healing, but the world still had a long way to go.

All of Davis's properties and holdings were seized and searched, all his secrets revealed. His horrific experiments were stopped, his machines destroyed. Any research that could be useful was handed over to ethical, educational institutions.

The world learned how he'd stolen his ability, how he'd lied, cheated, and manipulated to get ahead. Everyone knew he was responsible for the Vital kidnappings, for countless deaths in incidents like the one that killed the guys' parents. Everyone knew it was on his orders—in an attempt to assassinate Senator Christine Anderson—that an entire plane of civilians was shot out of the sky.

He killed my mother, but I took *him* down.

With Davis dead, his reputation in tatters, and no one willing to defend his memory or his legacy, Variant Valor started to lose steam.

The world was more stunned to learn of the Lighthunters' legitimacy. Their "coming out" went as well as we could've dreamed. They had insurmountable evidence to prove they were the "real deal," not to mention decades' worth of evidence to prove Davis was shady, manipulative, and a downright murderous psychopath.

At every turn, they preached peace between humans and Variants, vowing they were on the side of order and peace. It's what the Light demanded, and that included the human population.

After initial mistrust, the Human Empowerment Network began to calm down too.

The work Dot and Charlie were doing with other grassroots organizations across the world was helping. There were peaceful protests, Human-Variant community meetings, reconciliation speeches, forums, all kinds of small and large events in local communities all over the world that fostered cooperation and togetherness. Their main aim was to dispel fear through education.

As we drove through Bradford Hills—Lucian, Alec, and Ethan in an accessible SUV, Tyler, Josh, and I in Josh's Challenger—we had the windows down, enjoying the warm breeze. No armored cars tailed us. There were no security checkpoints to pass at the gates, no black-clad agents crawling over every inch of town or following every Vital.

The violence had stopped. Some residual unrest lingered in Bangkok, Moscow, Mexico, and a few other spots, but for the most part, the world was getting back to normal. People were getting back to their lives. Businesses were opening, schools were back in session, Bradford Hills Institute was back at full capacity. Some changes in staff had been called for, and a handful of students had been expelled after it was discovered they'd worked closely with Davis and committed serious crimes, but the reputation of the Institute was intact. Most people were just happy to get back to learning.

Me most of all.

I'd decided I wanted to major in genetics with a focus on Variant studies. I'd spent so much time not knowing what I was, then struggling to understand what it meant. I wanted to contribute to the wider understanding of what the Light was and how it functioned.

With the Lighthunters rejoining society and all the other Vivids coming forward, several new areas of study would exist by the time I finished my degree.

Lighthunters were working closely with Bradford Hills Institute and other prestige organizations all over the world to help identify which claims of Vivids were legitimate. There were, so far, forty-eight confirmed Vivids. Forty-eight of us in the whole world. About two dozen were coming to Bradford Hills next week to get to know one another and do some experiments.

Lucian, Victor, and Tyler had retaken control of Melior Group within days of Davis's death, but I still refused to continue our research sessions there. No one dared to make me stick to the contract.

Karen had died in the hospital a few days after the battle with Davis, and most of her research team had been disbanded while they investigated who knew of her treachery. Tyler's ability helped enormously, especially now that Davis's shield was dead and no longer protecting his people from being discovered. But it was a large organization, and things took time. Melior Group was doing a massive restructuring, and they let a lot of people go. Some were arrested and prosecuted, their transgressions going further than just disobeying orders.

Even so, I needed to not be surrounded by black-clad agents. I'd had enough of that. Further research and testing was happening in the well-equipped labs at Bradford Hills Institute with professors I knew and liked. They would be in charge of welcoming the Vivids and working with us all.

They were the ones I allowed to observe and gather as much information as possible the last time I glowed.

Zara was released from the hospital maybe a month after the altercation. Her injuries were extensive, and she'd have scars to rival Alec's, but she survived. Considering all that was revealed about Davis and how deeply his manipulations went, coupled with the fact that she'd cooperated and provided information early on, no charges were pressed against her. She was free to leave the hospital.

I appreciated beyond measure how selflessly she'd acted to help us bring Davis down, but I wasn't ready to forgive the way she'd betrayed me. I just had too much emotional baggage to wade through, and I wasn't sure we could ever get back to how we were at the beginning. But to make it safe for others around her, to give Dana a break from having to stick by her side twenty-four seven, and as a gesture of gratitude, I took her ability.

We did it under the watchful eyes of Bradford's professors, my guys all standing by to take the excess Light as soon as it was done.

We sat facing each other on the ground in the small research lab, legs crossed, and I took her hand. She smiled at me with a multitude of emotions in her face, but the one that seemed strongest was relief.

I pulled the Light out of her much more slowly than I had with Davis, careful not to take too much and kill her. She passed out anyway, collapsing onto her side as I dragged the last tendrils out of her. It weighed me down, the sheer force of that much Light making me grit my teeth as I glowed brightly.

But my guys were right there, ready to step in and take it all from me safely.

That was one thing I was sure of without a shadow of a doubt —they would always be there for me. They would always stand at my back, ready to support, defend, and love me in every way I needed, just as I would for them. We would lay down our lives for one another. After all the shit we'd been through, I knew there was nothing life could throw at us that we couldn't survive.

My Bond was complete and unbreakable. In them, I had the family, the connection, I'd craved my entire life.

We turned the corner, driving slowly through the manicured grounds of the memorial park. The rest of my family had already arrived and were waiting for us on the grassy area near the parking lot.

Olivia and Henry were standing in the shade of a tree, talking with their children.

Charlie and Ed were getting married in a few months, giving us all another positive thing to focus on. Ed had moved to Bradford Hills permanently and fit so perfectly with our family we sometimes forgot he hadn't been around from the start. He sometimes had to remind us to catch him up on inside jokes and conversations he hadn't been around for.

Dot, Kyo, and Marcus were looking for their own place in Bradford Hills—somewhere close to campus so Dot could finish her veterinary course. It still wasn't possible to marry more than one person, but the way Dot ranted about it, I had a feeling she would make it her own personal mission to change that law.

They were all dressed in bright spring colors—as if we were about to have a picnic and not a memorial.

Dot rushed over to me, her black hair shining in the sun, and gave me a hug.

"How you doing, girl?" She scrutinized me, but I smiled and pulled away.

"I'm good. Focusing on the positive memories. You?" Like me, she'd struggled with all the funerals we had to attend, each one reopening the wound of her own grief and making it hard for the skin to stitch over.

"I'm pretty good." She sounded a little surprised. "This one feels different."

"Yeah, it does."

I threaded my arm through hers, and we wandered over to the others while the guys helped Lucian out of the car.

"Hey, kitten." Kyo stepped forward and gave me a hug. Not to be outdone, Marcus lifted me clean off the ground when he hugged me.

"How you doin'?" he asked as he set me back down.

"Wishing people would stop asking me that." I raised my brows at him, and he flashed me a brilliant smile.

"It's because we care." Charlie nudged me, and I gave him and Ed hugs too.

"I know." I smiled at the way they linked hands as soon as their hugs were delivered. Their happiness was contagious, made even sweeter by the bitterness of all the recent loss.

"Evelyn." Olivia held me at arm's length, her gentle hands on my shoulders. "You look beautiful, darling." She pulled me into a hug and stroked my hair in a gesture that was so motherly I almost felt as if my mom were holding me.

"I love you, Auntie O," I whispered into her neck.

"I love you too." She pulled away and smoothed my hair before wiping her eyes discreetly.

Henry surprised me by going in for a hug too. He was a quiet man who traveled a lot for work, and out of everyone, I knew him the least.

The hug was brief but warm and not at all awkward. And if the hug was surprising, his words just about floored me.

"Your mother would be incredibly proud of you, Evelyn. I know I am." He nodded and turned to lead the way up a small hill, leaving me standing there feeling as if my chest were about to burst. I had to take a second to breathe through the emotion.

Lucian appeared next to me. "Let's do this." He gave me a smile, and Olivia pushed his chair up the hill—even though that damn chair was the best money could buy and was fully electric. I think she just liked feeling useful.

We climbed the hill as a group. We could've taken the winding gravel path to where my mother's memorial plaque was installed in a low wall surrounded by trees and flowers, but we took the most direct route, even if it wasn't necessarily the easiest.

As we crested the hill, I had to pause again.

Lucian let his chair race down the hill, a joyful laugh escaping him as he overtook Henry, and Olivia chased after him, half chastising and half laughing. The others jogged down behind them, but my Bondmates stood at the top of the hill with me in a line, looking down at the scene below.

I couldn't quite believe how many people had shown up.

A handful of chairs faced the plaque, and a simple lectern had been set up for speeches. The sea of people there to show their respects, to share memories of my mother, was overwhelming.

"She was loved." Tyler echoed my thoughts.

"More than you know." Alec nodded.

"So are you," Josh added quietly.

While many people were there because they wanted to remember my mother, many others had never met her—like the Lighthunters and some of the students from the Institute. They were there for me, to show their respect and support for me.

"How could she not be? Look at her." Ethan lightened the mood, and we all chuckled.

I adjusted my bag on my shoulder and headed down the hill to join my family and friends. Ethan, Josh, Tyler, and Alec were with me every step of the way.

I heard Alec thudding through the foyer and snapped my head up to check the time.

"Shit." I cursed under my breath. "Alec!"

"Yeah?"

"You may wanna skip the workout. We should probably head to the hospital soon." I leaned over my desk, rushing to finish the section of the research report I was working on.

Alec appeared in the doorway. "What do you mean? Now? It's happening now?" His eyes were wide, his shoulders tense. He looked like a really sexy, tattooed deer in headlights.

Before I could answer, Uncle Luce wheeled himself out of his office. Mine was next to his on the ground floor. I'd had it set up just before I started my PhD. As I researched how Vivid Light could be used to treat terminal diseases, it was handy to have a space to work from at home.

"Yeah, you may want to get going," Lucian said. "I'll meet you all down there later."

"Shit!" Alec ran his hands over his buzzed hair. "Should I change? Never mind. No time. Let's go." He waved his hands maniacally, trying to shoo me out of my chair.

I groaned and got up, reluctantly giving up on getting any more work done. "Alec, calm down. These things take time— sometimes days. We're not in any kind of rush."

"You don't know that," he argued. "Sometimes they happen fast. Really fucking fast. Like in the back of the car on the way to the hospital fast."

I chuckled as I took my time walking down the hallway; Alec buzzed around me like a toddler on a sugar high.

Josh came down the stairs just as Alec and I reached the foyer. He had my bag and shoes in his hands.

"Heard Alec losing his shit." He gave my Master of Pain a teasing grin. "Figured it was time to go."

Alec flipped him off as he grabbed his wallet and keys and I slipped my feet into flats.

Josh drove, the leather pads on his elbows stretching every time he changed gears. When he'd started teaching Variant studies at Bradford Hills Institute, he'd taken to wearing tweed. He was pairing the traditional, preppy Ivy League uniform with his band T-shirts and jeans, combining his two signature styles into one delicious one. When he wasn't at the front of a lecture theater, he was leading a program that provided Variant studies teaching in public, predominantly human, schools. All the girls had crushes on Professor Mason—human and Variant.

As we walked up to the maternity wing in the hospital, Tyler and Ethan got up from their seats in the waiting area.

Ethan wrapped me up in a big, warm hug and gave me a soft kiss that I just about melted into. He was in a white T-shirt but still had his chef pants on. He was the head chef at a painfully trendy restaurant in Manhattan and chasing his first Michelin star. In the next year or two, he planned to open up his own restaurant.

"We don't have time for this." Alec tried to wedge an arm between us, and we pulled apart, chuckling.

Tyler pulled me away from both of them with a hand around

my waist. "Would you calm down? You'd think it was Eve about to have a baby and not Dot, the way you're carrying on."

He gave me a kiss too, taking his sweet time—no doubt to irritate Alec. Tyler was the youngest headmaster Bradford Hills Institute had ever seen. One of the first things he'd done was create a new position—a human liaison who worked on building ties with human communities and broadening the Institute's admissions guidelines. Tyler had just come from a meeting in the city. His tie was loose, his crisp shirt rolled up at the sleeves.

I smiled against his lips and pulled away, putting Alec out of his misery.

"OK, which room are they in?" I asked.

"This way." Tyler took my hand and pulled me down the corridor.

Outside the door to Dot's birthing suite, Olivia sat casually flipping through the latest edition of *Variant Weekly* while Henry slowly paced the corridor, a very serious frown on his face.

We shared hugs as Alec scowled at us all impatiently.

Everyone else stayed outside as Alec and I went in.

"Your pain management plan has arrived." I grinned.

Dot looked up from her phone. "Thank fuck. The contractions are getting really close, and I'm more dilated than all the pupils of every rave attendee *ever*. I think it might be time soon."

"I told you so." Alec huffed, and I rolled my eyes.

"We're here now. It's all good." I rubbed his arm in a half-apologetic gesture. We'd all been giving him shit.

"Hey, kitten." Marcus gave me a kiss on the cheek, then gave Alec one of those thumping man-hugs.

I gave Kyo the same greeting, but he just stood in front of us looking kind of dazed.

"I'm going to be a father," he stated in a monotone, then blinked once. Alec and I shared a look.

Lucian was still the managing director of Melior Group, but he was looking to retire soon, and he was grooming Kyo to replace him. Having that kind of responsibility didn't seem to faze him, but the prospect of becoming a parent was proving a little intimidating.

"Yeah, man." Alec slapped a hand on his shoulder. "That's how this works."

"So am I," Marcus piped in from his spot next to Dot. "We'll figure it out."

Dot was having twins. After two years of trying to conceive naturally without success, they'd decided to try IVF. Dot immediately decided she wanted a baby from each one of her loves and insisted she be inseminated with both embryos. "Plus," she declared at family dinner one night, "it'll be good to get all my breeding out of the way at once." Miraculously, it worked.

"Shit." She cringed and leaned forward.

"Ace, you're up." Marcus took Dot's hand and waved us over with the other.

Alec rushed to his cousin's side and took her free hand. I held on to his arm and transferred the perfect amount of Light so he could take her pain away.

We'd perfected this process.

From time to time, after a really bad natural disaster or in a situation where it was difficult to get people to proper medical care, Alec and I volunteered our time to help manage pain—if it was safe, of course. Their protectiveness never really waned.

Alec had toyed with the idea of somehow making it his full-time work, but that would've required me to go with him everywhere he was needed, and I had my own scientific goals to kick. He'd also realized pretty quickly that he actually didn't want to spend that much time surrounded by people in pain. Even if he wasn't the one inflicting it, it still triggered bad memories. Yet he didn't want to stay with Melior Group either.

After Alec spent a few months moping around the house and bemoaning how useless he was and how he could just be "the house husband," Tyler slapped a pile of college brochures down in front of him and told him to get his shit together.

He was in his second year working as a specialized counselor at Bradford Hills Institute. He worked exclusively with kids with rare, dangerous, or isolating abilities. No one understood them like he did. He was kind of perfect for it.

Despite Dot's colorful evaluation of what stage of labor she was in, she actually wasn't ready to push for another few hours. We stayed with her the whole time, managing her pain through the contractions and then through the delivery.

Both babies were the picture of health, twenty little fingers and twenty little toes, wailing to announce their arrival into the world.

Alec and I stepped out to update the rest of the family while the nurses did their thing. Charlie and Ed had arrived too, and they all swarmed us for information.

"A boy and a girl." I grinned. "Both healthy. Dot did amazingly."

We all knew they were having one of each—Dot had left no aspect of this pregnancy a mystery—but it still felt as if I was announcing a surprise.

Henry started crying, which got Olivia going too. Charlie pulled a sniffling Ed into his side. Ethan got misty eyed, and Alec was somewhere between dazed and ecstatic after witnessing his first birth.

It was my first birth too, but I'd researched the fuck out of it. As soon as Dot announced she was pregnant, that became my side project. We even got together one night and watched a bunch of birthing videos together, a giant bowl of popcorn balanced on her giant belly.

Kyo and Marcus came out, kicking off another round of hugs, shouts of congratulations, and more tears.

We took turns going in to visit with Dot and holding little Jamie and Nina. I made sure I was sitting down when one of the fragile little bundles was handed to me, desperate for a cuddle but terrified I might hurt her.

Ethan was confident holding Jamie, the baby not even close to the length of his giant forearm. He cooed to him and even started singing a lullaby.

Josh wasn't remotely fazed by it either, holding both of them with assurance, although I suspected he was using his ability to make sure both precious babies were safe at all times.

Alec was still a little dazed when Kyo deposited a baby into his arms. His eyes were a bit wide, his shoulders more tense than I'd seen them in years. He looked down into little Nina's face and relaxed a bit, a smirk pulling at the corner of his lips, but he passed the baby off to Tyler quickly and heaved a sigh of relief.

Ty was uncertain and looked around the room for help.

"Just make sure you support her head." Marcus showed him. "And hold her like this. There you go."

Eventually he eased into it, rocking the baby. After a few moments, he cocked his head to the side and stared off into space as the rest of us chatted quietly around him. Then he smiled to himself, and his knowing gray eyes met mine.

I didn't know what truth had been revealed to him or if it was even related to having kids—I just liked looking into his eyes. He still gave me butterflies.

"Do you think you guys will have any?" Dot asked from her reclined position on the bed. I smiled at her and shrugged.

Maybe one day, but for now we had each other, and that was enough. We were happy.

THE END

***

Thank you for reading *Vivid Avowed*! I hope you enjoyed Evelyn's epic story. If you like paranormal RH, you'll love *Reverie and Redemption*.

I'm in love with three men. I'm just not sure if they're a dream come true or my worst nightmare.

It began with hearing voices - another step on my steady descent into madness. It was inevitable, considering the whole town hated me and I was the loneliest person on the planet.

I didn't really blame them. Everyone who got close to me ended up in the hospital. I'd be suspicious of me too.

When the three distinct, alluring voices in my head started to appear before my eyes as three distinct, gorgeous men I really started to question everything I thought I knew.

They called themselves *Dreamwalkers* and told me they were hunting the monster attacking all the people around me.

They won't leave me alone.

I'm not sure I want them to.

But am I the monster they're after? Or are we all in worse danger than I ever could've imagined?

One-click Reverie and Redemption now - https://geni.us/reverie-redemption OR keep reading for the first chapter.

ACKNOWLEDGMENTS

Writing and publishing books is an insane amount of work. So much happens behind the scenes before the shiny new story is released into the world – this process still makes my head spin. There is no way in hell I'd be able to do this all on my own!

For taking a chance on me, thank you to my readers. For being as excited about this crazy world in my head as I am, thank you to my ARC team, my Beta readers, my friend and PA Sam. For making me look way more professional and legit than I feel, thank you to my editor, cover designer and formatter. For making me feel like I'm not alone in this sometimes overwhelming book world, thank you to my author and writer friends. For your unwavering support of everything I do, thank you to my friends and family. For more than I can even express (but especially for bringing me coffee), thank you to the love of my life – John.

REVERIE AND REDEMPTION

Chapter One

The sun streamed through the tree branches high above, and the gentle breeze carried the sounds of birdsong. The forest felt welcoming, *wonderous*.

Filled with joy, I smiled up at the sky and held my arms out. A bird landed on my left wrist—a colorful little thing singing a trilling song—and I laughed. Another joined it moments later, and then more and more until I had birds covering both arms and shoulders like a scene from a Disney movie. These birds were my friends, the closest ones even snuggling against my neck.

Then, one by one, they started to take off, flying playfully around me, their wings carrying them higher and higher. I wanted to go with them and be free, but . . .

I frowned at my arms. The birds had pooped all over me, and now my arms were too heavy to flap. I couldn't fly. I stayed stuck on the ground while all my bird friends disappeared into the trees, taking their sweet songs with them.

The forest fell silent; the trees suddenly seemed denser, blocking out the sunshine. The only sound was the slow, almost too-quiet-to-hear ticking of a clock.

It started to snow. Within moments, it had piled over my feet, and when I finished cleaning the bird shit off my arms and tried to take off again, the snow wouldn't let me. Almost as if it was trying to hold me captive.

The previously vibrant, cheery landscape had turned gray and white, and the sole noise—that ticking—kept getting louder.

The snow had risen up to my knees.

Why was it snowing? Wasn't it summer? And where was that ticking coming from?

Nothing made any sense. I couldn't move. I'd be trapped in this spot, alone forever, unable to get away . . .

And then I felt someone, or *something*, watching me. I tried to turn, but the snow had buried me up to my hips now, and I couldn't see behind me.

And then . . .

And . . .

. . . then . . .

"*Wake up.*" The whispered words were both a demand and an invitation, a caress on my cheek that started to drag me out of my bizarre dream. The voice was distinctly male, with an edge of something like worry riding it.

I groaned and screwed my eyes up against the bright morning light.

As far as dreams went, that wasn't the weirdest one I'd ever had—not by a long shot. Maybe the snow was just wishful thinking, because sweat from the summer heat had already plastered my sleep shirt to my skin. I moved to peel the shirt off, and something poked me in the hip.

My eyes flew open. I wasn't even in my house, let alone in my bed.

I was in the fucking woods, being poked in the hip by a stick while the morning sun beamed down on me as if I were a plate under a heat lamp, waiting for the waitress.

I dragged a hand down my face, equally exasperated and unnerved.

This wasn't the first time I'd woken up in a place I hadn't gone to sleep. What worried me was what often came after.

Something tickled my shin, and I screamed, jolting to my feet and smacking at my legs. I jumped around on the spot, brushed my T-shirt down, shook out my hair, and cursed nature in a weird little anxiety dance. Once I'd assured myself nothing was crawling on me, I turned slowly on the spot to take in my surroundings.

All I could see in any direction were trees, ferns, patches of grass, the occasional bird. There was no sound of cars passing on a nearby road, no hiking track obvious in the dense underbrush, no sign of civilization at all.

Fuck.

I could literally be anywhere. My house had to be at least within a few hours' walk, but Gritton was nestled in a valley, surrounded by forest, accessible only by picturesque winding roads. I could've gone in any direction and ended up in a spot that looked just like this.

At least I still had my socks on. They were pooled around my ankles and filthy, but they'd provide some protection for my feet. Until I ran into a hungry bear. Then I wouldn't have to worry about my feet or anything else, ever again.

Funny that I focused on my socks in that moment, but better to count my blessings than fixate on how I'd probably die in these woods.

No one would even care. I doubted anyone in Gritton would even notice for a week or two, regardless of the fact that I was born there and knew most of the locals by name.

But my plant babies would wither and die.

Do it for the plants. I refused to die without even trying to get home.

I could simply pick a direction at random and hope for the best. But what if I just ended up deeper in the woods and starved to death?

Fucking fuck.

Paralyzed with indecision, I just stood there, looking around with my hands propped on my hips. I sighed and blew a random piece of hair out of my face. At least my hair was short enough that it wouldn't get all matted and caught on anything.

I needed to find a tree to climb so I could get some idea of which way to go, but there were no good trees around. All the ones I could see were giants of the woods, stretching hundreds of feet into the sky. None of the magnificent bastards had a branch within reach.

Guess I'd just have to choose a direction until I found a suitable tree.

"This way."

I whipped my head to the left and frantically searched the area with wide eyes. I'd all but forgotten the firm, deep voice I'd heard in that trippy state between sleep and wakefulness. I was fully conscious now, and I'd definitely heard it—clearer, louder, even a bit less worried.

Shit. Now I was hearing things. Maybe I'd already been stung by something that was giving me auditory hallucinations.

"Screw it." Figuring I had nothing to lose, I walked in that direction.

Really, Reverie? We're blindly following creepy disembodied voices into the deep, dark woods?

Most likely I'd just imagined the directions, my panicked brain creating voices from the rustle of the branches. I mean, my situation couldn't really get any worse, right?

I picked my way through the trees and bushes, careful to watch where I stepped. I walked for what felt like hours—but was realistically probably only half an hour—without spotting a single climbable tree.

Just as despair started to settle in, making me wonder if I should double back and try another direction, I saw it. One pine tree stood at least fifty feet tall, a dwarf compared to all the others around it, and it had a branch about waist high.

"Oh my god!" I rushed over to it, ignoring the pain in my feet. "You have no idea how good it is to see you, Mr. Pine Tree. I need to climb you. I hope you don't mind, but it is a matter of life and death."

Mine, and possibly someone else's.

But I couldn't think about that just yet.

I wasn't exactly an athletic type, but I managed to pull myself onto the low branch and swing my legs over until I was sitting on it. My hands and thighs were already getting scratched up, and I hadn't even climbed three feet off the ground. Doing my best to ignore the pain, I used the trunk to balance, wobbled into a standing position, and grabbed the next branch. This one would be harder than the first, even if I weren't already wrecked and injured.

Making sure my death grip on the branch was solid, I made myself look up. Not *up*, up, into the sky. Just ahead, so my brain could see what was in front of me instead of worrying about plummeting to what was below.

"Holy shit." I leaned forward. A path!

About a hundred feet away, a narrow track wound through the ferns and bushes and around the massive trees. It wasn't remotely visible from the ground, but from just a little bit of a height . . .

"Thank you, Mr. Pine." I kissed the branch, then immediately regretted it and spit out the mossy, earthy, gritty nature that had stuck itself to my mouth.

I scrambled down the tree and walked to the path. It was barely a goat track, but well worn. Without thinking about it too much, I turned left. Turning left had served me well the last time, so I just rolled with it.

Most hiking tracks looped around, went from one point to another, or connected to other tracks. I'd find my way back to a road eventually—hopefully sooner rather than later. By now, the late-summer sun had climbed high in the sky. My skin felt sunburned, my lips and mouth dry. I felt dehydrated and exhausted, but at least the packed dirt was easier on my feet.

After an hour or so, I rounded a bend and saw the end of the path. Rushing forward brought me to an intersection with a wider path, a wooden signpost standing nearby. I leaned against the post and released a sob of relief. Turning left had paid off.

The sign informed me I had reached Frank's Track. Arrows pointed in various directions, indicating the distance to landmarks. I was in the national park near my hometown, and I knew these hiking tracks.

It took about another half hour to walk to the parking area. The public toilets were filthy, but the sinks had fresh cool water. I peed, then drank and drank until my stomach felt as though it might burst, and then I sat in the shade for a while.

There wasn't a single car in the lot, crushing my hopes of begging some hikers for a lift into town. I considered resting longer, waiting to see if anyone showed up, but I knew that would just delay the inevitable. Now that I no longer had to worry if I'd make it through the day alive, I couldn't stop worrying about what I'd find when I got back.

With a resigned sigh, I got to my feet and started walking. Again. Gritton was only about another hour walk, but the mammoth trees lining the curved road provided shade, and the asphalt almost felt soothing on my feet after the rough treatment of the forest floor. I didn't pass a single car, the birds and an occasional rabbit my only companions on the walk.

Of course I'd gone and sleepwalked my ass to the remote woods on the opposite side of town from where I lived. I couldn't have been sensible about it and sleepwalked into the remote woods closer to my house. No, I'd have to walk down Main Street in my *Ghostbusters* T-shirt and my bright blue underwear with the hole at the seam of the left butt-cheek. Not to mention my filthy legs and arms, the tattered socks. As if they didn't think I was enough of a freak already.

I'd resigned myself to a life of loneliness, but that didn't make it easy. The stares and cold shoulders were a bitch to handle on a good day, let alone a day like today.

When Mr. Wallis's driveway came into view on the road

ahead, I started building up my emotional armor. By the time I'd walked past his property, I was holding my head high, my shoulders back and my expression stoic. There was no avoiding the walk through town, but I'd be damned if I did it while cowering or embarrassed.

More houses appeared, the properties getting smaller closer to town. By the time I came across the first person, I had a bit of a swagger in my step, as if I were exactly where I wanted to be, doing exactly what I planned.

The boys at Ziggy's Auto all stopped what they were doing, wiping their hands on rags as they stared at me. They never catcalled me or anything like that, but they never acknowledged my existence either.

"Boys." I gave them a jovial nod.

"Wait!" Travis stepped around the open hood of a car. He was a few years older than me and married. "Are you . . . uh . . . want some water or whatever?" He seemed confused—as if unsure why he'd even spoken to me. But he didn't hide the way he looked at my scratched-up legs, my dirty T-shirt, my disaster hair.

I slowed my pace in shock. He'd found a scrap of humanity and was actually showing me some kindness? I glanced up to the sky, sure it might collapse at any moment.

"Nah, I'm good." I waved him off, noting the narrow-eyed looks the others were giving him, and continued on.

Main Street was busy with the lunchtime rush, and I got plenty more reactions. People stopped in their tracks to stare at me, did double takes, craned their necks through the windows of the charming cafés and antique shops. Two elderly women sitting on a park bench openly tutted at me with disapproval.

"Mrs. Jones. Mrs. Douglas. Lovely day we're having." I gave them a wide grin. They'd been good friends with my grandparents; they used to pinch my cheeks and bring me home baked treats. Now I was nothing more than that woman the whole town wished would just disappear.

I forced down a shudder at the thought that they nearly got their wish that morning. Instead I just smiled wider.

The more they stared and whispered and steered their children out of my path, the more pep I forced into my step. I was practically skipping, my grin maniacal, by the time I crossed the main square and the people and buildings started to thin out.

None of them had even asked if I was all right. Dirt and scratches covered my arms and legs. My lips were cracked and dry. I looked as if I'd just escaped a serial killer in the woods. I'd known these people my whole life, and not a single one cared what had happened to me.

I'd stopped expecting anything from them a long time ago, but it still hurt to be treated as less than human.

The local school was on the edge of town. I just had to get past there, and then it was nothing but trees all the way up the winding road to my house on the hill.

"What the hell do you think you're doing?" Vera—Travis's wife—appeared from behind a tree, hissing at me like a striking snake. We'd gone to school together, had even been friends at one point. Now she was a teacher, and I was the town freak.

I kept my pace steady, not in the mood for any more friendly catchups with the locals. "I'm walking home. And what are you up to?"

"Can't you keep your weirdness private? There are children in there." She pointed to the school building behind her as another teacher marched toward us. Mrs. Upton had taught there since Vera and I were students.

I gasped and gave Vera a wide-eyed look. "You're right! How could I forget? They are so tasty before the age of ten. Thanks for the reminder, Vera. I'll come by for a snack later."

They both looked horrified, but I'd walked too far ahead for them to say anything else. I still heard Mrs. Upton's haughty comment though.

"Why is that girl still living in our town? No one wants her here."

Vera replied, but I couldn't make out what she said.

I'd asked myself the same question so many times over the years. Why did I stay? Everyone hated me here. I had no friends. I'd lost my whole family.

Why did I keep putting myself through this?

I'd tried to leave a few times—I'd even gotten as far as packing up half my stuff once—but I just couldn't make myself go. Maybe because at the end of the day, it didn't matter where I went, who I got to know. Everyone would leave me eventually. They'd either hate and fear me, the way my whole town did, or end up like my parents and my best friend and anyone else I ever cared about.

I pushed the thought out of my mind as I walked through the front gate of my property. Immediately, my shoulders loosened, and I could finally breathe. No one dared step foot past that gate, and that's how I liked it.

That was the other reason I couldn't bring myself to leave. This property, this house, was my sanctuary. I'd grown up here, and all my happiest memories had happened on this plot of land. It was the only thing that made me remember I was loved once. My parents were in every corner of this house, in the photos on the walls, in the furniture, in their bedroom that I hadn't been able to bring myself to open for years.

It was their home. Now it belonged to me.

A few steps up the walkway and the lush garden hid me from the road. At the end of the winding gravel path, I stomped up the front stairs.

"Fucking fantastic," I grumbled when I saw the front door wide open. "Couldn't have closed the door behind you when you went sleepwalking into the damn woods, Reverie? You're an asshole."

I wasn't really worried about anyone breaking in, but I did have a hosta plant in my sunroom that squirrels freaking obsessed over.

With a huff, I locked the door behind me and went to check on my plants. The polka-dot plant was drooping a bit, so I gave it a good watering, but otherwise my little indoor forest looked just fine.

"Pretty green babies," I cooed to them. "Momma's here to give you water and fertilizer and take care of you. I'd never leave you . . . intentionally."

The plants in the farthest corner whispered something.

I gasped, turning around to face them. Of course, it wasn't the plants—I loved my green babies, but I wasn't so far gone that I thought they could actually speak back to me.

Someone was in my house.

Would this day never end?

I reached for the ice pick I kept lying around to aerate the soil in the potted plants and brandished it in front of me like a knife. I was a split second away from calling out, *Who's there?* but I held it back, rolling my eyes. *Do not get slasher-flick-bimbo-murdered, Reverie. You're better than that.*

". . . is she . . ." The voice came again, from the same spot. Except I was staring right at it, and no one was there.

". . . but if she is . . . don't try . . ." That time it sounded like a different voice. It actually reminded me of the voice I'd heard in the woods. And it didn't sound so much like whispering now that I was focused on it—more like someone speaking really far away.

I stood there for another few moments and contemplated searching the house, but then I dropped my weapon and dragged my ass into the bathroom. Either I'd lost my mind or the exhaustion and dehydration were giving me auditory hallucinations again. Either way, I needed a shower.

After a good hour in the bathroom—scrubbing away dirt, wincing every time soap got into one of my scrapes, sanitizing each injury I could reach, and moisturizing my whole body—I put on my comfiest shorts and T-shirt and headed into the kitchen. My stomach growled almost constantly, *demanding bitch.* Grabbing Chinese leftovers from the fridge, I carried the box over to the couch and started wolfing it down cold.

With my belly full and my body clean and safe, I couldn't

avoid thinking about it any longer. *Who had fallen victim to the curse of just plain knowing me?*

It started when I was eleven years old: every time I sleep-walked, I'd wake up to discover someone I loved had been taken from me. And once all my loved ones were gone, anyone I even remotely cared about ended up being next.

So as much as it hurt, I couldn't blame the people of Gritton for staying away.

I hadn't sleepwalked in nearly a year though. I'd kept my distance even from those outside my town. I was a straight-up bitch to almost everyone I met. I literally had no friends; I didn't even have acquaintances. Who was there left to take?

My phone started ringing, the sound carrying through the empty house from my bedroom.

By the time I hobbled to my room, wincing from my sore muscles and scraped feet, the phone had stopped ringing. I pulled it off the charger to see half a dozen missed calls and a text message, all from the same person.

I called him back.

"Rev, hey!" Morris sounded rushed. He was my boss from the diner two towns over where I worked a few times per week. I didn't really need the income—my ginseng and herbs brought in more than enough for me to live comfortably—but I craved at least a little normality. I liked going somewhere where no one knew me, no one glared at me, no one hated me.

"Hey, Mo, what's up?" I gingerly lowered myself to the bed.

"Can you work tonight?" he asked.

The way I was feeling right now? No way in hell. I opened my mouth to say as much, but he kept speaking.

"Diana didn't show up for her shift this morning. Laura covered it, but now she can't do the dinner shift, so can you cover that?"

"Diana didn't show up? That's not like her." I squeezed my eyes shut and braced myself.

"Yeah." My manager sighed. "I got ahold of her husband

about an hour ago. She's in the hospital. Apparently, she just didn't wake up this morning. They're running tests."

"Oh my god." I felt sick to my stomach.

"I know. They have no idea what's causing it."

"Yeah, I'll take the shift. It's no problem."

"Thanks, Rev."

It was the least I could do—considering I was the reason Diana was in the hospital in the first place.

Keep reading - https://geni.us/reverie-redemption

ABOUT THE AUTHOR

Kaydence Snow has lived all over the world but ended up settled in Melbourne, Australia. She lives near the beach with her husband.

She draws inspiration from her own overthinking, sometimes frightening imagination, and everything that makes life interesting. She believes sarcasm is the highest form of wit and has the vocabulary of a highly educated, well-read sailor. When she's not writing, thinking about writing, planning when she can write next, or reading other people's writing, she loves to travel and learn new things.

To keep up to date with Kaydence's latest news and releases sign up to her newsletter here:

kaydencesnow.com/#newsletter

Join her reader group here:

facebook.com/groups/KaydenceSnowLodge

Or follow her on:

BY KAYDENCE SNOW

<u>The Evelyn Maynard Trilogy</u>

Variant Lost

Vital Found

Vivid Avowed

The Complete Evelyn Maynard Trilogy (including bonus content!)

<u>Devilbend Dynasty</u>

Like You Care

Like You Hurt

Like You Should

Like You Know

<u>Standalones</u>

Just Be Her

It Started With a Sleigh

Sand and Secrets

Reverie and Redemption

Expose Me